SWEET BLOOD OF MINE

OVERWORLD CHRONICLES BOOK ONE

JOHN CORWIN

FROM ZERO TO HERO?

Justin has ninety-nine problems, but a vampire ain't one.

When Justin discovers he has super powers, life gets a lot more interesting. But as he learns the ropes of his new supernatural life, he soon realizes he's not alone.

His parents are hiding dangerous secrets from him. The girl he falls for is sworn to kill him. A finicky felycan wants to make him his plaything. And a bounty hunter has his family in the crosshairs.

If that's not enough, his former best friend, Randy, wants to use his blood to create a vampire super-serum to build an army of bloodsuckers.

If he can't survive his other issues and stop Randy, Atlanta will be hip-deep in vampires, and Justin will be their juice box.

ISBN-13 978-0985018108

Printed in the U.S.A.

RAVEN HOUSE

BOOKS BY JOHN CORWIN

THE OVERWORLD CHRONICLES

Sweet Blood of Mine

Dark Light of Mine

Fallen Angel of Mine

Dread Nemesis of Mine

Twisted Sister of Mine

Dearest Mother of Mine

Infernal Father of Mine

Sinister Seraphim of Mine

Wicked War of Mine

Dire Destiny of Ours

Aetherial Annihilation

Baleful Betrayal

Ominous Odyssey

Insidious Insurrection

Assignment Zero (An Elyssa Short Story)

OVERWORLD UNDERGROUND

Possessed By You

Demonicus

OVERWORLD ARCANUM

Conrad Edison and the Living Curse

Conrad Edison and the Anchored World

Conrad Edison and the Broken Relic

Conrad Edison and the Infernal Design

STAND ALONE NOVELS

Mars Rising

No Darker Fate

The Next Thing I Knew

Outsourced

For the latest on new releases, free ebooks, and more, join John Corwin's Newsletter at www.johncorwin.net!

CHAPTER 1

I brandished the hall pass like a sword, ducking and slaying invisible monsters as I journeyed through the school hallway. I dodged the thrust from an imaginary ogre, parried, and gutted him with a sweep of my magical sword. Now faced with the evil sorcerer behind it all, I delivered my denouement. "My name is Justin Case. You killed my father. Prepare to die!"

I blocked his magical strike with the hall pass and beheaded him with a spinning swipe. The effort carried me off balance and I fell to my knees. Panting, I climbed unsteadily to my feet and took a long drag on the juice box I'd smuggled out of the classroom.

"Man, fighting monsters really takes it out of you." I shook the juice box, gauging my dwindling supply of sugary goodness. My bladder interrupted the precious moment, reminding me that my addiction to juice boxes came at a terrible cost—excessive urination.

I waddled down the hall, the generous spare tire around my waist jiggling beneath my XXL T-shirt. "Got me a hall pass and a juice box," I sang under my breath. "Ain't nothing better than a juice box and a hall pass."

I barged through the bathroom door just as Randy Boyle held out a glass vial to Brad Nichols and said, "You've never felt a rush like this."

Brad and Randy spun toward me. The vial shattered on the floor and reddish-brown liquid spattered.

"Shit!" Brad shoved past me and ran out the door.

"Sorry!" I backed away, but an iron grip squeezed my arm and flung me against the wall. The breath exploded out of my mouth. The hall pass clattered on the floor and my juice box tumbled from my grip.

Randy pinned me against the wall with an elbow and snarled in my face. "What in the hell are you doing in here, Justin?"

"I just had to pee!" I tried to wriggle loose, but couldn't budge an inch. "I swear I won't tell anyone!"

Randy's eyes seemed to flash red. He backed off and glared at me. "What do you *think* you saw?"

I blinked rapidly, still unable to process how Randy Boyle, of all people, could toss me around like a rag doll. He stood barely an inch taller and I'd seen twigs thicker than his arms and legs. He'd been relentlessly bullied in middle school—even more than me. And when he'd tried to fight me so he could climb a notch in the food chain, I'd kicked his ass.

Randy hadn't changed much in the past few years, and he certainly hadn't packed on any muscle. In spite of all the visible evidence of physical weakness, he'd hurled my tubby ass across the bathroom and held me against the wall like I was a waif.

What in the hell is going on?

Randy's eyes narrowed. "I asked you a question."

I gulped. "I don't know what I saw. I mean, I guess you could've been giving him cough medicine."

The other boy's nostrils flared. "You don't smell like the others." Randy sniffed around my neck, sending chills of disgust crawling up my spine. "You smell...sweet."

I clenched my fists, ready to take a swing at him if he tried to kiss me. "Must be my Axe Body Spray."

"No." Randy's eyes flashed again. "There's something else."

I wasn't about to give him a chance to critique my body odor again. I thrust my knee into his groin—or at least where his groin had been a split second ago. Randy blurred out of the way before my knee reached the target.

I blinked and pushed my thick glasses up my nose, convinced eyesight had just failed me. "Jesus, Randy, are you on horse steroids?"

The air burst out of my lungs again. It happened so fast, it took a moment to realize Randy had punched me in the stomach. He laughed as I crumpled to the floor, then knelt and inhaled deeply. "Hmm, yes, I know this smell. You need some time to ripen, and then you'll be my little bitch, Justin. It'll be just like it should have been in middle school."

I gasped for air. "I kicked your ass in middle school, Randy. Don't make me do it again."

Randy burst into laughter. "Oh, I'm not the same helpless kid anymore, Justin. You aren't either. You're fatter and weaker." He yanked me up so hard, I came off the floor and landed on my feet. Sniffed me again. "Just a little more time, and I'll harvest you."

"H-harvest? What in the hell are you on, Randy?" I pressed my back against the wall, desperate to get out of there.

Randy got an inch from my face and exhaled. His breath smelled metallic, like rust. He giggled. "I remember when we were friends, Justin. I remember when you abandoned me in middle school."

"Because you always took He-Man and made me play Skeletor!" I wrinkled my nose. "I got tired of playing the bad guys, Randy."

Randy snorted. "Damn, I'd forgotten about that." His amusement faded to a scowl. "But that's not why you abandoned me."

"It's one reason." I tried to slide sideways, but his hand smashed against the tile, leaving cracks. I flinched. "Fine! It's because Nathan and his goons kept bullying us, and you were a spoiled little jackass who didn't appreciate my friendship, so yeah, I distanced myself so they'd stay away from me."

The smile on his thin face looked ghoulish. "You threw me to the wolves, fatty." His eyes went distant. "Don't think I've forgotten. If I didn't have more important things to do, I'd break Nathan's legs and tea-bag him while he screamed." Randy moved his hand and backed away. He made a shooing motion. "Get out of here and keep your mouth shut, or you'll be the one with broken legs."

I grabbed the hall pass off the floor and ran like my life depended on it. I rounded the corner to the senior lockers and my legs turned to jelly. I slid to the floor and buried my hands in my face. My entire body trembled with fear and anger.

Memories flashed through the darkness.

RANDY AIMS *the stormtrooper at my Han Solo action figure. "Pew, pew, pew!"*

"Missed!" I say.

"No way! I got him that time!" Randy slides the stormtrooper right up to Han. "Bang!"

"Stormtroopers always miss," I remind him. This was the first time I'd convinced Randy to be the bad guys, and he hated it.

"Not this time!" Randy snatches Han from my grip and hurls him into the Millennium Falcon, knocking Chewbacca off the table and into the abyss. "He's dead, and I win."

I threw up my hands. "Fine, the Dark Side wins this time." I grab my juice box off the table and slurp the rest of its contents. A horn honks outside. I look through the window and feel relieved to see Mom waiting in her rusty old Volvo. "I gotta go."

"You hate it when I win," Randy says. "That stormtrooper hit Han and you know it."

"The good guys are supposed to win. I should've known you'd take the win even as the bad guys."

Randy scowls. "Even Han can't survive a headshot."

"Congrats," I say, "you murdered Han Solo and probably Chewbacca too." I walk down the long winding staircase, Randy hot on my heels, arguing why he won the entire way. I nod a few times, wave goodbye, and leave the mansion he calls home behind me. "Spoiled brat," I mutter under my breath. He's my only friend and I can hardly stand him.

"WHAT THE HELL HAPPENED TO YOU?"

I gasped and looked up. A shout of surprise escaped before I could stop myself. A face full of piercings, black lipstick, and heavy mascara stared back at me. "Sweet baby Jesus!"

"No." The girl raised a dark eyebrow. "I know the resemblance is uncanny, but I'm not him."

My eyes fixed on a little red cross painted just between her eyebrows. "But you have a cross—"

"Why are you cowering in the middle of the hallway?" The goth girl inspected me. "Drugs?"

I shook my head. "No."

"What's that red stuff on your lips?"

I touched my mouth. "Cherry juice box."

Her nosed wrinkled. "Jesus, you still drink from juice boxes?"

"They're my weakness." I rose on unsteady feet and debated telling the odd girl about Randy, but his threat of bodily harm sealed my mouth. I looked at her empty hands. "Where's your hall pass?"

"Hmf." She spun on her heel and stalked down the hall to the bathroom where Randy lurked. She flung open the door and went inside before I could shout a warning. She emerged a moment later and gave me another questioning look before heading down the hall, eyes wary like a guard on patrol.

"What a freak," I muttered. My bladder reminded me again why I'd gotten the hall pass in the first place, so I dodged around the corner to another bathroom and relieved myself.

When I returned to my homeroom class, Mr. Herman didn't even look up from his painting, or seem to notice that I'd been gone a lot longer than I should have. Bruce Dickens and Abigail Rogers made out in the back of the room, dry humping like two Christians practicing abstinence. Another group played poker, a pile of real money on their desks. Lacking instruction, everyone else did their own thing. Mr. Herman probably wouldn't have cared if an elephant riding a unicorn ran through the room.

I dropped into my desk with a groan. My entire body ached from the rough handling in the bathroom.

Jenny Matthews leaned close to my shoulder. "Little diarrhea problem? Did you shart yourself?

Annie Holmes giggled and leaned across the aisle toward her friend. "I saw him sneak a juice box out of the room when he left."

"Oh my god." Jenny snorted. "A senior in high school drinking juice boxes?"

I growled. "There's nothing wrong with juice boxes. I'll bet you can't wait to get some Sunny D every time you go home."

"Juice boxes. How sad." Annie shook her head and pursed her lips with false sympathy. "I wonder what Katie would think."

I stiffened in my seat. "Why would you tell Katie about juice boxes?"

The two girls giggled.

An angry retort died on my lips as a spike of pain stabbed into my forehead. Their faces went blurry and it was all I could do not to grab my head and scream. *What the hell is this? A nuclear-fueled migraine?* I jerked the glasses off my face in a vain attempt to quell the agony.

My mouth dropped open at what I saw next. The room was full of ghosts.

Hazy halos of light hovered around everyone's bodies. Bruce's and Abigail's ghosts wrapped around each other, misty figures of light doing the tango.

The headache vanished. I blinked and the room became unfocused. I slid my glasses back on and my eyesight returned to normal.

"Are you retarded?" Jenny exchanged a confused look with Annie. "Did you see that look on his fat face?"

"He's an idiot," Annie said.

I was still too stunned to reply. I turned away from them and looked down at my hands. "What's going on, man?" I pinched myself. "Am I going crazy?"

The bell rang. Desks screeched as everyone got up and headed for first period classes.

My phone buzzed with a text from Mark. *Got our swords ready?*

I cleared my head of other thoughts and returned it to more important things like Kings and Castles. My best friends Mark Dunbar, Harry Pots, and I loved to LARP—live action role play. I made weapons, shields, armor, and all manner of equipment for our group. I'd been working on three new swords for us to replace the ones damaged in the last battle.

Yeah. I'll show them to you later, I texted back. I couldn't wait to see their faces when they saw the works of art I'd created.

My excitement vanished the moment I stepped into the crowded hall-way, replaced by a sense of creeping dread. I scanned the mob for people I wanted to avoid at all costs during my journey to the next class —Nathan, Jenny, Annie, and now, Randy.

This was the first time I'd seen Randy in years. His parents yanked him out of school after he got caught bringing a gun to class. I suspected he meant to kill someone, but their money got him out of any serious trou-ble. When he returned at the start of this year, rumors said he'd been at a boarding school all this time.

I hadn't talked to him until today. I hadn't wanted to. Now I remem-bered why.

I made it to Calculus without incident. The dread vanished, replaced by happiness at being with fellow nerds, but mostly because of the golden goddess who sat to my right.

Katie Johnson beamed a brilliant smile at me when I walked into the room, the sun warming my face in an otherwise dreary world. Long blond hair spilled down her shoulders. Tanned legs spilled from beneath her skirt. Hormones spilled out of my brain and into my groin. I covered my crotch just in time with my book bag and slid into my seat.

"Hey, Justin." She smiled again. "Did you do the homework?"

I nodded and slid my papers to her. "Easy, peasy, lemon squeezy."

"You're so smart." She opened a notebook and compared mine to hers. "I only got two wrong this time."

"Nice!" I said. "I'm totes down to studying with you some more if you like."

Katie handed back the papers. "Totes?" She giggled. "I didn't know anyone said that anymore."

"Oh, um—"

She rolled her eyes. "I'm kidding, Justin." Katie looked up as the teacher, Mr. Hubble entered the room. "I'll need some help studying for that test this Friday. Maybe tomorrow evening?"

I shrugged, trying to play it cool despite the out of control hormones raging in my nethers. "Sounds good." I remembered Jenny's threat and couldn't stop myself from asking, "What do you think of juice boxes?"

Katie's forehead pinched. "Um, I prefer Sunny D."

"Yeah, me too." I tried to laugh it off. "I mean, heh, what else do teenagers drink?"

"Vodka for one thing," Katie said. "Tequila isn't bad either."

"Well, obviously, but I meant non-alcoholic because, um, everyone drinks vodka and tequila and sometimes even whiskey, which is what I drink all the time when I'm bored." I clamped my mouth shut to stop the train wreck of words.

Mr. Hubble opened his mouth to speak and the fire alarm blared. Nerds like me looked around in confusion and disappointment. The other students ran out faster than level one elves fleeing a horde of dark ogres.

"Everyone into the back parking lot." Mr. Hubble picked up his briefcase and left without so much as a backward glance.

I had a sudden fantasy about me and Katie all alone in the classroom after everyone had left. How she would snuggle up to me and praise me for being the Calculus god. How she wanted to calculate my variables. I blinked out of the fantasy and realized I needed to keep her in here at all costs.

"Probably another false alarm," I said to no one. Katie had slipped out along with everyone else during my moment. I groaned, got up, and headed into the hallway.

The empty hallway echoed with the obnoxious alarm. I saw the goth girl dash across the corridor. "Crazy chick." I wondered if she'd set off the alarm or simply decided now was a good time for a hardcore Goth jog. Angry shouting echoed from the hallway to my right. I hesitated, then allowed curiosity to get the better of me.

Treading on the balls of my feet, following the shouts, I went down to the Home Economics classroom and peered around the corner of the door. My worst nightmare waited inside.

CHAPTER 2

O kay, so maybe it wasn't my worst nightmare anymore. Randy had taken that slot handily after our last encounter, but the giant slab of meat named Nathan Spelman took a close second. Ordinarily, I would have turned tail and run, but instead I froze in disbelief.

Nathan had his meat-hooks wrapped around Katie and his lips pressed to her mouth. She writhed in his grasp and turned her face.

"Nathan, stop!" She struggled again. "I told you I don't date jocks."

"You should," Nathan boomed. "Come on, give me a chance."

"Let me go!" Katie shoved his chest, but she might as well have been trying to move a semi-truck.

I stood in the doorway for a stunned moment, unsure if my skills as a Kings and Castles woodland elf had prepared me to take on a challenge like this. Nathan could pass for an ogre. His neck had more girth than one of my legs, which was probably why he was an all-star football player. It would be suicide to attack that monster.

Then Katie started to cry.

Something in me snapped. Probably my sanity. But I couldn't care less. Nathan held her helpless in his iron grip. I might be short, chubby, and require a B-cup manzier, but I was still a man. I had to do something. In Kings and Castles, I was a level twelve woodland elf. Unfortunately, reality had graced me with all of five feet, six inches of height and the slender dimensions of the Pillsbury Doughboy after a few too many cartons of buttermilk biscuits. I needed a weapon to stand a chance, preferably a bazooka.

I sprinted to the janitor's closet. *Sprinted* might be too strong a word since I huffed, puffed, and begged god for a mercy killing by the time I got halfway there. The closet door hung open. I peered inside the small space and grimaced at the chemical fumes stinging my nose. A metal shelf held several containers of various cleansers. I supposed if Nathan needed a chemical bath, any of them would be perfect but they wouldn't do much good in a fight. I spotted the only serviceable weapon: a broom. It was a far cry from what the Lady of the Lake offered King Arthur, but I didn't have much of a choice. I grabbed it.

At that moment, my skull decided to turn inside out. A blinding flood of pain superheated my eyeballs and pounded on my brain like a midget playing whack-a-mole in my head. Another damned migraine! I dropped the broom and pressed both hands to my temples in a vain attempt to soothe the pulsating agony. My sight blurred and I fell against the nearby shelf. Spray cans rattled on the floor, and a bottle of something green shattered and spread across the tiles, overpowering the other scents with the cloying odor of pine.

The vice on my head loosened after a few seconds, the pain abating as though nothing happened. It felt like brain freeze only a gazillion times worse than the headache I'd had in homeroom.

What in the hell is wrong with me today?

A shriek from Katie reminded me an altercation with Nathan might supply a permanent fix for my migraine problems. I grabbed the broom off the floor and unscrewed the handle. I chugged down the hallway with my walrus-like gait and made it back to the classroom in time to see Nathan forcing his lips on Katie's tear-stained face. His massive arms held her immobile while she writhed in disgust. I was too angry at the sight to wait for my panting to slow.

"Release her!" I smacked the metal end of the broomstick on the ground and pretended it was my elven attack staff with a plus twenty chance of a critical hit, like say, in the enemy's balls.

Nathan snapped his attention to me, anger boiling behind his ferocious gaze at the interruption. Katie froze and her eyes widened with the same look I'd seen everyone give scrawny Jeff Nugent when he'd challenged monstrous Kyle Denton to a fight over a girl. Kyle had outweighed him by about a hundred pounds, been held back two grades, and was the first kid in middle school to grow a mustache and a goatee. Things hadn't ended so well for Jeff. I probably should have learned from his lesson, but I was a trained woodland elf who was too angry to be pooping his pants.

"Justin?" Katie said.

Nathan shoved her into a chair behind him and snarled. "If you know what's good for you, you'll get out of here and keep your mouth shut."

It just so happened I did *not* know what was good for me, so take that Nathan! I pushed my bottle-bottom glasses up my nose—to stall for time—and tried to speak, but my lips wouldn't move. Granted, I hadn't planned this out past—well, this point.

Nathan glared at me from across the room and probably decided I wasn't going to flee like most rational people would have at this point. He plowed through three rows of desks, sending them screeching and skidding to the sides, hands outstretched. I froze and nearly wet my pants. He lunged. I threw up the broomstick in a defensive gesture. He snatched it from me and snapped it over his knee like a twig.

Reason fled from me like a gibbering madman. I yelped before dodging to the side as Nathan threw the broken handle at me. One half nailed me in the head. I tripped on a desk. It flipped and I rolled over the top of it, somehow landing on my side while the desk clattered against the floor. Nathan laughed. I rolled onto my back in time to see him grab another student desk by its metal legs and lift it over his head like a club.

Katie screamed. "Stop!" She ran for the door.

Sheer panic, the kind that convinces your body to forget potty training, punched me in the guts. Agony paid a visit to my cranium once again in the form of a skull-shattering headache. In a few seconds, that desk was going to make the headache seem minor.

Time seemed to slow. The light in the room brightened. The odor of sour fear mingled with Old Spice and the chemical bite of industrial floor cleanser, attacked my nose. The volume of Katie's scream spiked to an eardrum-rupturing wail. My eyes swept across the room, picking out minor details I'd never noticed before. A crack marred the surface of the chalkboard. Someone had carved curse words on Mrs. Dalton's desk. Five number two pencils jutted from the ceiling tiles. Mustard stained Nathan's faded red T-shirt. A ghostly presence demanded my attention and drew my eyes to Katie's slow-motion fleeing form. It drifted from her body in a halo of steam, vanishing into the ether just inches from her skin. What was it? Gas? Vapor? A part of me could feel it. It felt hot and sensual and—

Holy crap a desk is about to crush my face!

Time sped up again. My hands shot up, palms out in a vain attempt to intercept the desk as Nathan swung it down on me. Life was at an end. Horrific images flashed past: How the impact would shatter both hands and crush my face to a bloody unrecognizable pulp. Only dental records would identify me after this mauling.

Plastic surgery, here I come.

Although plastic surgery might be a good thing. I could use a few tweaks and some serious liposuction. Lasik eye surgery wouldn't be bad either. It occurred to me that putting a positive spin on my imminent face smashing was a very odd way to be spending the last split second of my life.

The desk smacked against my hands with a loud *whack*. I gritted my teeth in anticipation of bone-crushing agony. Pain apparently had gone on holiday because it never arrived. I cracked open an eye. One hand gripped the front edge of the desk. The other gripped the vinyl seat attached by metal tubing to the rest of the desk. Nathan's scarlet face glared at me from above. He was trying to force it down on my face.

And failing.

This came as quite a shock to me. It didn't even feel like I was straining. I let my arms relax ever so slightly so I could bend my elbows. Nathan grunted in triumph. I shoved back with everything I had and let go of the desk.

Nathan's nose gave a sickening crunch. He bellowed and pinwheeled like a rollerblading ballerina on heroin, smashed backwards through several desks, and bounced off the wall. It was all over but the screaming—Nathan's screaming. I felt my undamaged face to make sure I wasn't dreaming. My glasses rested halfway up my forehead. I pulled them down over my eyes just as my body went limp as overcooked spaghetti. It was all I could do to wiggle my toes.

Katie knelt next to me, a radiant smile on her face. "You saved me, Justin!"

"Ungh," was all I managed to say. My eyelids drooped and everything went black.

I WOKE up with a cold compress on my forehead. I blinked and struggled into an upright position, squinting at the blurry room around me. I found my glasses on a stand next to the cot and put them on. The nurse's office came into focus. Thankfully, no nurse around. The last time I'd been here she tried to shove a glass thermometer up my ass because she didn't trust the new-fangled electronic ones.

I sneaked out of the room and into the hallway. Voices echoed from around the corner. I slipped back into the recessed doorway and froze.

"I ain't letting my best player get expelled 'cause of some little fat retard," said the familiar voice of Coach Burgundy. "What'd that little girl say about the incident?"

"Don't you worry none, I'll handle the boy." Principal Lee Perkins could have been the voice of Foghorn Leghorn with his genteel southern accent, but he wasn't nearly as funny as a giant talking rooster with his good ol' boy attitude. "I'll probably have to suspend Nathan for a day or two, just for show to keep the girl quiet."

"If she posts any of this on the line, we'll have hell to pay." Burgundy made a spitting noise. "Gotta make sure that don't happen."

"Don't you worry about the internet now," Perkins assured him as their voices faded. "We got this."

I trembled in anger and a little bit of fear. I didn't want to be on the principal's radar or the subject of Burgundy's wrath. Football was god in these parts, and the Quarterback Club could probably have me murdered for free. But I was also furious how they talked so casually about Katie.

Nathan was going to rape her!

I wished I wasn't so weak and helpless. If it hadn't been for pure adrenalin, Nathan would've smashed my face earlier. My entire day was going to hell in a handbasket and I had no idea how to turn it around.

Grabbing my books and going home seemed like a great idea. Screw the rest of the day. I just wanted to put as much space between me and this place as possible. I looked up at one of the hallway clocks and was shocked to see it was already three forty-five. Classes had been over for almost an hour and I'd missed the bus.

I smacked my palm on my forehead. "The entire universe hates me," I groaned.

My book bag sat behind the desk in the calculus classroom. I snagged it and grabbed my other books from the locker. Hell, I didn't even know if I had homework tonight or if I'd missed important lessons.

I went out the front door without being noticed by anyone except the janitorial staff and hurried through the parking lot and out of the still open gates. Across the road in a strip mall parking lot, I saw the goth girl talking to someone in a black sedan through an open window. I wondered if it was her drug dealer or the goth version of the Avon lady.

"Hey, kid."

I stiffened and turned. A tall twenty-something man in a leather duster and a flat-brimmed cowboy hat nodded at me as if he'd just finished a cattle drive out of Texas and was greeting the local townsfolk of Decatur.

"Yes?" I backed up a step.

"Hey, ain't nothing to be afraid of, kid." The man nodded his head toward the school. "I'm just trying to find out if the Slade kids go to school here."

"The who kids?" I scrunched my forehead in a confused look. "Slade? I've never heard the name before."

He took out a fancy looking smartphone and tapped on the screen. I noticed the logo of a half-peeled orange on the back and wondered if it was a custom case or some phone I'd never heard of. "Well, you're the twentieth person to tell me that, so I guess this isn't the place." He looked around. "Any other high schools around these parts?"

"Are you some kind of pervert?" I asked.

He snorted. "No, I'm a private investigator. I was hired by the father to see if his ex-wife is sending them to public or private school because she's asking for more alimony." He grimaced. "Nasty business, kid, but you can't blame a man for protecting his assets."

I wasn't sure if I believed him, but I nodded slowly as if agreeing. "Sure."

A breeze blew the flap of his duster away from his side, revealing a wooden rod in a holster on his belt. I pretended not to notice, but wondered if the guy carried nun-chucks with him.

Nun-chucks on a cowboy?

"Thanks for the help, kid." The man turned and crossed the road where a group of students loitered in the strip mall.

"Maybe I accidentally took LSD this morning." I hit the side of my temple as if that might click the cogs back into place, but nope, I hadn't dreamed this crazy day. I fidgeted with my smartphone and wished my parents weren't out of town on business. Unfortunately, I didn't have anyone else to call, so I hoofed it home.

I had a dozen messages on my phone, some from Harry asking why I wasn't home to show them the new swords, and several from Katie, telling me I was her hero.

I texted Katie first. *I'm just glad I could help. Did you report Nathan to the authorities?*

Next, I messaged Harry. *Dude, I'm sorry. Crazy day! Could you come pick me up from school? I missed the bus. I'll show you guys the swords.*

A mile passed before I got the first response from Katie. *No, I don't want the whole school finding out. They'll think I'm a slut!*

But Nathan freaking tried to rape you! I sent back.

Justin, please, no. They'll turn me into bad guy. It's easier just to let it go.

I messaged her again, trying to convince her to report Nathan, but she didn't respond. I was nearly home when Harry texted me back.

Hey, sorry, just got your message. It's cool. We can look at the swords tomorrow.

I blew out a sigh. The insides of my thighs were raw from chub rub, and the rest of me ached even worse. I trudged through the front door of the small square house I called home and locked the door behind me. The house was dead silent, but I was used to it. Dad was always out of town selling his art, and Mom was an accounting consultant always on the go.

It was probably for the best. Dad was one of those cool good-looking guys who probably never had a woman problem in his life, and my friends always commented on how hot my mom was. Apparently, I was the reason they stopped having kids because I came out fat, ugly, and nerdy. I didn't understand how their combined genes could've even made a creature like me.

I stared at my homely reflection in the mirror as I brushed my teeth. I was almost eighteen and still didn't have a lick of facial hair—just peach fuzz. An oily mane of dark hair hung to my shoulders. Even so, I wasn't sad. Hell, at least I had parents and a good life for the most part. I planned to graduate tops in my class and find a way to make a million bucks.

Assholes like Nathan and his football goons burned bright as the sun in high school, but fizzled out right after they hit the real world. Unfortunately, I had to deal with those flaming bright assholes tomorrow. I'd somehow hurt their almighty leader, and they'd never let me get away with that.

CHAPTER 3

The next day as I hopped on the school bus, all eyes locked onto me. Word had gotten around about my "fight" with Nathan. People whispered. Someone laughed.

"Congrats, Justin. You almost got our best football player expelled," said a guy from somewhere behind me.

I didn't turn to look. I didn't stop moving until reaching the back of the bus and settling into an empty seat next to the window. A wad of paper flew through the air and landed in the unoccupied seat ahead of me. I hunched down and looked out the window, watching as my tree-lined neighborhood vanished from sight, soon replaced by the tall buildings of downtown Decatur, Georgia, one of many towns swallowed up in the sprawl of metro Atlanta. It was all I could do to ignore the jibes and taunts lobbed at me, but I was in no mood to get my butt kicked by standing up for myself.

Somehow, the news about Katie's assault had gotten out. The administration put on a good show, but made up enough reasons to not expel Nathan, especially since Katie refused to come forward and share her side of the story.

I probably should have been more worried about the potential fallout, but all I could think of was Katie and how she'd reward me for coming to her rescue. *Hell, I might even get a kiss out of this!*

Three police cars, lights flashing, sat against the curb in the parking lot, forcing the bus to pull around them. Half a dozen cops shoved a struggling Ralph Porter out of the back door. He bucked like a bull, screaming and foaming at the mouth.

Everyone piled onto the side of the bus facing the scene.

Ralph roared and shouldered two cops away despite the handcuffs. He slammed another officer, sending the man tumbling nearly ten feet.

Oohs and *Ahhs* filled the bus.

Lenny Jones, one of the most redneck people in the school, raised a fist and shouted, "Fuck the police coming straight from the underground!"

"What the hell is that kid on?" the bus driver said.

One of the fallen cops got up, red-faced and scowling.

"Ralph's about to get shot!" someone said with excitement.

The cop drew a Taser and nailed Ralph in the back. Ralph wasn't a big guy—maybe five and a half feet tall, and lean. One shock from the high-voltage weapon should've knocked him on his ass. Instead, it just seemed to piss him off. He wrenched free from the other cops and charged the guy with the Taser.

The other police drew their Tasers and tagged Ralph mercilessly. He fell to the ground, convulsing, foam spraying from his lips. At last, he went still. The police hobbled him with leg cuffs and threw him in the back of the police car.

"Dude's on serious drugs," someone nearby said.

I wondered what sort of drugs could do that to a person. A figure stepped outside of the glass doors and watched the police. *Randy.* It didn't take a genius to make the connection. Whatever he was selling had done that to Ralph.

After the police drove away, the bus driver let us off. I waited for everyone to unload, then trudged into the basketball gymnasium where our beloved administrators corralled the students before homeroom began. I searched for Katie and found her sitting with Annie and Jenny as usual. The three of them looked at me then turned back to each other, glee in their eyes, mouths chattering at light speed. They could be talking about knitting sweaters for all I knew, but it didn't matter. It felt like every stray gaze was meant for me and every moving mouth gossiped about my fight with Nathan.

I wanted to sit next to Katie. Wanted to see her smile, the curve of her lips, and know the light in those jade eyes of hers was meant for me. Instead, I veered right, walked up the bleachers, and took the first empty seat I found. I cursed myself for my inability to man up and take my rightful spot next to her. Then again, what made me think I even had a chance? I wasn't exactly God's gift to women.

Goth Girl and two of her companions strode into the gym. Hoots and hollers rang out from behind me. I looked up and saw Nathan Spelman and the other football flunkies hurling insults at the odd group. My body went cold. I hadn't realized how close I was sitting to them. I tried to make myself small and unnoticeable. My generous proportions didn't cooperate. If the school board had almost expelled Nathan, why was he already back at school? I'd expected a suspension at the least.

Stupid jocks get away with everything.

Goth Girl stared at me as her troop tromped past in their platform shoes. Thank God they existed to take unwanted attention off me. I might be nerdy but at least I didn't look bizarre. She kept staring at me with such intensity that I turned away and checked for hanging boogers. I couldn't tell if she was sizing me up for a cannibalistic ritual or wondering if I might be a good recruit to her group of weirdoes.

I stared at my *Lord of the Rings* backpack instead and decided now would be a good time to catch up on homework. Pushing my worries away, I made the finishing touches on my History essay due in another week. Going to MIT was my dream. History class wasn't exactly going to get me there, but I had to maintain decent grades across the board if I wanted to stand a chance.

The bell rang. I jammed my books into my raggedy backpack until it was bursting at the seams.

"Whoops!" said a deep voice. A large foot connected with my History book and notebook, sent them skidding down the bleachers and into the crowd of students filing out of the gym. Pages of my essay scattered, floating down to the floor to be walked on.

Nathan gave me a sarcastic look of surprise as he and his group of guffawing toadies sauntered past.

"Letters to your mommy?" one of them said.

Pure rage infected my body. I gripped my Calculus textbook in white-knuckled anger. Thankfully, some rational part of my brain locked my muscles in place before they led me to certain doom. I packed up my other books and waited for the crowd of students to die down so I could find my book and essay. My heart pounded anxiously. All that work, probably rendered illegible from footprints.

I retrieved the book from the bottom bleacher as the last few students filed out of the gym.

"This yours?" said a familiar voice.

I turned slowly to face Goth Girl. She handed me a sheaf of papers with dirty footprints all over them.

"Yeah, th-thanks," I stuttered.

I hadn't noticed her eyes yesterday —an amazing violet hue lost in a sea of black eyeliner. Her gaze seemed to lose focus as if she were looking through my skin and into my mind. I felt very uncomfortable being the subject of that questing stare. I looked down at the trampled essay to avoid her eyes. When I flicked my gaze up again, she was already halfway out of the gym. I felt like a jerk for not being more grateful, but she creeped me out.

I made my way to homeroom—always an unpleasant experience with Annie and Jenny. Sure enough, their eyes widened the moment I stepped through the door. They huddled together and started whispering. Probably something terrible about me. I did my best to ignore them and dropped into my desk. I shuffled through my essay papers, wincing at the dirty pages. I had planned to type it out anyway. Just as long as I could still read it, I was good.

Jenny tapped my shoulder. "I'll bet you think you're the man now, don't you?"

Annie giggled. "Justin? The man? More like the juice box boy."

I gritted my teeth and tried to think of something witty to say. Nothing came to mind except possibly calling them demonic bitches which, while descriptive, probably would not help me out with their bestie, Katie. I made a show of reading my essay, pretending I hadn't heard them from all of two feet away.

"Guys are such creeps," Jenny said. "I don't even know why girls put up with it."

Annie gave the sigh of the long suffering. "Tell me about it. Like that skeezy Alan Weaver. He's such a stalker, always staring at Cindy Mueller like he wants to rape her."

I had a feeling these two would fit right in on a morning talk show some day, gossiping about movie stars, or maybe starring in one of the *Real Housewives* reality shows so they could tell a national audience about their terrible sex lives.

My eyes wandered toward the open door of the classroom. The hulking figure of Nathan Spelman towered just outside. He bared his teeth at me. Cracked his knuckles. Walked away.

I had the queasy feeling saving Katie had doomed me to an even worse fate.

CHAPTER 4

M y phone beeped as the bell rang for first period. My heart raced when I realized it was from Katie.

Want to study for calculus tonight?

Joy flooded me with warm buoyant ecstasy. Nathan could pummel me to a pulp. I didn't care. Katie liked me. Why else would she text me and want to study together? I was probably getting well ahead of myself but I had visions of me and Katie riding off into the sunset on a white stallion. Maybe even a unicorn. With wings. This was my chance to impress her with my mad math skills. She would fall in love with me, and BAM! Happy ending.

Buttercup, meet Westley.

Yeah, I'm totally delusional.

I could hardly wait for lunchtime so I could tell Mark and Harry the great news. I couldn't wait to tell them how Katie was going to fall in love with me, all thanks to the power of calculus.

Lunchtime arrived and I snagged our usual table. They arrived moments later. The two of them could have been brothers with their tall lanky frames and unruly brown hair. I delivered the good news about Katie and showed them her text on my phone the second they sat down. I'd been expecting some high-fives, a congratulatory speech, and maybe even some jealous looks. Instead, they wrecked my world.

"Dude, Katie just started dating Brad Nichols," Mark said.

The image of Brad buying drugs from Randy flashed through my mind.

The screen on my phone cracked from the intensity of my grip. "Brad Nichols?" My dreams of happily ever after faded to misery. "But I saved her from Nathan! What did Brad effing Nichols ever do for her?"

"It totally blows, man." Mark sighed. "I'm really sorry. But hey, I hear Gabby Hughes is available." He winked.

"Hope you made it home okay yesterday," Harry said. "We were bummed about not seeing the swords."

"Got pics?" Mark asked.

My mind was a million miles away. My heart ached. My stomach clenched. I wanted to throw up and roar with rage at the same time but ended up getting a bad case of hiccups instead. I grabbed my grape juice box and took a long draw.

I should've brought tequila instead.

I scanned the crowded lunchroom and spotted Brad sitting with a group of girls at another table halfway across the room. Katie didn't have the same lunch period or she might be sitting with him right this very moment. Brad had on his usual leather motorcycle jacket and bad-boy "I don't give a crap" smirk. He probably kept his black hair cropped close so he wouldn't walk around with dorky helmet-hair after zipping around on his crotch rocket.

I noticed Mark staring at Brad as well, a mix of jealousy and awe mixed on his face. "Don't tell me you wish you were him," I said even though somewhere in the back of my mind, a part of me raised its hand and shouted, *I want to be like him!*

Mark gave me a guilty look and locked eyes with Harry. "I dunno. I mean, we're almost done with high school and what do we have to show for it? It'd be nice to at least have a girlfriend."

"We're number one in Kings and Castles," I reminded them.

Harry shrugged. "So what? Don't get me wrong—I still love it." He glanced back over at Brad. "But why can't we have it all?"

Just great. Not only did Brad have Katie, but he was also luring my friends away from me. I wished fervently for the zombie apocalypse to strike so I could rescue Katie from the clutches of zombie Brad with a shotgun blast to his ugly face. I'd steal his motorcycle, grip Katie around the waist and pull her on with me before roaring away to safety. Scorching anger scalded my heart. It came unexpectedly in a boiling flood washing away all reason. My face grew hot and fists balled so tight my knuckles cracked.

CONSUME! KILL! DESTROY! A guttural voice shouted in my head.

My forehead felt like twin volcanos erupted in my brain. I clenched my teeth in agony and pressed my hands to my face. Something sharp poked my fingers. Powerful odors overwhelmed my nose. Armpit stench. Hair chemicals. Old Spice.

Why is it always Old Spice?

Underneath it all lurked something powerful. Something sensual. Something female. I unclenched my eyes, but all I could see were blotches of color and blurs.

Another pulse of pain jackhammered my brain and the headache vanished. My eyesight snapped to normal. Mark and Harry regarded me with wide-eyed concern.

"You okay?" Harry nodded at a mess of purple juice on the table. "Your face went beet red and you crushed your juice box."

Mark chuckled. "I thought your eyes were gonna explode out of your skull."

"I'm fine." The headache faded in an instant like the mother of all brain-freezes. I gave Brad Nichols the evil eye again and almost asked my friends what Brad Nichols had that I didn't. Stupid question. *Everything, of course.* Over the course of my short life I'd made choices. Unhealthy choices, obviously. I'd binged on juice boxes and comfort foods and made myself fat. I'd never worked out at a gym or expanded my interests beyond Kings and Castles.

In short, I represented the blubbery sum of seventeen-plus years of bad decisions and it was time to pay the piper. Maybe those choices were the reasons these horrific migraines suddenly nailed me out of the blue. I might be dying from a brain tumor but all I could think about was Katie. I wanted to steal her from Brad and make her mine.

Unfortunately, I had an acute streak of romanticism in me that wanted True Love, *Princess Bride* style. I wanted love and marriage before sex. Call me old-fashioned, but what could be better than having your first time with the girl of your dreams? *Probably having wild sex with lots and lots of hot girls*, said my second brain. My first brain chimed in agreement, causing me to wonder which brain was really the one in charge. *Ugh.* Why couldn't girls come with manuals? Or maybe even picture cards like the ones airlines used?

I looked up from my brooding. Mark and Harry gobbled down the school cafeteria mush and talked animatedly about our upcoming Kings and Castles tournament, my torment of no concern to them.

A patch of darkness caught in my peripheral vision. I glanced right. Large black-lined eyes stared back at me. Goth Girl. Her raven-dark hair cascaded like a curtain over the white makeup covering her face. I wondered who taught her how to do her makeup. It was way overdone for Goth, bordering on emo.

I looked behind me and then back at her. She was definitely looking at me, I decided. She quirked an eyebrow and scribbled something in a notebook.

Just great. Was she jotting down something about me? I could just imagine her notes: *Subject is still alive, but death by football players is imminent. Will drink his blood for the Dark Master. Long live Cthulhu!*

I arrived home from school. Dad's red Jetta and Mom's rusty Volvo sat in the driveway. We weren't poor, but they didn't seem to give a shit about updating their cars. I eased open the front door and whisked silently into my room. I didn't want to talk to them right now. They were such a happy couple and I felt like a complete loser when it came to love and life.

Oh boo hoo hoo. Stop feeling sorry for yourself.

Easier said than done.

Loud voices jerked me from my thoughts.

"It's foolish, Alice," my dad said. "They'll never let you or her come back."

"I don't care, David. I don't give a damn what they do to me," Mom said, the words raw with anger.

"But I do." The tremble of pain in my dad's voice stabbed me in my heart. What in the world was going on? Had something terrible happened?

I rushed from my room and crossed the hallway to their open door. My parents embraced, their tear-streaked faces red and tortured.

"Who died?" I asked, unsure what to feel since I didn't really know any of my relatives and I didn't think my parents would be this upset over one of my classmates.

They leapt apart like two teenagers caught on the couch, wiping tears from cheeks.

"Your aunt Petunia," Mom said, first as usual to regain composure in a pressure situation.

"Tragic," Dad said, offering me his trademark broad grin.

I stared at the two of them with narrowed eyes for a moment. They were hiding something, but Mom quickly slid her cool façade back in place. She crossed the room and pressed a hand to my head. "Are you feeling okay?" Her forehead wrinkled. "Why is your arm bruised?"

I sighed and pushed her hand away. "I'm fine. Everything is peachy keen and perfect in my life." I turned to walk out the door. "Which side of the family is dear Auntie Petunia on?"

"Mine." Mom's placid gaze met mine. "She was a fine woman."

"Since I've never met *any* of my relatives, I guess I'll have to take your word for it."

"Justin, we've been over this before," Mom said. "Your father's family and mine don't get along."

"That's putting it mildly," Dad chimed in.

She gave him an exasperated look. "David, please!" She turned back to me. "As a result, we're not on the best of terms with either of our families."

"But Aunt Petunia is special?"

"Yes."

Dad clapped his hands together. "With that settled, how about some supper?"

In the kitchen five minutes later, Mom dropped a microwaved meal in front of me. It made a moist squishy noise when the plastic tray hit the table. The poof of steam rising from it looked vaguely mushroom-shaped. I couldn't remember the last time she'd made something in the microwave. She loved to cook. I loved to eat what she cooked. That was part of the reason for the spare tractor tire around my waist.

Mom gave me a concerned look. "You have bruises on both arms and your neck."

"Getting kinky with the ladies, son?" Dad waggled his eyebrows.

Mom rolled her eyes and groaned. "I swear to god, David. He's still too young for your perverted sense of humor."

Dad snorted. "He's seventeen, Alice. When I was his age—"

Mom's eyebrows rose. "Please continue, honey. I'd love to hear this."

"—I was a perfect gentleman." Dad smirked and pushed away his microwaved meal. "Justin, do you like gladiator movies?"

It was my turn to roll my eyes. "Dad, you need some new movie quotes. That one's older than your buckskin rubbers."

He burst into laughter.

Mom threw up her hands. "Great, he's already corrupted."

"Well, I am almost eighteen." I shrugged. "I was bound to start talking dirty at some point."

Dad ruffled my hair. "Never be afraid to curse or tell a lady what you want, son."

Mom pushed his hand away and replaced it with her cool palm. She frowned and looked at Dad. "Something touched his aura."

I groaned. "Mom, won't you quit with that new-age crap?"

Dad's smile faded. "Better renew the protections. Just in case it's not nothing this time."

Mom went through her rituals, tracing symbols on my forehead. While it made me tingle, I prayed to god none of my friends ever saw the weird hippie crap my parents believed in.

"Should I get a pet rock to protect me while I'm at it?" I asked sarcastically. "I'll name him George, and hug him and squeeze him, and throw him at anyone who threatens me."

"Talk about older than buckskin rubbers." Dad shook his head. "Son, eat, um"—he looked at the nuked mush in the tray—"whatever in the hell that is."

"It's roast turkey, spinach, and mashed potatoes." Mom put her hands on her hips. "I don't always have time to prepare gourmet meals."

I scooped up a green gob and tasted it. "Pretty sure this is soylent green."

"Sometimes it's okay to eat people, son." Dad dug in and polished his off, grimacing the entire time.

Mom went down the hallway to her office, and I figured it was time for a father and son talk. "Dad, did you ever want a girl who was out of your league?"

He raised an eyebrow. "You mean like your mother?" He winked.

I'm strictly heterosexual and not incestuous or anything, but my dad is a fairly handsome man. I'd overheard Myra Bergdorf and another woman swooning over him in the grocery store once. Women would give him this really intense stare, like he was a celebrity or wearing chocolate body spray. The only woman who never looked at him that way was Mom. I guess being married helps you look past a person's charm. Unfortunately, I didn't have Dad's good looks or his chocolate BO.

He pushed away the empty microwave dinner and leaned back in his chair. "First of all, you're coming at it from the wrong perspective. No one is out of your league unless you put them there. Second, everyone has problems, even the hottest girls and the most popular boys."

"What sort of problems?" I asked.

"Bad home life, drugs, insecurities, teen pregnancy, the Catholic Church, genital herpes—"

"Gross!" I shuddered and hoped Katie didn't have the latter. "So what do I do?"

"Well…" he looked me up and down. "Women want a man to look like he respects himself."

"In other words, I'm fat."

He chuckled. "Yes, you are." Dad held up his hands defensively, as if I

JOHN CORWIN

might argue with him. "Nothing wrong with a little girth, son, but it wouldn't hurt to tone up a little." *99 Problems* erupted in his pocket. He took out his phone. "Business call. Sorry, I gotta take it."

I sighed as he walked away. All the toning up in the world probably wouldn't turn me into a lady killer like my dad.

My phone beeped—a text from Katie. *Still on for tonight?*

Despite the crushing sense of defeat upon learning about her and Brad, a tiny ray of hope blossomed. *I'm so optimistic it makes me sick.* I knew I was only setting myself up for another dose of hurt, but it didn't matter.

I agreed to meet her over at her place in half an hour. I spent the next few minutes putting on my best pair of cargo pants and an XXL T-shirt to cover my belly and B-cup tits. I brushed my shoulder-length hair to a silky sheen, then considered a nineties-style ponytail to add a pinch of action-movie bad guy to my look, but the thick glasses just murdered it.

I took Dad's Jetta and scooted over to Katie's house, singing *Friday* at the top of my lungs.

I parked at the curb near Katie's house and walked up the driveway. Soft sobbing noises emanated from ahead. Katie sat under the glow of the outside lights near the front door.

"Katie?" I stopped in my tracks. "Are you okay?"

She sniffled and wiped at her eyes. "Oh, God, I'm so embarrassed."

I sat down next to her. "What's wrong?"

She blew her red nose into a tissue and shook her head. The girl might be gorgeous under normal circumstances, but she was an ugly crier.

I didn't care.

She pulled out a fresh tissue and wiped her nose. "You know Brad, right?"

34

"Of course," I said in a tone that indicated Brad and I were old friends, even though my insides prickled with jealousy.

"He's a real jackass."

On the outside, I managed to craft a concerned look instead of smiling or laughing maniacally. On the inside I danced a jig. "What did the jerk do?"

"I've seen Rebecca talking to him a lot. He always tells me they're just friends."

I nodded solemnly. "Yeah. Not a good sign." Rebecca Simmons was one of the perpetual beauty pageant girls in the school. Pretty hot, I had to admit, but nobody topped Katie, not in my book. And what in the world was so special about Brad "I have a motorcycle" Nichols that made the girls want to talk to him? He didn't play sports, he wasn't muscular, and he seemed dumb as a brick. It had to be the motorcycle. That in and of itself probably added plus ten charisma to his character.

Riding the school bus was, by comparison, minus a million cool points.

"Jenny told me she saw Brad riding through Midtown with Rebecca on the back of his bike." Another sob shook her.

A wave of hot anger crept up my chest. How could guys like Brad get away with such bullshit? He had the most perfect girl in the universe crying over him while guys like me could only dream of even kissing a girl like Katie.

My brain abruptly decided now was the time to attack its bony prison again. Jackhammers pounded inside my forehead. Agony pulsed in my temples. Katie's face blurred and an incredible musky aroma tickled my nose. Steaming sexuality lingered at the edge of my senses, teasing me, beckoning me to take it and make it mine. A part of me reached for it. But a searing flash of agony ripped me back to reality. I winced and gritted my teeth but Katie kept talking as if nothing had happened.

"...I thought it was something really special. He told me he loved me. I just don't understand, Justin. I really need a guy's perspective on this. What do you think I should do?"

The headache vanished, leaving me in a slightly euphoric state as endorphins flooded my system. The blurry shape in my view sharpened into Katie's face. She looked at me, probably waiting for a response to Brad's outrageous behavior.

"Dump him," I managed to croak.

"Why can't I find a nice guy?"

I'm right here! I wanted to scream. Outwardly, I plastered a concerned look on my face. "Rebecca sleeps around. I hear she has genital herpes."

Katie sobbed even harder. It made me feel a lot better.

"I can't believe he would do this," she said between gasps.

I couldn't believe she was taking this so hard. Hadn't they just started dating? Was she really that head-over-heels in love with the guy? And then it hit me. My mouth spit out what my brain imagined without me meaning or wanting to say it aloud. "You slept with him."

Her eyes widened. Her face blanched. "Is it that obvious?" She blew noisily into a tissue. "Please, you can't tell anyone."

I couldn't believe she hadn't just denied it. "I won't."

A single tear trickled down her wet cheek. "I can't believe I let him be my first. We had so much fun together. And now I feel horrible." Sobs wracked her body.

I put an arm around her shoulders. At some point I might have fantasized about this moment, about squeezing Katie's hot body to mine, but the magic turned to ashes, leaving a bitter taste in my mouth and an ache in my heart. So much for true love. So much for riding off into the sunset.

Katie had wrecked her virginity against the uncaring shores of Brad Nichols.

I wanted to kill him.

When she finally calmed down—which took a while—she hugged me back. "I feel so bad for unloading all of this on you, Justin. You're such a great guy. I wish there were more like you out there."

"You want more overweight nerds in the world?" My voice sounded as dead as my heart.

She laughed. "See, nothing bothers you. I know we've known each other a long time but I guess we've never gotten to know each other."

A dull throb pulsed in my forehead. Great. All I needed was another headache. Katie's face blended into an indistinct blur as the pain increased. This cranial assault wasn't as sudden as the others. It crept from my forehead to the back of my brain and slithered down my spine, all ice, fire, and needles. I sensed that strange presence again. It was Katie, but at the same time it wasn't. Part of her ached to be free. Begged me to grab her by the hair and smack her on the ass.

Katie gasped. Our lips met. She pressed herself to me willingly and all thoughts of the world faded into bliss.

And then a bomb went off in my skull.

I wrenched away from her and the ghostly presence slipped from my grasp. The pain flashed away as quickly as it had come. I stared at Katie. She stared at me. I didn't know what to say about the last few seconds. We'd kissed, right? It hadn't been a dream? Maybe these migraines caused hallucinations. I didn't know what to think anymore.

Katie's huge green eyes focused on me. "Justin, that was…unexpected."

So we *had* kissed. "All part of my master plan for world domination." *Where in the world did that come from?*

She smiled. "I can't figure you out. You're brave—I mean just look what you did to Nathan. And now you've made me feel so much better tonight."

I noticed she hadn't said a thing about the kiss. Had she hated it? Loved it? I tossed out a joke to protect my feelings. "Probably my Axe body spray."

A giggle burst from her lips. "You're funny too." She looked at me for a moment and I could see the uncertainty looming in her eyes. "Justin, I really like you. But I don't know—"

"Hey, it's fine." I jumped up and brushed off my cargo pants. "Look, I have a Kings and Castles tournament this Saturday. You want to come?"

"Is that the restaurant with the jousting knights?"

"Um, not exactly. It's mostly a bunch of nerds clubbing each other with foam weapons."

"Ooh, that sounds fun to watch."

"Cool. I'll text you the details." I waved goodbye and made for the car before she could overanalyze what just happened. I felt heady. Unstoppable. *I kissed Katie Johnson.* Holy crap, I'd really done it. I hooted with laughter and smacked the steering wheel. I tried to forget mystery behind this flawless victory.

What were these headaches, these hallucinations, these bizarre sensations? Had they somehow helped me secure the kiss from Katie?

Or was I simply going crazy?

CHAPTER 5

Mark and Harry couldn't believe what I'd done when I told them in the gymnasium the next morning. Jenny and Annie sat in their usual spot but Katie wasn't there.

"You're fearless," Mark said with awe in his voice.

"Balls of steel." Harry slapped me on the back. "And she's coming to the tournament, too? You are the *man*."

I felt like the man. Kind of, anyway. I also felt a bit apprehensive about Brad Nichols finding out. The bell rang and I headed for homeroom down the barren cinder-block hallways of the school.

A commotion echoed from around the corner ahead. A few wads of notebook paper sailed into the hallway behind the hurrying form of one of the Goth guys I'd seen hanging with Goth Girl. Nathan and his gang rounded the corner, hurling insults and paper at the guy. I felt bad, but not bad enough that it was worth getting whacked.

One of Nathan's linebacker friends said something to the others then jogged after the Goth. He had something in his hand and I knew that whatever it was wouldn't be good for his prey.

Don't do it! Noooo! The rational part of my mind screamed at me.

I couldn't stand by and do nothing. So I tripped and fell right in front of the very large guy chasing down the Goth. The air exploded from my lungs as his weight thudded on my back.

The football player cursed at me. His buddies guffawed.

"Case you fucking moron." Nathan glared at me down his purple bruised nose. It didn't look as bad as I'd thought it would. From all the blood, I thought I'd broken it for sure.

The football player I'd tripped pushed himself up. "I guess you get the present then." He shoved an open plastic baggie toward my face with something inside that looked and smelled suspiciously like dog poop.

"Ahem," said an authoritarian voice.

We looked to see Mr. Turpin, my former boxer-turned-English teacher staring at us, his muscular arms bulging threateningly.

"Stay on task, Steve." His voice sounded gentle but with an edge, like butter on a sword.

Apparently Steve was the name of the buffoon who had almost smeared poo on my face.

"Aw, we're just playing around," Steve said.

Mr. Turpin stared at the baggie and then held out a hand.

Steve pshawed and handed it over. "Whatever." He shoved past me. "Guess we'll get something fresh for you later, Case."

Nathan bulled past me, eyes full of hate, and followed his pals down the hall.

A strong hand gripped me by the bicep and pulled me up. I turned, expecting to see Mr. Turpin's large hands on my arm and yelped as I came face to face with Goth Girl yet again. She drew in a deep breath through her nose. I could swear the girl was sniffing me just like Randy had. I pulled away from her, gently so as not to be too rude.

"Thanks." I backed up a step. "Are you following me?"

She snorted. "Yeah, that's it. I'm following you." She rolled her eyes. "Thanks for saving Ash."

"Who?" I asked.

Her eyes flashed. "Never give up." With that, she walked away.

"Kids these days." Mr. Turpin shook his head. "They never stay on task."

I had a feeling Mr. Turpin had been hit in the head a lot during his boxing days. He was a nice, soft-spoken guy, but he repeated, "Stay on task" like it was holy mantra even if it didn't fit the occasion. Then again, who was I to talk?

On the way home from school, Katie texted me, asking if I could study tonight. I told her I would after dinner.

As I approached home, a shout from inside grabbed my attention. I paused at the front door and pressed an ear against it. I heard indistinct voices but nothing loud enough to understand. I sneaked through the garage and around the pile of rakes and other yard implements that still looked new as the day Dad had bought them. The garage door didn't offer any better eavesdropping so I twisted the doorknob slowly and eased the door open into the kitchen. I peeked through the crack and caught a glimpse of my parents standing just inside the den.

"…won't happen to him," Dad said. "We would know for sure by now."

Mom sighed. "And I told you it doesn't matter. Everything depends on this. Everything. You need to keep it together or the Slades might—"

Slade? I stiffened at the mention of that name. It was the same last name of the kids that cowboy dude had asked about.

"Wait." Dad held out a hand and sniffed the air. He motioned Mom

41

further into the den and out of sight. "Do we need groceries for tonight?"

"Nope. Dinner is in the freezer."

"Not again."

"Yes, again."

A few seconds later, a door slammed shut. Something was seriously wrong with my parents. Arguments, microwaved dinners, and Dad sniffing the air like a coonhound. Maybe Aunt Petunia's death was screwing with their minds. And who were the Slades? A part of me wanted to ask my father, but I didn't want him to know I'd eavesdropped.

"Hey, son." Dad looked like a miserable person faking a grin. He reached into the fridge and grabbed a six-pack of beer.

"When did you start drinking?"

Dad popped open a beer bottle and took a swallow. He made a face. "I've always enjoyed a beer or two."

"Or six?" I stared at the bottles in his hand.

"Justin, I know you don't like to tell us everything. I was the same way when I was your age."

"I think keeping secrets goes for people of all ages." I gave him a pointed look.

He chuckled. "What I'm getting at is—"

"Sorry, Dad, but I've got a study date with a girl tonight and I really need to get a move on."

Dad took another swig of beer and winked. "That's great." He looked as though he wanted to say something else but instead took his beer into the den and tuned into a reality show featuring a bunch of women screaming at each other.

I nuked a meal in the microwave, gussied myself up, and went to Katie's.

"Hey Justin." she gave me an awkward hug.

I tried to say something witty but my brain failed me. "Hi." Where was all my bravado from last night? Apparently it took an extended vacation because we actually studied Calculus until nine. We didn't say a thing about Brad or our kiss. It was like it never happened. Or maybe I was supposed to man up and kiss her again. Why couldn't she just tell me what she wanted?

Katie walked me outside after we finished our homework. "Thanks for helping me out. I really appreciate it."

I could hardly stand it. She was so unlike most of the hot girls I knew—or knew of, in any case. She seemed smart and yet she fell for smack-tards like Brad. I tried to muster the courage to kiss her, but her hug came fast and her body language seemed to indicate a kiss was off the table.

Grow a pair and kiss her.

Yeah. It wasn't going to happen.

When I arrived at home, Dad was still up watching TV. A pile of empty beer bottles littered the coffee table. I went into my room and changed into cargo shorts and a T-shirt. The rest of the house was silent. "Where's Mom?"

Dad kept his eyes on the tube. "Girls' night out."

"Shouldn't you be doing a boys' night out then?"

"This is boys' night out." He motioned me over to the couch, thumbed the cap off another beer bottle, handed it to me.

"Seriously? Won't Mom kick your butt for contributing to the delin-quency of minors?"

"That's all life is, kiddo. When you've had enough contributions to your delinquency, then you're officially an adult."

"Deep stuff." I took a swig. Beer always tasted great for the first few sips then gross like carbonated toilet water. Of course this was one of those major father-son milestones and I wasn't about to spoil it for Dad or myself.

Dad turned off the TV and studied me for a moment. "About our earlier conversation—"

"Girls?" I asked.

He nodded. "Anything strange ever happen?"

His question struck a nerve. I narrowed my eyes, unsure if I wanted to confide about my hallucinations and headaches just yet. "Well, girls make me feel funny in my no-no place."

Dad snorted and clinked his beer bottle against mine. "Yes they do, son. Yes they do."

My dad wasn't the type to go after-school special on me, so I took a long guzzle of beer. "I'm going to take your advice."

"Advice?" He quirked an eyebrow.

"About toning up." I flexed a flabby bicep. "I'm gonna get buff."

He clapped me on the shoulder. "Atta boy."

I finished off my first beer and then a second. I felt warm, fuzzy, and happy, like drinking hot chocolate on a freezing cold day. I also felt very clever. Apparently alcohol increases charm and courage by at least ten points. I tapped out a text to Katie. Dad snatched my phone before I could send the masterpiece and put the phone out of my reach.

"Not a good idea." He chuckled. "You'll thank me in the morning."

"But everything is so clear. I have to tell her now."

"Yeah. Sure it is. That's your last beer, kiddo. Drink plenty of water if you don't want to feel like crap tomorrow."

I took his advice and drank water until I felt it might leak from my ears.

I woke up the next morning with only a mild hangover and a bursting bladder. My phone lay next to my computer. I looked at it and the text I had almost sent to Katie.

U R teh most beautiful perfect creature that will ever walk this Earth and I am ur king 4eva.

I grimaced and deleted the atrocity before my fat fingers accidentally sent it. Adults really do know what they're talking about sometimes. I thanked Dad under my breath for saving me from virtually castrating myself. A screenshot of the message would have likely found its way to social media if Jenny or Annie had gotten hold of Katie's phone.

I checked the clock and realized I'd never be ready in time for the school bus. I popped a couple of ibuprofen to quell the slight ache in my skull and got ready. I drove Dad's Jetta to school since he had a motorcycle if he needed to get out.

As I looked for a parking spot I noticed a mass of students milling on the wide sidewalk behind the school entrance. *Strange.* Usually everyone went inside, especially considering the cold and the freezing wind. Gray clouds scudded across the sky. Rain puddles dotted the asphalt. It was not a good day to be outside. I figured the principal must be running a fire drill.

After heaving my backpack on my right shoulder, I made my way toward the milling crowd and the doors to the school. My breath frosted in the cold morning air and my glasses fogged up a bit thanks to the knit cap I wore low over my forehead. I stopped for a moment to take off my glasses and wipe them. As I stood there I noticed how quiet the crowd had become. I pushed my glasses back on and looked ahead. Dozens of eyes stared back. I looked behind me expecting to see the latest pre-pubescent pop star step out of a limo. Nope, nobody there.

My stomach writhed and scurried away to hide in my bowels. Something was seriously amiss this morning. *Nathan.* He waited for me. I just knew it. I almost backpedaled and made a run for my car but that would only postpone the inevitable. I had to think my way out of this. The crowd parted as I reached the edge. Familiar green eyes locked onto mine as I stepped into an arena in the middle of the mob. Katie stood a few feet from the glass doors leading into the school. Next to her stood a person that made my heart freeze.

Brad Nichols punched a leather-gloved fist into his palm and grinned.

CHAPTER 6

I f there was ever a time for me to soil my underwear, it was now. Thankfully, that didn't happen. Brad approached, malice gleaming in his eyes.

Katie gripped his arm. "Stop, Brad. Please!"

He jerked his arm free and promptly ignored her. He looked me up and down. It didn't take long, considering I stood at least a full head shorter. He wasn't nearly as tall as Nathan but that didn't matter. I waited for him to taunt me. Instead, he buried his fist in my stomach.

My backpack fell from my shoulder. I staggered back, gasping for breath and wheeling to the right. A low hedge tripped me. My face planted in a puddle of muck. I jerked my head clear and took in a shuddering breath but got a mouthful of brown slime instead. Mud caked the left side of my glasses and dribbled icy fingers down my cheek. Through the right side I saw Mark and Harry snorting with laughter next to a couple of other guys I didn't know. They caught my gaze and sobered, apologetic expressions on their faces. Rage flared in my chest. I pushed myself to my knees. I didn't care what happened. I was going to beat the crap out of Brad.

Before I could stand, however, Brad grabbed my jacket and hauled me backwards over the hedge. He snatched off my knit cap and tossed it away before shoving me on my back. Cold water seeped into the seat of my pants. I tried to spring to my feet but my girth hampered me. I rolled onto my knees, soaking the front of my pants in a water puddle. My hands went numb with cold.

Katie gripped Brad by the arm. He shoved her away and she hit her head on the door. Raw fury flowed into my veins. *Do something, you fat idiot!* Pain burst into my skull. It wasn't from Brad this time. It was my stupid migraines flaring up again. Brad's fist caught me in the cheek. My glasses flew off. My jaw ached but didn't hurt nearly as much as it should have. I roared. Brad howled with laughter. I probably looked like an infuriated chipmunk.

"Look at the angry little pig," he said. Gales of laughter from the onlookers assaulted my dignity.

I jumped to my feet. He came at me again, fist cocked, eyes smug. I swung. My fist connected. His jaw made a terrible popping noise. His feet left the ground. An astonished look came over his stupid face as he fell right into the same puddle he'd put me in.

KILL. DESTROY!

Rage consumed me. I just wanted to tear Brad apart. My fingers reached for his throat.

The headache abruptly vanished, and with it, my anger. Everything blurred again. I felt my face, but of course, my glasses weren't there. I fumbled on the ground. A gentle hand touched mine and pressed the glasses into it. I put them on. The lenses were clean. I looked up, expecting to see Katie smiling at her new hero. Instead I choked back a gasp as Goth Girl swam into focus.

Katie hovered over Brad, tears in her eyes. She put his head in her lap and smoothed his cropped hair. My mouth dropped open. Why was she babying that asshole? I almost screamed in frustration.

Harry and Mark walked up.

"Holy crap, man!" Harry put a hand over his mouth to hold in laughter. "Didn't think you had it in you."

"I hope it was entertaining," I growled.

Harry smirked. "Look, man, it *was* kind of funny."

I lunged at him and knocked him on his butt. The smirk vanished.

"Thank God I have such great friends." I shouted for everyone to hear. "People I can count on when some asshole beats the crap out of me."

Mark placed himself between me and Harry. "What the hell, Justin?"

Harry leapt to his feet, pushed past Mark, and shoved me. "You idiot," he spat. "You never had a chance with Katie. You're just a delusional nerd."

Cold anger frosted my heart. Somehow, I kept clenched fists at my sides instead of flailing at him. I glanced at Katie as she helped Brad off the ground. She didn't even look at me. Instead, I met Goth Girl's eyes. She leaned on wall near the entrance, lips pursed.

Just inside the doors to the school, I saw Randy, a malicious glint in his eyes. He gave me a thumbs-up and vanished.

What in the hell was that about? I shivered as a cold gust of wind hit my wet clothes.

With the spectacle over, students filed inside the school. The nerd had won the fight, but none of them seemed impressed. I had a feeling videos would surface soon enough.

Goth Girl walked over to me when the crowd died down. "Trouble seems to follow you." She held out a hand. "I'm Crye."

"Uh." I took her hand and winced at her strong grip. "Justin." I shook my hand after she released it. "Damn, you've got an iron grip."

She chuckled. "And you have a nice uppercut." Crye shrugged. "I mean, your form is awful, but when you connected"—she smacked a fist into her palm. "Pow!"

"Truthfully, I don't even know how I did it," I admitted. "Pure luck."

"I heard you did a number on Nathan Spelman too." Crye arched her eyebrows. "Was that luck too?" Her nostrils flared.

"Are you smelling me?" I sniffed my armpits. "Do I stink now?"

Another chuckle. "You don't stink, but you look like hell. Maybe you should go home and clean up."

I looked down at my muddy clothes. Nodded. "Yeah, maybe I'll do that."

Crye rolled her eyes. "Nothing like high school drama to start the day."

"Or teen angst," I added. "I mean, I'm hopelessly in love with a girl who only wants a drug-using, herpes-infested, motorcycle-riding asshole for a boyfriend."

"Very angsty," she agreed. Shrugged. "Motorcycles aren't just for assholes though."

I looked around the parking lot as if searching. "You have a motorcycle?"

"Maybe." The bell rang and she sighed. "Oh, shit. Back to the angsty teenage drama that is high school." She punched me in the shoulder. "Go get cleaned up, hero."

I stood, somewhat stunned and a little shell-shocked as she went inside. I really hated to admit it, but I actually kind of liked that girl's attitude. I wondered if she was so Goth or emo, that she'd come full circle and was now in the irony stage.

Thoughts of Katie circled through my mind. For some reason, it didn't bother me nearly as much as it should have. My wet clothes in the freezing wind certainly did, though.

I grabbed my backpack off the ground and made a beeline for the Jetta, shivering violently from the gusting wind. My thoughts again gravitated to the fight and Katie doting over Brad. I couldn't help but feel sad and a bit betrayed, but what had I expected?

I was lucky to survive a fight with anyone, much less Brad.

My phone chimed. *Katie?*

No, a text from the wireless company, telling me my bill was ready to view. I sighed and tried not to think about her. A cheerful ding informed me the Jetta was almost out of fuel. I steered into a gas station.

As the gas gallon counter slowly ticked upward and the dollar amount skyrocketed to epic proportions, a low growling caught my ear. I looked at the dumpsters about twenty feet to my left. A pack of stray dogs snarled at a huddled form trapped between a brown metal dumpster and the brick wall bordering the refuse area. I took a few cautious steps forward until I could make out the shape of a perturbed cat. It arched its back and hissed at the dogs.

A large gray dog pounced. The cat leapt back. Huge slobbering jaws snapped on empty air. Why did the big guys always have to pick on the little ones? Bullies like Brad and Nathan and these stupid dogs were one and the same. Anger-fueled lunacy replaced the final dredges of logic in my addled mind. I ran at the dogs, yelling and waving my arms like an idiot. The big hound turned toward me, hackles raised, baring sharp and scary teeth. It lunged for my leg, teeth clacking. I shrieked and jumped back.

The beast snarled and charged. I swung my leg in an awkward defensive gesture. Somehow, my foot caught the dog right in the nose with a loud crack. He yelped and rolled on the ground while the other dogs whined and milled around. The little black cat had jumped to the top of the dumpster during the fray and seemed to be quite entertained. I reached for him while the dogs tended to their leader. I was afraid the cat might claw me but he settled into my arms and meowed happily as I raced for my car.

I miraculously remembered to pull the gas pump nozzle out of the fuel filler and to screw on the fuel cover even as I trembled like someone whose stomach had just informed them the Indian food they'd eaten was, in fact, about to tear their digestive system to shreds.

I sat in the car and put the cat in the passenger seat. For a moment, all I could hear was my own panicked breathing. I couldn't believe I'd done it. That dog could have rabies. It could have maimed me. I figured a good old-fashioned mauling would have fit right in with today's *fantastic* milestones.

The cat contemplated me with half-lidded eyes and mewed before curling into a ball on the seat for the ride.

My parents weren't home when I arrived. I went in and washed up, fed the cat some leftovers while I figured out what in the world to do next. The cat meowed, obviously seeing my distressed state, and arched his midnight-black fur against my hand to make me feel better.

"Thanks." I took a deep breath to calm my palpitating heart. "You're kind of a brave little cat, aren't you?" I took a moment or two to properly contemplate what I should call him. "Welcome to my world, Captain Tibbs."

He cocked his head to the side and meowed, a clear indication he loved his new name.

I checked the clock on the wall. It was almost lunchtime and returning to school seemed stupid at this point. I rubbed my belly and wished I had a magic wand to wave that would rid me of the blubber and replace it with a six pack.

I rested my face on my hands and closed my eyes while Captain Tibbs rubbed against my arms, happily purring and meowing.

I couldn't count on magic to miraculously transform me, but I could still do it. I just had to find the willpower to do it. I opened the fridge and found an assortment of fancy craft beers crammed in the middle shelf. Mom hadn't been grocery shopping and the only food I found was a single slice of ham with a sell-by date from a week ago.

It didn't taste half bad, but it didn't fill me up. I found stale saltines in the otherwise empty pantry, so I grabbed those. It was unconscionable that Mom had allowed my juice boxes to run out, so I contemplated the beer. A dark brew warned of high alcoholic content, so I started with that one first. The buzz hit me hard and fast, but it felt good, melting away the remaining pain I felt over Katie.

I tested a hoppy beer next, burped, and tasted the nuked lasagna I'd eaten the day before. Captain Tibbs settled into my lap and purred.

"Are you my new best friend?" I scratched behind his ears.

A warm, comfortable feeling spread out from my stomach. I tested a bitter stout beer next. Hints of chocolate and coffee soaked into my tongue and the warm fuzzies got even warmer and fuzzier.

Oddly enough, all the drinking didn't cloud my judgement at all. In fact, I had plenty of great ideas brewing upstairs. Beer, it seemed, was brain food.

Randy pulls a chocolate bar from the bag of candy he always brings to recess. As usual, he doesn't offer me any, but I'm content with my juice box and peanut butter crackers.

"Look, it's blubber boy and his sidekick stick boy." Nathan Spelman and his middle school pals roar with laughter at the lame joke and form a semi-circle around us.

One of them snatches the candy bag from Randy and pulls out the goodies. "Man, look at all this!"

"Don't you ever share?" Nathan rips open a candy bar and bites into it. "Mm, that's good."

"Leave me alone!" Randy shouts. "My parents will sue you if you touch me."

I scoot sideways, hoping to get closer to the teachers monitoring recess, but Nathan's pals block my path.

"My parents will sue. Wah, wah, wah!" Nathan rubs his eyes and makes blub-

bering noises then straightens and bumps his chest against Randy. "I could break you in half, stick boy."

I gather all my courage. "Can't you just leave us alone?"

Nathan snorts. "Protecting your sidekick, blubber boy?"

Fear clenches my heart, but I force myself to respond. "I always protect my friends."

The bullies close in around me. Randy takes off at a sprint, leaving me alone to face them. Nathan bursts into laughter. "Man, you need better friends." He knocks the juice box from my hand and squishes beneath his shoe. Grabs my last cracker and gives it to one of his friends. The other boy makes a show of eating it, then they leave for a group of cheerleaders.

I shiver with relief and look for my friend. Randy looks back at me from the safety of the teachers, not a hint of remorse in his eyes for abandoning me. At that moment, I wonder if he's even my friend at all.

CHAPTER 7

I woke up in my bed, a metric ton of agony pile-driving my head. I staggered to my feet and grabbed the ibuprofen bottle from the medicine cabinet in the bathroom then guzzled water to banish the cottony feeling in my mouth. Images of my dream about me and Randy in middle school played back in my mind.

Captain Tibbs hopped atop the counter and gave me a disapproving look.

"Why didn't you stop me?" I popped several ibuprofen tablets into my mouth and sat down at my desk.

He stared at me with luminous green eyes, and I figured I had lost some of his respect for drinking as much as I had.

My computer screen flickered on and a wall of words faced me. I had apparently composed a manifesto on Facebook about the sad state of humanity, bullying, and the depressing lack of juice boxes last night. Thankfully, I hadn't posted it. Under the notifications, I saw that I'd been tagged in a video.

My heart skipped a beat as I clicked it and watched the fight from yesterday unfold. Students laughed and cheered as Brad tossed me over the hedge and into the mud.

"God, he's pathetic," said a familiar voice.

A snort. "Tub of lard loser."

The camera angle shifted for an instant, and I caught a view of Harry and Mark sneering at me while Brad dragged me into the freezing water puddle. My fists clenched and anger surged.

You pieces of shit.

The worst part was that I couldn't disagree with them. It was insanely painful watching my rotund figure wallowing around helplessly. When I punched Brad, my mouth dropped. I paused the video and tried to measure just how far he'd come off the ground. Two feet? Three?

Christ, how hard did I hit him?

I saw a gaunt face in the crowd, a gleeful smile on his face. I backed up the video and focused on that face, on Randy Boyle, as he watched the fight unfold. He seemed disinterested until my punch cleaned Brad's clock. Something flashed in his eyes—satisfaction, maybe?

Why is he so interested in me?

I didn't know, but I had to find out.

The usual insults and arguments infested the comments section of the video, but one theme was clear—no one could believe I'd delivered the finishing blow. Even worse, Jenny and Annie commented that I'd stalked Katie and creeped her out. They praised Brad for defending her and chalked up my victory to a lucky punch.

Those lying bitches!

This spawned an entire thread of people volunteering to kick my ass or report me to the cops. Yesterday made the previous day seem like nothing by comparison, and today promised to be straight out of the bowels of Hell. I briefly considered asking my parents to homeschool me so I'd never have to go back, but they weren't around enough to do that.

Besides, I had to get good grades if I wanted to become rich and rub it in the faces of my tormenters at the first high school reunion. A sigh escaped me. I had no choice but to tough it out.

High school drama, here I come!

Captain Tibbs sat atop my computer desk and watched me with pity. *You can do it!* his green eyes seemed to say, and he was right. I could handle this.

Dad grinned when I staggered into the kitchen. "Well, well, well, look who had fun at the expense of my beer last night." His eyes focused on my face. "Did you get into a fight?"

I looked down. "I'm sorry, Dad."

"About the fight or my beer?"

"Um, all of the above?"

He snorted. "You don't look too beat up, so I guess you won."

"The other guy got cocky and I got lucky." I shrugged. "I guess even clumsy nerds win sometimes." I did a double-take at Dad's eyes. Instead of dark blue, they looked pale and icy. His skin seemed paler than usual too.

He slapped my back. "That's my boy." His lips pressed together. "As for drinking, you didn't drunk text did you?"

I shook my head. "No. I must have passed out before I did anything too stupid."

He clapped me on the shoulder. "Good job. Look, I really didn't want to work another Saturday, but I gotta get on the road. Hopefully I'll be home tonight."

I'd completely forgotten it was already the weekend. "Can I use your car?" I asked.

He nodded. Tossed me the keys and grabbed the ones for his motorcycle. "Have a *wonderful* day, Justin." He chuckled as if he cracked himself up and left.

Mom hurried out of the bedroom, looking lovely in a radiantly white dress. "I've got to go too, sweetie." She kissed my cheek and inspected my eye. "I don't approve of drinking or fighting." Mom sighed and put a hand on my forehead. "I suppose it's a male thing."

"Why does everyone around here work on a Saturday?" I asked.

She kissed my cheek. "When your father found you passed out on the floor in your room, he put you in bed."

"You're not mad?"

She smiled and shook her head. "I married your father, son. It takes a thick skin to survive this family."

"Yeah? Are there some stories I don't know?"

Mom's lips pursed. "Maybe. Your father put leftover pizza in the fridge."

Cold pizza for breakfast sounded like a winner to me. "Thanks, Mom."

She kissed my cheek again and went outside. I heard voices and looked through the peephole. Dad sat on his motorcycle talking to Mom. He shook his head at whatever she said. She threw up her hands and argued something. I wished I could hear what they were saying through the door.

Dad pointed a thumb over his shoulder toward the house. Mom nodded, said something else, and kissed him on the cheek. The Harley roared to life. Mom grimaced and plugged her ears as Dad drove off.

I opened the door. "What was that about?"

"I'm just mad we have to work today." Mom got in her car and waved goodbye as she backed out.

I went back inside and saw Dad's briefcase sitting on the floor. He must've forgotten it. I grabbed the car keys, ran outside, and revved up the Jetta. I turned right at the next street since Dad always seemed to go this way and hurried to catch up. As I passed the old Suburban Plaza, a strip mall, I saw Dad park his motorcycle and head for the barber shop.

He must not be in such a big hurry after all.

Dad walked up to the barber shop, turned right, and went into the laundromat next door instead. The parking lot was packed, so I had to park at the far end.

"What in the world is he doing in a laundromat?" I tried to make sense of it. We had a perfectly functional washer and dryer at home. Hell, he hadn't even brought any clothes with him. An awful thought crossed my mind. *What if he's meeting a girlfriend?*

I left his briefcase in the car and sneaked up to the window. Like the other businesses in the old strip mall, long plate-glass windows yellowed with age offered a view inside. A flickering neon sign advised passersby the laundromat was open twenty-four-seven. I edged to the end of the glass and peered inside. Dad sat, one leg crossed over the other, watching a couple of gray-haired women as they tossed clothes inside a washer and gossiped.

He continued to watch them even after they took adjacent seats and pulled out smartphones, holding up pictures of grandchildren. Did my dad have a fetish for old ladies? Was he a stalker? *Gross!* I almost wished I hadn't even found out.

Fifteen minutes later, Dad stretched, stood up, and headed for the door. I hurried into the barber shop next door so he wouldn't see me. Old Larry, the barber, stopped shaving some poor kid's head with a pair of clippers and gave my shaggy mane a hungry look.

"Justin Case? I haven't seen you in over a year, boy. Looks like I'll need to haul out my dog hair trimmers to get through the mess on your head."

Dad walked past the window. His eyes were deep blue, his skin tanned and healthy. My jaw dropped open at the stark difference from what I'd witnessed at the house. I hid my face behind a magazine and peeked out until the cycle rumbled to life and Dad took off for parts unknown. "Thanks, Larry, but I changed my mind."

I went outside and watched the motorcycle vanish over a hill. A part of me wanted to follow Dad and see where he went. Another part didn't want to know anything else at all. *Old ladies? Laundromats? What's next, I find out my parents are swingers?*

I was already feeling a bit delicate thanks to the bathroom assault, headaches, hallucinations, losing my best friends, getting into a fight, and finding out I never had a chance with Katie. I didn't need to discover something potentially devastating about my parents as well.

It's better just to accept this laundromat fetish and move on.

I went back home and dropped onto the couch, uncertain what I should do with myself for the day since I was on the outs with Mark and Harry and there was no Kings and Castles tournament this weekend. After a few minutes of hesitation, I raided the hidden box of cash my parents kept in Mom's closet.

Neat piles of twenties sat inside a red John Madden shoebox. I'd often wondered why my parents kept so much money in a shoebox nestled amidst Mom's other shoeboxes. One might wonder what originally brought me into Mom's closet to search through her shoe boxes. It wasn't because I enjoyed wearing high heels. It was because I wanted to find hidden Christmas presents one year.

Maybe my parents secretly own the laundromat and put the cash from it into this shoebox. Maybe they run a drug ring out of there.

Endless possibilities circulated through my imagination, but right now the only thing I wanted to do was take some money and enjoy a day at the movies. I got the money and drove down to North DeKalb Mall. The new Avengers movie was out, and I was dying to see it. I ran by the food court and grabbed lunch to kill some time before the movie started.

As I bit into a burger, I saw Crye, her black hair curled into Princess Leia buns, mascara artfully traced from her eyes to her cheeks as if streaked by tears. She peered around the corner of a kiosk at something to my left. I looked left and saw a group of preppies.

A girl in a short plaid skirt, white blouse, and nerdy glasses pranced around the group while sucking suggestively on a lollipop. One of the guys, his jeans torn and faded in the most stylish way possible, adjusted a bowtie and nodded as a slightly older man spoke to the group.

The older man sported a thick goatee and wore an Affliction T-shirt, bejeweled jeans, and a gray hoodie—obviously unaware his ensemble went out of fashion years ago. Not that I could really talk about fashion. I still thought cargo pants and Old Navy T-shirts were pretty cool, mainly because I could stuff all the pockets with snacks.

The group broke off into pairs, scattering in all direction. Crye seemed intrigued by this development and left cover. She sauntered through the crowd, eyes locked on Affliction Dude, or so it seemed from my angle.

What is up with that chick?

I took another bite of burger and thought back to the other times I'd seen her lurking in the hallways since the start of school. I knew of her two Goth buddies. Both of them had been around at least since my freshmen year before they'd thrown on all the gear and makeup. Crye, however, had only started at Edenfield High this year. I had no idea what she really looked like.

Maybe she's a crazy stalker.

Rumors circulated that she'd been kicked out of her previous school. I wondered if it was because she liked to follow strange men in the mall.

Now I was really curious. I thought about stuffing my food back in the bag so I could get up and follow Crye, but the movie would start in twenty minutes and I wanted a good seat. On the other hand, real life intrigue interested me nearly as much as a superhero movie.

I stuffed the rest of the burger in my mouth and put the fries back in the bag. Grabbed my drink and scooted back my chair. Walking fast wasn't exactly my forte, but Crye and her quarry weren't in any hurry.

Crye loitered outside a bookstore, holding book in hand while looking at Affliction Dude. The man stopped in front of a leather couch just inside Macys and rubbed it with a hand. A salesman approached him, but backed off at a glare. Crye tensed at the silent exchange.

The salesman's eyes stared straight ahead as if in a trance. He unzipped his pants and dropped them, revealing tight-whiteys. He dropped onto the couch, spread his legs, and put his hand down his underwear.

Affliction Dude grinned and backed away. A little girl screamed. A woman shouted. The salesman jerked, eyes blinking as if he'd just woken from a dream. His mouth opened wide with horror. He jerked up his pants and ran away even as the woman continued to shout at him.

What in the hell was that?

Crye slid the book back on the wire kiosk and headed after Affliction Dude. I stayed a safe distance back and followed. Before I'd gone very far, a hand gripped my arm and guided me into a side hallway. I barely had time to register the change in direction when Randy's gaunt face dominated my view.

"Book shopping, Justin?" He revealed red-stained teeth. "Let me guess— comic books?"

For a moment, I couldn't form words, just a strange stuttering sound as I desperately tried to figure out what had happened. Finally, I said, "What?" in a long, drawn-out stupid voice.

Randy tapped a finger against my temple. "You're really slow, Justin. Didn't you used to be smart?"

I tried to push Randy away, but I might as well have tried to move a buffalo. His strength in the bathroom hadn't been a figment of my imagination. I strained and wriggled, but I couldn't so much as budge his skinny little ass. "How are you so strong?"

"Well, it's not exercise." Crimson-stained teeth gleamed. "If you have half a brain you'll figure it out." He dug a finger into my left boob. He muffled my cry of pain by clapping a hand over my mouth. "You're such a weak little tool."

Tears blurred my eyes as he twisted his finger. "Mphh!"

The pressure relented. The pain faded. Randy leaned forward and sniffed my neck. "Damn, you're close. Must be a late bloomer, Justin, because I've never seen your kind take so long to hit puberty."

His hand left my mouth and I gasped for breath. "What are you talking about?" I wanted to run, but a cage of arms and hands trapped me.

Randy put a finger in his eye and gently scooped out a tinted contact lens. Beneath it, his iris looked red. His eye began to glow with an inner light. It didn't flash or gleam red from an overhead light—it actually glowed. He bared his teeth. Canines extended to sharp points nearly half an inch longer than his other teeth.

Another "Whuuuuuuut?" escaped my stunned lips. *This can't be real. This cannot be real!*

Randy popped the contact lens back in and suddenly, he was back to being his normal stick-figure self. "Don't go far, Justin." He gently slapped my cheek. "I've got plans for your sweet blood."

In a blur, he vanished. I wobbled on my feet, knees like Jell-O brand gelatin, and slumped against the wall. For several minutes, I couldn't even move.

"Can't be real. Gotta be a trick of some kind." I pushed myself up and took a deep breath. My French fries lay scattered on the floor and my drink had spilled. The bathrooms were a little further down the hall, so

I went inside and splashed cold water on my face until I felt slightly calmer.

"He's punking me." I paced back and forth in front of the mirror. "Vampires aren't real. Vampires are not fucking real!"

A bathroom stall came open and a man peered out, forehead furrowed, eyes wary of the lunatic talking to himself about vampires. He edged around me, quickly washed his hands, and left. I checked the other stalls to make sure they were empty before another crazed soliloquy.

"Randy tricked me somehow." I'd seen dozens of videos with elaborate jokes and fake magic tricks. In one, a guy appeared to levitate because he sat on a wire frame hidden beneath robes. In another, a girl made her eyes glow with contact lenses.

I snapped my fingers. "He didn't remove a contact lens, he just pretended to and left in a red one." I frowned. "But how is he so strong?" I couldn't explain that part, but then again, I hadn't worked out a day in my life. Randy might be all skin and bones, but that didn't mean his stringy muscles couldn't be strong.

I pulled up my T-shirt and inspected the bruise forming on my man boob. Randy could really injure me unless I learned to defend myself. It was time for a power up and a makeover. I had to take the unicorn by the horn and shit my own rainbows, because nobody else was going to do it for me.

CHAPTER 8

My decision to turn over a new leaf didn't start off well. Captain Tibbs jetted out of the house the moment I opened the door to the house.

"Wait, where are you going?" I chased after him.

He returned a curt meow. *So long and thanks for all the fish.* Then he vanished into the neighbor's hedge. I ran to the other side and tried to find him, but Captain Tibbs had sailed away. "Are you kitten me?" I shouted. "This catastrophe ruined my caturday!"

Captain Tibbs wasn't swayed by my puns and didn't come back.

"Damn, I'm kind of sad." I took a moment to appreciate the brief time I'd had with my feline friend, hoped he didn't get run over by a car, then went into Mom's closet for more cash to fund my transformation.

"Ahem?"

I spun around and found Mom directing a questioning eyebrow at me.

"Um, you're home?"

"Are you trying on my high heels?" She narrowed her eyes. "Do you play dress up in my clothes while I'm gone?"

"No!" I threw up my hands defensively. "Absolutely not! That's not why I'm in the closet."

"Son, if you like to do that, it's fine." She offered a smile. "I'll support you no matter what."

I shook my head vehemently. "I was going to steal some money from your shoebox."

Mom frowned. "American money?"

It was my turn to frown. "What other kind of money is there?"

She blinked. "Oh, of course. What do you need it for?"

"A gym membership, maybe some new clothes."

Mom nodded. "That's fine, honey." She motioned me over, took my hand. "But first, we need to talk."

I gulped at the tone in her voice. "About what?"

She made me come out of the closet—literally, not figuratively—and took me into the den where we sat on the ugly plaid couch. "I have to go on an extended trip. I might not be back for a few weeks."

"Another China trip?" I asked.

She nodded. "It means I'm going to miss your birthday next Saturday."

I tried not to let my disappointment show. "I understand."

"I thought we could celebrate tonight instead." She touched my hand. "Is that okay?"

The clouds forming in my horizon dissipated. "That would be great."

"Excellent! Decide where you want to eat, and we'll go, okay?"

"Awesome!" I rubbed my hands together gleefully, already thinking about the possibilities. "Wait, is Dad coming home tonight?"

Mom nodded. "I ordered him."

I pumped my fist in the air. "Woot!"

She kissed my cheek, frowned. "Did something happen today?"

"Please don't start with the aura stuff today, Mom, please?"

Her cool hand touched my forehead. Lips pursed, but she didn't press me on it. "Fine. I've got work to do." She got up and went into her office.

When Dad got home, I picked out a nice steakhouse for us to go to. Afterward, we went out for ice cream and took a walk around Decatur Square. I had such a good time that for a while, I forgot about my problems.

Sunday rolled around, and I lounged in pajamas playing video games all day. I thought about the gym, but procrastination felt so much better than busting my ass in a weight room. As Sunday night darkened the skies, the reality of Monday loomed like a shadow in the dark. I'd tried to put on a brave face, but the video of my fight now had hundreds of views and comments.

Most of them weren't friendly towards me. The one person I'd hoped would put in a good word for me hadn't. Katie remained quiet on the matter. Then I found out why.

She'd unfriended and blocked me on Facebook, as had Mark, Harry, and a dozen others. Of the few high school people who remained on my friends list, only Jimmy Buttafuoco said I was cool for sticking up for myself. He wasn't doing me any favors since he'd been voted most likely to become a pedophile.

I'd defended myself against a bully and my reward?

Social pariah.

MONDAY, arrived and the anxiety in my chest grew palpable—a living malevolent creature with claws in my guts, heart, limbs. I couldn't think straight. I decided to take Dad's car since the school bus would be a pure nightmare.

Every head seemed to swivel my way as I walked into school. I avoided the gymnasium like the plague, sticking to an empty hallway nearby.

In homeroom, Jenny directed a gleeful smile my way and shook her head. "Look, it's Rocky!"

Annie laughed. "Stalker boy got his ass kicked"

I pshawed. "Did you watch the same video I did? I knocked him out cold."

"Hah!" Jenny smirked. "You landed a lucky punch."

"Meh, whatever." I gave a dismissive wave of my hand and tried to play it off.

"Such a douche," Annie said. "Forcing yourself on Katie and making her kiss you. I'm glad Brad kicked your ass."

"And blah, blah, blah, high school drama!" I held out jazz hands and shook them for effect. *What in the hell did Katie say about our kiss?* I turned in my seat and tried to ignore them, but they kept on needling me with names and insults.

My vision blurred and I winced in anticipation of another headache. Instead, the room snapped back into focus and my head only tingled for a split second. My hand hurt, however. I clenched something painfully tight. Upon closer examination, I realized I held the snapped-off corner of my desk. I hastily tossed it into my book bag before anyone noticed the vandalism.

I must be going insane.

The bell rang and I jetted out of there.

At lunch, I discovered how Andy Dudowitz, the obscenely fat kid, felt.

He and his palpable body odor occupied a table in the corner all to themselves because nobody wanted to be within smelling distance of him. I couldn't even find a seat. Everyone locked me out with angry glares or derisive laughs. Even Andy shook his massive head when I looked his way. Mark and Harry glared darkly at me. I was positive even the lunchroom ladies would reject me at this point.

Crye caught my eye with a wiggle of her finger. I hesitantly wandered over. Today she wore enough metal piercings in her nose, mouth, ears, and tongue to construct a battleship. Next to her sat a short guy with a hazardous amount of eye shadow and a red Mohawk flopped over to the side. Beside him was an Asian guy with dark spikes of thick hair and eyeliner radiating like war paint beneath his eyes.

I sat uneasily next to Crye. If she sneezed, the flying metal would probably kill me.

"Hi." The trailer hitch in her mouth clacked against her teeth.

I tried not to gag.

"Awesome job against Brad, dude," said the Asian Goth guy. "I'm Ash Falls." He nudged the Mohawk guy, "is Nyte Cradle."

"N-y-t-e," Nyte said.

I'd already figured out how to spell their names since Crye had written them in depressing Goth letters all over a notebook titled *Poems of Dark Souls*.

"Where'd you come up with those names?" I asked.

"They are our true names," Crye said in a mysterious voice. "You have your own waiting to come from the darkness of your soul."

I blew out a breath. "Mine is probably Stinky Crap."

Crye snickered. "Nice, Stinky. By the way, I was just kidding about the true names stuff. We like to act weird and mysterious since everyone expects it."

Nyte and Ash laughed.

"It's cool, looking angsty and different," Ash said, "but mainly we just hate people because they're idiots."

Nyte snapped his fingers. "Bingo."

"No truer words." I grinned. "Do I have to wear eye makeup too?"

Ash laughed. "Yeah, the more the better."

A part of me wanted to ask Crye why she'd followed that guy at the mall, but I didn't want to alienate the only people who let me sit at their lunch table.

Despite the cold shoulder from the general high school populace, I wasn't ready to trade in my cargo pants and sneakers for black leather pants and platform shoes. At least I had someone I could talk to and sit with, even if they were a bit touched in the head and on the creepy side. Then again, that described me perfectly.

As I left the lunchroom I ran into a meat wall, bounced off it, and landed on my ass. I looked up at Nathan Spelman.

"Oh, excuse you." Nathan smirked down at me. I tried to get up, but he put a hand on my head and pressed me into a sitting position. "Well, well." He crouched, keeping his sweaty palm on my head while other students walked past with wide eyes and/or smiles, depending on their current opinion of me.

"I want to make something crystal clear, stalker boy. You get within a hundred feet of Katie Johnson, and I'm going to smear you from one end of the hall to the other. Won't be enough left of you to put in a bucket."

"You get to stalk Katie but I don't?" I couldn't believe what I'd just said. Something was wrong with my mouth today. I needed to get it checked before someone punched my teeth out. Although that moment might be upon me.

Nathan popped me on the side of the head. For him it was probably a love tap. I felt my brain hit the side of my skull and stars danced in my eyes. "You better keep your mouth shut about things you don't understand."

Anger pounded in my chest and the next words just shot out of my mouth. "You're probably right. I don't understand rapists."

Next thing I knew, I was face down on the floor looking at a smear of blood on the tiles. My glasses were gone. Someone shouted. An authoritative voice roared for everyone to shut up and move on. I pushed myself to my knees and saw a blurry figure standing over me. I found my glasses a few inches from the blood smear and put them on. The blur resolved into the face of Ted Barnes, the Vice Principal.

"Go see the school nurse, boy." He stabbed a finger in that general direction.

I groaned and looked around for Nathan. He was gone. "Nathan Spelman just beat the crap out of me."

"Funny, looks like you just slipped and fell. Now go get cleaned up."

"Are you kidding me? I'll bet he has one of my teeth lodged in his fist."

"You want to get suspended, boy?" I shrank back as Mr. Barnes and his gleaming bald head invaded my personal space. "I suggest you listen to me."

It didn't take long for the gray porridge I call my brain to see where this was going. Mr. Barnes was a member of the Quarterback Club. I hadn't made too many friends by confronting Nathan. Mr. Barnes wasn't about to cut me a break, especially when it involved a football player.

I pressed my lips together so I wouldn't say anything else stupid. My upper lip hurt like hell, but my jaw seemed intact. I traced my teeth with my tongue and didn't find any unexpected gaps or wiggly ones. I skipped the nurse and went to the bathroom instead, halfway expecting a biker gang to jump me the moment I went inside.

After washing off the blood I took a good long look at myself. Lank, greasy hair hung past my shoulders. Scratched and battered glasses teetered crookedly on my nose. My split lip looked like the king of all cold sore outbreaks. My chubby, ashen face needed a tan.

"Jesus, I look like shit." I pulled off my glasses and wiped them on my shirt. It was hard not to feel sorry for myself. Hard not to feel worthless and unwanted. I agreed with Crye. I hated people. Not all of them. Just the bullies, the drama queens, and the sheeple who around them.

Mr. Turpin raised an eyebrow when I entered English class. "Did you have an accident, Mr. Case?"

"I tried to beat the crap out of someone's fist with my face."

"I see." He regarded me for a moment then started the day's lesson.

I wondered how a guy could go from boxing one day to teaching English the next. Maybe he hadn't taken too many blows to the head, or maybe English was something you didn't need many brains cells to teach—or learn for that matter. When the bell rang, Mr. Turpin motioned me to his desk.

"I take it Mr. Spelman and his ilk are the cause of your bloody lip?"

"More or less."

"It doesn't matter how big they are if you knock them down first."

Wow, what a nugget of useful information. "Uh, thanks." I edged toward the door. "I'll remember that." I walked down the hallway shaking my head. How in the world was I supposed to knock down the big guys? What did that even mean? Crazy old boxer dude. What he should have told me was to work out until I had huge muscles and then smack Nathan in the nose with a set of brass knuckles.

I kept my head down for the rest of the day and managed to make it through without another incident. When I got home, Dad wasn't home yet, and Mom was off on her work trip to China.

Rows of canned goodies stocked the pantry and juice boxes fought for room with Dad's craft beers in the fridge. I grabbed blue raspberry and slurped half of it down before taking a breath. I stopped and stared at the box of liquid sugar in my hand, then went to the bathroom to stare at my fat face. My stringy hair. My oversized clothes.

Despite everything I'd been through, here I was falling straight back into old habits. I didn't stand a chance against Randy or Nathan in my current form, and saw diabetes in my near future.

I was comfortable with myself, but was it healthy to stay this way when someone like Randy could kick my ass?

I shook my head. "No. I can't keep doing this to my body." I went into the kitchen and dumped the juice box in the trash can. I opened the fridge door and slid the trashcan closer, then scooped all the juice boxes into the trash. I loved my parents, but they were enabling me to stay unhealthy.

"No more!" I raised a fist to the heavens. "I will be made anew!"

Time to say goodbye to the old and hello to the new.

CHAPTER 9

Change is an easy word to say but a pain in the ass to follow through on. So I started off easy and made a checklist on my computer:

1. *Join Gym*
2. *Haircut*
3. *New Clothes.*

The list looked so tiny on the vast expanse of empty computer screen, but at least it was a start. It was particularly pitiful in light of the fact that I had stayed up most of the night making that list and doing research. I'd once heard someone on TV say, "It's all about the G-T-L. Gym, tan, and laundry." At the time, it seemed like awfully shallow advice. But maybe they were right. I looked like a shaggy overweight slob and felt horrible. Why should anyone else like me?

I went into Mom's closet and looted the rainy day shoebox again. Since Mom hadn't cared when she caught me before, I emptied half the shoebox and stashed the cash behind a fake panel I'd built into the drywall in my closet a couple of years ago. Money might not make me happy, but it could fund a transformation.

It was two in the morning when I finally fell asleep.

THE NEXT DAY during classes my head bobbed every few minutes. I actually face-planted on my desk in homeroom which amused Jenny and Annie to no end. My eyelids felt like they had tiny but chubby sleep fairies hanging on the lashes and pulling them closed. I think I must have sleep-talked something to that effect while dozing because Nancy Sanders asked me if sleep fairies gave out money for eyelashes. Then she giggled hysterically. Our Literature teacher was not amused.

At lunch I took a seat next to Crye and gang. "Hi." I hoped they hadn't changed their minds about letting me sit at their table.

"Hey." Crye yawned so hard and wide her jaw cracked. Apparently I wasn't the only one pulling all-nighters. Even the powder-white makeup and dark rings of eyeliner couldn't hide the sag in her eyelids.

Ash eyed me. "You go to a rave or something last night?"

"Nah. Just did a lot of reading." I bit into a soggy square slice of pizza and forced it down my throat while mulling the list I'd made. "Do you guys think I'd look better if I cut my hair?"

Ash shrugged. Crye stood up and walked around the table, her black Victorian-era dress rustling as she walked. She wound some of my hair around her fingers and sniffed it. I noticed her black fingernails matched her lipstick.

Her violet eyes seemed to peer right into me. They were not the peaceful color of flowers, but sparkling, fiery, and full of life despite the dark bags under her eyes.

"Do you wear contacts?" I asked. I couldn't stop staring into those amazing irises.

She jerked from her reverie. "Yes—yes of course. Nobody has eyes this color."

"Looks cool," I said lamely. I'd almost said "beautiful" but figured that would've been over the edge.

Crye stared again at my hair as a tarot card reader would look at a fortune. "Your hair is a mess."

"I know that, but—"

She put a finger to my lips and shook her head, so I shut my mouth. Sometimes the hardest part of asking for advice is actually taking it to heart. I'd done things my way for long enough and look where that got me: relying on a Goth chick for fashion advice.

Crye held my hair so it stood on end. She looked from Ash to Nyte to me and grunted like a doctor who'd just found a potentially hazardous anomaly in someone's brain scan. "You have coarse hair. I think you should cut it to about six inches and spike it."

"Spike my hair?"

"Her mom owns a fancy salon. I'd listen to her," Ash said.

Today Crye wore her long black hair straight with a simple part down the middle like the matriarch from the Addams Family. The day before she'd adorned it with pink-bowed pigtails. If it weren't for the shrapnel-like piercings all over her face and the deathly white makeup, she might actually look cute. I could almost stand everything except the nose and tongue studs. The hygiene issues those posed made me want to barf.

"I can get you a friend's discount," she said.

A lump formed in my throat. I couldn't understand what I'd done to deserve a friend's discount from people I'd more or less looked down upon until a day ago. I hadn't done a thing to deserve the kindness of these people except turn myself into a social outcast. I cleared my throat, but my reply still came out a little gravelly.

"Thanks," I said. "I'll do it." I gave her my number and went to class.

After school, I went to a gym I'd passed a million times before on the way home, and inquired about personal training.

"I want someone who will really whip me into shape," I told the skinny guy who signed me up. I hoped he wasn't a trainer. His arms looked like noodles and his round belly jiggled beneath his shirt.

He pursed his lips and looked me over. "I know just the person."

I looked around the gym and spotted several people wearing blue trainer shirts then pointed out a stocky black guy with arms thicker than this guy's waist. "How about him?"

"George?" He tsked. "He's booked right now. I can put you on the waiting list."

I scanned the area but the other trainers looked just as out of shape as their trainees. I wasn't about to waste money or time. I needed results. "Yeah, put me on his list, please."

"In the meantime, I'll put you with one of our best, Vic."

Vic sounded like the name of a swarthy Italian guy from New Jersey. A guy who could teach me street smarts and help me get six-pack abs all at the same time.

"Sounds good, thanks." I paid for two months up front and hoped by then I would know what I was doing and wouldn't need a trainer anymore. My parents might not like me stealing from their rainy day funds all the time. Then again, maybe they'd pay for my gym member-ship if I just asked them to.

"Why don't you go get suited up?" the guy said. "I'll get Vic."

"Sure." I went into the locker room and nearly ran into the naked, wrinkly ass of an old man. He had a foot up on a bench, the other on the floor, and meticulously inspected his low-hanging ball sack.

"Yep, it's a groin pull, Frank." He looked sadly at another man and shook his head. "I don't know how women use that damned leg machine!"

I went around a row of lockers for some privacy then quickly changed into gym shorts and a sleeveless T-shirt to show off my chubby arms. I examined myself in the mirror, flexing and grunting. One thing was for sure—I had way more sag than bulge—except in the tummy area. I pulled up my shirt and grabbed a roll of pale jelly belly. My navel ran deep enough to store fifty cents worth of dimes. My man boobs sagged like that old man's balls.

Vic has his work cut out for him.

I left the locker room and looked for someone fitting the profile of a low-level thug from a New Jersey mafia family before giving up and going to the trainers' desk. A redhead with ripped abs and enough freckles to form constellations on her otherwise forgettable face looked up as I approached.

"I'm looking for Vic."

"That's me." She flashed a freckly grin. "Justin?"

"Yeah," I tried not to voice my disappointment. I needed someone like George to get me in shape, not an aerobics queen. I hoped George's waiting list wasn't too long. "How does a girl get a name like Vic?"

"Short for Victoria." She shrugged. "You can call me either. Just don't call me Vicky. Can't stand that name."

She hopped up and motioned me to follow. After the dreaded weigh-in, she calculated my body fat percentage first with calipers and then with an electronic device I held in my hands. I think I maxed it out. Then she measured my biceps, my chest, my waist, and my legs. By the time we finished, half of the thirty-minute session had passed and the desire to pump iron activated my mouth.

"What's all this for?" I asked.

"We're setting a baseline," she explained. "Otherwise we can't measure progress." She looked at the numbers she'd collected and shook her head. "Besides, you won't last more than ten minutes."

"Gee, thanks."

Six minutes later sweat drenched my clothes. I staggered aimlessly in a haze of breathless agony, ready to drop dead on the floor. Victoria made me walk back and forth until the incredible cramps in my sides faded. All in all, I'd lived down to her expectations. On the bench press I'd struggled to push up a meager ninety-five pounds. I hadn't been able to do a single pull up, even with weighted assist. I'd nearly strained a muscle doing military press, and fallen over backwards trying to squat ten-pound weights on the barbell.

Other nearby patrons seemed both disgusted and amused.

"It's normal to do crappy your first day in the gym," Vic said in a not-so-reassuring way. "A month from now you'll be doing much better."

"A month from now I'll be dead." I felt as though I might keel over at any moment.

"Drink two gallons of water between now and tomorrow." She handed me a sheet of paper. "I prepared a list of foods you can have. Stay away from everything else."

I glanced at the list: chicken breasts, wild-caught fishes, whole grains, and all the green vegetables I wanted. "I don't know how to cook."

"It's easy. Just broil chicken breasts. Google for recipes and you'll be okay."

"Is broiling the same thing as boiling, but with an R in the middle?"

Her mouth hung open a fraction. "Google it."

I wondered if there was anything Google couldn't help me with. "What about fat-free microwave dinners?"

"Absolutely not. Anything processed is crap. You know all the agony you went through today?"

"Yeah."

"Do you want it to be for nothing? I'm not lying when I say eighty percent of body composition is what you eat. Exercise can only do so much. Garbage in, garbage out."

I sighed. "Okay. I'll do whatever it takes."

She flashed straight white teeth. "See you Wednesday. Rest well until then."

I gulped what felt like a gallon of water from the water fountain before I left and still felt thirsty. I turned to leave so my fat bottom wouldn't keep other parched souls from enjoying a drink and plowed into a cute girl in tight gym shorts and a yellow tank top. The fabric adhered to drool-inducing curves. "Sorry." I tried to get out of her way.

"You are rather hardcore," she said in a proper British accent. "It is quite awesome, dude."

"That's me," I said. "Zero to hardcore in ten minutes." I wondered if she was making fun of me or if the British naturally had issues using the words "dude" and "awesome".

She laughed, deep throated, sexy, and hormone-sizzling. Compact but muscular and a little shorter than me, she wore her yellow blonde hair in a tight bun. A pink flush accented her fair skin. If she'd been working out, it didn't show. Not even a sheen of sweat glistened on her body.

"I'm Stacey." She held out her hand.

I took it, noticing how warm it felt. "I'm Justin."

"You are *quite* the handsome one." She ran a finger up my arm.

My hackles rose. My vision snapped like someone had put a picture on a rubber band, pulled it taut, and let it go. Two sexy blondes smiled back at me and blurred out of focus. I massaged my forehead and rubbed my eyes under my glasses, trying to ward off the inevitable headache.

"Are you quite all right?"

I pinched the bridge of my nose and opened my eyes. The dizziness faded and my eyesight returned. I looked into her amber eyes. Her pupils weren't round. They were vertical slits. I massaged my eyelids again, convinced my eyesight had gone crazy. "Just a headache," I said. "Must be allergies."

"I was just about to depart," she said. "Would you be so kind as to walk me to my horseless—my auto-mobile?"

"Sure," I said in a very cool and experienced manner so as not to give away the sudden tidal wave of hormones threatening to overwhelm me on the spot. One workout and I already had a hottie after me! Things were looking up.

Okay, so I was probably counting my chickens way before hatching—and possibly even before the eggs were laid—but the rough workout combined with a sudden flush of testosterone made me dangerously full of myself. I grabbed my keys from the locker room, forcing myself to walk in a composed manner though I had a sneaking suspicion she'd be gone by the time I came back out. When I returned, she was still there. *Amazing.* She flashed her pearly whites in a full-lipped smile that almost caused an accident in my pants. We stepped outside into the pleasantly chilly autumn night.

"This time of year is simply delightful." Stacey inhaled deeply. I hoped she didn't get a whiff of my BO. She grabbed my arm and drew another deep breath. "You smell delicious. So sweet."

Sweet? Hadn't Randy said the same thing?

Her sensual touch banished all thought from my mind. I adjusted my shirt to hide the tent pole trying to form the Smurf village with my shorts. "Yep, it's a great time of year." We walked toward the side parking lot of the building. I wondered if maybe I should ask her to go with me somewhere to grab a bite to eat when something like warm, wet sandpaper rasped up my arm and to my shoulder. I snapped my focus to the aforementioned shoulder.

Stacey was licking it.

"What are you doing?" I jerked away from her. It wasn't that I minded a girl licking me, but something felt plain wrong her tongue.

She gripped my chin and forced me to look into her eyes. Vertically-slit pupils widened into bottomless swirling pools. Consciousness faded. My vision snapped again and I staggered backwards, breaking the hypnotic embrace of her eyes.

"Your kind is so luscious," Stacey said in a low purr. "So sweet. But so hard to convince."

"My kind of what?" I backed, tendrils of cold fear spreading through my stomach and into my chest. "Sweaty fat boys?" *Am I hallucinating again, or is this real?*

She bared her teeth like a lion about to pounce.

I ran.

CHAPTER 10

Usually I wouldn't flee from cute girls, but this time I made an exception. Something was seriously wrong with this chick. I huffed and puffed and bee-lined for my car near the back of the dark parking lot. I looked behind me. Stacey was nowhere to be seen. I stopped and doubled over, an acute hitch stabbing my side.

I panted like a three-legged Chihuahua in a greyhound race. My legs felt like molten rubber. Every muscle screamed for relief. I cursed Victoria and her hardcore workout. I cursed my terrible physical state and scanned the gym parking lot for any sign of Stacey. Was this a joke? One of my haters punking me?

Anger scoured the fear from me. I clenched my teeth. I was willing to bet by the time I got home, there'd be a YouTube video of chubby Justin fleeing from a pretty girl. *Those butt sphincters!* I looked around one last time but Stacey—if that was her real name—had vanished. I clutched at the stitch in my side and hobbled toward car.

A warm hand touched my neck. I shrieked like a brain-damaged goat. Stacey stood behind me. *Just great.* Now they'd have video of me screaming too.

"You think this is funny?" I yelled. "Who put you up to this? Katie? Brad? Harry? Randy? Cthulhu?"

Stacey's plump scarlet lips stretched into a languorous smile. Her black pupils vertically split a sea of sparkling amber. Whoever had done her makeup had done a great job. I really needed to get them to help me out for Halloween.

"I am unacquainted with these people of whom you speak. Perhaps we could continue this conversation at a more comfortable location." Her British accent became even more clipped and proper than before, making her all the creepier.

"Ha, ha." I faked a British accent of my own. "And I am the Dread Pirate Roberts, you scoundrel!" I turned to walk away.

An iron grip clamped onto my arm and spun me around. Stacey bared her teeth and pressed me against a black SUV. I struggled uselessly. Images of Randy and the mall flashed through my mind.

Her smile widened to reveal long sharp canines. No, this woman wasn't using makeup or lighting tricks. She was strong as an ox. Her feline pupils dilated. Contact lenses wouldn't do that. Maybe Randy hadn't been faking it. Maybe vampires were real.

Holy shitballs!

I was about to die or become fatally anemic.

"You smell divine," Stacey said. "A pity I couldn't convince you to accompany me to my home. I would so enjoy taking my time with you. Your kind is exceptional, so much better than ordinary kine. So raw and emotional."

I didn't know what in the world "kine" meant. It wouldn't matter shortly. My track record with women was about to get markedly worse. Or maybe being sucked dry by a vampiric hottie was a decent way to go. Except I wouldn't be around to brag about it, which was kind of depressing.

"Shhh. Just relax." Stacey licked her lips. "I promise you'll enjoy this."

I squirmed. "You're going to kill me!"

She shook her head. "No, I am not a killer, but I do love fear." Stacey pressed my shoulders against the van. I struggled like a mouse under a cat's paw, but might as well have been clamped in place by steel bands. She pressed her pert nose to my neck and inhaled deeply.

"Such a tender fledgling." She licked me with her sandpaper tongue again. I wondered if this was the same as sniffing a warm apple pie before devouring it.

"Maybe it's my Axe body spray." My voice trembled and my body shook. I drew upon every bit of willpower I had left and rammed my knee into her stomach. My knee met a plate of steel. I yelped. The girl must do serious ab workouts.

She laughed. "Such spirit. Such fear." Her nose nuzzled my ear playfully. The faster my heart thudded in my chest, the louder she purred with happiness.

"What are you? A vampire?"

She let out a deep-throated laugh. "My little lamb, you are so precocious." Her hot lips pressed against my neck and traced up to my ear, leaving a trail of goosebumps. She nibbled my earlobe. I expected the sharp sting of those fangs at any moment.

Stacey faced me with half-lidded eyes. The purring grew louder and her eyes widened until she seemed to gaze into my very soul with those luminous amber moons. Something tugged at my fear as though it were a fish swimming in a sea of emotions. A part of me resisted the pull, jerking and flailing. Another part of me rejoiced in the sheer ecstasy of the moment. But the numbing warmth only increased the terror slamming my heart against its ribcage. I fought harder but my will faltered. Those eyes had the gravity of stars and I was a helpless planet about to be sucked into oblivion.

Something vaporous drifted from my eyes and toward her, a tunnel of misty white light. Terror trapped a scream in my throat. The light resisted the pull and slowed to a crawl. The tension increased yet again and the terror in my heart climaxed. The light reached her eyes.

Fireworks exploded in our faces. Red, green, and blue flared like the destruction of a tiny star between our noses.

Stacey rocketed backward, slammed into the side of a white BMW, and left a Stacey-sized dent in the door. She fell to the ground, screaming and covering her blackened face. My face felt sunburned, but the explosion hadn't hit me for some reason.

While she writhed on the pavement mewling pathetically, I kicked her. It wasn't exactly the gentlemanly thing to do but I didn't care. It was, however, the wrong thing to do. My foot met an iron ribcage and crunched.

I yelped and hopped around on one leg. Unless I procured a rocket launcher, I wasn't going to do anything to hurt this vampire woman. So I did the only thing I could do. I limped very, very quickly back to my car, whimpering from the pain in my possibly broken foot Stacey's wet-cat yowls echoing in the cold night air. I revved up the Jetta and peeled out like demons were on my tail.

About halfway home I broke into sobs. "This can't be happening. This did not just happen. I'm going insane. I am insane. I'm freaking insane!" My eyes burned and watered. My vision blurred. My brain throbbed. I felt drunk or high or both. My eyesight returned to normal.

I swerved around a corner just as a pregnant woman stepped into the road in front of me. Her face flashed in the headlights. I slammed on the brakes but it was too late. Eyes squeezed shut, I waited for the thud of body on metal. The sound never came. I leapt from the car and staggered around it. No body. No sign of anyone at all. But a woman had been there! Her face—my God, her face. She'd looked just like Mom. I dropped back into the car as my eyesight blurred again. Hallucinations again. I was losing my mind.

A baby cried in the distance. I tried to pinpoint the sound but it came from all directions. A woman screamed. Something inhuman seared the air with a roar of pure agony. What was going on? *I'm going insane, that's what.* I shoved the car back into drive.

Somehow, I made it home although I almost plowed into the mailbox. I got out and staggered up to the door. I half expected to see a crazed Stacey streaking down the road after me. Thankfully, no. I barely remembered locking the front door behind me and then shoving furniture against it. Shoving more furniture behind my bedroom door. Then the floor greeted my face.

I wake up, panting, heart thudding in my ears. A baby's screams echo down the hall. I climb down from my bed and grab the plastic sword Daddy gave me for my sixth birthday. My palms sweat. I tighten my grip and step into the dark hallway. Wails echo down the long corridor. In one direction lurks darkness. Bright light beckons the other way. I turned for the light. Pictures line the walls, but I can't make out the faces. The harder I look, the blurrier they become.

The baby screams. Why was it screaming? Was someone hurting it? I ran toward the shrieks. My padded pajama feet make little noise as I run for the light. But the light only seems to move further away. The faster I move my legs, the slower I go.

"I'm coming!" I shout in a child's tiny voice. "I'll save you!" I brandish my toy sword, ready to meet any threat.

The light frames a dark shadow in a doorway ahead. A tall hat perches on top, and a long walking cane rests in the right hand. I stumble, trip, and fall to my knees. Dark dread writhes around my heart and squeezes. The air frosts in my lungs. Vapor puffs from my mouth.

The figure holds out its hands. A woman screams in agony.

"No!" I cry. "Stop it!" But I can't move. I can't make the bad man go away. I am helpless to save my—

My ringing cellphone startled me awake. My ears hurt. My head hurt. Every part of me simmered in raw agony. I pushed myself off the floor, pulled the phone from my pocket, and stared with bleary eyes at the screen. It was Crye. I answered.

"Your appointment is at ten AM.," she said in a voice entirely too chipper. "Don't be late!"

"Isn't it a school day?"

"Teachers' work day. Don't you remember the announcement?"

"Oh. Okay. I'll see you soon." I pushed myself up onto my knees. *What a nightmare.* It had to have been a nightmare. Vampires did not exist. Hot girls that approached sweaty smelly fat kids after a workout also did not exist. I was positive of that. And what was with the pregnant woman and the screaming baby? Maybe Stacey had slipped me some heroin.

I loved Kings and Castles. I loved pretending that wizards battled ogres and knights rescued damsels—or dudes—in distress. K&C was equal opportunity, after all. Battling with foam swords against real people dressed as imaginary foes was more fun than anything I'd ever done.

The mere thought that supernatural creatures might exist absolutely terrified me. If predators like Randy and Stacey existed, who kept them from killing the rest of us normal people? Were there superheroes, or was I doomed to play the victim and die by the fang?

My pounding heart sent tremors through my sore muscles. Pure adrenalin must have fueled my effort to shove furniture against the doors.

I had to accept facts. Vampires—or something like them—existed. I was probably in mortal danger. I needed protection, but I didn't know who to contact. Until then, I needed to surround myself with people. Being alone was a recipe for, well, me being eaten by that demon chick, Stacey, or sucked dry by Randy.

Getting a haircut was the perfect way to achieve my objective, and possibly gain a few style points as well.

As I showered, images of Stacey with her amber eyes and fangs flashed through my mind. I got out of the shower and regarded my long wet mop of hair in the mirror. Then I noticed hand-shaped bruises the color of rotten blueberries on my biceps. I looked at my foot. A nasty greenish bruise covered my toes. My injuries once again I reminded me that last night really happened. Stacey existed. Randy existed. I might never see Stacey again, but Randy was another story.

I touched my long hair. An undercurrent of apprehension gripped my nerves. It seemed almost funny getting a haircut frightened me more than the supernatural.

I'm more afraid of change than vampires and demons put together.

I shivered.

After dressing, I removed the furniture blocking my bedroom door and the front door and looked for Dad, but he was nowhere to be found. I wondered if I'd locked him out of the house with my furniture blockade, or if he was still out of town. I hadn't heard a thing from Mom since she left, which was unusual. She typically texted me while on business trips.

I sent Mom a text. *Hope your trip is going OK.*

My phone buzzed a moment later. *Unable to reach this wireless caller.*

I blinked a few times, and scrolled back through the text history under my Mom's contact. The number looked right. Maybe her phone didn't work well in China.

Dad's motorcycle wasn't in the garage, so I sent him a quick text.

Coming home tonight?

I really wanted an adult presence around. Just the thought of spending another night alone with monsters lurking outside made my bowels twitch.

I took the Jetta to Crye's salon in East Atlanta Village, a neighborhood still struggling to cross the divide from gangster to hipster. A cute girl in jeans and a tight pink T-shirt sat at the reception area. I stared at myself in the mirror on the wall behind her to keep my eyes off her creamy cleavage. The tight fabric of her shirt gave her breasts enough extra oomph to make me a fan for life.

I was a hopeless romantic, but the lure of this girl's anatomy made my hormones boil.

She smiled at me. "Hey, Justin. Be just a few minutes."

I blinked. "Um, hi?" How did she know my name? Had Crye told her what I looked like?

Knowing my luck she's another vampire chick. Maybe I won't have to get my hair cut after all.

The girl raised an eyebrow. "Don't be nervous. I told Mom you needed all the help you could get."

I rubbed my eyes and looked closer. No makeup. No eyeliner. No piercings. Her skin looked flawless, not a hole in sight. I'd been right. Without makeup, Crye was beyond cute.

My mouth decided to inform her exactly what I thought before I could stop myself. "You look like an angel."

Her full lips spread into a lovely smile. "I've never heard that one before." She giggled. "I'll bet you use that line on all the women."

I shook my head, still in a trance. "No, never. I'm terrible with women."

Crye laughed again.

"Oh, god. Oh, my god, I am so sorry." I waved my hands defensively as my brain finally came to its senses. "I didn't mean to get all creepy. I had a really rough night, and I'm not thinking straight."

Her eyes saddened. "So I don't look like an angel?"

"Yes, yes, of course. You're gorgeous!" I grimaced and hissed a breath between my teeth. "Crap, I'm sorry. I got creepy again."

"No, it's not creepy, Justin." Crye touched my hand. "Always say what you want around me, okay? You're kinda weird, but I like your spirit."

"You do?" I frowned. "What's there to like about it?"

"After all the bullying and beatings you've taken, you keep getting back up and moving forward." She shrugged. "It's like you have this unstoppable sense of optimism."

My mouth hung open at a complete loss for words. No one had ever said that about me before, but when I really thought about it, it felt right. "Thanks, Crye."

"Don't call me that around here." She winked. "Use my real name, Elyssa."

Burning angels fall from the heavens. Demonic creatures tear themselves from the earth and hurl themselves toward a massive army. Overhead, darkness collides with light. Lightning ripples through the clouds. Thunder rumbles and the shockwave throws me to the ground.

The cold embrace of death wraps around my body.

"I'll never let you die." Her face blots out the sky, raven hair trailing across her shoulders, violet eyes filling me with hope even as Armageddon rages around us.

A furious scream fills the air and a flash of superheated light consumes us.

I threw up an arm and shouted. "Sweet baby Jesus!" The mirror reflected my terrified expression.

Crye—Elyssa leapt to her feet, eyes wide. "You hate my name that much?"

I spun around, arms raised defensively. No demons, no angels, only hairstylists with scissors. *These hallucinations have got to stop.* I managed a weak laugh. "I think I'm going crazy." *Why did I just have a daydream with Crye in it?* Maybe I liked her more than I realized. Maybe I wanted her to join my Kings and Castles group.

"Maybe you need a nap." Her nostrils flared, eyes narrowed as she approached me. "Do you wear body spray?"

Before I could answer this non sequitur question, a tall brunette with an imperious gaze, long legs, and epic cleavage—yes, I'm obsessed with boobs—interrupted the conversation. She pursed her lips and stared at me. "You were right, dear. This one needs serious work." She spun on her heel and hooked a finger over her shoulder at me. "This way."

"Ooh this is gonna be fun." Crye's violet eyes sparkled. I stared at those lovely gems, wondering why she still wore colored contacts without her Goth garb. "Better hurry," she said. "Mom's impatient."

I hurried to the chair where her mom waited, towel in hand. Women filled most of the chairs, their hair tended to by fabulously dressed men and tired-looking women. A cross between ammonia and roses scented the air, no doubt a toxic cloud from hair chemicals.

"Thanks for doing this, Mrs., um..."

"Call me Leia."

"Thanks, Leia." It felt strange calling Crye's mom by her first name. And she looked so young too. If not for her imperious adult attitude, she and Crye could be sisters. I forced my eyes from her cleavage and plopped in the chair. Leia spent the next several minutes washing my hair, then shooed me over to a salon chair. I took a seat and stared at the mirror. My hands trembled as I thought about the irrevocable change in my immediate future. It wasn't too late to get up and run. Leia's hand clamped onto my shoulder.

Now it's too late.

Her hand on my shoulder reminded me uncomfortably of Stacey. My neck felt very warm where she'd licked it, like the hot ice lotion athletes slather on sore muscles. I hoped it wasn't infected. I stared at the right side of my neck in the mirror. It looked redder than the moon-white skin around it.

Leia left for a moment then returned with a spray bottle. She stood behind me and appraised my hair with an arched eyebrow. Her nostrils twitched. "You should probably not wear body spray." She rubbed her nose. "The scent is a bit much."

Despite all my joking, I really didn't wear any sort of body spray. *Must be pheromones.*

Leia went back to inspecting my hair, grunting as if uncertain any amount of hair styling would improve my appearance.

Movies depict major lifestyle changes as quick and easy, using a video montage of exercise, proper eating, and professional grooming all set to an upbeat pop tune. In real life, it was proving to be traumatic, time consuming, and slow as molasses. I'd need all the pop songs in the world to get through this change.

"Elyssa seems to think you'd look better with spiky hair," Leia said after staring at my mop.

It took a moment to remember Crye had another name. "Yeah," I croaked. My eyes met hers and I realized with a start that her eyes sparkled violet like her daughter's.

As if on cue, Crye appeared at my shoulder and looked me over appraisingly. "Dye his hair black and go with long spikes."

Leia pursed her lips and stared for a moment. "Do you want him to look good or maniacal?"

"Both."

"Um, can we go more for the good look?" I asked. "I already look crazy."

Crye grabbed my shoulder. "Just go with it, you big scaredy-cat."

"I don't want to look stupid." I almost said "freakish" but I didn't want to hurt Crye's feelings since she'd suggested the style.

Leia raised an eyebrow. "Let's begin, shall we? I have a full schedule today."

I reluctantly nodded. Crye went back to the front desk. Leia started by lopping off most of my hair with scissors. I closed my eyes and tried to steady my breathing so I didn't whimper. After she cut my hair, she dyed it darker black with something that reeked like burning tires and barf.

When she finished, I stared at the finished product in the mirror. I hardly recognized myself, aside from the pale chubby face and thick glasses. I mentally added *Contact Lenses or Geek Chic glasses* to my list of improvements.

Instead of a nerdy fat kid, I looked like a cool chubby kid. Leia had cut my hair a little shorter than the six inches Crye wanted, but I was secretly relieved the new 'do wasn't too outlandish.

"Not bad," Crye said when she came over to inspect the new me. "New glasses, new clothes, and you'll almost be respectable."

"I was meaning to ask about that." I used the mirror to direct my gaze to Leia. No way in hell I'd take fashion advice from someone who thought Goth attire was stylish. "Do you have any opinion about what kind of clothes I should buy?"

"I always have an opinion, child," Leia said. "But I have too much to do to chat about fashion." The back door squeaked open and a serious man in tight black clothes stepped inside. Crye and Leia exchanged a look, then Leia whisked away. She took the man by the arm and escorted him into a back room.

"What was that about?" I asked.

Crye blinked. "Nothing. Just a hairstylist who's always late."

"Oh." I wondered why she sounded nervous about it. I thought back to the mall. "You know, I've been meaning to ask you—"

"You need clothes." Crye glanced at a pink *Hello Kitty* watch on her wrist. "I get out of here in an hour."

"Please, nothing Goth," I said.

She shook her head. "Yeah, no. Goth isn't for you."

"Oh, well that's cool. What kind of clothes do you have in mind?"

"I asked Renaldo to help." She pointed to a young male stylist who laughed and gestured in the exaggerated way I'd seen only gay men do.

"You asked a gay guy to help me?"

"Hey, you want fashion advice. Gay guys are the best."

"Maybe for picking out curtains," I grumbled. Renaldo looked to be in his early twenties. He wore a baby-blue button-up shirt tucked into dark jeans that a wild animal must have savaged given the rips in the fabric on the thighs. Come to think of it, he looked as fashionable as the people I'd seen in the mall.

I held up a hand to ward off Crye's reply. "I saw you following some dude in the mall the other day."

Her eyes flared, but she blew it off with a shrug. "I was at the mall, but I wasn't following anyone."

"Yeah, you were." I looked around to make sure her mother hadn't returned. "The guy had on an Affliction T-shirt. He looked like an old guy trying to dress to impress younger people."

"I don't know who you're talking about." Crye's voice frosted. "I was probably just walking the same way." Her eyes narrowed. "How did you know I was at the mall? Are you stalking me?"

"Hey, don't turn it around on me." I took a breath. Sighed. "Look, I'm sorry. I shouldn't have brought it up. It just looked like you were following him."

"Well, I wasn't." She clapped my shoulder hard enough to make me wince. "Now, back to gay men and their superb fashion taste."

I nodded, and looked at Renaldo again. His ensemble of torn jeans, dark red tie, and blue vest looked really spiffy, but I could never pull off that look. Whatever I got would have to be XXL. If I wore clothes as tight as his, I'd have a muffin top. "I have to admit, he looks pretty stylish."

"He's hot and fashionable," Crye said. "Too bad he's not into girls."

"Wow." I quirked my lips. "Did you just call a guy 'hot'? Never expected that from you."

"I am a girl, stupid. And I'm not batting for the other team, if that's what you were thinking."

She wore way too much pink to be a lesbian or a Goth, for that matter. Not that I was an expert on either. I glanced at the approximate location on her nose where she usually wore a stud, wondering how large a hole those things left, but her skin looked perfect, unbroken. I couldn't spot any holes in her lips either. The studs must have teensy-tiny pointy things on them unless they were fake clip-ons. For some reason that made me feel better. It'd be a waste to mar such great skin with a bunch of holes.

I followed her back to the front and took a seat next to a middle-aged woman with a mountain of teased up bangs in the shape of a claw. I looked in the mirror behind Crye's desk and did a double take at the new me. I looked so much better. Then I noticed the red skin on my neck. It looked like a rash. Surely I wasn't going to turn into a vampire, was I? I would have felt the urge to drink blood if that were the case. Also, vampires didn't have reflections.

Despite all evidence pointing to the contrary, I worried that I might burst into flames when the sun hit me. But I didn't know anyone I could ask for advice. Maybe Google could also give me the cure for vampirism. I sat back and Googled furiously on my smartphone until Crye walked over and lightly booted my foot with hers.

"Ready?" she asked.

Renaldo appeared from the back. He looked me up and down, his head shaking the entire time. "Cargo pants? Old Navy?" he said in a decidedly deep and not-gay voice. "We need a complete rebuild."

"Can you help?" Crye pressed her hands together in prayer as if I had some severe medical condition that only a miracle drug could cure.

"I'll do my best. Let's head to the mall."

I was glad I brought plenty of my ill-gotten cash with me. Several hundred dollars later, I had a nice wardrobe though I felt like a piece of meat. Every time I tried on jeans or slacks, Crye and Renaldo took a critical eye to my ass to make sure the pants looked fitted. I was exhausted. Crye and Renaldo only seemed to draw energy from the experience like window-shopping vampires.

I took my two helpers out for a nice meal to thank them for their help. Afterward, Renaldo gave me a hug. "Ah, my little creation. You're going to knock their panties off." He kissed Crye on the cheek and waved goodbye as he hopped in his sporty red convertible and sped away.

"I'm going to collapse." My weary muscles ached and my injured foot felt stiff as a board.

Crye smiled and punched me on the shoulder. "You survived and that's all that matters."

"I guess." I drove her to her car. "Thanks. For everything."

Crye opened the door, hesitated, then kissed me on the cheek before getting out. "You look good, Justin."

As I watched her get into her car, a tear trickled down my face. I felt immensely grateful and happy that I'd met her. We hardly knew each other, but I felt like I'd known her for ages.

She's my only true friend.

Well, Ash and Nyte were too, but I felt closer to Crye—Elyssa, whatever her name was. I decided to stick with the name Crye since she preferred it at school. Calling her by two different names would only confuse me.

I drove home, my heart happier and lighter than it had been in ages. Dad lay on the couch when I walked inside. He looked rough, unshaven, and smelled like gasoline and exhaust fumes. His knuckles looked bruised and dirty, and I wondered if he'd been in an accident.

Dad stretched and sat up. "Hey, kiddo." He blinked. "You got a haircut?"

I nodded, spun around in my new jeans and T-shirt. "Got some new clothes too."

"Nice." He rubbed his unshaven jaw. "Um…"

I prodded him when he didn't finish the thought. "Um, what?"

He dismissed it with a wave. "Nothing. I'm just beat from riding the motorcycle all day." Dad rubbed his eyes and I noticed they looked pale again.

I really wanted to ask him about the laundromat, but another part of me didn't want to know any deep, dark secrets that might scar me for life. I hoped there was an innocent explanation, but the way my Dad had looked at those old women made me shiver at the memory.

"You okay, son?" Dad went to the fridge and grabbed a beer. He touched his throat. "What happened to your neck?"

I almost told him that a demon woman had given me a hickey, a vampire classmate had repeatedly threatened me, and that I'd hallucinated about running into my pregnant mother with the car, but decided I didn't want my father thinking his son was insane, so I settled for a white lie instead.

"Oh, a girl licked my neck and kissed it."

He clapped his hands together. "Nice!" He popped the top off the beer and took a swig. "Were you on a date?"

"Yeah." I hated piling on the lie, so I cut it short. "I started working out too. I'm gonna go jogging before it gets too late."

Dad held up a hand, palm out. "Don't leave me hanging."

I gave him a high five and felt really guilty for taking credit. I'd been a victim, not a stud. Still, I'd sleep easier with him in the house.

He checked his watch. "Damn, I gotta go pick up something for work. I'll probably be back late."

My forehead scrunched. "Didn't you just get back? What's kept you traveling so much lately?"

"Lot of art galleries want my advice." He framed my face with his thumbs and forefingers. "There's a lot more to hanging art than you'd think." Dad squeezed my shoulder. "Glad to see you taking care of yourself, Justin." He sighed. "I just wish…"

"Wish what?"

Dad looked me in the eyes. "It doesn't matter who or what you are, it's what you do that's important. I'm proud of you, son."

I was both confused and incredibly happy. "You're proud of me even though I'm fat and not handsome and muscular like you?"

The side of his eyes tugged down slightly. "I am proud of you for who you are. I just hope that you'll always feel the same way about me and your mother."

The way he said it sounded like he felt ashamed for something. *The laundromat and old ladies, maybe?* I decided to stick with the positive and save whatever bad secrets he had for later. "I do, Dad."

He ruffled my hair. "Oops, didn't mean to mess up the new 'do." Dad grabbed a duffel bag and waved goodbye before vanishing through the door.

I went into my room and pulled out sweatpants and a T-shirt. A dull ache worked up my spine and into the back of my head. The pain spread, growing steadily worse as I disrobed. Pinpricks in my forehead grew to stabbing pain. The skin on my neck throbbed. I rushed into the bathroom, desperately searching for ibuprofen. Vision blurred. Legs went weak. Blinding pain exploded.

Agony overwhelmed me.

CHAPTER 11

I threw up so hard I blacked out for a moment. I flailed for the toilet. My fist connected with something and made a horrible crunching noise. My muscles twitched, tightened, and contracted so fast I fell into a shuddering heap and cracked my head on the bath-tub. How I kept a grip on consciousness, I don't know. My bones felt as if they were disassembling into jigsaw puzzle pieces while evil brain fairies tap-danced inside my head. I writhed and tried to scream but only rasping groans escaped my tortured throat.

Heat flared in my chest, spreading fire along my skin. Between spasms, I cracked an eyelid and looked at my hands. Blood oozed from the pores. It soaked my clothes. Wet warmth dribbled down my scalp and covered my eyes. I screamed silently. Pain overwhelmed me once again and mercifully stole consciousness away.

Some undefinable time later I awoke in the fetal position on the floor. A puddle of crusted blood, vomit, and god only knew what else pooled in the middle of the white tile. My body felt lighter than air and I wondered if I'd just died and was having an out of body experience. I looked around but didn't see a spare Justin lying anywhere. I pinched my blood-covered skin. It hurt. I was alive despite the obscene amount of bodily fluids on the floor.

Or was I?

My stomach clenched. What if I'd turned into a vampire? I looked in the mirror. Blood covered my face, my neck, and everywhere else. I opened my mouth and said, "Ah," to check for fangs. My teeth looked normal, albeit a little yellowish. Gross. I was going to have to do something about that. The sun shined through the bathroom window. I stuck out a tentative hand and braced for flames. The sunlight warmed my skin, nothing more. My skin was not flammable, or at least no more so than the average human's.

What had happened, then? Was this the result of my body fighting an infection? Bad Indian food? It looked like I had spilled every gallon of blood in my body on the floor, the walls, and even the ceiling. I decided to make a doctor appointment ASAP. I'd heard of growing pains, but this was ridiculous. I stripped and stared at my body in the mirror. The bruises on my arms were gone. The red spot on my neck had vanished. I wriggled my toes. They felt good as new. Aside from my usual pallor and fatness, I looked normal—well normal for someone who worked in a slaughterhouse. Something crunched underfoot. I lifted my foot and saw a bit of porcelain. Then I noticed the toilet. The side of it gaped open. I stared at my fist. No bruises, no broken bones. Had Stacey done something to me, or was this a continuation of the awful migraines and blurring vision issues that intermittently plagued me? Maybe my encounter with her had triggered an even worse episode.

It was Wednesday, but this called for a sick day. I called into the school and faked my father's voice. "Justin won't be in today. He vomited blood last night."

"Okay," the school nurse said. "Tell him to drink plenty of fluids."

"Yes, I will." I hung up and stared at the awful mess. This was going to take a while.

After a bucket of bleach and a whole lot of scrubbing the bathroom sparkled. My stomach growled, but we only had junk food in the pantry. All those juice boxes sat in the garbage, but I resisted the siren call of sugary goodness.

I showered, and went to buy groceries. Since I had just vomited blood I decided to go organic for once. As I entered the grocery store, a strange aroma tickled my nose. In addition to the odor of breads, chicken, beef, and the slightly sour odor of spilled milk somewhere to my left, there was a mélange of perfumes, a touch of armpit body odor, and something more. Something that made my second brain perk up and take notice.

What in the world made me think there was spilled milk to my left? I followed the odor and saw a puddle of white at the other end of the aisle. The stench overpowered my nose from twenty feet away. I evacuated the area and went about the business of procuring healthy treats for my belly, starting with meat. Every scent cut into my olfactory senses. Beef, chicken, pork, all marched up my nostrils hand-in-hand with odors I didn't recognize and did not ever want to recognize. Some people ate really gross stuff.

Separating one odor from another proved difficult unless I picked up a package and sniffed it, which made me look like an anally retentive shopper and nearly made my eyes water. I grabbed a package of organic free-range chicken breasts and pushed my glasses up my nose as I read the nutrition information—no chicken hormones for me.

I poked myself in the forehead instead because my glasses weren't there. I felt my face and my head to make sure I hadn't somehow shoved them into the wrong place. Considering the thickness of my goggle-like eyewear, they were hard to miss. My hands confirmed my glasses had indeed gone AWOL.

Somehow, I could see just fine.

I looked toward the produce department at the far end of the store. I read every word on the small sign. *Radishes - $1 a bag!* The package of chicken fell from my hands and rattled the metal cart when it landed inside. I noticed how sharp colors and contrast seemed. Every little detail hummed, shined, and smelled vibrant—alive. It was like calibrating a dull TV image into something warm and colorful. If the grocery store looked this good, I wondered how a sunrise would appear.

This was crazy. I had to be dreaming. I pressed my hands to my cheeks to confirm I was awake. A woman perusing beef passed by me. I caught the scent of the underlying odor that had bewitched me earlier. Except it wasn't so much of a scent as a presence.

Breathing through my nose didn't matter. I smelled her with my mind. That was probably one of the dumbest things I had ever thought. *Smell her with my mind?* What kind of sense did that make?

At the moment, it made all the sense in the world.

"Hi." I waved.

She turned and looked at me with one of those I-don't-have-time-for-you-to-hit-on-me looks. She had to be in her twenties. The furrow of her brow, the slump of her shoulders told me she'd left college behind and entered the crush of real life. Something burned beneath the surface, buried beneath mounds of worries and cares and responsibilities.

It appeared as curling wisps of glowing vapor, a nimbus trailing behind her as she walked, or hovering around her when she stopped to inspect a packet of round-eye steaks here, and lean ground beef there. It thrummed with her base desires. Her lusts. Her carnal nature. I wanted to touch it, to make it mine. A wisp of my own darted from me and latched onto one of those seductive vapors. Tickled it. Hers curled, stretched, and wound itself around mine in a lovers' embrace.

The woman's eyes widened. She licked her lips like a nervous school girl about to be kissed for the first time. "Hi," she said in a throaty voice. Her anatomy turned on the high-beams, figuratively speaking. She pushed a lock of brown hair behind her ear and smiled.

I slipped an arm around her waist and kissed her, pressing my lips feverishly against hers. She grabbed my butt with one hand and squeezed. The other hand went straight for my crotch. I heard noises in the background: shrieks, cries of dismay, and the tap of a heavy foot against the tiled floor. I didn't know who or what made that racket. I didn't care. Nothing could make me pull away from my meat-market love goddess. My sexy little filet mignon.

I got your beef right here.

"Take it outside, you two," said a gruff voice.

I ignored the pesky voice. I pulled her body closer to mine. Felt her clutching desperately at my belt.

Someone gasped. "Oh my God, what are they doing?"

"Perverts!" a woman shouted.

"Dear Jesus, strike these sinners down!"

I had only eyes, ears, hands, and now tongue for my grocery store Aphrodite.

Someone jerked me mid-kiss from my simmering Amazonian love princess. I spun, disoriented and stared at the large security guard responsible for ruining my romantic moment with—with—um, whoever that woman was.

"You two gonna have to leave if you keep that up." He crossed his arms and delivered a no-nonsense look. Behind him stood a group of horrified onlookers, mainly old people and moms with young kids.

"Mommy, what's that in his pants?" asked a little boy.

I opened my mouth to say something but the sheer mortification of what I'd just done froze the words in my throat. I was also keenly aware of what exactly was in my pants and fighting to get free for my horrified audience. I spun around. The woman I had just been dry humping scurried away, shoulders hunched.

I took her cue and grabbed my shopping cart. My face burned. I took cover in the restroom for a few minutes trying to figure out what in the hell had just happened. No way she'd jumped me for just my looks. Not even new jeans and shirt could make a woman jump me like that. Whatever it was, I had to be very careful. Otherwise, I might end up on the news with a nickname like the Grocery Store Chicken Choker, or Beef Boy.

I took a deep breath and left the safety of the bathroom. I needed healthy treats to continue my quest for wellness. I had chicken. Time for veggies.

It became evident after a few seconds that I still sensed that alluring feminine odor whenever a woman was near—attractive women, mainly. The older or uglier they were, the less magnetic the smell became although it was never disgusting or repellant—they all had similar desires, wants, and needs crying for release. I ignored them the best I could and got the heck out of there before I went porn-star on one of the cashiers.

My mind raced as I sat in the Jetta and tried to figure out what was going on with me. It wasn't puberty. I'd already grown hair in all the right places and my voice had changed from a squeak to something resembling a nerdy baritone. Whatever it was started last night. Or maybe it started when Stacey tried to suck the life force out of my eyeballs. I wasn't about to start looking for her again even if she did have answers. In fact, I was kind of scared to go back to the same gym. Of course if I saw her there, I'd confront her in front of everyone so as to avoid a repeat molestation. Maybe that was what I should do. Then again, a woman that powerful might just mind-rape everyone and make us her little bitches.

Unfortunately, Victoria expected me to show up in a few hours. Vampire mistress or not, I had to go and figure out a way to convince Stacey to cough up some answers. I drove to the hardware store and looked for a toilet. It was all I could do to resist the copious number of hormone-laden women flaunting their femininity while they shopped for great values on home improvement items.

Or maybe that was just me and my new phase of hyper-puberty.

I couldn't sense their thoughts so much as feel the sexual cougars lurking behind the civilized façade they wore in public. I grabbed the cheapest crapper I could find and rushed to the front of the store with it tucked under my left arm. It was only when the cashier gave me a startled look that I realized how odd it must look for a chubby kid to tote around a heavy toilet one-armed without breaking a sweat. In fact, it hadn't even occurred to me that the toilet must be something heavy.

Despite her confusion, a part of her grew aroused by my display. Vaporous tendrils of feminine allure hung before me, waiting, wanting, begging. All I had to do was—

"No!" I shouted and scared the crap out of the poor girl. She jumped back a foot from me. "Uh, sorry." I pointed at my ear. "I'm talking to my idiot friend on a teeny tiny Bluetooth headset. Really rude, I know." I paid and got out of there.

I asked, and Google supplied me with a stir-fry recipe. My stomach hated me for taking so long to feed it, but loved me again once I shoved the passable meal down my throat. Dad still wasn't home. Still no texts or calls from Mom. I wondered what in the world kept her so busy that she couldn't take a moment to type out a few words to her son. I went to my room and did a double-take when I passed Mom's office. Her laptop sat on the desk, and it was on.

Since when doesn't she take her laptop with her and who left it on?

The desk was immaculate, every bit of paper filed away and each item on the desk lined up perfectly with its neighbor. Mom was OCD when it came to cleanliness and pretty much everything else. Which was how I knew she would never leave her laptop behind and especially not on unless she was nearby. I rushed to the garage, but her car wasn't there. The odor of fresh exhaust fumes tickled my nose.

Someone was just here.

I went back into her office and clicked on the internet browser minimized on the task bar. It popped up a window that said, *Transfer Complete. PI Services will receive the money within two hours.*

"What the hell?" I looked at the sidebar menu and realized this was the bank website. Considering it hadn't automatically logged out yet meant that I'd just missed the user by minutes. Only one person was irresponsible enough to leave the laptop open to a logged in bank website—Dad.

Mom got onto him all the time for leaving on her laptop. Since Mom never let me mess with her laptop, I decided to snoop. Maybe it would offer clues about her business trip. I checked her credit card statement, but it hadn't been used in ages. I soon discovered why. My parents didn't need credit. Their checking account had a positive balance seven digits long.

"Six million dollars?" My voice rose to a squeak. "Where in the hell did they get this kind of money?" Nearly every transaction was a cash withdrawal or wire transfer. *No wonder that shoebox is always full of money.*

But if they were that rich, why did they drive such old cars? Why did we live in such an ordinary house? Dad's words came back to me. Were my parents up to something I wouldn't be proud of? Accountants didn't make that much money which mean it had to be from Dad's art-related work. Maybe Aunt Petunia left us a fortune through her will.

Or perhaps my parents were criminal masterminds.

I scoured the computer for more information but found no information about where the money came from or where Mom had gone on her trip. I was about to leave the computer when I noticed a folder at the root of the hard drive—*Copy of hash codes.* I wasn't a computer expert, but this wasn't a normal system folder.

My porn stash was hidden in a folder named *Device Drivers* on my computer. I doubted Mom harbored porn on her hard drive, but it could be the perfect place to stash a criminal paper trail.

I opened it and found a bunch of files that didn't open when I double-clicked them. I assigned them to a text viewer program, but received a screen of programming code with bizarre symbols I'd never seen before. It struck me as very odd because unless Mom was a secret hacker or computer genius, she couldn't have written this stuff.

Had she made this folder copy by accident while removing other files? I didn't know but I wanted a copy of my own just in case it might be important to figuring out where she'd gone. I grabbed a flash drive from my room and copied the folder over before shutting down the laptop.

I wanted to analyze the files some more, but my phone notified me that Victoria awaited.

The moment I entered the gym, I knew it had been a terrible mistake. Not because Stacey the vampire was there, but the sheer volume of sweaty, sexy women threatened to overload my senses. I had to think about baseball so hard I felt the veins in my head bulging. Everywhere I turned, sexual desires and longings threw themselves against me. It was insane. I knew what a victim of Viagra over-dosing must feel like. I pulled my T-shirt down a bit further over my shorts and found Victoria in the free-weights section of the gym. The dense cloud of male stink in this area overpowered the feminine allure of the cardio section. Weights clanged, men grunted in agony, and two muscular guys flexed in front of the mirrors that ran along every wall.

Just my kind of place.

"You ready?" she asked.

"I guess." I was not looking forward to the torment awaiting me.

We went to the bench press first. She stacked on some meager weight. I pumped it up and down, no problem. She added a couple of larger plates. No problem there, either. I was so surprised, I forgot to be impressed.

Victoria arched an eyebrow at me. "Are you juicing or something? That's over two-hundred pounds and you're not even breaking a sweat."

I shrugged. "I had orange juice this morning."

She gave me the stink-eye.

Victoria slid on more forty-five pound plates until both sides of the barbell could hold no more. Just about every dude in the testosterone-soaked iron-pumping section of the gym stared at me with unadulterated jealousy. The barbell creaked and sagged dangerously on each end. I pushed it up and down several times without a hint of exhaustion. Victoria stared open-mouthed.

"I don't believe it." She waved her hands in the air over the barbell, apparently looking for invisible wires. "This isn't possible unless you were totally faking it the other day." Victoria grunted and jerked on the barbell without so much as budging it.

"Lemme see that." A guy roughly the size of a buffalo, with bulging arms and a shaved head stepped up to the plate. He lay down on the bench, muttering curses to himself. Then he started slamming his chest with alternating hands, roaring obscenities at full volume. "Mother fucking do this! You got this shit! Make momma proud!" He pushed on the barbell. His face went from pink to purple in about two seconds. His veins bulged and pulsed alarmingly.

"Do you need a lift-off?" I asked.

He roared. He screamed. He said terrible things about his mother and his upbringing. He sagged and gave up. Stood. Glared at me. Then held out his fist for a bro-bump followed by the asteroid explosion that makes life worth living.

"You're the real deal." He shook his head. "Man, you gotta tell me what you're on."

"Teenage hormones." I shrugged. "It's all I got."

He wandered away, cursing and mumbling. A few other muscle-bound dudes grumbled to themselves. I could make out most of what they said despite the mournful howling of a country singer on the ceiling speakers. What in the world had Stacey done to me?

"We're not done yet." Victoria's face glowed redder than her hair. She marched me down a hall, into a private office, and sat down on the corner of a desk. I sat opposite of her. She looked *pissed*. "What kind of joke is this?"

"It's not a joke."

"You come in here weak as a lamb Monday, now you're pumping more iron than humanly possible. Look at you! You're chunky, not muscular."

"Thanks. I appreciate that."

"Something's going on and you're not leaving until I get some answers."

My vision seemed to shift. The ghostly halo formed around her. I realized with a start it was exactly what I'd seen around my classmates that day in class. On impulse, I latched onto hers just like I had the woman in the grocery store. Victoria's scarlet face paled. Her eyes widened while her mouth formed a shocked "O". I stood. She jumped up and attacked me with sloppy, wet kisses. Then we fell on the desk in a tangle of limbs and clothes.

My second brain demanded I rip off her clothes and go all the way as a hand ran up her bare calf, her toned thighs, and further onward to glory. The hopeless romantic in my other brain told me to resist. Feral instinct controlled me, shoved my intellect to the side. Victoria was apparently gripped by the same instincts because her hands fumbled with the knotted drawstrings on my shorts as a war of thoughts raged in my mind.

Rip off her clothes. Pull her hair. She is yours. Dominate her!

What about true love? What about saving your virginity for the perfect woman? This is your gym instructor, for god's sake! Snap out of it!

The hopeless romantic part of me was right. I was about to blow my virginity on a woman I hardly knew, much less loved.

My body refused to listen. Victoria had a death grip on my shorts. I tried to think about baseball. No good. I focused on Katie, her long blonde hair and tanned legs. For a moment, I thought it worked. Then my hands moved to help Victoria with my drawstrings.

I felt like a puppet on strings. Unbridled carnal lust gripped me by the balls and I couldn't do anything to stop it. *What teenage boy wouldn't trade places with me right this moment?* What kind of a moron was I? Wasn't this what I really wanted? To have women want me? Why else had I asked Crye—Elyssa—to help me?

Elyssa.

Fiery violet eyes flashed in my head for a brief second. My body froze. Victoria laughed in delight as she pulled loose the knot. I jerked back. Bolted for the office, spinning around as Victoria's death grip on the drawstrings pulled them clean out of my shorts. I stumbled back into the gym proper and bowled over a guy warming up with stretches. After apologizing and pulling up my shorts, I casually walked for the exits as if I had not almost had sex with my trainer and dropped my drawers in front of a strange man.

Despite my frayed nerves, I felt recharged and better than ever. I felt as if I were taking a part of Victoria with me. I once read in Cosmo that losing your virginity was like that. Technically, I hadn't lost my virginity, but I could have if I'd really wanted to, and wasn't that almost as good? I jogged through the rows of treadmills lining my path to the gym exit and pumped one fist in the air—since my other hand held up my shorts.

Today, a boy nearly became a man!

Startled looks greeted my burst of post-almost-sex enthusiasm. I didn't give a crap. I stepped outside, barely resisting the urge to skip like a child with a lollipop. The skin on the back of my neck prickled. My improved senses interpreted this information. Something female but not quite human approached from behind. Entering the dark parking lot with little more than my carnal jaunt on my mind had been a mistake.

The hot sensation burning between my shoulder blades felt alien compared to what I'd sensed from the women inside the gym, but something about it seemed very familiar. I spun in time to see Stacey's delicate white fingers reaching for me.

I grabbed her by the shoulders and jacked her against a windowless child molester-themed van. She cried out in surprise. Her eyes widened in delight. Thankfully, the elastic band on my shorts managed to cling to my waist instead of dropping to the ground.

"My little morsel. You've changed." She smiled prettily and with a touch of innocence.

"Don't try your tricks with me. What are you?"

Her irises, swirling amber pools of hypnosis, tried to draw me into their depths. I shook off the effect and reached for the sexual vapors steaming around her as I'd done with Victoria. They slipped away from me like smoke in the wind. Stacey flashed a wicked smile and purred. She jerked her arms free, spun us around and pinned me to the van. Then she licked my face and peppered me with hot kisses.

"You." Kiss. "Are." Kiss. "So." Lick. "Desirable, my tender little morsel."

I tried to push her off me but despite my newfound strength, she had leverage and was in better shape. I wasn't entirely helpless, though. I ducked under her arms and crawled away on my knees. My shorts chose this moment to fall down. She clutched her ribs and burst into hysterical giggles.

"What's so funny?"

"You are a true delight. It's such a bloody shame I cannot drink you in." She inhaled a deep breath and regained her composure, though a radiant smile lit her face. "I could still offer you a great many physical pleasures. You are the first of your kind in many, many years that has tried to lure me into his embrace. How intoxicating."

"First of all, I didn't try to lure you." I stood up and covered my tighty-whities with my shorts. "Second of all, you have fangs and a very scratchy tongue. Are you a vampire?"

Her full red lips curved into an alluring smile. "You have no tutor to educate you in the ways of the Overworld?" Her delighted laughter filled the parking lot. "Perhaps I shall take you under my wing. You must promise to keep me happy. Very happy. We will have such fun, my lamb."

"The Overworld?"

"Consider my offer, little lamb, and you shall have your answers."

"How am I supposed to find you?"

"Worry not your pretty little head." She pecked a kiss on my cheek. "I will find you." With that, she dashed away into the darkness, her legs a blur.

Yep. She was a vampire all right. And this did not bode well for me.

CHAPTER 12

School seemed so unimportant I almost didn't go. But I dragged myself out of bed and got ready anyway. I couldn't afford to miss classes. After my make-out session with Victoria, the urge to fling my virginity to the wolves of desire burned like hot coals in my tender bits. I'd taken certain "precautions" but worried about another complete loss of control. I would dive into an ocean of hot feminine hormones inside that high school.

But I had no choice.

Crye smiled at me the moment we made eye contact when I entered the gymnasium. She wore full Goth battle gear complete with a spiky chain from ear to lip. I couldn't reconcile this Goth creature with the cute girl at the hair salon. It was like seeing a cheerleader at a heavy metal concert. The incongruities blew my mind. Others apparently didn't care for her garb either as the general vicinity of the bleachers remained clear of students. I walked up the stairs and sat next to her.

"Where are Nyte and Ash?" I wondered if their real names were as innocuous as George and Fred.

"Running late." She yawned. Fatigue underlined her eyes in dark patches that showed through her makeup.

"Something wrong?"

"No, just tired. I'm so sick of school you couldn't possibly know."

"Seems like a waste of time. Maybe we should do homeschooling."

A giggle erupted from her. It reminded me of the cute girl in pink, not this Goth chick with scary makeup.

"You look much better today." She looked me up and down. "There's something else different though. What is it?" Her nostrils flared slightly and her pupils dilated noticeably.

I looked down. "Maybe it's the clean underwear."

Crye snorted. "No, it's something else." An apple clocked her in the back of the head. "Ouch." She rubbed the spot and flicked her gaze behind us.

I grabbed the apple and looked up the bleachers. Nathan and a group of his football buddies howled with laughter. I growled and stood. Crye grabbed my arm and tugged me back down.

"Let it go," she said. "I'm used to it."

"Those assholes hit you," I said.

"And what are you going to do? Be my valiant knight? Go up there and get your butt kicked by the entire football team?"

"I can't just sit here and let them do that to you." I glared up at the guffawing jocks. "Besides, it's only half the football team."

She looked at me with those pretty violet eyes for a moment and touched my hand gently. A smile warmed her gaze. "Thanks."

Heat flushed my face. "Sure," I said. "Uh, no problem. I say words a lot and never back them up with action."

She laughed again. I liked the sound of it.

"I know this is going to sound kind of mean," I said, "but why do you cover a perfectly pretty face with all that Goth stuff?"

I could see her blush even through the makeup. "You think I'm pretty?"

Not only had I caught her off-guard with that question, but myself as well. It was far bolder than what I'd meant to say. I looked away shyly then forced my gaze back to hers. "Don't let it go to your head or anything."

She grinned as the bell rang. "I guess I've spent my life building a thick skin. It's nice getting a compliment every once in a while."

"Maybe you'd get more if you didn't have on the Goth shields all the time." We grabbed our book bags and walked to the gym exit.

She gave me a searching look for a moment before shrugging. "See you at lunch."

I watched her vanish into the crowd of students and wondered if I'd hurt her feelings with that comment. I also wondered what she was hiding from me. There was definitely more to her than met the eye.

Homeroom was only marginally bearable. Annie and Jenny did their best to tick me off, sniggering and hurling mean words my way.

"Somebody has a new Goth girlfriend," Jenny said.

Annie snorted. "I hear they bang heads really good."

"I'll bet she's got piercings all up and down her cooch. Is that true, Justin?"

I ignored them.

"Oh, he's embarrassed, Annie. Maybe we hurt his feelings. Can you hurt the feelings of a stalker?"

"Only if you get a restraining order," Annie said.

They burst into fits of laughter.

"A haircut and new clothes don't mean you're not a creepy pervert," Jenny said, trying to punch through my cold-shouldered disregard.

Their sex vapors, as I decided to call them until someone instructed me otherwise, hung nearby for the taking. But I didn't have the slightest desire to touch those vile things. The thought of giving those bitches any pleasure made me cringe.

Jenny poked me in the back with the sharp end of a pencil. I turned around. "What is your problem?"

"You and your creepy friends are," she said. "Katie told us you've been stalking her. She saw you at the mall following her."

"Bull shit." *What the hell is she talking about?* "I haven't set eyes on her."

"You should watch out," Annie piped up in her nasal voice. "Brad is out for payback after your lucky hit."

"And he just got a new Harley," Jenny said as if that should strike the fear of God into me.

I felt an evil grin spread across my face. "Maybe I'll wrap that scooter of his around his scrawny neck."

Jenny gave me a *Yeah, right!* look. "How's a ball of lard like you gonna do anything to Brad Nichols?"

I grabbed the corner of her desk and snapped off a chunk with a loud crack. She jumped and shrieked along with half the class. I smiled the coldest smile I could muster, although I'm sure it looked more crazed than anything. "Oops." I handed her the fragment.

She raised her hand and shouted for Mr. Herman.

He looked up from his artistic rendering of Simon and Garfunkel. "What the hell do you want?"

"Justin broke my desk." She held up the piece of desk as proof.

Mr. Herman squinted at it, then at her desk. "Just glue it back. Now shut up and leave me alone."

Jenny bonked me on the back of the head with the wood but it didn't hurt. She scowled. "I'm gonna make your life miserable, you low-life creep."

"Your very existence already does that." I stuck out my tongue.

The next few classes consisted of a string of people trying to make my life miserable with rude comments, gestures, and outright hostility. I noticed Katie was no longer in my calculus class. Alan Mueller informed me she'd transferred to another teacher the day before.

Christ almighty! Was my presence really so unbearable?

Despite my anger, I refrained from breaking another desk. Something told me that keeping my new strength under wraps might be a good idea. No telling what top-secret government agency would capture, tranquilize, and vivisect me once they found out a teenager could break desks with his bare hands.

Apparently, Katie had spread some untrue rumors about me as well. Given my nobody status, it was no surprise everyone believed her.

Lunchtime mercifully arrived. I joined Crye and gang at the usual table.

Nyte gave my clothes a once-over. "Looking better."

"Not too mainstream?" I asked.

He shrugged. "You are who you are. That's not for us to decide."

I grinned. "It's good to see there are decent people left in this place."

He nodded solemnly. "I know. One less person who isn't a steaming pile of shit."

"Apparently, you and I are an item." Crye smirked. "At least that's the gossip."

"I heard," I said. "Will the dumbassery never end?"

She pursed her lips. "Oh well. Sticks and stones may break my bones but —" An orange plopped down atop her mashed potatoes and splattered her lacy, chocolate-brown dress with the nuclear-flavored gravy only found in school cafeterias.

My jaw clenched. I snatched the orange out of the brown muck and shot a glare toward the only place it could have come from. Nathan and two sniggering linebackers sat at their usual table with several cheerleaders. I stood up.

"No!" Crye said.

Nyte and Ash both grabbed me but I shook them off. "I'll be right back."

I forced back my rage and calmly strolled to Nathan's table. Despite the confidence in my new strength, I really didn't want to get into a full-out battle royale. I could be suspended or even booted out of school. Knowing how the principal and upper brass felt about the football players, they wouldn't hesitate to protect their interests.

Nathan had his back to me while the other players and cheerleaders watched me the entire way. They told Nathan about my approach because he tried to get up when I reached them. I put my hand on his shoulder and pressed him back down into the seat so hard the metal legs groaned.

"Oh, don't get up on account of me," I said with a big grin. I took the orange in my other hand and fought back the desire to crush it in his face. Instead, I squished it into his mashed potatoes until the orange was a pulpy mess. Nathan struggled to stand. I kept him down with very little effort.

One of the linebackers stood up. I couldn't remember his name or his real position on the football team, so I called pretty much all of the ones I didn't know linebackers. It made things easy on me.

"Who the hell do you think you are?" He walked around the table.

I smiled the friendliest smile I could, although it probably looked maniacal on my pale pudgy face. I was going to have to work on practicing my grins.

He took a swing at me. I jumped back and watched his slow-motion fist smack into Nathan's ear. Nathan yelped like a puppy. I turned and walked back to the table while Nathan and his pal yelled at each other. I took a seat and calmly wiped orange bits and mashed potatoes off my hand. Then I bit into the burger that the lunchroom ladies had probably cobbled together from dead alley cats.

Crye shook her head. "That was about the stupidest thing I have ever seen. Are you looking to get yourself killed?"

Ash's mouth hung open. "I thought it was pretty cool."

"I don't condone physical violence," Nyte said. "Although you forced them to perpetrate it on each other, in which case I whole-heartedly approve."

A smile cracked Crye's angry reserve. "Okay, so it was kind of artful. But still so stupid that I want to smack you in the face."

I grinned. "You want to kiss me? In front of everyone?"

"I'm serious, Justin. Don't ever pull that kind of stunt again. I'm a big girl. I can take all the idiocy these morons dish out."

I shrugged. "Fine. I won't wear my shining armor to school anymore."

Nyte and Crye's eyes suddenly widened. A hand gripped my shoulder.

"Come with me, boy," said Mr. Barnes.

Every instinct told me to dive headfirst through the cafeteria window and make my escape. My next instinct was to break Mr. Barnes' hand and throw him through the cafeteria window. Common sense told me to act innocent and deny everything. So I stood and followed without a single word. We went into the main office. The secretary looked up at me with a knowing frown. I was sure she'd practiced it a million times in the mirror so students would know just how badly they were about to get it.

I returned a vacant toothy smile, the one a village idiot might give to the townsfolk as he's being led to the gallows. I saw my reflection in the mirror hanging behind her desk and realized even this attempt looked freakish and crazy. I really needed to practice my facial expressions. Maybe take acting classes. This was just sad. As an aside, I was glad to see I still had a reflection. Whatever horrific but undeniably cool STD Stacey had given me had not—yet—turned me into a creature of the night. If that had happened, then I'd probably go pants-on-head crazy on Mr. Barnes and to hell with the consequences.

I had never been to the principal's office. Mr. Barnes directed me to a seat in front of a scarred and worn wooden desk, then closed the door and left me alone while he ostensibly went to get the principal. Lee Perkins, the principal, was every bit the football stooge Ted Barnes was. They were both grand poobahs of the Quarterback Club and the things I'd heard about the club's underhanded activities made the mafia sound like a bunch of angels.

Mr. Perkins stepped solemnly into the office. He looked a lot like Colonel Sanders after eating a few tubs too many of fried chicken. Mr. Barnes followed close in his considerable wake. I gave them my best innocent look.

"I hear you've been up to all sorts of no good," Mr. Perkins said in his old-school and somewhat genteel southern accent. "I got half the school demanding your head on a silver platter, boy."

"Why, whatever for, sir?" I held onto my legs to keep my hands from trembling.

Mr. Barnes slapped his hand on my armrest. "You don't take that tone with us, boy." His redneck twang made him sound a touch inbred.

"Now, now," said Mr. Perkins. "I'm sure we don't need to tell young Mr. Case how to act before his superiors." He winked at me. "Do we?"

I decided to play it safe and shook my head.

"We got several eyewitness accounts that you attacked Nathan Spelman in the lunchroom today. That's assault and battery, boy. I've got some good friends down at the police station. Some of those good old boys could educate you on the formalities involved with those charges."

I wondered if he realized "boy" was no longer applicable to most of the males he spoke of or if he might be a pedophile at heart. "I was just returning the orange he dropped," I said. "I'm sure there are plenty of witnesses who will back me up."

Mr. Barnes chuckled. "I don't know 'bout you, son, but I'd put more stock in red-blooded all–American athletes like Nathan than the table of devil worshipers you've fallen into league with."

With considerable effort, I kept my mouth shut. "Would you like me to apologize to Nathan for returning his orange? He dropped it quite some distance because it landed in my friend's mashed potatoes."

"How 'bout you hold your tongue, boy," Mr. Barnes said.

At any moment, I expected him to tell me to squeal like a pig.

Mr. Perkins leaned back in his chair and rested his arms atop the hard knot of condensed fat he called a stomach. "I don't see much other recourse but to suspend you for three days or give you a week of after-school suspension. I suspect that suspending you will only give you free license to wreak your havoc upon society in general, which would reflect poorly on our fine institution. Therefore, I'm going to hand you over to Marjorie Foreman."

Ms. Foreman? I blanched. I knew this because my face felt like it had been splashed with ice water. "I didn't do anything. Nathan threw an orange at us. His own friend hit him in the face." The desperation in my voice sounded pathetic.

He smiled. "I'm sure that's the story you'd have us believe. Unfortunately, it simply does not hold much water with either of us."

My jaw tightened. "Maybe if I join the football team then everything I do will hold water with you."

"Well, now, boy, I think you just earned your little devil-worshipping girlfriend a week of after-school suspension with you. Does that sound about right, Ted?"

Mr. Barnes nodded, eyes overflowing with malicious glee. I felt my non-violent resolve crumbling. I wanted so badly to beat the ever-loving crap out of these useless slags that it hurt. Rage boiled deep inside the pit of my stomach. But I couldn't act out my fantasies. For one thing, I really would go to jail or be an outlaw. I didn't want to flush my normal life down the shitter. So I kept my mouth shut while they gloated and had their fun. Super-strength or not, there wasn't a thing I could do and it sucked.

CHAPTER 13

Crye sat in the waiting area, her face grim as I left Mr. Perkin's office. "Thanks so much for getting me after-school jail," she said.

"How did you know they suspended you? They just told me."

"Yeah, well Barnes and *Jerkins* told me I earned detention for using my feminine wiles to encourage you to commit an act of violence."

"That's a load of crap!" What I'd said to the principal hadn't mattered. Those lying bastards planned to give her detention no matter what. I almost turned around to pummel the two of them. Instead, I grabbed Crye's hand and dragged her through the hallway and out the front doors of the school.

"I don't have time for all this drama!" Crye shook her hand loose. "If you could just keep your mouth shut, things would go a lot smoother for all of us. Nathan and his goons came over to the table and threatened Nyte and Ash after you left. He said they'd hold them down and pull out their piercings with pliers."

"You've got to be kidding me. And these are the smacktards our upper brass will do anything to protect?" I managed a growl of sorts, although it sounded more like indigestion.

"That's right, Justin. Get mad. Go crazy. So far it's helped out a lot."

I turned on her. "What do you want me to do?" I yelled. "Let them throw apples at your head and oranges at our table and make fun of us? Is that what you enjoy? Does it make it easier to cut yourself with razor blades at night so you feel better?" I turned to walk away then rounded on her again. "I hate feeling like crap. I hate seeing them do this kind of thing to you, Elyssa, because despite all the effort you go through to cover yourself up with this Goth mask, I think you're someone special."

Tears welled in her huge eyes and tracked mascara down her white-powdered face. It looked horribly gruesome but it wrenched at my heart. She shook her head slowly, then turned and walked away.

The rest of the day became a numb blur. People made cruel comments about me and my friends. At least a couple of nerds with balls of steel approached and congratulated me on doing something about Nathan. Mark and Harry passed me in the hallway with new girlfriends and gave me withering looks of hatred. It didn't matter what I did or what super-powers I possessed, I was a pariah.

To make matters worse, the hot languid vapors from every female I saw distracted me constantly. Thankfully, the lust factor wasn't out of control like it had been with Victoria. So long as I could keep myself from latching onto the sexually-charged wisps, I wasn't in imminent danger of making out with random girls. I wondered if losing my virginity would put a stop to the merciless, simmering desire radiating from my groin or if it would only make things worse. I found myself quoting the *Princess Bride* over and over again to remind myself true love was worth waiting for.

When the final bell rang, I decided to take my books to the car before reporting to detention. I stopped in shock just outside the door. It looked like an army of cocaine-fueled street artists had attacked the back sidewalk leading to the parking lot with chalk. Alien symbols and patterns enclosed in circles covered every square inch of concrete. Because of the hedges on one side and an industrial-sized air conditioner on the other, it was impossible to avoid walking over them. Apparently the artist didn't care.

Most students barely gave the drawings a second glance as they stomped over them. A figure in a cowboy hat leaned against a midnight-black 1967 Impala. I wasn't an expert on old cars, but I'd seen every episode of Supernatural and would've known Dean Winchester's car anywhere.

Except the person leaning against the car wasn't a fictional character. It was the guy who'd stopped me in front of the school the other day and asked me about the Slade kids. He watched the exodus of students with keen interest, gaze locked especially on Garth Reed, a tall, exceptionally pale kid who was probably one link of DNA away from being albino.

When Garth reached the end of the sidewalk, my new enhanced sight picked out the disappointment furrowing the cowboy dude's face. *Is he some kind of pedophile?* I had a mind to confront him. With my new super strength, I might as well do something good.

I heard a gasp and turned around. Crye's eyes locked onto the sidewalk, then scanned the parking lot.

"Who drew those?" she asked me.

I shrugged. "They were already here."

The final dregs of the student body filtered out. Crye knelt at the edge of the first pattern and gritted her teeth. "What the hell are Arcanes doing here?" She muttered it under her breath, but my new enhanced hearing picked it up just fine.

Arcanes? Okay, this was really freaking me out. I reached out for her, hoping to apologize for my outburst earlier and also to find out what she meant by Arcanes, but she dashed down the sidewalk.

I started to follow, but someone gripped my arm and turned me around.

127

Ted Barnes confronted me with his shiny bald head. "Don't forget your detention, boy."

I opened my mouth to explain that I simply wanted to put my books in my car, but decided I'd have more luck teaching the laws of thermodynamics to a jar of pickled pigs' assholes than this idiot.

"Who in tarnation scribbled devil signs all over the sidewalk?" Barnes shouted at no one in particular. He hollered at a janitor down the hallway. "Pedro, I need a cleanup pronto."

"It's too late," I said in a mysterious voice. "The entire school is possessed. The devil owns us now. All hail Cthulhu." I moaned like a zombie and walked away, leaving Barnes with a perplexed look and hopefully a healthy dose of fear in that shit-stain he called a soul.

The Punisher, aka Ms. Foreman, awaited me in her room after school. She was a short, sweet-looking black woman with oversized glasses and an absent-minded aura about her. In other words, my worst nightmare. That little façade of hers masked the true nature of the demonic beast lurking beneath.

I'd made the mistake of crossing her my sophomore year in English by making some smart remark about her glasses. She hadn't even sent me to the principal's office, but gave me a motherly smile and an after-school detention cleaning out toilets that scarred me for life.

Crye entered the room a moment later. Ms. Foreman looked her up and down. "Well, now. This just won't do, will it?" Condescension dripped from her words. "I can't have you assisting me with all that dangerous jewelry." She reached into her desk and pulled out a plastic bag which she handed to Crye. "Now you just put away all that jewelry and scrub that horrible makeup off your face. Don't you worry, now. I'll give young Mr. Case some busywork until you get back."

The busy work consisted of taking chalkboard cleaner and, starting with her chalkboard, going to each and every class, spraying them with the noxious stuff, and wiping them down until they sparkled. Five rooms later, I knew what huffing gas did to the human brain. *This chalk-board cleaner is murdering my brain cells.*

Crye joined me in classroom six. I expected her to scowl or shout at me. Instead, she ignored me and that hurt even worse. We cleaned several chalkboards like this until I couldn't take it anymore. "Look, I'm sorry for what I said earlier. Just say something to me. Please."

She hit me in the head with a chalkboard eraser.

"Ouch!"

Crye nodded in satisfaction. "Now that we have that settled, thanks."

I rubbed my head. "Seriously? You bonk me on the head and then thank me?" *Girls are insane.*

"For being my friend and standing up for me. It pisses me off when you fly off the handle and do something stupid without thinking it through. You're just a nom—I mean Nathan is huge. He could tear you apart."

"That makes total sense," I said. "You thanked me for something that ticks you off. Argh!"

"Do I hear talking?" Ms. Foreman's voice echoed in the hall. She poked her head in the door. "Now, now, children. No talking during detention."

We nodded. She smiled sweet as a razor-laced caramel apple and vanished into the hallway. I looked back at Elyssa. She looked so much better without all the makeup and piercings. I hated the name Crye. From now on, even if she beat me for it, I'd call her Elyssa, Goth makeup or not.

I meant to ask her about Arcanes and why the symbols on the back side-walk made her gasp, but didn't want to upset the apple cart. Elyssa hadn't responded well to my questions about stalking Affliction Dude in the mall. I had no doubt she'd look unfavorably on questions about mysterious patterns, pedophiles in cowboy hats, and whatever she meant by Arcanes.

Arcane hardly made sense in the context she'd used it. It literally meant "obscure or mysterious", but she'd used it like a plural noun. Maybe I hadn't heard her right. Maybe she'd said *markings* or something that sounded similar. It was just one more question I had about this strange girl.

ELYSSA SURPRISED me by wearing normal clothes to school the next day. Dark jeans, a pink T-shirt, and leather boots. Silky black hair framed fair skin unblemished by foreign metal.

Damn she's gorgeous!

She smirked at my confusion when she walked up the gym bleachers toward me. "Commandant Foreman demanded I not wear my devil makeup until after our tour of detention is finished." She clicked her heels and saluted for added effect.

I snorted. "No offense, but I like normal, non-goth Elyssa better."

She punched me in the shoulder. "There's nothing normal about me."

I saw the fierceness flash behind those lovely violet eyes and nodded. "I know, Elyssa. I know."

Elyssa blinked, caught off guard and backed up a step. She looked like a kid caught with her hand in the cookie jar. "Hey, I've—um—I gotta get to class."

"But the bell hasn't even rung for homeroom yet."

Before I could stop her, she spun and hurried out of the gym. I hesitated a moment, then got up and went after her. I walked around the empty halls, but she was nowhere to be found. The hairs on the back of my neck prickled. I spun and intercepted the hand reaching for my arm.

Randy's eyes flashed with surprise but he recovered with inhuman speed, jerking his arm free and slamming me against the wall. "You've ripened." He flashed red-stained fangs. "I'm ready for a taste."

It felt like my first encounter with him all over again, fear spreading like poison in my veins. *You've got super powers now, idiot! Use them!* I kneed him in the groin. He twisted to the side, but I was still fast enough to nick him. With a roar, I jerked my arms free. Randy blurred left. A hammer blow caught me in the jaw.

I spun. The world wobbled. Another blow caught me in the shoulder blades. My face met the floor. Weight dropped onto my back. Randy grabbed my hair and jerked up my head, baring my throat. "Damn, Justin, you're a lot stronger, aren't you?" He chuckled. "New haircut, some fancy jeans." He pulled my arm behind my back and put pressure on it until it felt like the arm might pop out of the socket.

"Ahh," I groaned, unable to move or resist. "Go to hell, Randy."

"Hey, you even have a cute girl now." Randy sighed. "Too bad your blood is a hot commodity in my circles."

"Vampire circles, you mean?" My voice rasped through a tight throat.

"Don't struggle or this will get very messy." A pinprick jabbed my neck. I gasped, wondering if this was what a vampire bite felt like. Seconds passed like an eternity. "All done," Randy said. "Well, except for my taste."

I felt his hot breath on my neck. "What did you do to me?"

"Just took some blood." Randy growled. "I'm not gay, Justin, so don't take this the wrong way."

I felt his breath quicken on my neck. Sensed his growing excitement. The bell rang and Randy jerked away. I put everything I had into my free arm and pushed up off the ground as hard as I could. We flew up five feet. I heard a sickening *pop*. Agonizing pain shot through my shoulder.

Randy fell off and landed on all fours, fangs glistening, an animalistic snarl on his face. "You little shit!"

I saw a plastic syringe of my blood rolling across the floor. I reached for it, but agony exploded in my dislocated shoulder. I must have blacked out for an instant, because when I came to, Randy was gone. A stampede of feet thundered through the hallways. I didn't want anyone to find me like this so I struggled to my feet, arm hanging uselessly at my side, and staggered to the nearest bathroom.

It just happened to be the boys' room where I'd first encountered Randy and Brad days ago. My complexion had a greenish cast to it. A red bump formed on my temple, and a thin trickle of blood dried on the side of my neck where Randy had jabbed me with the syringe. A rush of endorphins rescued me from the throbbing pain in my arm. I'd never had a dislocated shoulder and had no idea what to do about it.

It was all I could do not to fall to my knees and barf.

In the movies, the tough guys rammed themselves against a wall, or just grabbed the affected arm and shoved it into place. In theory, it seemed either might work, or it might just cause me to scream, puke, and pass out. I didn't want to end up unconscious on the bathroom floor. The other kids already talked badly enough about me. Finding me in that condition would only add fuel to the fire.

I heard people coming toward the bathroom so I hid in a stall and waited. A group of boys came in arguing about who would win a fight between Thor and Hulk. When they left, another pair of voices echoed against the tiles.

"Where's Randy? Man, if those steroids he's selling are half as good as he claims, we can finally get on the football team."

"Then chicks galore, dude."

"He said something about a new and improved version coming real soon." Dry hands rasped together eagerly. "This shit is gonna be the bomb!"

"Totally dope!"

"Off the chain!"

A pair of hands high-fived. They continued talking about future conquests with Randy's super drug, overly optimistic about who they'd bang. Their happy bragging turned to cursing when the final homeroom bell rang and Randy still hadn't shown.

What in the hell is this drug? It didn't take a genius to connect the dots between my blood and this steroid. Randy could've taken his "taste" as he put it, but he'd opted to fill a syringe first. If he planned to unleash a supernaturally enhanced drug to the high school populace, that could wreak havoc. I had to find out more, preferably with my arm back in the damned socket.

After the disappointed boys shuffled out, I emerged from the stall, debating how to get my arm back in place. *Should I see the nurse?* It seemed like the only sane option. Oddly enough, the red swelling on my temple had already visibly receded, and though my arm hung loose, my shoulder wasn't killing me.

Do I have super healing too? I stared at the lump on my temple, but didn't see it changing right before my eyes.

"Justin?"

I sucked in a breath and turned toward the door. Elyssa frowned back at me like a parent who'd just caught their kid misbehaving.

"What are you doing in the boy's bathroom?" I felt more vulnerable, as if her being in here was like seeing me take a dump.

"Your arm!" Elyssa's gaze flicked between the lump on my temple and my arm. "What happened to you?"

I grasped for a reasonable excuse that didn't involve vampires. "Nathan," I said lamely. "I don't know how to get it back in the socket."

Elyssa bared her teeth. "That animal. Why didn't you go to the nurse?"

"I hate this school and almost everyone in it. I don't want anyone knowing about this."

She pursed her lips, nodded. "I don't know how you aren't moaning in pain right now. You must be tougher than I thought."

"Endorphins," I explained. "Believe me, I passed out at first."

Elyssa touched my shoulder just outside the gap between the arm bone and the socket. "Lean against the wall."

"Whoa, hang on." I backed away, wincing as my arm swayed. "Since when can you reset dislocated arms?"

"Since I did it for my brothers all the time growing up." A wan smile tweaked the corners of her mouth. "They play rough."

"You have brothers?" I felt intrigued by this rare insight into her family. "Any sisters?"

"Shut up, and brace yourself against the wall."

I did as she ordered. "You don't like when I ask questions, do you?"

As if in answer, she gripped my arm and popped it into the socket. Pain blinded me. My eyelids fluttered open. Elyssa's beautiful but concerned face filled my view. I moaned in pleasure. "I heart you, Elyssa."

Her fair cheeks flushed. "Talking in emojis now, Justin?" Elyssa sighed. "You need to get your ass off the bathroom floor and take it easy."

I felt drunk on endorphins. "Winkey face, devil face, heart."

Elyssa giggled. "What is wrong with you?" Her gaze softened and she pressed a hand to my cheek. "Dammit, Justin, stop. Please." She tugged me to me feet with surprising ease. "You've really shed some weight, haven't you?"

My senses returned and with them, a heatwave of embarrassment. I looked at her and lost myself in those violet sparklers of hers. *Holy shit.* Whatever I'd felt for Katie seemed like an elementary school crush compared to the emotions swelling my chest right now. Elyssa was smart, and strong. She made me laugh and helped me look at life in a completely different way. She'd been there for me when no one else was. My god, she'd just reset my dislocated arm!

Is this true love? Is this girl my one and only, or are the hormones doing all the talking again? I tried to speak, but my heart was so full right then, I couldn't think of what to say. I just wanted to feel Elyssa's lips on mine and wrap my arms around her.

"You're not on drugs are you?" Elyssa asked. "You look dazed."

"Drugs, yeah." She was my new drug. "Will you go with me, yes or no?"

Her dark lashes fluttered. My super ears heard her heart beat a little harder and faster. Just as suddenly, her face tightened and her pulse slowed back to normal. "Justin, get to class. I'll see you later."

She turned me in the direction of homeroom and gave me a light push to send me on my way. I blinked out of my stupor. "Why were you in the boy's bathroom—" I broke off my question by the time I turned to face her because she was gone.

Elyssa wasn't at lunch that day. Harvey and Phuc—Nyte's and Ash's real names—hadn't heard from her either.

"She's real private," Ash said. "I gave up asking where she disappears to all the time."

"Disappears?" I said. "Like Clark Kent does to Lois Lane?"

He nodded. "Maybe not quite like that, but she'll get real serious all of a sudden and just walk away without a word. This one time, she didn't come back to school all day."

"Do you see her after school much?" I asked.

Nyte nodded. "Yeah, we go to some Goth clubs. We know a lot of people on the scene."

"How did you guys meet?" I asked.

"Here at school." Ash shrugged. "It was like one day she showed up, and the next thing I knew she was in the gang."

"Our tiny gang," Nyte added. "I literally have no idea why someone as smart and hot as Elyssa would want to be our friend."

Ash nodded in agreement. "It's like she wears the makeup to hide how pretty she is."

I couldn't disagree with them.

"All the guys stare at her without her makeup, but since she hangs out with us unpopular rejects, nobody wants to risk their rep by asking her out." Nyte smirked. "Besides, she's only got eyes for one guy in this school."

My heart sank. *No wonder she was so stand-offish.* I closed my eyes in silent prayer. *If it's Brad Nichols, I will murder him.* "Shit. Who?"

Ash and Nyte exchanged amused looks.

"What's wrong?" Ash asked.

I waved away the question. "Nothing, I just—" I bit back a sob and looked miserably at the two of them.

"Dude, are you in love with Elyssa?" Ash made a strangled noise as if trying to hold in laughter.

Nyte looked concerned. "Justin, don't cry, man."

"Yes, dammit. I didn't even realize it, but—" I was too sad to finish my thoughts. "Who's the lucky douchebag she likes?"

Ash burst into laughter. "Man, you're a whiz at calculus, but dumb as a brick when it comes to women."

Nyte chuckled. "That describes us perfectly too, you idiot."

"Okay, yeah, we're dumb too." Ash waved it off. "Anyway—"

"Elyssa totally digs you, man!" Nyte slapped me on my sore shoulder.

I gasped in pain and hissed a breath through my teeth.

"Wow, thought you'd look happier than that," Ash said.

Tears burned my eyes. I wasn't crying because of pain, but joy. *Elyssa digs me?* "But she doesn't act like she likes me."

"From what I gather she has a super-strict family." Nyte grimaced. "Not to mention two older brothers who'd probably kick your ass."

"I met her mother." I shrugged and winced. "She seemed nice enough."

"They're always nice until you date their daughter." Ash offered a sympathetic smile.

"I'd get my ass kicked for her," I said. *Or would I?* After all, I had super powers now. Her brothers would be in for a big surprise if they tried anything.

"WHERE WERE YOU AT LUNCH TODAY?" I asked Elyssa at after-school detention.

She picked up a bucket and a scraper since our next task was to dislodge the gum from classroom desks. "Girl stuff."

"Like, um, bleeding?"

Elyssa gave me a withering look and shoved the bucket into my arms. "Get started in here. I'll start down the hall."

"But, but, I thought we could scrape gum together."

She shook her head. "You ask too many questions, Justin."

Before I could object, she left. I went after her, but Ms. Foreman stepped into the hallway, hands on hips. I spun around and went back into her classroom to get started. Unsurprisingly, the desks in her room were pretty clean. I imagined she'd benefitted from more child labor than a Chinese shoe factory in this state-funded gulag of lower education.

Elyssa vanished before I could talk to her after detention ended. Ms. Foreman was impressed with the amount of gum I'd collected. Using my

137

super strength, I'd simply picked up and flipped over each desk with one hand, then scraped the underside with the other, raising my efficiency by over a hundred percent. Yes, I'd actually calculated it.

I dumped the bucket into the garbage, put it up, and raced into the parking lot. Elyssa was nowhere to be found. A hot spike of strangeness triggered my danger reflexes. Stacey sauntered from behind a school bus, clapping her hands in a slow rhythm.

"Why are you giving me the slow clap?" I asked. "And why are you being such a creepy stalker?"

She tsked. "Not nice, my little morsel. Not nice at all." She brushed her hand across my cheek.

I sighed and rolled my eyes. "What's not nice is sneaking up on me, not to mention trying to suck out my soul."

"I feed on fear, not souls."

"No means no, Stacey."

She smirked. "You are entering decidedly dangerous territory, my dear toy. Have you thought further about the deal I offered you?"

"Becoming your sex slave? I don't think so."

She walked behind me. Much as I didn't like the thought of a very strong, not to mention fanged, woman standing at my back, I stood my ground. She wrapped her arms around my chest and nipped my ear. Then, of course, she licked me.

I spun and pushed her away. "Will you stop licking me? Your tongue feels like fine-grit sandpaper and it's gonna give me a rash."

"But I like you," she said. "Can you not see that?"

"What, with all your posturing and calling me 'morsel' and 'toy', blah, blah, blah? And you talk like a pretentious idiot. Maybe you've been around a while, but you should probably use the lingo we use in this century, not two centuries ago."

Her eyes glistened, large amber pools. Tears welled precipitously before spilling down her cheeks and over trembling lips.

"Look, I'm sorry. I didn't mean to hurt your feelings."

"Why do you not like me?" she asked plaintively.

Freaking women and their abilities to turn the tables on you. Not two minutes ago she acted super-cool and condescending, and now she sounded like the only girl I ever broke up with back in fifth grade. I put a hand on her shoulder. "Look, I'm sure you're not all bad, but you have to admit, it's not polite to suck people's fear out of their eyeballs."

"But it is my nature."

"Just like the scorpion and the frog? That's a cop-out."

"It is not a cop-out." She reverted back to her haughtier tone, wiping away the moisture on her cheeks. "Think about my proposal, Justin. You are in grave danger. I can protect you from those who would do terrible things to you, and I would teach you to protect yourself." She ran her hands slowly down her curvaceous hips and smiled. "In return, you may enjoy all I have to offer. I will show you just how inventive we older women can be in bed." She ran her fingernails up my jeans-clad leg and squeezed my ass.

I leapt away with a yelp. "Will you cut that out? What kind of danger am I in?" *Besides Randy the vampire and becoming your sex slave?*

She smiled and shook her head. "I will only tell you that it is right before your eyes. You have no idea who or what you even are."

"Yeah, well Google hasn't helped me a bit." I sighed. "Look, I have deep personal beliefs that prevent me from having sex with you. Maybe we could just mess around a little?" The thought of selling my body to her appealed in an egotistical sense, but little else. If her tongue felt like sandpaper, what would her private parts be like? The thought of that was enough to banish my stiffness issue on demand. I tucked that unpleasant thought away for future use.

She wrinkled her nose. "Mess around? What rubbish is this? I want someone to be with me, not a one-night stand."

"You want to go steady?" I was utterly perplexed.

"I want a committed relationship. What is wrong with that?"

I laughed at the innocent blink of her big round eyes. "Are you an old-fashioned vampire?" *Do vampires suck fear out of eyeballs?* I knew all about vampires from reading books and watching movies, but there was so much variation on the theme, maybe real vampires did more than just drink blood. I tried to ask the question, but Stacey continued with the conversation at hand.

"Are not intimate relations a great deal more enjoyable with someone you like? Especially when you can practice frequently and learn new things?"

"But we hardly know each other." I paused. "Wait, we are talking about sex, right? Not blood sucking, because I don't want to be anybody's snack pack."

She broke into a deep-throated laugh. "I speak of normal but fantastic sex, you adorable little man. Blood sucking is not a requirement." She giggled. "I will give you more pleasure than you can imagine."

"I'm a teenage guy, so I can imagine quite a lot."

"Give it your full consideration. I fear if you take too long, it will be too late for me to protect you." She paused and pursed her lips. "And, Justin, I am not a vampire."

"Then what are you?" I felt some relief at this revelation, though that didn't mean she wasn't something worse.

She traced her fingernails through my hair and gave a wicked grin as I shivered. "Perhaps you will figure that out with your clever little mind. Eventually."

"Are you the reason I changed into whatever I am?"

One corner of her mouth rose in a lopsided grin. "I'm afraid that, my dear, is all you."

With that, she sped across the parking lot, her body a blur, jumped halfway up the three-story school, and then cleared the remaining half by vaulting to the roof from a window ledge. The darkness swallowed her.

"Badass!" I ran as fast as I could toward the school. My legs moved faster than I'd ever thought possible. The ground blurred. Wind whipped against my face. *What a rush!*

I tripped on the curb. Smacked into the side of the building. Rebounded, and skidded backwards on my ass. I rolled around on the ground holding my shin, sucking in my breath.

"Oh, god that hurt." I picked myself up. The blood on my scraped hand clotted within seconds and the injury faded to almost nothing as I watched, spellbound over the next few minutes.

I waited for the pain to recede, then jogged back and forth in the parking lot to get the feel of my faster legs. Whenever I tried to go too fast, my reflexes couldn't keep up with the rest of my body and I ended up tumbling to the ground or colliding with one of the tall lamps in the parking lot.

It seemed that my new abilities didn't come with a set of instructions. I would have to practice my hyper-speed running, while learning to dodge, jump, and avoid obstacles. My new quick healing could patch me up fast, but falling down at super speed still hurt like a bitch. "It might help if you practiced in grass instead of asphalt, you idiot."

A more disturbing thought occurred to me. Even with my newfound strength, Randy had still kicked my ass today. Until I learned how to protect myself from his ilk, my super powers meant nothing.

CHAPTER 14

My muscles felt as though they'd been through a grinder when I woke up the next morning. Apparently, running at super speed was just like regular exercise to my enhanced musculature.

I stripped and went into the bathroom for a shower. As I passed the mirror, I noticed something odd about my chest. No, I hadn't grown more than the few wisps of hair that sprouted from my left nipple a couple of years back, but my man boobs appeared noticeably smaller. I touched my left pectoral. My finger met a layer of hard muscle hiding under the flab. My stomach also looked slightly less paunchy and doughy than before. I flexed my biceps. Meh, they still looked pathetic, but at least they weren't sagging.

This revelation made my morning a bit brighter despite the lack of sleep. I thought about suspension with Ms. Foreman. I thought about Elyssa. I was actually looking forward to staying after school. I couldn't wait to see Elyssa in the gym. My brain, the spoil-sport it was, decided to play back a few choice samples of my disastrous experiences with humans of the female variety. Dark clouds blocked the rays of feel-good sunshine, squashing all my warm fuzzies of the morning. My track record with girls resembled a zombie apocalypse.

Maybe Ash was right—maybe Elyssa really did like me, but she wasn't making this easy at all. I just hoped her parents weren't crazy religious nuts who wouldn't let her date. I could suffer through an ass-kicking, but going to church was another level of hell.

Just take it slow. Really slow. I wondered if I should take it anywhere at all. So far I hadn't discovered what I'd become. If I started anything with Elyssa, people like Randy might use her against me. But the only way to navigate this new world was by entering a serious relationship with Stacey, the British supernatural chick.

While she might help me defeat Randy, that would kill my chances with Elyssa. I mulled over the frustrating situation all morning as I prepared for school. I'd hoped for a light bulb moment, but ended up with a cranial power outage.

I couldn't just let Randy continue to bully me. He'd stolen my blood and probably had a new and improved batch of his super steroid drug brewing right this very moment. Somehow I had to stop him.

I need someone to train me. Someone who didn't demand sex, blood, or soul-sucking as payment. My parents were still AWOL. Even if they were here, I wondered if confiding in them was wise. Most supernatural abilities weren't inherited from parents, but derived from the bite of a werewolf, the sting of a vampire fang, or radioactive spiders.

"Did anyone bite me in the past couple of weeks?" I asked myself. Since my migraines and the odd surges of strength happened even before I'd met Stacey, it meant my turning point occurred somewhere around the time I'd first encountered Randy.

That steroid drug! I imagined the red liquid splashing on the floor just a few feet away from me. Had I somehow inhaled the fumes? I snapped my fingers. "That has to be it because I started seeing things right after that."

It seemed the mystery was solved, but what did that make me? Maybe Stacey didn't know about the steroid drugs Randy sold and mistook me for something else. I had just bitten off a lot of food for thought, so I started a flow chart in my notebook as a thinking aid.

Justin inhales super steroid > Randy sniffs Justin > Randy thinks Justin's blood can improve steroid.

I stopped right there. Randy said I smelled sweet. I needed to ripen so he could harvest me. If his steroid drug created me, had it caused a mutation in my blood? The would explain his desire to fill a syringe with the red stuff so he could recombine the mutations with his steroid.

The mere thought of what he might do to the school populace with that steroid scared me. What if Nathan Spelman and his kind got a hold of the drug? Not a nerd in that school would escape without a wedgie or worse.

When I got out of my car in the school parking lot, I nearly collided with Katie. I jumped away from her. God only knew what would happen if someone saw me near her. Principal Perkins—or Jerkins as Elyssa called him—might sentence me to the electric chair.

Katie smiled. It wasn't a warm smile, exactly. More of an *I-have-your-balls-in-a-vice* smile. "Hello, Justin," she said in a tone that could freeze sunshine.

"Hi." I turned to leave.

"I can't believe I wanted to be friends with you. It makes me feel gross to even think about it."

"Cool story, bro." I was amazed how little her cruel remark fazed me. The part of me that wanted to ravish females detected something off about her emotional state. If I had to guess, I would say she might be lying. It wasn't like I could read her mind, but I could sense insincerity rolling off her, buried in waves of anger. Loitering beneath it all throbbed a white-hot pulsar of sexual energy. I had to think about

Stacey and her possibly sandpaper-lined unmentionables to keep Justin Jr. from getting too riled up.

She glared at me. Everyone seemed to glare at me nowadays. "You should watch your back. I know a lot of football players who'd love to teach you a lesson."

"Are you doing the deed with them too?"

She slapped me. It stung like crazy but I smiled through the pain.

"Were you always just a fake friend to me, Katie? I understand being pissed about me kicking your boyfriend's ass, but this is ridiculous."

"No. I used to genuinely care for you, Justin. Then you got creepy. You made me kiss you and got in a fight with Brad. Then that video went viral. My parents saw it, Justin. Do you know how mortified I was?"

"Look, I wasn't trying to be a creep, okay? I'm a friggin nerd with little to no experience with girls, and I thought you liked me. I'm sorry I kissed you, and I'm sorry I fought Brad, but he really didn't give me a choice." I threw up my hands. "I've had enough high school drama for a lifetime, so if you really want more, maybe you should go binge on One Tree Hill on Netflix."

"I don't like drama either, Justin!"

I was beginning to figure out that people who claimed to hate drama were the most dramatic people of all. "Can't we just call off this little war and be civilized again?" I wasn't sure I wanted to be friends with her, but getting everyone else off my back would be just peachy.

Her bottom lip trembled. "I don't think I can, Justin." A tear trickled down her cheek. "How would it look if I forgave you after all the pain you've put me through?"

Oh my effing god! I had to bite my tongue. Otherwise I would have explained in no uncertain terms how Team Katie had started all this. Instead, and with great pain, I took the high road. "You'd look pretty good, actually. Magnanimous, even." I hated myself for not calling her out on her bullshit, but was willing to do whatever it took to make my life a little better so I could peace-out of high school and survive the journey to the real world.

Katie shook her head and reached a hand out to touch mine. She jerked it back like it had touched a hot stove. "Things have gone too far. It's too late for us to ever be friends again."

Well, I tried. "I'm sorry to hear that."

She sighed. "I don't really regret being friends with you." Her face flushed and she looked away. "I treasured our friendship, Justin. I know you think I'm a horrible person for putting Brad over you, but just because I didn't want to date you didn't mean I valued you any less."

"Hey, I get it. I mean who would want to date a chubby loser anyway?"

"Please don't say that. You're not a loser."

I thought of Elyssa, my newest crush and how she didn't want to get involved with me. *Maybe I am a creeper. Maybe Ash was wrong about her liking me and that's why she's avoiding me.* The self-inflection stung because it felt right. I'd been in Katie's friend zone and hopped right into Elyssa's without missing a beat.

My optimism faded and it was all I could do not to laugh and cry hysterically at Katie's comment. "You're wrong. I'm social poison to anyone who gets near me now. Besides, I kind of understand things a little better than I did then." I reached a hand toward her, thought better of it, and lowered it. "Can you call off the dogs? Please?"

"I can't. I don't control them." She wiped away tears. Her gaze settled on something behind me and widened slightly. "Be careful, Justin." She hurried away.

Before I could turn around, the sound of a fist hitting an open palm alerted me to yet another confrontation. I turned to see Nathan and three of his biggest buddies baring their teeth and trying to look menacing. Instead, it appeared as if they strained to drop a deuce in the parking lot.

With great effort, I kept my silence. What else could I do? If I fought them, I'd lose politically. If I did nothing, they still won.

"What did I say about harassing Katie, you little stalker?" Nathan sneered. "Looks like we're gonna have to teach you a lesson real soon. You won't know when or where, but it could come at any second."

"I'll bet your parents are so proud." I turned and walked into the building. The morning was starting off so well I could hardly wait to see what came next. The bell rang for homeroom and I groaned. It was too late to get to the gymnasium to see Elyssa. "Damn," I muttered. My heart sank. I missed her already. Then again, maybe she needed space.

I wanted so badly to believe Ash and Nyte. The moment I revealed I had a crush on her, Elyssa's signals hadn't been mixed—they'd been outright clear that she didn't want more than friendship with me.

I've got to cool it. I'm not worthy of her.

A part of me wanted to impress Elyssa. I could bend steel bars. I could outrun any non-vampire in the school. I could cut myself and heal within a day or less. I could also seduce any woman I wanted.

A shudder ran through me. *No!* What use was that power when all I wanted was true love? Maybe it was just teen hormones making me silly for Elyssa. Maybe it would pass just like my feelings for Katie had. It didn't matter. I wouldn't abuse my powers like that. I'd been bullied nearly every year since fourth grade. I'd been forced to eat mud, had shit thrown at me, and endured the threats of bigger and stronger kids.

I wouldn't stand for it anymore and I sure as hell wouldn't perpetrate it on anyone weaker than me. Either Elyssa liked me or she didn't. What-ever happened, no matter how it broke my heart, I would move forward. My life's journey had hardly started and it was too soon to give up now.

147

Lunch rolled around. I noticed immediately something vastly different at the Goth table. In the place of pale-faced mascara-slathered individuals with nauseating amounts of piercings, sat two dejected guys. Ash was unsurprisingly Asian under all the makeup he usually wore. The name Phuc kind of gave it away. Next to him sat a pale kid with a ginger complexion. If not for the dyed floppy Mohawk, I wouldn't have known it was Nyte.

Ash sported a dark bruise under one eye. A fresh scab stood out on Nyte's swollen bottom lip.

I slid into my seat. "What happened?"

Ash's forehead pinched. "The principal informed us we were no longer allowed to wear our devil-worshipping costumes."

"And he hit you?"

He shook his head. "No, that happened when Nyte and I left the mall last night. Three big guys in ski masks did this." He pointed at his eye.

"And one of them jerked out my lip ring." Nyte's face flushed scarlet.

I winced. "Jesus, man. Are you okay?"

He touched his swollen lip. "I'm better today. Yesterday, not so much."

"I don't get how the principal can control wearing makeup. It's against freedom of speech." I nodded toward Lisa Gibbs. She slathered on so much foundation her faced looked like a field of dried mud. "How come she can coat her face with makeup but you can't?" I turned toward Nathan and the jocks. "How about those letter jackets? If they can wear those, you should be allowed to wear your Goth gear."

Ash gave me a *What can you do?* shrug. "Yeah, I mean we could fight this in court." He looked at Nathan. "But if we do, I have a feeling those guys will put on their ski masks and come after us again."

I caught a smirk from Nathan and the world flashed red. This couldn't continue, but what could I do about it? I'd already tried physical violence. That had just ticked them off more and caused them to go after my friends. I glanced back at Ash and Nyte. I hadn't known them long but it was true—they were my friends. They'd brought me in when times were tough and stood by me. Mark and Harry had revealed their true colors the moment it suited them.

None of it could be helped now. I had to figure out a better way to take Nathan and his fools on their own turf. Unfortunately, I hadn't gained super thinking powers to go with my hyper libido.

"Where is Elyssa?" I asked.

As if on cue, she entered the lunchroom on the far side. Her shoulders slumped and the dark rings under her eyes looked more pronounced than ever. Her face brightened when our gazes met, but she quickly broke eye contact. My stomach fluttered. The world seemed so much better knowing she'd be next to me in a moment, but it also seemed that much sadder with the realization I would probably never be anything more than her friend.

"You two feeling any better?" Elyssa asked Ash and Nyte when she sat down.

They nodded.

Ash's fist tightened. "I'm still furious."

Despite my new abilities, I felt powerless in the face of such bullying. "We've got to put a stop to this crap."

"How?" Ash asked, interest sparking in his eyes.

"I'll come up with something. I have to."

"I HOPE you're not getting their hopes up for nothing," Elyssa said that afternoon in detention. "I'm going to be really mad with you if you are." The violet in her eyes seemed paler and less fiery than usual. Her skin had gone from fair to pale. It gave the impression that her sleep deprivation was even worse than usual.

"Is something wrong?" I whispered, glancing back down the hall for any sign of our warden, Ms. Foreman.

She looked thoughtful for a moment before apparently reaching the conclusion she didn't want to tell me something. Oddly, I could barely detect her feelings as I did other girls, and the usual emotional runoff that accompanied most females wasn't there. It was like she guarded her feelings with the Great Wall of China. I could have dropped the leash keeping my inner beast at bay and possibly sensed more, but I didn't want to violate her. I cared too much for her to do that. Even worse, I might lose control and bad things could happen. If she was The One, I didn't want to ruin anything.

She finally answered. "I'm just tired."

We'd moved from prying gum from classroom desks to the lunchroom tables. The table Nathan and gang usually sat at had mounds of the stuff glommed underneath. I wondered if Ms. Foreman asked them to do it so her servants would have something to do. Thankfully rubber gloves protected my hands from the nasty stuff. I didn't want to touch anything that had been chewed by someone else's mouth, especially Nathan's. Elyssa didn't seem to mind.

"Doesn't this gross you out?" I asked.

She shrugged. "I've done worse."

"Your parents make you shovel horse poo or something?"

She giggled. "No." She tossed a chunk of fossilized gum at me. I flinched and swatted it out of the air.

At least she's not so distant today. I didn't know why she seemed more comfortable around me and I didn't want to ruin it by expressing my feelings.

"Ahem." Ms. Foreman stood at the door to the cafeteria, just five feet away. The piece of gum hung in her hair.

It was all I could do not to burst into hysterical laughter or scream in a fit of pure panic.

"Well, children, I can see this job is much too easy for you," she said with a mirthless giggle. "Follow me."

Dread formed a bubbling cauldron of acid in my stomach as she took us back into the kitchen and handed us rubber coveralls. They stank of rancid grease and industrial detergents.

"Put these on," she commanded.

"What are these for?" I asked.

"Now is not the time for questions, young man. Both of you. Put these on." She smiled as a torturer might smile while yanking toenails from a victim's feet.

Elyssa slipped into hers without a word. I followed suit. Heck, if a girl wasn't complaining, I guess I wouldn't either.

That didn't last long.

Five minutes later we stood before the school cafeteria grease traps. These weren't small. They were industrial-sized ones, big as kitchen sinks, and they belonged to a school cafeteria where the food already looked like garbage. The mutated organisms cooked in this kitchen probably created a serious biohazard. I couldn't believe she could make us do this. Wasn't this against child labor laws? The vacuum station which usually sucked up the grease was broken. It meant we had to scoop the gunk out by hand and dump it into thick plastic bags for disposal.

Ms. Foreman had obviously used this as punishment before. She had the janitor show us how to pop the lids off the traps while she made a quick exit.

"You kids must've really ticked her off," said the wrinkled old man with a chuckle. "I wouldn't wish this on my ex-wife."

"It can't be that bad." Elyssa held a large metal scoop and a flat-bladed scraper.

He wheezed out a laugh. "Oh it's bad. I just hope you got strong stomachs and a weak sense of smell."

I almost insta-barfed when he popped the lid off the first trap. The fumes and odor drifting from it smelled like rotting carcasses slathered in dog vomit and feces. It looked even worse, black pools of liquefied life forms with bits of corn and other random garbage floating on top. Elyssa wrinkled her nose, took a couple of deep breaths, then got on her knees and started scooping. The janitor left us, his laughter echoing down the hallway as he went.

"What in God's name do your parents make you do at home?" I asked. "How can you stand the stench?"

"Gotta learn to filter it out," she said.

"Filter it out?" I gagged. Your parents don't make you shovel horse poo. They make you shovel horse carcasses."

Ms. Foreman apparently knew about the odor and never showed her totalitarian face while we worked, sweated, and, in my case, fought an intense gag reflex. If you've heard the expression "I wouldn't touch that with a ten-foot pole" then add another thousand feet and you'd know how I felt just looking at the tub of putrescence. Somehow I managed to choke down the constant urge to vomit and started scooping. By the time we finished, it was almost eleven. Neither of us had particularly enjoyed the exercise, but I still felt closer to Elyssa, as if by sharing such a horrific task it had bonded us even tighter.

I tried to convince Elyssa to save a bit of the rancid grease so we might decorate Ms. Foreman's office with it. Elyssa gave me a look which would stop a charging bull dead in its tracks, so I took that as a "no".

Ms. Foreman smiled in a kind, yet purely evil way as we came to tell her we were done. *Doesn't she have a family to go home to? A basement of imprisoned orphans to feed scraps?* What teacher in her right mind wanted to stay at school all night?

Ms. Foreman checked her watch. "Goodness gracious, children. It certainly took you long enough." She giggled gleefully, reminding me of a wicked witch. "If the janitor gives his blessing, perhaps I can find something less demanding for you two tomorrow. You may go now."

We trudged out to the parking lot. I felt for Stacey's presence but didn't sense it. I did *not* feel comfortable knowing that creepy chick might lurk nearby.

"Well, this has been an interesting week," I said. "In a way, I'm going to kind of miss it once tomorrow is over."

Elyssa stopped and glared at me. "You're insane, aren't you?"

"Maybe a little." That brought a tiny smile to her lips. "Seriously, though. What's wrong with you today?"

"I already told you that," she said. "I didn't get enough sleep."

"Why not? Watching too much late night TV?"

"Is it really that important to you?"

"Yes, because you're important to me."

She sighed. "We're not going down this road again are we?"

"What road?"

"The one where you do stupid crap because you want to protect me or get all touchy-feely."

I tried to resist the lure of expressing my feelings for her. Clearly, she didn't want to be more than friends. But her words triggered me and I couldn't stop myself. "If caring about what happens to someone is touchy-feely, then I'm sorry. I'm not a real man. I'm just an idiot who believes in common decency."

"Save your feelings for someone who needs them, Justin. In case you hadn't noticed, I was doing quite fine until you started showing concern. Just look where that got us."

"You ungrateful—" I shut my mouth before anything really nasty slipped out.

"You want gratitude?" She belted out a scornful laugh. "So that's what this is about. You do it to feel good about yourself." She gave a knowing nod. "Why don't you find someone else who can show you the gratitude you so desire?"

I stood there, fists clenched and blood pressure rising. *Don't do it, Justin! Don't ruin this!* I walked over to her. Grabbed her around her slender waist. Pulled her to me and planted a kiss on her soft lips. She tensed. I braced for a possible knee to the groin. Instead, she melted against me and let out a soft moan.

Elyssa smelled like spring flowers, leather, and a little bit like the grease traps. It was an odd, but unexpectedly nice combination. Her body burned hot against mine. The caged animalistic part of me clawed at the flimsy barrier I'd erected to keep it at bay. I couldn't hold it off much longer. I broke off the kiss before the dark side of my lust tore down the wall. I stared into Elyssa's large tremulous eyes. Her raven locks framed the creamy fair skin of her face.

My god, she's beautiful.

I brushed a stray lock from her face and tucked it behind her ear. My heart pounded, so filled with desire and yearning, I had to take a deep breath.

She looked so vulnerable and scared that I wanted to kiss her again. But I couldn't. It was all I could do to hold back my demonic sexual urge. When "demonic" becomes a common adjective you use to describe yourself, you know you have a problem.

"Why'd you have to go and do that?" she asked softly, tracing her finger along my chest.

Pleasant chills tickled my skin beneath her touch. "Because I really like you."

"Why do you like me?"

I groped for an answer but the only thing that came to mind was, "I just do."

"You just do? Aren't you supposed to tell me how beautiful my eyes are, and how firm my ass is?"

I laughed. "Well, both are true."

"Have you been looking at my butt? How do you know it's not all saggy without my skinny jeans to hold it in place?"

"Only one way to know." I gave her a slap on the rear. "Gee, do you work out?"

She gave me a playful push and giggled in a girlish way I thought I'd never hear again.

"I—I wasn't sure you liked me, Elyssa." I swallowed the lump in my throat. "When I told you how I felt, you pulled away."

Sadness tugged the corners of her eyes. She took my hand and idly traced the palm with her fingernail. "Justin, we need to take this slow. I have an…unusual home life and I'm afraid you might not want to be with me anymore once you get to know me." A single tear glistened at the corner of one eye. "My father wouldn't want me dating. I mean, I'm not supposed to fall for anyone, especially not here! You're so normal and I'm—"

I interrupted her with a kiss. "It's okay." I took her hand and kissed the smooth skin of her wrist just beneath the palm. I put her hand to my cheek and closed my eyes. It felt good. It felt like…home. "I don't think a crazy family will drive me away, Elyssa. This feels right."

Her lips brushed mine. "I hope so."

I pulled her in for one last lingering kiss before she got in her car and drove away.

For the first time I could remember, everything felt perfect, but memories of Katie seeded my optimism with doubt. Thoughts of Randy made me realize that Elyssa might be a target once he found out I had a girlfriend.

Randy had proven he could still beat my ass. If I wanted to protect myself and Elyssa, I had to gain control over my powers. I had to stop him.

CHAPTER 15

The insistent beep of my alarm clock awoke me extra early the next morning so I could get to the school gymnasium in time. On the way out, the house phone rang. Nobody ever called that line but telemarketers and I almost ignored it until I saw the caller ID—*Private Investigations*. I snatched the handset off the cradle.

"Yes?" I tried to muster a deep voice.

"This is Willis. I couldn't get you on your cell so I called the backup number you gave me."

"Mhmm."

"I've decided not to pursue this any further. Ever since that Conroy fellow showed up at our offices and warned us off the investigation, weird shit has been going down. Thousands of rats swarmed our offices two days ago. Yesterday every car in the parking lot turned upside down —on their freaking roofs. Oh, and that's not even the best part. Today, my wife's stupid little Chihuahua came up to me at breakfast and told me—in English—I had one more day before really bad things started happening."

"He talked to you?" I gasped, trying to keep my voice disguised despite the crazy stuff this dude was telling me.

"Look, I've dealt with the Overworld plenty, but this is way out of my league."

"The Overworld?" Stacey had said that word.

He didn't seem to hear my question. "My secretary told me she was outta here if I don't do something. Frankly, I'm this close to checking out myself. I don't care if you believe me or not. I'm done. I'll refund half your fee. And by the way, I think they have someone tracking you because a bounty hunter came in here asking questions the other day. You'd better watch your back."

The line went dead. I stared at the phone for a moment. Dad had mentioned the Conroys before. Who were they? Why was he trying to find them? And how could a dog talk? Before my transformation, I'd never have believed such a crazy story. Now I wasn't so sure. Why had my father hired this guy in the first place?

I checked my text history. Mom still hadn't responded to me, and Dad still wasn't home. Things were officially way off with my home life. I called Dad and got his voicemail. I sent a text but didn't hold my breath on a response. Dad hated texting.

Despite all the questions brewing, I hurried out the door so I could get to school.

Elyssa had saved me a seat on the bleachers next to her. I pecked her on the cheek and took her hand in mine. *Carpe diem!* I thought, because I wasn't sure how to say "Seize the hand" in Latin. I was determined not to make a waste of this relationship by being timid.

Ash and Nyte showed up. Neither looked the least bit surprised at the sight of me and Elyssa getting fresh.

Ash glared up the bleachers at Nathan and his dimwitted toadies as they harassed a group of bespectacled nerds reading a Kings and Castles rule book. "I wish I was bigger and stronger. I'd punch those goons until their noses broke."

I knew the feeling. Unfortunately, raw power hadn't helped me one bit in my quest to overcome the bullies of either the normal or supernatural variety. Especially not when the bullying ran up the chain of command that was supposed to prevent it.

"Fighting isn't the answer." Elyssa's eyes darted to me. "Especially not with the football worship in this place."

"But they've stolen our dignity," Ash said. "They've taken our very identities."

Elyssa sighed. "This is high school, not real life. These morons think they're the big fish, but they're swimming in a small pond."

"More like a cesspool," I said.

She grinned. "Exactly. Anyway, once we're out of here, you'll never have to worry about them again. Nathan and his roid-ragers will get some random girls preggers and drink themselves into obesity by the time they're thirty. Those prissy cheerleaders will lose their looks after whoring around and doing drugs in college and will end up living with rednecks in trailer parks."

"Do you have a crystal ball?" I asked. "This is amazing. She can predict the future and it's beautiful."

"You think I'm joking." Elyssa raised an eyebrow in disdain. "I know what I'm talking about. The circle of life you've heard about just keeps on repeating itself in high school after high school across the nation. God knows it feels like I've been to all of them."

"What you're forgetting is we'll have a whole new set of douchebags to deal with in corporate America," Ash said.

Nyte shook his head fiercely. "I will *never* work for the man."

"Are you gonna be a rapper?" Elyssa asked. "'Cause they're the only ones allowed to use that term."

I chuckled. "I've never seen a ginger rapper, but maybe that's the fresh new twist everyone craves."

"I'll be Carrot Ice." Nyte flashed a gang sign and pretended to nibble on his finger like a rabbit with a carrot.

We groaned.

"Nom," I said.

Elyssa stiffened. "How do you know that word?"

"He's nomming on his finger." I raised an eyebrow. "You know, the Cookie Monster goes nom, nom, nom when he's gorging on cookies."

Elyssa's expression relaxed. "Oh, yeah."

Ash's forehead pinched into a V. "What does nom mean to you?"

"Nothing. I just didn't hear what he said the first time." Elyssa looked down at her hands. Her fingernails were cropped short—no nail polish on those digits. I'd never noticed that before. For someone who kept her hair Pantene perfect, it seemed odd she'd skip out on the manicures.

The bell rang, so we stood to leave. Ash scooted first into the stream of students walking down the bleacher steps since he was closest to the end. Nathan barreled down the steps behind him and plowed into his back. Ash jerked like a car had struck him and plummeted down the three remaining stairs while his books and papers scattered onto the basketball court.

"Watch that last step," Nathan said. "It's a doozy." The two thugs, who I'd learned were named Adam and Steve, guffawed like it was the funniest thing in the world and kicked the books further onto the hardwood court as they walked past him.

Elyssa clenched my arm so tight it hurt. I winced, but she didn't notice, instead focusing a glare of pure hatred on Nathan. I touched her hand. "Loosen up a little?" I gasped.

She blinked as if coming from a trance and stared at the hand cutting off my circulation. "I'm sorry."

We hurried down to help Ash gather his books. Some other students stopped to help as well. I recognized some of the nerdy types that had supported me in my war against bullying among the helpers. At least not all of humanity was doomed.

"Are you okay?" I asked Ash.

His head drooped. "My dignity has dropped to an all-new low."

I saw Nyte, his neck glowing red, hurrying away. "I'll see you later," I said to Elyssa and kissed her on the cheek, then rushed to catch up with Nyte before he did something stupid. He entered the boys' room. I hoped he wasn't following Nathan in there. The results would not be pretty.

Nyte stood alone at the back of the bathroom, banging his fist against the cinder blocks with all his might and sobbing. I didn't know what to do. I wasn't sure I'd want anyone bothering me in the middle of a melt-down. I opened my mouth to speak, then thought better of it and snuck back out. I stood in the hallway trying to decide what to do when he burst out of the bathroom, face composed, eyes red.

"You okay?" I asked.

"No. Not even a little bit. I have never wanted to physically harm anyone in my life. But I want to kill Nathan. I want to stab him with a sword."

"I can't let you do that, but I can show you how to stab people with fake swords."

He cocked an eyebrow. "How?"

"Maybe you guys would like to join me for Kings and Castles this weekend. I don't have a squad anymore, but I'm still team leader. I'll register you guys and we can build some weapons and kick some butt."

"I've heard of that tournament. Maybe it would be fun to pretend-murder someone." He shrugged. "I'll probably suck."

"We all suck at something. The important thing is to have fun." Those words sounded strange coming out of my mouth. Winning K&C used to be the only important thing in my life. Elyssa had changed my outlook on everything that had once been such a vital part of my existence. K&C hardly seemed important anymore. Since ending my friendship with Harry and Mark, I hadn't devoted another minute to building fake weapons or prepping for another tournament.

Still, it could be fun having the gang join me in a tournament.

Lunchtime arrived and I told Ash and Elyssa about K&C. "The tournament is tomorrow morning. I figure we could whip up some foam weapons tonight if you guys want to come over after school." That, of course, depended on whether or not Ms. Foreman let Elyssa and I go at a decent hour. Maybe she'd have mercy since it was Friday.

"Kings and Castles?" Elyssa asked.

I wasn't surprised she'd never heard of it. "Yeah, like Dungeons and Dragons played out in real life with fake weapons."

Her eyes flashed. "Oh my God, you are such a nerd."

"So are you."

She pecked a kiss on my cheek. "Yep. Sign me up."

I looked at her and thought back to the strange path we'd taken to meeting each other, namely the day Randy first threatened me and then again when I'd saved Ash from being smeared with dog poop. "Why'd you tell me to never give up when I saved Ash from dog poop that day?"

She shrugged. "I don't know. It looked like maybe you could use some encouragement."

"You felt sorry for me?"

Her face flushed. "Don't let this inflate your ego, but I guess I kind of admired you for what you did. You protected someone you didn't even know from a bully."

"You admired me?" I was a bit shocked at her admission. I had done something to impress the tough girl.

She sighed. "Oh, I just knew this would make you feel too big for your britches. It was only a little bit of admiration anyway."

I gave her a hurt look. "Only an itsy-bitsy teeny bit?" I held my thumb and forefinger in measurement.

She laughed. "Maybe even a little less than that."

Seeing her smile filled me with desire. I wanted to kiss her. I didn't even care if the entire lunch room saw it. I would stand on the table and declare my undying devotion to her. But the bell rang and the moment passed.

That afternoon, Elyssa and I kept our mouths shut and worked hard. Ms. Foreman let us go at five. She probably wanted to spend a nice relaxing Friday evening at home, torturing the kidnapped children in her basement.

I ordered pizza on the way home. Ash and Nyte were already at the house when I arrived, and the pizza showed up a few minutes later.

Amazingly, Dad was home. He sat in Mom's office working on her computer when I walked inside. I had so many questions for him, my head nearly burst. Since I didn't want to ask them in front of my friends, I clammed up and bided my time.

Dad ruffled my hair and grimaced. "Ah, damn. I shouldn't do that in front of your friends."

Ash grinned. "I think it's cool."

"We're the product of terrible home lives," Nyte said. "Tortured souls and all that."

Dad chuckled. "The more angst and pain, the better. I really need to devote more time to making Justin miserable."

I didn't want to say it, but his and Mom's activities lately already caused me some serious doubts and confusion. Before I let him leave this house again, we were going to have a pow-wow.

The doorbell rang. I answered it and Elyssa stepped inside.

Dad's eyes flared with surprise. "Holy smokes, son. How'd an ugly punk like you get her to hang out?"

Elyssa giggled. "Thankfully, I can look past Justin's ugly outside. I mean, he's kind of terrible on the inside too, but I like that."

Dad belted out a laugh. "Well, looks like you all have things well in-hand. I'm gonna run down to Melton's and grab a burger."

I gripped his wrist. "Dad, I need to talk to you about some really important things later, okay?"

His gaze sobered at my tone. "Yeah, I think we do need to talk. Can it wait until the morning, though?"

"Just as soon as I get back from Kings and Castles, tomorrow afternoon, okay?"

He nodded. "You got it, kiddo."

After Dad left, I grabbed weapon-making supplies and we sat around eating pizza and making swords. It was the most fun I'd had in ages.

Ash held up a sword he'd made. It flopped like a wet noodle.

Elyssa laughed. "That thing needs Viagra."

I disassembled his weapon and showed him how to use PVC pipe to stiffen it. Elyssa built two small swords, one for each hand. She twirled them around like she knew what she was doing while we watched in amazement.

"I wanted to be a majorette," she told us with an embarrassed shrug.

Ash and Nyte made standard medium-sized broadswords—at least I think that's what they were going for. They were so lumpy and covered in duct tape that a kindergartener might have made them.

"This is going to be a blast," Nyte said, his eyes alight. "I've never done this before."

"Well, let me give you guys some quick pointers before tossing you into the thick of things," I said.

I took them outside and gave them the skinny on how squad logistics worked, and how to keep an eye on each other's backs. Then I showed them the basics of swordplay. While I was no expert on swordplay, I was still much better than most of the people in K&C thanks to the fencing lessons I'd taken a couple of years back. Not that it really translated all that well to foam swords.

After Ash and Nyte said their goodbyes, I leaned against Elyssa's car and pulled her in for a kiss.

"You're not a bad leader," she said with a hint of admiration in her voice.

"Holy crap. Did I just hear another compliment escape those lovely lips of yours?"

She gave me a passionate kiss that left me panting. Nodded. "You're a different person than the one I met. You've grown more confident." She chuckled wryly. "Maybe too confident at times."

"True," I said with a grimace. "Now, can I have another one of those magnificent kisses?"

I pulled her lips back to mine. Her scent intoxicated me. The touch of her body against mine was like being kissed by the sun. I ran a hand up her neck, clenched her hair at the nape, and gave it a gentle tug. She moaned. I groaned. Her teeth nipped my neck and I shuddered with pleasure. Fire rushed from my stomach and flooded my veins. My dark side slammed against its cage like a wild beast. Control faltered.

I jerked away and took a few steps back. It took everything I had to keep myself contained. Thinking of baseball just didn't help.

"What's wrong?" she asked.

"I don't want to take things too fast," I said. "I'm just so attracted to you that I'm afraid I'll do something I might regret."

"You're a romantic, aren't you?" She tsked. "Silly boy."

"Actually, yeah, I am. I want my first time to be special." I braced for her response, scared that she might laugh.

She nuzzled my cheek with her nose. "I'm okay with that."

I felt relief, but then another scary thought entered my mind. Before I could resist the urge, I blurted out the question. "Are you a virgin?"

She laughed. "One-hundred percent grade-A certified virgin." She flashed a smile and took a bow.

I almost leapt with joy. My heart lightened until I thought I might float away. *This girl must be The One.* "Do you want your first time to be special?"

She pressed herself against me and gave me a kiss that left me breathless. "How special do you want it to be, my knight in shining armor?"

Our bodies hovered so close I knew she could feel exactly what she'd done to me. "Are you saying you want to have sex?"

She raised an eyebrow. "I'm not saying anything. Why do you have to put things into words? Can't you just flow with the feelings and see what happens?"

That would be very dangerous. My hyper-active sexual sense was hard enough to control around girls I didn't like, much less a girl I was falling

166

in love with. And the spell it wove wasn't real. I had done so little exper-
imentation with it that I really didn't know what the extent of my ability
was. Most guys with my "problem" would gladly use it on women left
and right without a second thought. Maybe guys like Nathan didn't have
a conscience when it came to such things, but I wanted to know that the
girl I made love to was doing it because she was as in love with me as I
was with her.

How disgustingly romantic.

"What happened to taking things slow?"

"I know what I said, but…" She smiled and looked down. "This isn't easy
for me to say, Justin, but being around you makes me want to stop
talking and thinking. What if today was our last day alive?"

Her comment hit close to home. What if Randy drained all my blood? I
touched her chin and brought her gaze up to mine. "You're right," I said.
"I talk too much."

"Yes you do." She kissed me again and shivered. "Have you been working
out?" She squeezed my arm.

"A little."

"You're losing weight too. I hope you're not on one of those crash diets."

"Nope. Just eating healthy."

She traced a finger along my chest and looked down. "So, about my
family. Maybe you can meet them Sunday."

"Do you mean your parents?"

"And my two older brothers, Jack and Michael."

"Wow, I got names."

The corner of her mouth inched up in a lopsided smile. "I don't talk
about family much. I sort of dig you, though, so maybe it's okay just
this once."

167

"You *are* a hard ass. I guess contending with two brother does that. How much older are they?"

"Jack has five years on me and Michael is seven years older."

"Are you close?"

"Oh yes," she said with a distant look to her eyes.

"They're in college?"

"Jack is. Michael works for Dad."

"What kind of business?"

"The family business."

I shrunk away with a feigned expression of fear. "You're in the mob?"

She chuckled, but it almost seemed that she didn't find that to be far from the truth. "We're in the security business."

"Ah," I said, as if that explained everything. Maybe her dad made her work late for his company, though it was hard to picture Elyssa dressed as a rent-a-cop. That would explain the fatigue I often saw in her face.

"If you really think you're up to it. I have to warn you that my dad is a very serious person. He's a special kind of asshole, especially when it comes to boyfriends."

"What did he do to your other boyfriends?"

A wistful smile cast sadness into her eyes. "You're really the first guy I would call a boyfriend. The last guy didn't last the five minutes it took for me to come downstairs to meet him."

"Are you kidding me? What did your dad do to him?"

"He mostly stared at him."

"Your dad sounds scary."

She nodded, face serious as a heart attack. "He is."

CHAPTER 16

I didn't sleep well that night. Maybe it had to do with nervousness about my new K&C squad. Maybe it had to do with Elyssa's dad. I dreamt of a man with military buzz-cut and glowing eyes. He stared at me until I ran screaming.

I woke up in a panic with my fist embedded in the bed's headboard. Nobody with glowing eyes stood at my bedside, so I extricated my fist and got ready for the tournament.

Elyssa waited for me in the parking lot. I froze in my tracks and stared. She'd braided her long black hair into pigtails that hung to her shoulders. She wore knee-high platform boots. Fishnet stockings and a black skirt showed off muscular legs. She obviously worked out. She looked so amazingly hot I wanted to run away with her and forget everything else.

"You like?" She grinned at my stunned silence.

I nodded. "Me likey so much." I almost drooled.

Ash and Nyte showed up moments later. They wore variants of Goth attire. We looked like the army of darkness rather than elves. I didn't care. They had also used white and black face paint as a sort of camouflage. Yes, it was definitely a departure from green-cloaked elves.

"Did Kiss join the army?" said a familiar voice.

I turned to find Harry smirking at our group. Mark and two other girls dressed as forest elves flanked them. I offered a cold look in return then turned back to my squad without a word. Elyssa cocked an eyebrow and gave me a lopsided smile. She took my arm and we walked to join the milling mass of the elven army.

Harry and his gang trailed behind us. "I wonder who's going to be the cannon fodder today," he said.

"I think the girly boys will go first," Mark said.

Harry laughed. "If Justin doesn't get distracted by the prostitute they hired to join them."

Red exploded in my eyes. I raised my fist and whirled. Something dead-stopped my arm. Harry backed away and tripped over Mark's sword, landing heavily on his back. He looked like he'd about crapped himself. Elyssa's warm hand held firmly to my bicep, preventing my arm from completing the punch I really wanted to connect to Harry's stupid face.

"What did I tell you about being heroic?" she growled.

I took deep breaths and calmed myself. How was I supposed to protect a girl who got ticked at me whenever I tried to protect her honor? This was going to take some serious getting used to.

"Yeah, that's right. Keep walking," Harry shouted as we left them behind.

"Are we allowed to kill teammates?" Nyte asked.

"There's no rule against it," I said. "But let's hit the enemy first and get to those assholes later."

We lined up with the rest of our allies. The Dungeon Masters, dressed in their long flowing robes and fake Methuselah beards stood atop a tall tower in the middle of the battlefield.

"Ten minutes until battle commences," one said in a well-practiced announcer's voice.

We produced our weapons for inspection by the brightly-clad faerie referees.

One of them held up Elyssa's dual swords. He balanced them in his hands then twirled them. "Wow, these have great balance. They're just like ninja sai short swords."

She beamed. "Thanks. If the balance isn't right, what good are they?"

"Totally." He looked lost in her eyes, the poor nerd.

"Ahem." I handed him my beautifully-designed long sword.

He glanced at it, hefted it, and handed it back without a word. I felt mildly offended. Elyssa chuckled.

"I guess all of us can't be foam sword masters," I said with a huff.

"I'm a perfectionist." She pecked me affectionately on the nose.

I lined up my squad and gave them last-minute pointers, then led them to the left flank. Nyte and Ash flushed with excitement. Elyssa stared across the makeshift medieval village separating us from the Conanites, the enemy army. Pine trees lined the town perimeter and just beyond that hung the yellow ropes guarding the outer boundaries. To our right was the parking lot and bleachers for those who enjoyed watching nerds beat the crap out of each other.

I pointed to a walled-in fort in the middle of the battleground. "There's the goal," I said. "We make it there, and we're good as gold."

Elyssa pointed to a smaller hut lined by a thick hedge. "Why not there?"

"It doesn't have a wall."

"The hedge is thick enough to keep people from running through it and it's a smaller place to defend. We can't be flanked."

I gave her a curious glance. "I've been doing this a while. Any time my squad took and held that center fort, we survived."

She shrugged. "Okay, fearless leader."

A gong sounded and the battle started.

The armies rushed forward to battle with a roar. Nyte and Ash went down in the first skirmish. Elyssa whirled, struck, parried, and took down enemy squads whenever they attacked. She even knocked foam arrows from the air before they struck us. Elyssa made me look like a rank novice. After several small battles, she and I burst through the enemy's last line of defense.

Elyssa became a blur, her swords blocking, thrusting, slashing. The referees looked as confused as me but called out each kill as my girl-friend cut through the enemy like butter. I took out a couple of strag-glers. The gong chimed. Elyssa had just finished off the enemy king. Harry and Mark gaped at her. I gaped at her. The faerie refs gaped at her. She looked at us and went red in the face. The rest of our army roared and rushed over to offer congratulations.

After the celebrations died down and seventy percent of the guys present had asked for Elyssa's hand in marriage, I managed to drag her away from the ululating mass.

"Where in the world did you learn to fight like that?" I asked. "You're amazing."

She looked anything but happy, however. In fact, she looked downright embarrassed. "Too many kung-fu movies, I guess."

"Yeah, it doesn't work like that." I cocked my head like a curious dog. "You've taken martial arts, haven't you?"

"Yes," she said a trifle too quickly. "My dad made me take lessons and I guess it came in handy today."

I wasn't sure if that was the whole truth, but it felt truthful at least. Besides, I was too much in awe of her to think straight. I wanted her so badly right then that it was all I could do not to drag her into one of the huts and get busy. "I want you," I said.

She grinned. "You're so easy. All a girl has to do is whirl a sword, kill a few enemies, and you're ready to go." Her throaty laugh raced through my nervous system like a sexually charged lightning bolt.

I realized that if I started kissing her there would be no stopping myself. I closed my eyes and thought of baseball. *No good.* I thought of Stacey's sandpaper tongue. That didn't work. I took deep breaths and thought of Stacey playing baseball. Nothing quenched the unbearable heat of my desire for Elyssa.

"Well?" she asked, a bemused expression in her fiery eyes.

"I—Maybe we should go get cleaned up."

She rolled her eyes. "Seriously? You want me. I want you. What's wrong with that?"

"Nothing, but—"

"That's right. Nothing is wrong with sex. You and I are both eighteen. Barely legal but adults." She bit my earlobe.

"I'm not eighteen yet."

"Funny, I thought today was your birthday." She produced her smart-phone from some secret place and held the screen to my face. Her calendar had *Justin's Birthday!* in big bold letters surrounded by little hearts.

"I'm eighteen?" I had forgotten all about my "special" day.

"Answer my question big boy. Why can't you let nature take its course? Are you afraid?"

"No, of course not." *I'm petrified.* Partly due to my nearly uncontrollable psychic effect on girls and partly because Elyssa was a force to be reckoned with. She was going to think something was terribly wrong with me if I didn't act like any other testosterone-fueled teenager. "I just want it to be special. Not rushed because of spur-of-the-moment feelings."

She sighed. "I think someone's been watching one too many after-school specials."

My sexual energy plummeted and the little sex-obsessed demon perched on my shoulder poofed back to his hot abode underground where he could sulk about my idiocy. Now that I could safely kiss her, it felt awkward. We walked back to the cars in silence, though Ash and Nyte more than made up for it by jabbering incessantly about how cool their ten minutes of battle had been.

"Let's go grab some pizza to celebrate," Ash said.

"I've got to get home," Elyssa said. "Maybe another time."

"Me too," I said. "Great job, though, guys."

"I'll go with you, Ash." Nyte climbed into Ash's gargantuan periwinkle Ford.

They drove off leaving me and Elyssa standing near her car in the almost empty parking lot. She gave me an intense look of longing before pressing herself against me and delivering a kiss that curled my toes. My hands slid to the small of her back. She grabbed one of my hands and pressed it to her chest. I almost lost control over bodily functions.

A demon-possessed fever overcame me. My sex-starved sense slammed against its tin-foil prison. I picked up Elyssa. Twirled us around and set her on the hood of her car. She wrapped her legs around my waist and squeezed my body to hers. Her fingernails raked down my back. Spikes of pure pleasure shivered across my body. All thought of resistance vanished. More than anything on Earth, I wanted to be with her. I was ready to give it all to her. She pressed my hand to her thigh and moved it slowly upward. My heart pounded. The caged creature in my mind roared.

SWEET BLOOD OF MINE

And then I lost it.

The flood of carnal hunger burst through the psychic dam. It clawed for the steaming sensuality bursting from her like solar flares. It snatched at those tendrils and for an instant, caught them. The tendrils slid from my grasp, insubstantial as smoke, and retreated. Strong hands gripped my shirt and flung me like a rag doll. I slid on my back across the gravel parking lot until a tree stump stopped me at the edge. I opened my eyes. Cold metal pressed against my throat. Warm liquid trickled down my neck. Twin violet stars pierced the dusk and stared down at me.

"Elyssa?" I croaked.

She straddled me. Tears poured down her cheeks and dripped on me. "You filthy monster," she said, sobbing. "You almost had me, didn't you?"

"What are you talking about?"

"I should kill you this instant." She bared her teeth, sobs wracking her body.

The cold metal pressed harder against my skin. Every heartbeat thrummed against the blade, causing another trickle of hot blood to run down my neck. I held my breath for fear of opening an artery.

"You lured me with your sweet talk and charm and I ran in like a stupid little mouse."

"My charm?" I rasped.

She choked on her sobs. "Damn you to hell, Justin. Why? How could you be a monster?"

"Please tell me what's wrong, Elyssa. I don't understand! Please tell me what the hell is going on!"

Her glowing eyes sprang open and I waited for ultra-violet lasers to scorch me. Her face was pale, bloodless. Her lips curled into a snarl. I gasped as her canines lengthened into pearly white stilettos. They looked like Randy's fangs, but sparkly clean instead of bloodstained.

She stared at the blood trickling down my neck. Her nostrils flared. She licked her lips and lowered her face toward my neck. She jerked back, shaking her head as if warding off a dizzy spell.

"You've led me on. Used me. You knew all about me and my family, didn't you?" Cold anger and betrayal frosted her voice. "It's all been a ploy."

"I don't know a thing about your family." I felt dizzy either from a lack of blood or the realization that my girlfriend was a freaking vampire. Despite that terrible revelation, I didn't care. *I love her!* "Elyssa, it's me, Justin. I would never do a thing to hurt you. Please tell me what's going on."

She stared into my eyes for a long moment before abruptly standing and backing away from me. I noticed a long iron-gray blade in one of her hands. "Explain, then, but don't come a step closer or I'll finish you."

I touched my neck and crimson stained my hand. "Are you a vampire?"

She stared at me again, divining the sincerity of my questions before answering. "You really don't know, do you?"

A hysterical laugh burst from my lips. I remembered how she'd held me back from Harry earlier and how tightly she'd gripped my arm the other day. It hadn't occurred to me because I was so unfamiliar with my newfound strength. Elyssa was as strong if not stronger than I was. "Are you like me? Do you have super strength?"

"Oh no," she said with scorn in her voice. "I'm nothing like you."

"But you're as strong as I am. I can't control this problem I have. I didn't want it to happen!"

Elyssa sobbed, fresh tears welling in her eyes. It broke my heart to see her in such pain. To see the pain that I'd caused with my ignorance. She backed away from me as one might back away from a poisonous snake. "I don't want to hear it, Justin. Just stay away from me. Don't talk to me. Don't ever come near me again."

"Please, no, Elyssa. Don't go!"

She wiped the tears from her eyes and gave me a look that bordered between pure hatred and longing.

I ran toward her. She held the knife up in a defensive position. "I'm not lying. I will kill you if you come near me again."

"What do you think I am?" My voice sounded broken, pathetic.

"You're a fucking demon spawn."

Ice stabbed me in the chest. "A—a demon? No!" I pinched my arm. "I'm human!"

"No." She shook her head. "You're not."

"But—but Elyssa. I love you." My voice sounded so broken and desperate that I hardly recognized it as my own.

She clenched her teeth and screamed. "Shut up! Shut up, you filthy, lying monster!" Then she slammed the door of her car and roared out of the parking lot.

I stood in the gathering dusk alone with my tears.

Happy Birthday.

CHAPTER 17

I stood rooted to the spot, agony ripping at my insides, until light faded and darkness took the sky. I somehow gathered the willpower to go to my car and get in. I cried like a baby the entire way home. Women were my kryptonite. Even the one that loved me now thought I was a monster—a demon, no less. And maybe I was.

She was a vampire, but I didn't care. *She's wrong. I'm not a demon!*

One thing was true. My newfound abilities caused more pain and harm than good. I couldn't beat up bullies. I couldn't protect my friends. Everything I did backfired and hurt the people I cared about.

I wasn't even sure I had friends anymore. What would Elyssa tell Ash and Nyte? She had known them much longer than I had. If she sat with them in the gymnasium at school, I wouldn't be able to. Not without getting stabbed in the throat with a pencil.

One thing was for sure. I wasn't meeting Elyssa's parents on Sunday.

Elyssa's mother, Leia, popped into my mind. I remembered her eyes. Her violet eyes. Just like Elyssa's. I didn't have violet eyes. My eyes did not glow that I knew of. Or maybe they did and I just hadn't looked into a mirror at the right moment. I wondered if her entire family consisted of fanged violet-eyed people. The Vampire Brady Bunch. But if she was a vampire, why didn't she have bloodstained teeth like Randy and red irises? And why wouldn't she give me straight answers?

The first question was probably a matter of simple hygiene or mixing baking soda with toothpaste. The second question wasn't so easily answered unless vampires didn't all have red or violet eyes.

I walked inside the house. Dad was nowhere to be found. I had questions for him, damn it. He'd promised we would talk, but his motorcycle was gone and he didn't answer his cell phone.

Who were the Conroys? Where had Mom gone? Had I been born, or did my parents summon me from the pits of hell?

I went into my room and locked the door. I looked like a zombie. Dirt caked my face. Dried blood crusted my neck and a thin red line ran from the left side of my throat to my Adam's apple. I couldn't believe Elyssa had done that to me. No wonder I'd thought she was hiding something from me. She had been. My girlfriend—ex-girlfriend—was a vampire ninja assassin.

Damn, that's badass.

The way she'd handled those swords during the tournament blew me away. She knew her stuff.

But I was still just as in the dark now as I'd been the day Stacey had attacked me. Except now I knew my super ex-girlfriend was a vampire, I was possibly a demon, and Stacey was something completely different. What was it with me and supernatural chicks?

I don't want to be a demon!

Elyssa had to be wrong about me.

I went down a checklist, trying to deduce what I might be. I wasn't a vampire, a werewolf, a leprechaun, and definitely not a merman. The list went on and on, but nothing quite matched my symptoms.

179

Nothing I'd read in urban fantasy novels had prepared me for this predicament. I didn't glow, glitter, or grow fangs, but I could seduce any woman in a heartbeat. Correction: I could seduce any *normal* woman. Apparently the supernatural ladies knew how to defend themselves.

I thought demons possessed people, not seduced them into sex.

I took a shower during which I alternated between sobbing and moments of stoic silence. This was worse than all my disastrous relationships rolled up into one big ball of pain.

Katie may have broken my heart in two, but Elyssa had shattered it.

I was the perfect candidate for a soap opera acting career: Plenty of drama and an unhappy ending to all my romantic endeavors. I found myself staring at the computer screen. Just staring at it without a clue as to why I'd sat down there in the first place.

I searched for *demon spawn* and came up with hundreds of results—mostly stories about mythical beings who feasted on the souls of young girls. Apparently, I was doomed with this curse. I didn't even know what to call my symptoms. I almost posted to WebMD:

Please help! I have this psychic sexual sense which lets me see these sex vapors emanating from women. Then I ravish them.

Sincerely, Unintentional Molester

Then I stumbled upon a clue that almost made sense: *Incubus – a demon that seduces women in their sleep.*

I read on about it, but it spoke of possession and visiting women in their dreams. The seduction part was spot-on, but everything else, not so much.

I scribbled thoughts on a bit of paper. The *vapor* as I called it was a sexual feeling that my mind interpreted as a ghostly halo surrounding people, but more noticeably, females. It had to be telepathy of some sort. But I couldn't read minds, only hints of emotions around that sexual core of energy. A light bulb sparked on. I sensed sexual energy and bits of emotional energy. Psychic energy.

I searched on those terms and came up with everything from yoga to people gluing energy stones to their foreheads. I also discovered every conceivable way to enlarge my manhood. Not even Yahoo Answers had anyone asking about super strength combined with the ability to make women rip off their clothes.

The term *incubus* came up several times, but no definition of it offered an *Aha!* moment. I found a website detailing hundreds of supernatural creatures including one that sounded like me—a dark faerie. The Unseelie, or evil faery, used its sexual lure to trap females while it drained them of beauty and life. But certain things didn't add up. Faeries were ancient, according to the website, immortal, and they didn't have children. So unless another evil faerie had done something to me and put me up for adoption, I didn't know how I could possibly be one. Deep down, I didn't really want to admit that I was a faerie either, because it sounded girly. But at least it was a start.

I flopped on my bed and spent some quality time staring at the ceiling as my maudlin emotions dragged my spirits into the gutter. Somehow, I slept. On Sunday, I sat on my bed, staring at the wall—the ceiling needed some alone time. Agony gripped my heart.

I called Elyssa and got her voicemail. "Please call me back," I said. "I don't understand what's going on." After an hour, I called her again. After the fifth time, I gave up. She wasn't going to call me back. As far as I knew, she didn't have a social networking profile on any of the major websites. I didn't even know where she lived.

I called Ash.

"Hey, Justin," he said in a cheery voice. "Man that was so awesome yesterday."

"Yeah, it was fun."

"You know, I want to thank you."

"For what?" I was surprised Elyssa hadn't called him and told him not to talk to me.

"You've really been a good friend," he said. "This isn't easy for me to say, but..." He took a deep breath. "I haven't had a lot of real friends besides Nyte and Elyssa. You're for real, man. Thanks for being there for me."

I choked up all of a sudden. My voice cracked as I tried to speak. "Sure. Thanks for being there for me, too."

"Any time." He chuckled. "We're gonna go out for burgers later if you want to join us."

"You, Nyte, and Elyssa?"

"Ha, like you wouldn't know if she's coming. I have never seen her happier, man. I'm so glad you guys met."

I felt tears coming on again and clenched my teeth to stiffen my upper lip. "Maybe I'll join you later." I tried desperately to keep my voice even.

"Cool. Just text me if you can make it."

I hung up, as salty tears burning my eyes. "Screw me." I flopped down on my bed. I'd even forgotten to ask him if he knew where Elyssa lived. He would probably wonder why in the world I asked. It seemed like something a boyfriend should know. Besides, if Elyssa thought I was a demon, what would her family say? Much as I needed to get out of the house, I couldn't force myself to go out with Ash. I would only be a miserable mess.

Sunday passed in a haze of pain.

I woke up to Monday. A tiny shard of hope that I might be able to talk to Elyssa lodged in my heart. But she wasn't in the gymnasium that morning. Ash and Nyte didn't know where she was. I searched everywhere for her in the hallways between classes. During lunchtime I looked but couldn't find her in the cafeteria. Ash figured she must be sick. I felt sick to my stomach. I left the cafeteria and went outside. A figure sat on a bench near the tennis courts on the side of the school.

Elyssa.

She whirled to face me when I was twenty feet away. She relaxed somewhat when she saw it was me, but her hands remained in a defensive position. "What are you doing here?" she asked.

"What are *you* doing out here?" I shot back. "This is silly. I'm no demon, Elyssa. I'm just a guy like any other. Okay, maybe I'm not quite like any other, but I would never hurt you."

Her eyes iced over. "Get away from me."

"I'm not going anywhere until you tell me what's wrong."

"You don't understand do you?" She grabbed her sandwich and stuffed it back into the bag. "You're a demon spawn. The thought of having kissed you makes me want to vomit. You're not even human."

"What are you talking about?" Anger coiled around the sorrow. I walked toward her with my arms up. "Look at me. I'm human as you are."

"Your kind is anything but human."

"I'm getting really tired of people telling me what my kind is like. I don't even know what my kind is! And in case you hadn't noticed, you're a vampire!"

She gritted her teeth. "You don't know what you're talking about." She walked toward me with menace in her eyes.

I backed away in case she pulled another knife on me. "I love you, Elyssa. I didn't want to do whatever the hell it was my body tried to do to you. I can't control it. Can't you help me?"

"You wouldn't know what love is if it ripped out your heart, Justin. It's a human emotion." Raw emotion boiled in her voice. She shoved roughly past me. "If my father found out about you, he'd kill you."

"Kill me? What did I ever do to deserve death?"

"Violating Overworld law, for one." She bared her teeth. "And my father despises spawn."

Dread coiled around my heart. "Please, I'm not evil. If I'm a demon, I promise I'm the good kind!"

"Stay the hell away from me." She walked a few feet, spun around. "And you'd better not harm a hair on Ash or Nyte or I will hunt you down and hang you by your intestines."

"So you're going to take them away from me too?" I shouted. "You're just going to rip everything I care about out of my life?"

"Damn, you put on a good show, Justin!" She threw up her hands. "Your kind is incapable of caring about anything. I guess you'll discover that before too much longer and I won't feel so bad about having to put you down."

Then she walked away.

I punched the wooden bench so hard it split in half. I punched it again and again until only a pile of pulp remained. My hand ached. Splinters jutted between my knuckles and blood ran down my fists. Within minutes, the skin pushed the splinters out. The blood stopped flowing. My hands looked good as new. If only it were so easy to heal my broken heart.

Hunger gripped my stomach. I spotted my bagged lunch sitting on the ground where I must have dropped it earlier, so I took it and devoured it. I was still hungry but now I was thirsty too. I went to a water fountain and drank, but nothing seemed to quench my thirst. My stomach rumbled. I went into the bathroom and washed my hands. When I looked into the mirror, a stranger looked back.

Well, not exactly a stranger, but a miserable guy who looked just like me but with ice-blue eyes instead of hazel ones. Those eyes were haunted. That face was very pale. This stranger, the poor fool, didn't have a chance at happiness.

It was then I realized my eyes looked just like Dad's had that night.

What am I, Dad? Am I really a demon?

Two guys I didn't know burst into the bathroom. They were laughing so hard that tears of mirth poured down their faces.

"And the bear wiped his ass with the rabbit," one of them said, slapping the wall with each convulsive guffaw. His friend collapsed against the wall, holding his ribs and howling with laughter.

They kept repeating the sentence over and over again. Apparently it was the punch line to some joke I'd never heard but wished I knew so I could laugh along with them.

Something tickled my senses. It was faint, but emanated from both of them. I reached for it with my mind and latched on. This was completely unlike what had happened with me and Victoria. With her, it had been like drinking a milkshake through a large straw. This was like drinking unsweetened tea through a tiny stirring straw—pleasant if you're really thirsty, but not as tasty or satisfying. My mind sucked greedily on it anyway. The gnawing hunger diminished. Their laughter faded as they did their business and left.

I glared at myself in the mirror. Icy blue eyes darkened to hazel. My skin regained color. I had just fed upon another person's joy.

I really am a monster.

CHAPTER 18

A river of icy fear ran through my body. Elyssa was right. I was
a soul-sucking creature of nightmares and would never know
love. I would never again feel her arms around me or her soft
lips against mine. I would never know the joy of making love with her,
or any other woman for that matter. My make-out session with Victoria
had been as fake and phony as a blowup doll. I could seduce any woman
but never win her love. Even worse, I apparently had to leech emotions
from other people to satisfy my hunger.

I didn't want this life. I wanted my old life back. I wanted Elyssa back.
Tears fought their way into my eyes. I clenched my teeth and gripped
the porcelain sink with both hands.

"Stop crying you stupid freak." The sink cracked and shattered in my
hands. I backed away and fled the empty bathroom before someone
came in and reported me for vandalism.

"Aw looky, someone's been crying," said a familiar voice. Nathan's
leering face came into focus through the haze of anger, fear, and
loathing I felt.

I clenched my fists so tight my knuckles crackled like fireworks. I thought my hands would bleed. It took every ounce of willpower not to beat Nathan into a bloody porridge of skin and crushed bones that instant. Something in the back of my head screamed, *Do it! You're a monster anyway. They never accepted you as a human. What makes you think you'll ever be accepted by any of them, you demonic freak?*

I didn't care if Nathan or his crowd liked me. I only cared about three people, and one of them loathed me. Other students chimed in, ridiculing me as I walked through the locker-lined hallway.

Something hard smacked against the top of my head. I saw stars for a brief instant and heard raucous laughter break out. I turned and saw Steve guffawing and pointing at his class ring which he'd cleverly turned palm-down to smack me on the head.

Flames of anger licked at my heart, simmering my blood.

KILL. DESTROY.

The inner voice roared for death. It demanded a bloodbath.

I could do it. I could kill everyone here.

The thought made me sick. Every last one of them deserved a good beating, but not death. I turned and walked away, the roar of laughter echoing behind me.

"Hello, Justin." Mr. Turpin stood in his classroom doorway watching me.

"Hi, sir." I stopped walking and stuffed my hands in my pockets. "Did you need something?"

"You've changed." He looked me up and down. "You look much stronger than before."

His statements made me uneasy. "I work out, if that's what you mean."

Mr. Turpin's gaze seemed sharper than usual, and he wore a very uncharacteristic smirk. "You don't have to take the bullying, Justin. You're not the weak boy from a few weeks ago."

"Are you saying I should fight them?" My forehead pinched. "Fighting them wouldn't do me any good. It would just get me in trouble."

"If you had the power to get away with it, would you?"

I blinked a few times, wondering if Mr. Turpin knew more about my situation than he let on. On the other hand, his question was spot on. I did have the power to beat the ever-loving shit out of anyone in this school, and I was probably fast and strong enough to get away with it. But that wasn't me. I didn't want to abuse my power like Randy, I wanted to—I sucked in a breath—I wanted to use it for good.

I shook my head. "No. I know what it's like to be bullied. If I had the power, I wouldn't use it to bully others."

He pursed his lips. Nodded. "Interesting." Mr. Turpin folded his thick arms. "I'll see you in class, Justin." He turned and went inside the classroom.

Elyssa thought I was a demon—a monster. Maybe by definition I was. What I had to do was prove that I was good. If actions spoke louder than words, then I needed to stop moping around and spring into action.

I took a seat in my next class and jotted down the dots in my notebook.

Elyssa knows about supernatural creatures.

Her father hates demon spawn.

Elyssa carries a freaking dagger with her.

She is a ninja.

She has fangs.

Her family runs its own security business.

Elyssa followed Affliction Dude.

Is Affliction Dude a supernatural?

Once I jotted down my suppositions and questions, I connected the dots. A bigger picture slowly formed. Elyssa had admitted receiving martial arts training. Her K&C performance also pointed strongly to weapons training. All her late nights and sneaky habits indicated to me that she frequently worked in the family's security business. If they truly were into security, and Affliction Dude was a supernatural criminal, then in that context, Elyssa's mysterious behavior made sense.

On the other hand, Affliction Dude might have hired her family to watch his back. In which case Elyssa was protecting and shadowing him from a distance. Somehow, I felt that wasn't the case. It seemed Elyssa was tailing him, not looking out for his well-being as he perused the women's lingerie section of Macy's.

My goal was simple—stalk Affliction dude and bring him to justice. Another connection lit up the neurons in my brain.

Randy was at the mall that day.

Randy sold illicit steroid drugs—possibly supernaturally enhanced by my blood or vampire blood. There was still a chance inhaling the fumes had transformed me into a superhuman. I wished I'd remembered to bring that up with Elyssa, but she probably wouldn't have believed me anyway.

I was probably grasping at straws, but what if Randy had been at the mall to meet with Affliction Dude and his gang? Maybe that was his supplier.

I snapped my fingers. "Yeah!"

Half the class jumped at my sudden outburst and the chemistry teacher, Mr. Heisenberg, shouted in alarm.

"What in the world, Justin?" The teacher rubbed a hand over his shaved head.

I looked at the variables scrawled on the board. "Oh, the formula just suddenly made sense to me."

"Oh, well, I'm glad you're excited about chemistry." Heisenberg glared at Tommy Smith who snored gently with his head on his desk. "If only everyone was that excited."

Cindy Mueller raised a hand and waved it. "I'm excited, sir!"

Heisenberg sighed. "Aren't you always?""

Right after class, I jogged up and down the halls looking for Randy in all the boys' bathrooms. I found Brad Nichols preening his hair in the last bathroom. He saw me in the mirror and snarled.

"You're dead meat, Case." Brad punched a fist into his palm. "You ready for round two?"

"No." I folded my arms and stayed a safe distance. "What kind of drugs is Randy selling?"

His eyes narrowed. "He never got the chance to tell me about it, thanks to you busting in on us."

"You didn't meet with him again?"

Brad bared his teeth. "I ain't got to tell you shit, Case."

I resisted the urge to jack him against the wall. It seemed to work in all the formulaic CSI shows, but I didn't trust its effectiveness in a school bathroom. *Use your brain, Justin!* "I know you don't have to, but I heard the stuff he's selling doesn't work as advertised. He's spiking it with stimulants so people think it's working, but it's just making them hyper."

Brad frowned. "That's not what I heard."

"Well, one of my friends took it and puked blood, so I'd be careful." I shrugged, backed away. "Just be careful."

"That son of a bitch better not have lied." Brad stepped toward me. "Don't think you're off the hook, bitch."

"Dude, are you even with Katie anymore?"

Brad burst into laughter. "I was never with that idiot. Dude, I was nailing three other chicks when I got with Katie."

My blood began to boil. "Yeah, you're a real stud, Brad. You won the genetic lottery with good looks, but you're a grade-A certified shit stain on humanity."

Brad roared and punched me with everything he had. His fist cracked against my jaw. I didn't even flinch. He screamed in pain, holding his hand. "What the fuck?"

I grinned. "Better get that looked at, Brad." I opened the bathroom door, stopped and looked back. "Maybe get checked for herpes while you're at it." Then I left, walked around the corner, and waited.

We still had five minutes before the next class started. I hoped letting Brad injure his fist against my face hadn't ruined my plan. Brad burst out of the bathroom, fist wrapped in paper towels. Curious students looked at his hand, but no one stopped him on his way toward the gym at the other end of the hall.

I weaved between students, ignoring any jibes that came my way and followed Brad. He walked to the left of the gym and entered a service corridor. When he vanished into the double doors at the end, I peered through the crusty windows until I saw him go around the corner, then went inside.

"I want the shit now." Brad's voice echoed down the hallway.

"I'm still waiting on a new batch," Randy said. "Did you find others who are interested?"

"What about the temporary stuff? You said it'd give me a taste of super strength."

"I have a few vials left, but the new batches are going to be the real deal." Randy sighed. "Look, dude, you're obviously pissed about something, and what happened to your fist?"

"Nothing," Brad growled. "Just give me the boost. I have a score to settle."

"Whoa, biker dude. Hang on." Randy laughed. "I can't just go handing it out so you can go berserk on someone. Remember, we don't want a lot of attention."

"God damn it, Randy. Give me some or I'll kick your ass!"

I tip-toed to the corner, glad the sounds of students talking in the hall outside covered the sound of my footsteps. As a vampire, Randy probably had super hearing like me and I didn't want him to hear me coming.

"Did you really just threaten me, boy?"

Brad grunted. Cried out in pain. "Stop!

"Don't like having your nipples pinched, Brad?"

"Stop it, please!" Brad sobbed. "It hurts!"

"Yeah, kind of like the time you punched me in the nuts to impress those girls in middle school, you piece of shit." Randy laughed. "If I didn't have a mission, I'd have torn off your ball sack and made you eat it."

"I'm sorry," Brad moaned. "I just need—"

"Shh," Randy said. "Just go with the flow and it'll all be good. I'll let you know when the new batch is up, okay? I'm supposed to find out more today."

"Fine." Brad's voice trembled.

"Now, get the hell out of here."

I scurried back out of the corridor and went into the hallway just as the bell rang. I was in business. All I had to do was follow Randy after school and I'd find his supplier.

When the final bell rang, I dashed outside to the parking lot and waited for Randy to make an appearance. I searched all the faces, but even as

SWEET BLOOD OF MINE

the crowd dwindled, still no sign of him. It wasn't until after the crowd died down that a skinny figure in a hoodie walked out, the hood drawn over his face.

Though I couldn't see his features, I knew it had to be him. "Vampires burn up in sunlight," I reminded myself. As if to prove me wrong, Randy pulled back the hood and looked around. He didn't glitter, but he also didn't burst into flames. After a few seconds, he pulled the hood back over his face.

"Maybe he's not a vampire," I muttered. "Or maybe vampires operate differently in the real world." For all I knew, they didn't even turn into bats.

Randy climbed into a black SUV with dark-tinted windows. I got into my car and followed at a safe distance, hoping Randy didn't know what kind of car I drove. Traffic was already heavy and grew thicker as we drove towards the Atlanta skyline. He took I-85, got off on the service road, and took a right down a street between a hotel and a corporate park.

His last turn took him past the sign of a prancing neon horse. *Pink Pony* flickered just beneath the bucking mare. I'd never been here, but I'd heard of the place. Thankfully, I had plenty of my parents' cash on me.

Randy walked straight into the strip club like he owned the place. The bouncer at the door simply nodded at him. I parked at the back of the lot and headed inside. Security at the door took three bucks for parking and opened the door.

The burly man grinned. "Have fun, kid."

"Woot," I pumped my fist. "I loved naked girls."

"Freaking virgins," the bouncer muttered as the door closed.

Music boomed on the inside. A fully-clothed stripper on one of several stages spun around a pole for the sparse crowd. I sat at the bar and watched the creepy-looking guys feed her dollar bills as I scanned for Randy. I saw my quarry talking to a brunette dancer at the bar. He flashed some cash and the pair vanished into a section marked VIP.

I wasn't sure if I should follow, so I turned back to the creepy men watching the dancer on stage. One old guy wore large 80s sunglasses and a detective cap straight out of Sherlock Holmes. Another rubbed his nipple through a hole in his dirty undershirt. A bouncer with glasses leaned lazily against a wall, seemingly unconcerned with the creep-fest.

"Want a private dance, hon?" asked a smooth voice in my left ear. "I'm Raven."

A lovely dark-haired girl in a translucent negligee stood behind me, her hands resting on my shoulder. Chocolate brown eyes blinked alluringly beneath fake eyelashes. The unicorn tattoo over her pierced belly button was sort of sexy and she smelled good, but her sex vapors—her aura—felt cold and dead.

"How private?" I asked, trying to keep the quaver out of my voice.

She gave me a sugar-coated smile. "Don't be nervous, sweetie." she rubbed my arm affectionately. "I'll be gentle."

She seemed to really like me. *Of course she seems to, dummy. That's her job.*

"How much?" I forced myself to think about this logistically. I could use her to keep an eye on Randy.

"Well, a lap dance here would be ten, a dance in the private lounge is thirty, and a dance in a private VIP room is two-fifty."

"Two hundred and fifty?" I had a grand stuffed in my pockets, but that was still a lot.

"That's right." She fluttered her eyelashes. "It's more intimate back there."

I really wanted to be more excited about it than I was, but this girl was a guttering candle compared to Elyssa's fierce flame. *Just use her to get into VIP.* I flashed a grin. "Let's do it."

She took the cash and led me into the back room where Randy had gone. Curtained rooms lined the hallway. I heard moaning from the first one on the right. Raven held a finger to her lips and smiled, then slightly parted the curtain.

The brunette Randy went with was naked and bent over a chair. My mouth dropped open when I saw his scrawny little ass flashing back and forth. The pure sexual energy from the woman flushed my inner beast from hiding and my pants got a lot tighter.

Raven pulled me along to the back room. A faux leather couch squatted against the back wall and a foldout chair sat in the middle. She got on my lap and started grinding. "Is that a wad of twenties in your pocket, or are you just happy to see me?"

"Both?" My voice broke.

She laughed softly. "You are adorable, honey." She pressed my face into her breasts. "How'd you like a full treatment for that stack of twenties?"

I froze up. "Uh—"

She laughed again. "Well, if you just want the dance, let's go over the rules, okay?"

"Okay," I said, voice cracking.

"I do all the touching. You," she said putting my hands to the sides of the chair, "have to keep your hands to yourself. Otherwise, I'll have to get the bouncer to come and take you away. And you're too cute for me to want to do that to you." She smiled and tapped my nose with her finger.

I nodded and white-knuckle-gripped the sides of the chair. She laughed.

"If you're really good, I might give you a feel even without the extra money."

I pushed back against the beast inside me. Seeing Randy and that dancer had nearly unleashed it.

It slammed against the bars of my willpower. *Take her! She is yours.*

195

With those sorts of thoughts, maybe I really was a demon.

A new song began. Raven—if that was her real name—twisted her body in a slow rhythm. She bent over, displaying her panties then straightened in a slow languorous motion. She slid the negligee from her shoulders with well-practiced flourishes. I wondered how many hundreds of times she'd done this same exact dance for other men. In the back of my mind, I could hear, feel, smell, and almost taste the white-hot hum of sexual energy from the club. Her touch aroused me and stoked the beast even more. I gritted my teeth and prayed for the song to be over.

Raven slid the negligee down her shoulders to reveal her breasts. "You get to spend thirty minutes with these. Wouldn't you like to touch them?"

"Thirty minutes?" My voice trembled.

"It's not two-fifty for one dance, sweetie."

I can't last thirty minutes with a naked woman.

My vision shifted, revealing her cold, impersonal aura. Tendrils reached from mine to hers. I fought them back, but it took everything I had. My pants felt like they were ready to split open and the effort of holding back made me dizzy. If I didn't leave, this would spin out of control.

I jumped up, depositing Raven gently on the floor.

"What the hell?"

"Look, I have a girlfriend. I can't do this." I headed for the curtain. "I'm so sorry."

A genuine smile spread over her face. "That's so sweet."

I stepped into the hallway just as Randy emerged from his room. I stepped back into mine, peeking out.

"What are you doing?" Raven pressed up against me. "Oh, I just saw the guy from down the hall leaving. I felt weird walking out with him."

"Yeah, he's a regular. I think he knows the management or something."

I turned toward her. "He's here a lot?"

She nodded. "He's best buds with Spike, the night manager."

I grimaced. "Who the hell names their kid Spike?"

Raven laughed. "His name is as real as mine."

"Raven is your real name?"

She snorted. "You're hilarious. No, that's not my real name. I think Spike's real name is Fred or Bob, but I don't ask him a lot of questions. He's creepy as hell."

"Does he like Affliction T-shirts? Have a goatee?"

Raven's eyebrows rose. "You know him?"

I quickly realized I should've kept my mouth shut. "I thought I saw him outside."

"Odd, he doesn't usually get here until eight." She shrugged. "Probably came in early."

Randy was gone and it didn't seem like Raven knew why he met with Spike, so I went down the hallway and peered around the corner. Randy stood at the bar, his back to me. I walked casually toward the dark back corner and took a seat where I could watch him without him seeing me.

An hour passed during which I had to suffer through four lap dances to as to not appear out of place. Affliction Dude finally showed, then he and Randy went into a back room and didn't come back out.

I yawned. It was nearly eleven and still no sign of Randy. I went outside and noticed his car was gone.

"Dammit!" I face-palmed. They must have left via a back door.

My first night of sleuthing had uncovered some connections, but I was such a noob, I'd let my quarry escape.

197

If I was going to prove to Elyssa that I was a good guy, I couldn't let it happen again.

CHAPTER 19

W hen I got home and stepped out of the car, a familiar heat blossomed between my shoulder blades.

"I warned you and you didn't listen, did you, my love?" said Stacey.

"Love?" I turned to face my cute and rather frightening stalker. "What do you know about love?"

Stacey showed her lovely teeth and purred. A breeze blew back her hair and I noticed her ears had pointy tips like an elf...or a Vulcan. "I know far more than you, little lamb."

I walked over and gripped her shoulders. She pursed her rosy lips and purred louder.

"Am I a demon?" I asked. "Something like an incubus?"

"A demon?" She giggled. "Now, now, dear. I will tell you nothing until you agree to my stipulations."

I reached for her psychic energy but it slipped away from me like smoke in a breeze. The sensations I drew from her were so different as to be almost alien.

"You will find I am not so easily captured nor tantalized as mortal kine, love. I will teach *you* how to please me." She wrapped an arm around my waist and pulled me closer. She rubbed her head against my chest and inhaled.

I was oh-so-tempted to give in to her demands right then. What more did I have to lose? I extricated myself with some difficulty from Stacey's firm embrace and walked down the driveway toward the house.

"You're leaving me again?" she said in an angry tone. "Are you not even curious about what I have to offer?"

"Of course I am." I looked her up and down. She was undeniably sexy and cute but that not entirely human part of her gave me the creeps. Catlike ears. Rough tongue. Feline eyes. Was she some sort of cat woman? My internal catalogue of fantastic creatures grew by another entry. I wondered if she could turn into a cat. Shape-shifting didn't seem all that far-fetched anymore. Maybe she was some sort of werecat. "I made a counter offer but you refused."

"I have explained myself quite thoroughly," she said and sniffed.

"What is it with women and disdainful sniffing?"

She scrunched her forehead and gave me a puzzled look. Light from a streetlamp reflected eerily off her amber eyes just like a cat's would. Her vertically-slit pupils dilated until they were round.

"You are one strange cat." I meant it literally.

"I am exceptional."

"You'll get no argument from me, Cheetara, but I don't like your catitude."

Her eyebrows pinched into a V. "Who, pray tell, is Cheetara?"

"That's for me to know and you to find out." *My turn to be mysterious, babe!* I made one last play for her help. "Have you ever wanted to be a hero?"

Her nose wrinkled. "I have tried my hand at that and went rather poorly."

"There's a kid I go to school with. He used to be normal, but now he's a vampire and he's got some shady dealings going on." I leaned closer to her. "I'm a total noob. I need someone with experience to train me in the ways of the Force. I need a teacher who can help me control my abilities. Will you be my tutor?"

Stacey smiled slyly. "If you agree to my terms, perhaps I can help you." She took my hand. "Some free advice—stay away from vampires. Do not try to be a hero, love. You will only end up dead."

Well, I tried. "With great power comes great responsibility. Giving up isn't an option."

Musical laughter tinkled from her red lips. "You naïve little darling. I would so dearly love to keep you safe from harm. I promise I would love you to death."

"See, that's the kind of creepy stuff that drives away guys." I backed away. "Mentioning the whole love and death thing together. It scares us." I paused and decided to take a stab at her identity. "You're a werecat, aren't you?"

Her eyes widened and a smile lit her face. "You're a clever one, my lamb. Perhaps that will be enough to keep you alive." She stood on tiptoe and kissed me on the cheek with hot lips, then sprinted away into the darkness. *Not so fast,* I thought. I wanted to find out where she lived. I dashed after her and tripped over a tree root on the other side of the street, nearly braining myself on a low stone wall. I climbed to my feet and brushed the dirt off my pants. A sigh escaped my lips. What good were super powers if my reflexes couldn't keep up?

Damn it, I need a sensei or a Jedi master.

I went inside. Still no Dad. Still no texts from Mom. It didn't take a genius to realize they weren't on business trips, and it had to do with all the money in the bank. Maybe it even had to do with me. I might be a demon. Maybe I was possessed. Maybe Randy's steroid drug had changed me. It stood to reason my parents knew something and they'd vanished right around the time it started happening.

A message blinked on the landline phone. I checked it. Another private eye had left a message, telling Dad he was off the case after a single black cloud appeared out of the clear blue and rained frogs on his agency. The Conroys again.

"Why is he hiring private eyes?" I tried calling the number but got voice-mail. Then again, it was past midnight.

I wondered if Dad might be stalking women down at the laundromat again.

I jogged to the strip mall but he wasn't there, staring at old women with those strangely blue eyes of his. Then it hit again. His eyes and mine were the same color—hazel. And his had been ice blue that day—the same color mine had turned. Was he a demon too? I snatched a bottle off the ground and hurled it angrily, expecting it to fly a few feet and smash into the pavement. Instead, it sailed across the parking lot, over the strip mall, and out of sight. Enough with the mysteries and igno-rance. I had to find Dad and demand answers.

THE EXPRESSIONS on Ash's and Nyte's faces went they saw me enter the gym the next day told me they knew about the state of affairs with Elyssa.

Ash shook his head sadly. "I'm really sorry about you and Elyssa."

"Sucks, man." Nyte flushed red.

Since they hadn't broken out the pitchforks and torches, Elyssa prob-ably hadn't mentioned I might be a demon.

"Uh, what did she tell you guys?" I asked.

Ash frowned. "Just that things didn't work out and she was taking a break from the group."

That sounded like one of Elyssa's rational reasons. Of course it was utter crap. I felt ill just thinking about her. My knees turned to jelly and my stomach soured. I dropped onto the bleachers, trying desperately to keep from crying and throwing up all at the same time.

Ash squeezed my shoulder. "I really thought you two were a great couple."

I couldn't answer. It took everything I had not to sob uncontrollably. The bell mercifully rang. I got up and stepped into the aisle to walk down the stairs. Feet pounded behind me. My hackles rose.

I leapt back just as Nathan's shoulder rammed the empty air where I'd been. Caught off balance, he tumbled down seven stairs before face-planting with a crunch on the hardwoods below. He howled in pain, rolling in a spreading pool of blood. His nose looked broken—again.

Laughter rippled across the bleachers. His football buddies rushed down to help him. Concerned cheerleaders sprang to his side and soon all the pretty people loudly admonished the crowd.

Mr. Barnes rushed inside. He saw Nathan bleeding profusely on the gym floor and yelled for the nurse. His eyes locked onto me. He glowered. Walked over to Adam and talked to him. I tried to attune my hearing so I could pick up on the conversation, but the general hubbub formed a sonic barrier against eavesdropping. Adam pointed at me, a scowl on his face. Barnes gave a nasty grin, one he'd likely practiced over and over in the mirror, and motioned for me to come to him.

Ash and Nyte collectively groaned. I gritted my teeth and strode toward Mr. Barnes. I knew nothing I said would exonerate me. If only my brain had gotten an upgrade in addition to my brawn.

Kill them all, the beast whispered. *Power is yours to take.* I might not be a demon, but I was definitely possessed by something. It wasn't exactly evil, but carnal, lustful, and above all, cocky as hell.

Unfortunately, I didn't have an angel preaching tolerance in my other ear, just a nerd with glasses, his nasal voice reminding me that physical violence led to expulsion and jail.

No prison can hold us!

Screw you, demon. I agree with the nerd.

"So you've graduated to tripping people, Case." Barnes sneered. "March yourself down to the principal's office and wait there."

Adam and Steve smirked at me. Aside from their hair color, they could have been clones.

"Looks more like a case of steroids interfering with motor coordination," I said.

"You little—!" Adam sprang at me, grabbed me by my shirt and tried to shove me. I held my ground and smirked.

His eyes flared in disbelief.

I turned to the Vice Principal. "I do believe he just physically assaulted me, Mr. Barnes."

"I didn't see anything." Barnes revealed a crooked-toothed grin. "But I heard verbal assault which I'm adding to your report."

My face burned. Rage suffocated the last shred of resistance and the cautious nerd within me hightailed it out of there. Everything seemed to slow as the adrenalin in my body spiked. I balled my hands into fists. I would crush these morons. These bugs. The demon agreed.

WE ARE POWER INCARNATE!

A familiar face caught my eye. Elyssa stood in the doorway. Her eyes glistened with sadness. Or were they narrowed in contempt? I uncurled my hands and let my arms drop to my sides. A tear sparkled like a diamond down her cheek. She turned and walked away.

The beast retreated into its cage and sulked.

I trudged down the hallway to the office and took a seat in front of the secretary.

"Back again already?" She tsked. "Kids these days."

I ignored her. The image of Elyssa haunted me. I closed my eyes and saw her smiling, face full of light and love. I opened my eyes and saw Mr. Perkins's ass in my face as he flirted with the secretary. My super sense of smell did me no favors, either.

She laughed. "Oh Mr. Perkins, you're such a card."

He turned to face me. "Into the office, Case."

I walked in and sat down, resigned to my fate.

"You still haven't learned your lesson, I see." He leaned back in his chair with an alarming shriek from the springs. He rested hands on his rotund belly. "I suspect Ms. Foreman will be sorely disappointed to learn her detention wasn't enough to set you right." He tapped his lower lip and an evil smile curled his lips. "I may just have a cure for you, boy."

I smiled as I left his office moments later. That idiot thought he was punishing me? It was all I could do not to laugh out loud at the secretary's confused look.

"What are you smiling for, boy?" She huffed. "Rotten kid."

Ash and Nyte waited anxiously to hear what had happened when I joined them for lunch. When I told them about my punishment, they grimaced in horror.

"This is an outrage," Ash said. "They'll murder you."

Nyte's mouth dropped open. "Dude, you're gonna get destroyed!"

"I think they'll be surprised." I flexed my fledgling bicep.

205

"You've been working out?" Nyte asked.

I nodded.

Ash covered his face. "I can't bear to watch."

Nyte sighed. "I'm definitely gonna watch no matter how bad it is. Maybe I should video it for posterity and proof."

"Proof of what?" Ash said. "Homicide?"

I sighed. "Calm down, guys. Nobody's getting murdered. Trust me."

"What do you want for your epitaph?" Ash asked. He waved a dismissive hand in the air. "Never mind. I'll come up with something. It'll have to mention how bravely you faced your doom. How you loved, lost, and faced death with dignity."

"Or soiled himself," Nyte added.

"Lay off with the melodrama." I laughed it off. They were killing my confidence.

As I left the lunch room, Tweedledum, Tweedledumber, and Tweedle-dumbass pushed themselves off the wall where they'd been leaning, obviously waiting for me. Nathan with his very bruised and bandaged nose tried to smile while his two lackeys imitated chimpanzee grins. Word of my punishment had spread predictably fast.

"You're all mine, Case," he said in a stuffy-nosed voice. He poked me hard in the chest.

"Sorry, Nathan, but I only go for girls, not apes."

Nathan roared and grabbed my shirt.

"Save it for the field, Mr. Spelman," Ted Barnes said from a few feet away.

Nathan reluctantly let go of my shirt. He smoothed it out with a grue-somely bruised smile plastered on his face. "You're right, Mr. Barnes. I wouldn't want to get his street clothes all dirty."

Mr. Barnes smiled. "Very good." He glared at me. "Go to class before I get even more creative with your punishment."

I shrugged and walked down the hall. As I passed the corner of the senior lockers hallway, a hand reached out and jerked me around the corner. Elyssa slammed me against the lockers with a bang.

"Ow!" I rubbed my head.

She glared at me with steel in her eyes. "You have to get out of this punishment."

"Is this your idea of foreplay?" Her scent, laced with anger, leather, and oil, intoxicated me.

"Shut up and listen to me. You can't go through with this."

"What do you care? I'm a demon, remember?"

"You may not be human, but those football players are. You don't understand what will happen if you harm them and the authorities find out."

"Authorities?" I raised an eyebrow. "Please explain it to my poor, ignorant self, Elyssa."

Her lips pressed into a firm line. "You're probably just playing me, but, fine. I'll play along."

"I'm not playing you or anyone else." I wanted to grab her by the shoulders but would probably pull back bloody stumps if I did.

"The Overworld has laws governing supernaturals and noms—normals. The authorities could kill you for infractions."

"That's why you did a double-take when I said noms." I tried to lean forward, but her supernatural strength pinned me to the lockers. "Are you a supernatural detective?"

Elyssa bared her teeth. "I'm a damned disgrace for not taking you in."

"Have I broken any rules?"

She laughed with derision. "Oh, yeah. I also don't see the high-and-mighty demon spawn tossing their young into the public school system. They look down on everyone."

"Am I demon possessed, or are demons physical? Inquiring minds want to know."

Elyssa backed away. "I'm not playing this game anymore." She waggled a finger. "Damn, you're good. Years of freaking training. Finally get my own mission and get duped by demon spawn. Are you even eighteen?"

I ignored the question. "Why warn me about Overworld enforcers killing me?" I rubbed my now-healed throat. It didn't hurt, but my heart pounded painfully at the thought of what she'd done and what she'd promised to do. "I thought you wanted me dead."

Elyssa looked away. "You don't understand. I don't expect you to. Maybe you didn't try to trick me into loving you but—"

"Wait, so you do love me?" Hope welled in my heart.

She growled and pounded a locker, leaving a fist-shaped dent. "Stop it, Justin. Stop it!"

I grabbed her shoulders, to hell with the consequences. "Look at me and tell me you don't love me. Do it and I'll never bother you again."

"I don't love you," she mumbled.

"Look at me when you say it!"

She looked at me, eyes dull and faded. "I don't love you."

I let her go. My heart turned to lead, the heavy lump sagging in my chest. "Well, if there are agents out there looking to kill me, I guess it would be a mercy."

I turned to leave. Her hand gripped my shoulder.

"Please, listen to me, Justin."

I pushed her hand away but didn't turn to face her. I couldn't let her see the tears welling in my eyes. "Why? What does it matter? I'm just playing you, remember?"

"It just does. I—I don't want to see you hurt."

I took a deep shuddering breath. "You're not doing a very good job of it." I walked away and left her standing there.

CHAPTER 20

I t took longer than I'd expected to put on a football uniform but not as long as it had taken the outfitter to find one that would fit me. He'd measured me at five feet, eight inches and a hundred-eighty pounds which came as a surprise to me since I'd been five feet, six inches and nearly two hundred pounds of pure lard just a few weeks ago. Most of the football players ranged from six to seven feet and their gear made them appear even bigger. I looked like a munchkin in a forest of lumbering giants.

"Good luck." The outfitter wore a dubious expression on his face. He probably planned to forward my measurements on to the undertaker.

I wondered if I died if I would turn to dust and freak everyone out or if a demon ghost would streak out of my nostrils and possess someone else. I hoped not. If someone like Nathan got these powers, he'd molest every woman in the county.

Coach Burgundy yelled at me the moment I stepped onto the field for practice, shaking me from my thoughts. "Get your ass over here, Case!" The short, stout man brandished a porn 'stache, beer-keg belly, and a large purple-veined nose. How a man of his physique could coach football made no sense. Then again, the football team's one-and-three record didn't exactly scream success.

The offensive coordinator, Coach Wise, lived up to his title, hurling offensive remarks while demonstrating an IQ at odds with his last name. He impolitely urged me to increase the pace of my hell-bound posterior. He was short, fat, and ruddy with a shaved head. I gave him an offended look then trotted over to Coach Burgundy.

"Show us what you got, kid." Burgundy pointed to a long row of tires.

"Do I pick them up?" I asked. A vague memory of having seen these before rattled in the nearly empty football database stored in my brain, but I wasn't sure what the deal was. Maybe I need to roll them somewhere.

Laughter rose from the assembled football players.

"Retard," someone said.

Coach Wise clarified with a little constructive screaming. "You little idiot, you run through them!"

I ran at them. My foot caught on the first one and I smacked face-first onto a tire. Guffaws and loud laughter echoed across the field. My face burned with humiliation. I could beat the tar out of those idiots but I couldn't run across some stupid tires? I stood up, brushed myself off, and started over. This time I took it slower. I focused on my feet. My eyes roved ahead and picked out the pattern. My feet got the message and painstakingly made it the rest of the way through without tripping me up. Still, I'd done it at sub-turtle speed. Coach Wise yelled at me to turn around and come back faster.

I think he just wanted me to bust my butt again. I came back a little faster, almost losing it on a row of larger tires in the middle, but eventually made it. Nathan, huge and intimidating in his uniform stood watching, helmet tucked under his arm. He scowled when I made it across unscathed. His swollen, plum-colored nose sported fewer bandages. I

211

couldn't believe he was practicing. I guess his nose hadn't been broken, just sprained—if that was even a thing.

"Can't wait for blocking practice, Case. I'm gonna show you pain."

I glanced at his nose. "I think you're already showing me pain."

A chorus of disdain and hoots rose from the players. Some of them razzed Nathan while others clearly expected to see me carted to the morgue by the end of practice.

The next exercise consisted of Coach Wise standing atop a contraption with skids on the bottom and large pads on the side. It seemed to belong on a ski slope, not a grassy field. Thankfully, I didn't have to go first this time. I watched players ram their shoulder pads against it, pushing the thing while Coach Wise hurled insults questioning their sexual preferences, parental lineage, and physical strength. If this was what passed for motivational talk in football, it was no wonder jackasses like Nathan abounded.

"Case, Meyers, Riggs, Heyward, get your butts out here," Coach Wise said in his lovely mellifluous voice.

Three other guys trotted out with me. Coach Wise barked out some commands. We lined up. He blew the whistle. We charged the sled. I rammed into it with my shoulder and pushed for all I was worth. Coach Wise blew his whistle like a maniacal traffic cop. I stopped and looked around, confused. We'd pushed the sled about twenty yards. Correction: I'd pushed it. The other three guys were picking themselves up out of the dirt. Apparently, I'd pushed it so fast that they'd fallen flat on their faces.

"What the hell is wrong with you, Case?" Coach Wise said, his entire head glowing scarlet. "You have to time it with the team, you moron."

"Sorry."

We turned the sled around and lined up again. This time I paced myself and gave only a little effort so the others could keep up. After several more inane exercises, Wise divided us into offense and defense. Nathan lined up on the defensive line. His two buddies, Adam and Steve, took positions just behind the line. Apparently they really were linebackers.

Coach Wise lined me up in what I learned was the tight end position. Nathan walked over and said something to the coach. They both sniggered like little kids, whispering back and forth. I knew I wasn't in for a good time. Nobody was lined up directly across from me, but Steve, who hovered just behind the defensive line, graced me with a sneer. Super strength or not, these guys knew what they were doing and they had mass on me. They could cause me some pain if they hit me just right.

We huddled around the quarterback.

"Tight dump on three," he said. He grabbed my practice jersey. "That means you."

"I have to drop a deuce on the count of three?"

"No, you dork. Run out about ten feet and cut straight left. Look for the ball right when you cross the middle."

I remembered seeing a football game where some guy got absolutely clobbered trying to catch a ball across the middle. My future as a target practice dummy became clear. I sighed and took my position.

The quarterback started his call. "Green forty-five! Green forty-five! Hut. Hut. Hut!"

Both lines exploded into action. I hesitated. Jetted forward a few steps. Cut left. Made a mad dash across the middle. My senses spiked. Every color brightened. Every breath and creak of equipment in my ears coordinated sounds with a location. Other players appeared to slow a fraction—or perhaps my perception just sped up.

Adam's cleats kicked up dirt as he rushed me from my left. Nathan turned, eyes locking onto the target, namely, me. Steve approached from behind. The quarterback cocked back the football. His arm catapulted forward. The ball rocketed toward a point feet away where I would meet the football and my body would meet Nathan and friends. According to my calculations, I would catch the ball about a split second before Nathan and Adam pounded me from the front and Steve rammed me from behind.

Fuck it. I'm going in, bitches!

I caught the ball. Lowered my shoulders and clenched my teeth. Plowed into Nathan and Adam. They were heavy guys, dense with muscle, not to mention their bone-filled heads. I was lower to the ground, though, and a hell of a lot stronger. Plus, I was ready for them. It felt like I'd punched through a brick wall, but I came out the other side and ran twenty yards before I tripped over my own feet and plowed a furrow through the grass with my facemask.

I stood up sputtering and digging dirt and grass out of my eyes. I had to take off the helmet to get it all out. I turned to see Nathan flat on his back and Adam rolling around clutching his knee. Coach Wise stared at me with a combination of naked horror and wonderment.

Steve pulled Nathan off the ground. Nathan limped a little, shooting looks of pure hatred at me. Then he and Steve helped Adam off the field and onto the bench.

Coach Wise stormed over to me and grabbed my jersey. He pulled me in for a close-up of his crooked yellow teeth and rotten tobacco breath. Turned his head to the side and spat a dark glob on the ground before glaring at me again. "You ever played football, son?"

"No."

Coach Burgundy spoke with Nathan and Steve. They looked at me. Burgundy grinned and nodded.

Oh, crap.

They lined me up as a running back next. I wasn't sure if I was the half-back, the three-quarters back, or the fullback, but I knew I was going to get the ball. I was supposed to run straight through a hole made by the big guy playing center and the guy to his left. I couldn't remember the position names, but I guessed it didn't really matter. Nathan lined up where the hole would form. Steve crouched right behind him. Adam, sitting on the sideline, had ice on his knee, so at least I didn't have him to worry about.

"You're gonna feel pain, Case," Nathan said. "It's time for the pain train!" He flexed and roared.

The quarterback barked the signs. I saw him turn with the ball. I ran forward and felt the ball thump into my belly. It was a good thing the real running back had told me how to receive the ball or I probably would have just knocked it on the ground.

Again, my senses kicked into hyper-drive. The hole in the line opened, except it wasn't a hole for me to escape through so much as it was a hole for Nathan and Steve to come in and pound me to hamburger. I ran straight at them. This time I put a little arm action into the mix and shoved Nathan away. Steve glanced off my other shoulder, but his hands gripped my jersey. I ran, dragging him behind me for ten yards until another player dove at my legs and knocked them out from underneath me.

Nathan howled in pain, holding his arm. I'd knocked him back a few feet. Steve pushed himself up slowly. He looked dazed. Coach Wise walked over and grabbed me by the facemask. He dragged me over to Coach Burgundy.

"Wise tells me you ain't never played football," Burgundy said. "That true?"

I nodded.

"You juicing, boy?"

I knew this time they weren't asking about orange juice. "You mean steroids? No."

"You gotta pass a drug screening anyway. Go give the nurse some piss and blood."

"Why do I need to pass a drug screening?"

He chuckled. "You want to be a part of the team, don't ya boy?"

"No, not really." My eyes widened in horror. That meant I'd have to see Nathan and his goons every day, not to mention practice football.

"I think if you want to stay in the good graces of the principal, you'll do what I tell you, boy. I think you want to graduate, don't you?"

Coach Wise spit a glob of brown between my shoes. "Now git outta here and give the nurse what he told you to, Case. And have your ass out here for practice tomorrow."

"But—but—" I sputtered, unable to offer a defense. I face-palmed and turned for the locker room. About halfway there I heard footsteps running behind me. I spun, preparing to defend myself, then noticed it was Ash and Nyte.

"That was freaking epic!" Nyte clapped me on the shoulder pad.

Ash shook my hand. "Simply amazing, Justin. I didn't think you had it in you."

"And it's all on video," Nyte said. "Epic!"

"Yay," I said glumly, pumping my fist. "I should've just let them beat the crap out of me."

"Why?" Ash said.

"Because now they want me to take a drug screening so I can play on the team."

"What?" they both asked in unison.

"And if I don't, then they threatened to make things harder on me."

"Oh, man." Ash's nerdy accent drifted a little more Asian than usual. "I wasn't aware they could add you to the team this far into the season."

Nyte snorted. "Dude, this is the South. Football coaches are gods down here."

I went into the locker room and changed clothes. I probably should've showered first, but I wasn't thinking straight. I walked to the nurse's office. She was still there, puttering around and mumbling to herself. She took my blood and then I peed in a cup with a screw-on cap. I worried she might want to grip my privates and make me cough. The last thing I wanted was a little old lady violating me. Thankfully, she did not.

I was famished by the time I got out of there, and not just for food. If the nurse had touched me in my no-no place, I might have lost control and the results would have destroyed my sex drive forever. I shuddered.

Darkness descended as I drove home. The hunger grew, clawing at my stomach and demanding I feed.

"No!" I slammed the steering wheel. A wave of dizziness overcame me. The road blurred. Snapped back into focus. Tail lights flashed feet away. I slammed on the brakes and avoided rear-ending a pickup truck by inches.

I cursed and pulled into the next parking lot I came to. A Chinese buffet beckoned me and my stomach to come hither. But I hungered for more than food and it was driving me out of my mind. This was torture.

My stomach whined again, growling its displeasure with me. "Just normal food," I told it. "No molesting girls."

I wasn't sure it was my stomach that needed talking to.

I ran into the restaurant and piled a plate high with beef and broccoli from the buffet table. It smelled divine. My stomach did the happy dance but my inner demon snarled at the insult. It didn't like being ignored. The waitress who filled my water was old, fat, and had hair

JOHN CORWIN

growing from a wart on her chin. That could be really, really good or really, really bad depending upon just how desperate my soul-sucking tummy wanted energy.

I dug into the food, inhaling it. Eating that much food should have stuffed me. Instead, I felt as hollow and ravenous as ever. The craving felt no different than typical hunger pains, but strange visions appeared before my eyes. Most people, even guys, now had steamy halos of energy floating around their heads or a glowing nimbus drifting like fog around their bodies. The creature within me stirred. I drooled. I wiped my mouth with a napkin and squeezed my eyes shut. I had to get out of there before I did something terrible. Especially if it involved getting it on with another dude or my waitress.

"More water?"

I looked up and stared into the dark liquid eyes of a gorgeous Asian girl. "I—uh..." Pulsating white tendrils streamed from me and latched onto the girl's halo. I knocked my glass off the table as I reached useless hands toward the ghostly tentacles to stop them. It was way too late.

Her eyes grew heavy-lidded. Her pupils dilated, eclipsing brown irises. She dropped the pitcher of water onto the floor where it clattered against the tiles and splashed on her shoes. A brief moment of silence ensued. The restaurant grew still around us. Then she launched herself at me. My self-control shattered. Her soft lips met mine, pressing hard and filled with the desire to consume me. She nipped my lower lip. Giggled. Jumped on me, locking her legs around my waist and peppering me with kisses. Then she got personal. She pulled my T-shirt over my head and kissed my neck. Bit it. Ran her tongue along my earlobe and whispered exactly what she wanted to do to me in my ear.

I swept dishes and Chinese condiments off the table and sat her on top of it while the din of breaking glass and clattering silverware filled the restaurant.

What are you doing? A horrified but tiny voice screamed from somewhere within my head. I pulled back from the girl for a

218

moment. Threads of energy swirled like tiny vortexes from her halo and into me. Her essence glowed bright, welcoming and lustful.

FEED. DEVOUR!

My body strained to resume what it had been doing a moment before, but the sane part of me wondered if I was killing the girl.

SHE IS YOURS!

The malevolent spirit inside me felt just fine with it. In fact, it *wanted* me to do it. *I care!* I didn't want to be an evil demon. Even if I was nothing more than a monster, it didn't mean I had to be a complete jackass about it.

Why do I still care? Elyssa hates me. And the power I have—I should use it! Why shouldn't I experience love and happiness?

But this wasn't happiness and it sure as hell wasn't love. It was pure, simple lust—nothing more. Besides, what if I drained her completely?

Cold water splashed against the side of my face. Another pitcher full of ice water dashed against the cute waitress. I sputtered. She shrieked. My connection to the girl evaporated. My former waitress, the one with a pre-pubescent goatee shouted in Chinese. The girl gave a horrified look at the mess she and I had created and wailed in confusion. Tears filled her big brown eyes.

"I am so sorry!" I held out my hands defensively. "Please, forgive me!"

I threw two hundred dollars on the table and fled. Hopped in my car and screeched out of the parking lot.

"I can have any woman." I sighed. "But all I want is Elyssa."

I took a deep breath before I suffocated from the oppressive maudlin atmosphere. The powers I had were wrecking my life. So far I'd achieved nothing. Every time I'd tried to overpower my oppressors, I only ended up further and further under their control. If I'd just let the beating happen at practice, I'd be done with my punishment. Now I had to join the freaking team.

Using my abilities obviously drained my supernatural energy levels but I had to use them if I wanted to survive football. I couldn't quit football because the principal and his lackeys had me by the short hairs. That meant these cravings would continue. That meant violating more unwitting females.

I couldn't do that. That poor waitress could get fired and it was all my fault. If I didn't figure out a way to fix this, I'd eventually do something terrible and attract the wrong attention. Elyssa had warned me. Stacey had warned me. I was backing myself into a very dangerous corner.

Even worse, football would keep me from finding out what Randy was up to.

My phone beeped with a text message from Ash. It had a link to Facebook and YouTube. I clicked the link and stared in horror.

Nyte had posted clips from football practice. I was there for the world to see, me plowing through two giants like they were packed with feathers. My supernatural abilities were bared to the world.

CHAPTER 21

I couldn't rid myself of the knot dangling like a lead weight from my stomach the next day. I wondered how many people in the school had seen Nyte's video and put the pieces together even though Nyte thankfully left out names and his account wasn't associated with his true identity. No telling how many people Nyte had shown it to. Just what I needed: a video showing my inhuman strength.

Where in the hell were my parents when I needed them the most? Dad had never returned after I saw him Friday. He had no idea the kind of pain I'd gone through with Elyssa, or the football shit storm I had to deal with now. I was genuinely worried about Mom, and just getting pissed at dad.

Pissed!

That thought segued into another shock of realization. I had given a urine and blood sample to the nurse yesterday. What if I really wasn't human? What kind of results would the lab return?

Oh my God.

This was trouble. I had to swap those samples with someone else's.

Maybe I could talk Ash or Nyte into giving up some bodily fluids for my sake. I'd have to lie and tell them I was on steroids or purple drank.

I skipped the gymnasium and rushed to the nurse's office. The little old lady wasn't there. Instead, an oxymoron gazed sleepily at me.

"Yeah?" said the male nurse. He was a tall, heavy-set guy with tiny eyes and a blimp for a head. I couldn't understand how anyone in the health-care industry would let themselves go like that. He had to be pushing three-hundred pounds.

"I left some, uh, fluid samples here yesterday, and I was wondering if they were still here."

"Nah. Nurse Godwin took all that to the lab this morning. She'll be back soon with the results, so I wouldn't sweat it."

Sweat broke out on my forehead. "Where is this lab?" My voice rose into a panicked squeak.

His eyes narrowed. "Something you're worried about?"

My mind grasped frantically for some excuse. "I ate powdered bull testi-cle, and someone told me it would jack up my testosterone levels. I'm afraid it might show up bad on my test."

His eyes relaxed and he laughed. "Those homeopathic remedies are so fake, dude. You don't have a thing to worry about. Besides, they started the drug screening tests at six this morning so they're probably already done."

I bit back a string of inventive curses but tucked them in cranial storage in case the need for such atrocities ever arose again. I left the office. Instead of going to the gymnasium where trouble always found me, I snuck into my homeroom class and sat very still, hoping Mr. Herman wouldn't look up from the large mural of Sonny and Cher he painted on the wall. He turned his head, as if pure animal instinct warned him. I was, I realized with a jolt, a predator in every sense of the word. True, I didn't prey on men. Although I had fed on those guys in the bathroom.

It had just been laughter, though, no kissing. Surely that didn't put my sexual preferences into question, did it? I shuddered.

"Thank you," he said, then turned back to painting.

"For what?"

"For laying out that punk Nathan Spelman. I can't tell that inbred gorilla to do anything. He's got the collective head of the administration up his fat ass."

"Laying him out?"

He chuckled. "I saw the video. I was watching a Deep Purple video when a colleague sent me the link."

Oh no. Nyte, I'm going to kill you.

I started sweating again. "How did you know it was me?"

He put down the paintbrush and turned to look at me again. "The faculty knows about your punishment. Those idiots in the main office can't keep anything a secret from us. I figured you'd be in crutches next time I saw you."

"Is there anything I can do to stop them from making me play football?"

"This is the South, kid. It isn't progressive California or the Great White North where basketball is king. These good old boys have got you by your young boys whether you like it or not."

"Can you teachers help me?"

He snorted. "Why? After what I saw, you have nothing to be afraid of."

Except I did. If Elyssa was right, I had plenty to worry about. And what if I accidentally killed someone?

I received a lot of curious looks and stares during the day. I wanted to wear a paper sack over my head so people wouldn't know it was me. After English class, Mr. Turpin waved me over to his desk. I wondered if he was going to give me more useless advice about making sure to knock down big people before beating the crap out of them or ask me strange questions.

He leaned back in his chair and said, "You seem to be a natural at football, Mr. Case. I saw the videos and must say, I'm impressed."

Elyssa had been right. What a horrible mistake this was turning out to be. "I really overdid the energy drinks. All that caffeine and sugar, you know."

An amused smile crept across his face. "I'm sure. It appears this football season will be far more interesting than I'd anticipated. Perhaps Nathan and his friends will learn that you're not such easy pickings after all."

"I really don't want to play," I said. "In fact, I'd just as soon quit."

"Actions have consequences, Mr. Case." His eyes seemed to judge my reactions. "In the grand scheme of things, this is rather insignificant. You can learn and move on."

Mr. Turpin was just chock-full of advice lately. "I don't know about moving on. I feel kind of trapped."

"Trapped? Oh, yes." He chuckled. "Unfortunately, it appears that our good Coach Burgundy has a vested interest in keeping you on the team."

"So I've heard."

His smile vanished as he leaned forward. "There are ways to fix such problems, however."

Something in his face made my blood run cold and I wondered if a few wires had been knocked loose in his boxing days, or maybe short-circuited something essential. Surely this guy wasn't suggesting I do terrible things, was he? "What do you mean?"

His eyes narrowed and he pursed his lips for a moment. "I'm sure you'll do what you need to do, Mr. Case. Good luck to you."

"What does that mean?" I asked.

He twirled a pencil between his fingers in a way that reminded me uncomfortably of Elyssa's prowess with a dagger. "People become very different animals when backed into a corner. I wonder, what sort of animal will you become?"

That was a damned good question—one that I had no answer to. "A teddy bear?"

Turpin flicked the pencil. It shot straight up and stuck into the ceiling to join six others above his desk. "We shall see."

I gulped and went to my next class. *I'm beginning to think I'm the only normal person at this school.* The administration was the good-old boy mafia. Mr. Herman and god only knew how many other teachers wanted me to beat the snot out of Nathan. Mr. Turpin wanted to see me cornered just to see how I'd react. Elyssa might want me dead.

"Yep, I'm screwed."

At lunchtime, I hurried to the cafeteria and shoveled my home-cooked stir-fry down my throat. By the time Ash and Nyte arrived at the table, I was getting up to leave.

"Where are you going?" Ash asked.

"I gotta study. Didn't have time last night." I waved goodbye and headed out to my real mission. Since I wouldn't have time to stalk Randy after school, I prowled the bathrooms in the hopes I might discover more about his supernatural steroid serum.

I finally heard his voice echoing from within the bathroom closest to the gym.

"Not yet. Soon," he said.

"Damn, Randy, we've been waiting a week on the new V," an unfamiliar voice replied.

"Can't help it. You'll be the first to know when it's out," Randy replied.

"Is the new batch of V really as good as you say?" another voice asked.

"Maybe better." Randy chuckled. "I sourced some new ingredients. Anyway, I gotta go."

I slipped around the corner and peered at the bathroom exit. Two bro-meisters trudged out in oversized jeans and baseball jerseys. Randy emerged nearly a minute later and headed toward the gym. He veered left into the service corridor where Brad had confronted him the day before. I waited until he vanished inside then counted to twenty to give him plenty of time to get where he was going before I went in. Just as I began my approach, Elyssa stalked past the gym, peered into the crusted windows on the door leading into the service corridor. I ducked back into cover and peeked at her just as she slipped inside.

What's she doing trailing my perp?

Apparently, she'd connected the dots from Affliction Dude to Randy. I crept up to the door and opened it just enough to slide inside. The background hum of the HVAC system covered my footsteps, but it also muffled the conversation coming from ahead. I reached the corner and peered around it.

Randy sat in a worn vinyl chair, legs crossed, a cocky expression on his face. Elyssa stood opposite him, face grim.

"...would do a much better job," she said. "Why do you think I got kicked out of my last school?"

"Because you sucked?" Randy said. "I don't want failures working for me."

"I didn't get caught. The other dealers got pissed and drove me out." Elyssa shrugged. "If you want distribution, I can do it. Women want V as much as the guys."

My heart froze. Eyelids fluttered. I felt dizzy. *Elyssa wants to work with Randy?* Here I thought I was the bad guy, the one playing with people's emotions. Instead, it was the girl I thought I loved.

I couldn't breathe. I just wanted to run out as fast as I could, but instead watched in horror as Elyssa worked a deal with Randy.

"Well, we do need girls on the inside," Randy said. "But you gotta take the V if you wanna deal the V. Comprende?"

"Deal. But I won't be your guniea pig. I need the good batch, not this half-assed shit you've been peddling." Elyssa leaned against a support beam, eyes narrowed. "I still have connections at other schools too."

Randy rubbed his hands together and grinned. "Awesome. In that case, I'll try to get you in on our next meeting with the big guy."

"When's that?" Elyssa said.

"Depends." Randy shrugged. "They're testing a new ingredient. If it works out, I gotta source it. I'm working that angle now."

"What new ingredient?" Elyssa pursed her lips. "You guys aren't newbs. Why add something new to the mix now?"

"Because it's the missing link." Randy's lips flattened. "I'm sure of it." He shrugged. "Anyway, keep an ear out. I'll text you when it's time. Probably this weekend or early next week, is what I hope."

Elyssa pushed off the wall. Nodded. "I hope V is everything you promised, or the deal's off. Got it?"

Randy backhanded the air. "Yeah, whatever."

Elyssa started walking my way so I tiptoed as fast as possible to the exit and skirted into the shop classroom. Heart aching, I watched her exit the service corridor and vanish from sight.

My ex-girlfriend, the drug dealer.

AFTER SCHOOL LET OUT, I trudged down to football practice. Thunder pealed in the dark sky, followed shortly by rain. It perfectly complemented my mood. Elyssa wanted to work for Randy. That meant my plans for taking him down wouldn't change her mind about me. It would just piss her off. Had she ever loved me? Had it all been a ploy?

Even drug dealers fall in love. If Elyssa was truly a criminal, what did it say about my type of supernatural that she considered me the monster? On the other hand, she didn't seem to know that my blood was probably the new ingredient Randy wanted. If I found out she'd gotten close to me just to take my blood, that would've crushed me—again.

Knowing what I did, I should've hated Elyssa for what she put me through, that self-righteous hypocrite! But no. My heart still yearned for her. All I wanted was my little drug queen back in my arms.

God, I'm pathetic.

I changed into my gear and headed to the practice fields. A couple of players I didn't know gave me grudging nods of respect—or maybe it was fear—as I approached. Nathan and his bunch glared at me.

So what else is new?

After pushups, sit-ups, jumping jacks, and something they called burpees—which had nothing to do with burping—we had to run the tire gauntlet, push the sled, wash, rinse, repeat the same stuff from the day before. Afterward, they put me in as a running back.

Bryan, the quarterback, grabbed my jersey in the huddle. "I don't know why the hell they're putting you in this position. You don't know a thing about football."

I jerked his hand loose and looked at the mix of concerned and angry expressions in the huddle. "I don't have a choice. I'm stuck with you and you're stuck with me." But I had an idea to unstick me from this mess.

I got the ball on the first play, of course. Nathan lunged at me. I let him take me out. He rammed me into the ground. It hurt, but not as bad as I'd feared. I still gave everyone a good show, limping back to the huddle. The next play took me right into Steve's arms. He roared in triumph as he picked me up and slammed me bodily to the mud, pumping his fists and laughing. Nathan gave him a high-five and kicked a clod of dirt on my jersey while I got up. Three plays and three painful tackles later, Coach Burgundy called me over to the sideline. Finally. An end to the madness.

"You ain't a bad actor, boy," he said with a grin. "But this ain't the Glee Club and you ain't fooling nobody 'cept them idiots out there."

"I just got lucky yesterday." I shrugged. "My powdered bull testicle supplement wore off."

"I don't think so, boy." He shoveled a fat pinch of tobacco into his mouth. "I think you don't want to play." He spat and looked out at the players. "Them's some good kids out there. You may have the strength, but far as I'm concerned you're just a piece of cowardly trash compared to them."

"Thanks for the encouragement, sir," I said with every ounce of sarcasm in my body.

"I'll tell you something else, boy. I don't care how you feel about playing. If you don't straighten up and fly right, then your grades will suffer."

"You'd force teachers to fail me if I don't play? You can't get away with that."

"You think I can't? I own this school, boy."

"You don't own all the teachers. There's no way they'd go along with you."

Burgundy crossed stubby arms and smirked. "Why don't you just test that little theory of yours and see what happens?"

From what Mr. Herman had told me in homeroom that morning, the teachers wouldn't lift a finger to help me if it meant protecting their jobs. "Fine, fail me then. I'll just move to another school."

"Maybe *you* can. But can your friends?" He hawked and spat a glob between my shoes.

My mouth fell open. Who did this fat turd think he was? God, obviously. I wished I had a recorder on me. I would nail him to the wall. Surely the cops would do something about it if nobody else would. At that moment, however, I had no choice but to comply. I would bide my time and revisit this conversation with him tomorrow, only then I would bring a recorder.

"Fine. But leave my friends out of this."

He slapped me on the butt. "Atta boy. Now get back out there."

"What's the matter?" Nathan asked in a whiney, mocking voice as I rejoined the team on the field. "Coach finally see you ain't worth crap?"

I ignored him and the shoulder bump from Steve as I passed through the defensive line and back to the offensive huddle.

Bryan sighed and shook his head. "Bulldozer left." Yet another variation on the same play we'd repeated so Nathan and buddies could pound me into the dirt. I could tell he was getting as sick of it as I was, but Coach Wise hollered the plays from the sidelines like a crazed hillbilly drunk off his ass on moonshine.

I looked back at Coach Burgundy and snarled behind the facemask. I looked at Nathan. He bared his teeth like a chimp. I wasn't sure who I hated the most right then, Coach Burgundy, Nathan, or myself.

I got the ball. I smashed past Nathan, but pulled my punches so it wouldn't look too spectacular. I dodged left to avoid a lunging Steve, and then sprinted, only to trip over my own feet. Heaven help me if the coach thought I was faking that. I pounded the dirt with my fist only to have the breath pounded out of me as Adam and Steve piled on.

"Enough of that," Coach Wise said in his usual quiet manner, veins pulsing in his forehead like blue fire hoses ready to burst.

Bryan helped me up. "How can you be so good one minute then clumsy the next?"

I shrugged. "I've never been very athletic. Not unless you count fencing."

"You made fences?"

I groaned.

After practice I sat in my car and stared out at the dark, empty parking lot. Thoughts of Elyssa and her betrayal swirled in my head. Then again, she hadn't exactly betrayed me. I'd thought she was a good person—a hero of the mysterious Overworld. Instead, she'd turned out to be a criminal.

Or had she?

I face-palmed. What if she was just playing Randy so she could get close to Affliction Dude? Maybe it was all a ploy and I'd just overreacted.

I wanted that to be the truth so badly, I refused to even think about the alternative—that she was a lying scumbag.

I had other, more immediate issues to deal with. After using so much energy at football practice, the ravenous hunger had returned. No matter how hard I tried, I couldn't ignore it. I had no choice but to feed.

I went to a restaurant and found a cute girl headed for the bathroom. Between the men and women's restrooms was a family bathroom with a lock on the door.

"Hi." I let the demonic hunger control the vaporous sex-seeking tendrils.

The girl gave me a look. "What the fuck do you want, creeper?"

Her words knocked me back a step. "Well that escalated quickly. I just said hi."

"Yeah, while I'm going to the bathroom? Leave me alone, creep."

I latched on to her halo. She stopped dead in her tracks, lust filling her eyes. I opened the family bathroom door and ushered her inside. Straining against the desire to ravish this mean girl, I let the energy flow into me even as I fended off her kisses. Carnal lust drew me to swift arousal. My hand reached for her leg.

Control, damn it! What would Elyssa think?

Her violet eyes and raven hair filled my mind. Pain filled my heart. The girl burst into tears and the energy soured. At least the hunger was gone for now.

When I got home, I looked in the garage for Dad's bike. He still wasn't back. His promise of answers on Saturday had been a lie and I was furious with him. Where was Mom? Why was he hiring PIs to find the Conroys? For all I knew they were both dead, dragged to the bottom of a lake by cement galoshes.

I was so pissed with them and so frightened for them, I could hardly sleep. I called Dad's cell ten times in a row and texted him a small essay.

Answer me, you son of a bitch! Where are you?

I TRIED to keep tabs on Elyssa at school the next day, but she didn't meet with Randy—at least not that I saw. As for my arch nemesis, he vanished after lunch and didn't come back. I even wondered if he was actually taking classes and asked around. None of the teachers I asked knew of him. Then again, I couldn't ask every last one of them.

Later at practice I saw Nyte, Ash, and a handful of students sitting in the bleachers.

Wow, my very own fan club.

I waved at my friends then looked for Coach Burgundy. The sheriff and two deputies huddled in a group with him. *How convenient.* I'd hidden an MP3 recorder in my pants, intent on capturing incriminating evidence. He waved me over.

"Here's that boy I told you about." Burgundy slapped me on the back.

"He don't look like much." The sheriff sized me up with his eyes. "You sure he's up to it?"

"Don't let his size fool ya, Roscoe. This boy's the real deal." He slapped the sheriff on the shoulder.

Roscoe looked me over like a prize coonhound before nodding. "We got a lot riding on this, boy, so don't let us down."

My brilliant idea of recording the coach fizzled like a cigarette in a urinal. If he and the sheriff were in cahoots, who else was in his pocket? As if to answer that question, the local city police chief strolled over, a grin on his rugged face. He towered over the Sherriff, tall and broad-shouldered. He slapped Roscoe on the back and shook hands with Coach Burgundy. I turned and scooted away, my tail between my legs.

Despite its location in metro Atlanta, the good-old-boys club was strong as ever in Decatur. The only authorities I could go to at this point might be the GBI or the FBI. I wouldn't have been a bit surprised to see representatives from those agencies show up and give Coach Burgundy a grin and a slap on his fat ass.

After the usual warm-ups, I endured practice handoffs without a defensive line to counter me for half an hour.

"Why do we keep running the same drill over and over and over?" I asked Bryan.

"Repetition helps muscle memory. Your body will know exactly how to respond to a play under pressure."

I wished it helped my brain memory too. I felt like such an idiot for getting myself in deeper and deeper with every move I made.

Soon the defensive line joined the offense for practice. Nathan and his buddies overloaded the left side which, as they knew, was my destination.

"C'mon, Nathan. Let's do real practice," Bryan said when he walked to stand behind the center.

Nathan sneered. "Shut it, Jones. I'll do what I want."

Bryan sighed and barked the call. I took the ball, noticing that my body did indeed know how to receive it better after all that repetition. I decided at the last second that plowing through three huge guys would look way too suspicious, so I squirted around them and to the outside. The safety dove for me as I ran into the end zone. Coach Wise whistled the play to stop.

I turned in time to see Nathan hurtling toward me, murder in his eyes. At the last second, I stepped aside and tripped him. He rumbled, bumbled, stumbled, and face-planted in a mud puddle with a loud splat. The handful of students in the bleachers cheered. I turned to them and flourished a deep bow. Coach Wise whistled until I thought he was going to pop an artery and spray-paint the field.

"Spelman, you cut that out right now, boy. Practice like you know you should."

Nathan pushed himself up, mud dripping down his face and practice jersey. He looked like he wanted to kill us both. Nathan stopped short of murder and instead shot me a glare that might have caused a bowel evacuation in the prior version of me. Instead, my bowels ignored him. I tossed the ball to Coach Wise and was about to turn away from the small crowd when I noticed two figures seated at the top corner of the bleachers, well away from everyone else.

They wore black hoodies pulled over their heads, jeans, and gloves. Large sunglasses covered their eyes but I saw hints of pale skin. They looked to be in their twenties at least. Definitely not high school students. Definitely nobody I knew. I caught myself staring and turned away quickly.

Were those the people Elyssa had warned me about? Were they vampire buddies of Randy's? Sick dread formed ice in my chest. I had to be careful. Very careful.

Before practice ended, the crowd of onlookers doubled in size. Nerds, cheerleaders, and people I had never seen before showed up to watch the Nathan versus Justin show. At least that's what Nyte and Ash called it. They'd taken down the videos after I begged them, but it didn't mean others weren't posting their own. I toned down my performance enough so hopefully people wouldn't wonder. But I couldn't overdo it or Burgundy would complain and threaten me again.

I watched the hoodie people from the corner of my eye. By the time practice ended, they had vanished. But that didn't mean they weren't watching me. My teeth chattered despite the sweat pouring down my face.

"I got you on the roster for the game tomorrow," Coach Burgundy told me after practice. "You rest up and eat a good supper. I want you at your best for the game."

Relief settled over me. I had almost forgotten about the blood sample I'd given the nurse. Since the FBI and a dozen other federal agencies weren't converging on me right this minute, maybe they'd discovered nothing unusual in my fluids.

"Yes sir," I said. It was all I ever said to him these days. He owned me and he knew it.

I left practice and decided where I would go to "eat". No matter how carefully I conserved my supernatural energy, my inner demon wanted to feast. If this kept up, I'd have to choose a different place to feed every night to stay off the supernatural radar. A mall, a restaurant, a library— it didn't matter.

At least now I had an emergency stop button. One thought of Elyssa was all it took to destroy my mood.

I *hated* it. On the one hand, I wanted sex so badly that my "boys" seemed ready to explode. On the other hand, every time I kissed a girl I felt like I betrayed Elyssa. I saw her face and smelled her hair when I closed my eyes. My soul was with her, not the strangers whose essence kept me sane.

Unfortunately, football doomed me to a depressing future.

CHAPTER 22

I t was almost midnight when I got home that night. I'd driven all the way to the west side of town to avoid shitting too close to where I lived.

"You are becoming quite the predator, my little lamb," said Stacey as she dropped lithely from a tree in the front yard of my home.

I squeaked and jumped three feet off the ground. "Can I just give you my cell number? Please?" I put a hand to my heart. "You're going to give me a heart attack." For a split second I'd actually thought she might be one of the anonymous watchers from football practice.

She laughed and stalked toward me, the light from a nearby streetlamp glinting off her reflective eyes. "I will give you free advice, my sweet. Do not spread out your attentions too widely. It makes you far more noticeable."

"You gotta be kitten me." I winked. "I'll be more careful." I tried to put on a brave face, but her warning set off alarms in my head. I was walking a minefield without a metal detector. Those ivory-skinned peeps with the hoodies might be the very mines she was talking about. It was only a matter of time before I triggered one.

"You are too adorable, my love. I imagine quite soon you will see the error of your ways and come to me." She snuggled up to my chest and purred.

I sighed and wondered why the cute ones also had to be psychotic. Her head jerked up suddenly, and she sniffed the air like an animal sensing danger. She hissed and a claw dug into my back. I yelped and leapt away from her, muscles tensed and ready for danger.

"What is it?"

She didn't answer me. Her amber eyes gleamed with feral wariness. I also noticed her fingernails had extended into three-inch claws. Maybe I'd triggered one of those mines she'd told me about after all. She sprinted away, her legs a blur.

I looked around the immediate vicinity for a threat but sensed nothing. Whatever it was could wait. I charged after my pesky stalker. Running and dodging over roots, curbs, rocks, banana peels, and all of the little things that make running at super-speed super perilous came a lot easier.

I couldn't believe how much I'd improved. *Must be all the football practice.* My mind communicated faster with my legs, spotting obstacles farther away. My arms chugged back and forth, aiding my balance around sharp turns.

Stacey leapt over a six-foot wooden fence. I cleared it with a single bound, but a low-hanging branch on the other side nearly took off my head. She ran through the back yard and vaulted a swimming pool, flipped in mid-air and rolled sideways over the fence. I jumped, but my timing was off. My left foot splashed cold water when I landed, but my right foot somehow caught the edge. I shook it off. Hopped over the fence and into another backyard. A dog nipped at my heels as I pursued Stacey over a chain-link fence and into yet another yard.

We zigged through residential streets and zagged through old closed-down office parks. My wet shoe squished in a staccato rhythm until the speed dried it out a bit. She increased her pace, zooming, down a road where abandoned buildings and decrepit houses loomed. I recognized Scottdale, a derelict town to the east of Atlanta.

I sped up. My feet drummed against the pavement. Wind whistled past my ears. Stacey ran down a road crumbling asphalt road lined with dilapidated brick buildings. She bolted left and sprinted several feet up the side of a red-brick warehouse, pushed off from the wall to catch the window ledge of a neighboring warehouse. Without pausing, she bounced from the ledge up to the roof of the other building and disappeared. I groaned. Football hadn't taught me a thing about urban bouldering.

I ran up the side of the building. It was much easier than I'd expected, centrifugal force lending false gravity against the brick. I turned and leapt for the window ledge. Instead of grabbing it, however, I plowed through the boarded-over window and slammed head-first into a metal railing on the other side. It rang like a gong.

The pitch black room blinded me. A blue-tinted light flickered off and on. I caught glimpses of worn bricks, rusty metal railing, and a long drop to broken concrete. It took me a moment to realize the light wasn't from an external source—apparently I now had night vision. It wasn't up to the challenge and went out, plunging me back into darkness.

I stood, a bit woozy from the impact. Something rustled below in the darkness. Something hissed—or did it scrape? I couldn't be sure. There was a loud thump. The metal catwalk shuddered and groaned. Two glowing yellow orbs appeared ten feet away. My breathing faltered. I felt a serious need to soil myself. Whatever the thing was sniffed the air with what sounded like a huge snout.

I decided not to wait to find out what it was. I dove out the window, sheer panic giving me flight. I grabbed onto the roof of the opposite warehouse and pulled myself up. The moon was dim, but a shadowy form appeared in the window where I'd been. It sniffed the air. I stood still, hardly daring to breathe. Could it see me? What was it? Had I shit my underwear?

I felt certain of one thing: Stacey lived nearby, possibly in one of these abandoned buildings. I no longer had the desire to stick around and find out. But I wasn't exactly sure which way was home. A deep mewling preceded a loud thud as the creature landed on the roof next to me. Glowing eyes met mine. It was a house cat. Correction: a *gigantic* house cat. Bony armor-like protrusions ran along its spine. Saber-toothed fangs protruded from its muzzle. Thick, sinewy muscle coiled beneath bristly fur.

Holy shit, did He-Man lose Battle Cat?

Any other time I would have thought it looked pretty badass. This time, however, I squeaked, backing up until a brick chimney checked my retreat. Not good.

The cat hissed and sliced the air with razor-sharp claws the size of sabers. I dodged left just in time to avoid being sliced into salami. The chimney crumbled to pieces from the force of the blow. I grabbed an old two-by-four from the roof and held it like a sword in front of me. The cat swatted it and shaved a foot off the length. I gulped. It lunged. I jumped to the side and brought the board down hard on the cat's head. The board splintered and the monster kitty howled in pain. It lunged for me in a graceful, terrifying surge of death. My foot caught on an exhaust vent and my back slammed against the roof. The creature pinned my chest with one large padded foot. Its claws extended just enough to prick my skin. If it extended them any further, they would skewer my heart. Of course it could always chomp off my head too.

I pushed against the tiger-sized paw. It didn't budge. The cat sniffed me. I bunched my legs, bracing them against the cat's stomach. Before I could heave, it batted me with its other paw, knocking me momentarily senseless. It opened its mouth wide, revealing jagged rows of ivory stilettos set against its fangs. This was it. The bite that would end it all.

A shadowy figure blurred past. Silver flashed. The cat's eyes widened. It

239

made a brief yowling noise that turned to a gurgle. Then its large head dangled to the side, hanging by a vine of muscle and thudded against the roof, narrowly missing my head. Its legs went limp and the body crashed atop me, knocking the wind from my lungs. Gouts of blood poured onto my face. I sputtered and wiggled desperately. Somehow, I managed to get enough leverage to push the carcass off my chest. I scooped blood off my face and out of my eyes. I pulled off my shirt. The front was sodden with scarlet, but the back was relatively untouched, so I used it to wipe off my face. I tossed the shirt aside and looked for my savior.

Nobody was there.

I sniffed the air, trying to use my enhanced senses to pick up on something. All I smelled was the coppery odor of fresh blood. Then I threw up. After I threw up, I laughed and sobbed. It seemed an impossible juxtaposition. I shook from fright, but happiness at my continued existence gave a manic tinge to my laughter.

"Thanks!" I said in a conversational tone. I hoped for some response, but none came.

After getting my bearings, I set off for home. It took longer because I stuck to the roads. I'd had enough of leaping over fences for the night. I trashed my bloody clothes and got in the shower. Rivulets of hot water relaxed my muscles, scarlet with cat blood. As I dried off after the shower, I studied my body in the mirror and realized the pudginess on my belly was almost gone. My arms boasted slightly more muscle than a week ago. My legs had bulked up. Unfortunately most of my new jeans now ended above my ankles and my belts wouldn't go any tighter—they had run out of notches. I was growing up rather than out, as my old body had done.

Thoughts of my mysterious savior troubled me. I had no complaints about my rescue, but who or what had killed that huge feline? Had they been in the neighborhood already or were they following me? Even my new muscles and strength had been no match for that oversized alley cat. Surely, whoever it was wanted me alive because they could have killed me along with the creature. I had too many mysteries competing for space in my overwhelmed brain.

If only I could grow smarter, now that would be something.

I tossed another pair of jeans I'd outgrown into a pile on the floor. It looked like Elyssa, Renaldo, and I would need to make another trip to the mall. Except...Elyssa had left me. The agony of loss stabbed my heart. I bit back a sob and lay down in bed. I wanted to forget her. To forget this pain. I didn't want to be in love with her. My heart didn't care what I wanted. It still beat for her. It still longed for her embrace and the feel of her soft curves pressed to my body. I saw Elyssa's smile, her lips, her violet eyes shining with desire.

A line of women, complete strangers, waited to fulfill my hungry future. But they would never, *could* never be who I needed. Who I wanted. The girl who filled the Elyssa-sized hole in my heart.

Damn, I miss you.

PEOPLE I HAD NEVER SPOKEN to in my short life came up and slapped me on the back, shook my hand, or gave me the brofist when I walked into school Friday morning. My ass was dragging thanks to the late-night jaunt after Stacey and the supernatural fuel tank was running low.

"Good luck at the game tonight," said one dude.

Adam Gosling and his group of nerdlings came by my seat in the gymnasium. "Here's a video with our assessment of your strengths and weaknesses according to your practice sessions." He handed me a flash drive. "Please beat the crap out of Lanier High."

"Why do you care about football?" I asked him. Adam had the muscula-ture of a toothpick with an oversized olive-shaped head balanced atop it and glasses that made my old bottle-bottom ones look thin in comparison. Fat or thin, most of his squad had "nerd" written all over them. Then again, I would have fit right in not too long ago.

"Gerald Ledbetter, my arch nemesis, goes to Lanier High. He won the state science fair last year, narrowly defeating my genetically modified potato battery. It's a matter of pride."

"But this is football, not science."

He shrugged. "It would make me feel better. His older brother, Marty, is their quarterback and Gerald won't shut up about him."

"Oh. Well, I'll do my best." I looked at the flash drive he'd given me. "Thanks for this. I'll check it out."

"You're a true inspiration, Justin." Randy looked me up and down. "You've gone from corpulent to athletic and improved yourself measurably." He gestured at the nerd herd behind him. "We're all going to the gym and eating more responsibly now." One of the chubbier guys in his group stuffed a Twinkie in his mouth about the same time Randy finished that announcement. Randy sighed. "Except for Theodore. I'm afraid he's a lost cause no matter what."

I was touched by this, but didn't know what to say. If ever an after-school moment had presented itself, this was it. Instead, I said, "Kick ass." *Wisdom and insight. I have it all.*

Randy and group cheered.

Something drew my eye to the door at the far end of the gymnasium. Elyssa stood there watching as people came by to wish me good luck, give me cookies, and one girl even gave me a pair of panties. I grimaced and hoped they were clean.

I looked at Elyssa. She stared back at me. I wondered if that was longing in her eyes or wariness. I could make out every detail of her fair-skinned beauty with my enhanced eyesight. I traced the line of her jaw and longed to smooth back the stray raven-black lock against her cheek. I wanted so badly to run over, hug her, and feel her melt against me. If only for an instant. Her attention meant more to me than the circus my life had become.

Even if she is a drug dealer.

"You okay?" Ash shoved yet more of my gifts into his now-bulging backpack.

"No. I'm not."

He followed my gaze and saw Elyssa. "Oh, man." He patted my back. "That sucks. I really wish you two could work things out."

"I don't think it's going to happen."

Nyte sighed. "Why can't life be like the *Princess Bride*? I would climb the Cliffs of Insanity for a girl like Buttercup."

I gave him a look of disbelief. "You like the *Princess Bride*?"

"Best movie ever," Ash said.

Nyte nodded. "Real life sucks."

I looked at Elyssa again and swallowed the knot in my throat. "Yeah. Pretty much."

Even homeroom had become more bearable as news of my football feats spread.

"You're looking great, Justin." Annie touched my bicep and sighed. "Who'd have thought you'd be any good at sports?"

"Are you on steroids?" Jenny asked.

I glared at them. "Seriously? You two are my friends all of a sudden?"

"We've always been your friends." Jenny's eyes grew wide and innocent.

"What?" I sputtered.

"Don't get yourself worked up." Annie patted my back. "You need to conserve your energy for the game."

I rolled my eyes, turned around, and pulled out some homework I needed to finish. I'd received offers from several of the nerd herd to help me catch up with my school assignments, but I'd turned them down. Completed work did me no good if I hadn't done it myself. I might stink with women, but maybe I could still get into MIT where I could seduce all the nerdy girls I wanted.

My stomach growled with desire and not for the first time that morning. My pursuit of Stacey and narrow escape from the huge cat last night had left my beast famished but I'd been too tired and depressed to hunt another victim. After seeing the way Elyssa had looked at me this morning, I decided I didn't want to refill that soul-sucking reservoir. I didn't want football. I didn't want fame. I didn't want all the fake friendships my peers had to offer.

I just wanted her.

I could hardly concentrate on my homework between my insides aching and thoughts of the girl I loved. I wondered if she really did love me. She'd practically admitted she did—or had—loved me. But I was slowly becoming the monster she feared. Especially after all the things I'd done to sate the raging beast inside me. Most guys would think I was crazy for not whoring it up with every hot chick I came across. I would trade it all for the girl with the violet eyes.

The school held a pep rally right after lunch.

The fun just never stops.

After all the nonsense was done, I quickly changed back into my street clothes from the new football jersey which reeked of fresh vinyl. Students filed out of the gym. I chased Elyssa down the hallway and grabbed her arm. She tried to pull away, but I held on and dragged her into an empty projector room. She took my thumb and bent it to the side. Pain lanced up my arm. I yelped and jerked it away.

"You're so damned mean," I said.

She shoved me against the wall and backed up a step. "How many times do I have to tell you to leave me alone?"

I wanted to confront her about her dealings with Randy, but none of that mattered to me. She could be the drug queen of Atlanta and I'd forgive her, if only she'd take me back.

"You love me and I know it," I growled. "I've seen you looking at me."

She snorted. "Oh yeah? That's all you've got? Pathetic."

"I can't stop thinking about you. You're all that keeps me sane."

She slapped me. My ears rang and I staggered back. "Leave. Me. Alone. I don't know how much clearer I can make it. You are demon spawn. Do not touch me again."

I lunged and tried to kiss her. My lips met hers about the same time her knee met my stomach. I went down in a heap, groaning and gasping for breath. She knelt beside me.

"Are you okay?"

I tried to laugh, but it hurt too much. "No, I'm not."

"Good," she said. "Maybe your felycan girlfriend can kiss it all better."

Before I could ask her what that was, she disappeared. Thanks to all the research on the supernatural, it didn't take long to piece it together. Werewolves were also called lycans. It wasn't too much of a stretch to call feline shifters felycans. Before I could be happy about solving that minor puzzle, it hit me.

Elyssa knew about Stacey.

CHAPTER 23

"Damn, Justin, you've gone from zero to hero." Randy leaned over me.

I sprang to my feet quick as a cat. "Just when I thought you'd stopped bothering me." I briefly considered asking him about Elyssa, but reconsidered. I didn't know if she was for real or faking it with the drug dealing.

"Busy with the boss." Randy shrugged. "I'm here with a business proposition."

"Business with a vampire?" I narrowed my eyes.

Randy leaned against the wall and folded his thin arms. "Your blood is primo—even better than expected. I don't like beating it out of you, Justin. It's just counterproductive, you know?" He smirked. "I'd rather you gave me some willingly every week. In trade, you'd get a thousand dollars."

"What, exactly, would my blood be used for? Making your drug?"

"Helping people." Randy gave a double thumbs-up. "We're working on something that will change the world, but it needs a little more oomph. Your blood gives it that."

"Somehow, I find that hard to believe." I crossed my arms and mimicked his stance. "In fact, I've learned enough about the Overworld, that I suspect what you're doing is illegal."

"No." Randy pushed off the wall. "It's legal, and you can be a part of it." He stepped outside. Stopped. "Pro tip, Justin—take the deal. You'll be happier you did."

I did not like the way that sounded.

I had to stop Randy's criminal enterprise. It wasn't about proving anything to Elyssa anymore. It was about protecting the other kids in my high school. God only knew what that supernatural blood-enhanced serum of his would do to normal kids. I wondered what effects the other batches had. I just hoped I could pull it off. The thought of fighting vampires scared the hell out of me.

I'd gone from mega-nerd to super-stud in the eyes of my classmates, but beneath the water, my legs churned uselessly. I was a duck swimming against a raging river, narrowly avoiding the rocks. In the end, I'd go over the waterfall and end up broken at the bottom.

Or, I could just flap my little duck wings and fly away.

Damn. Even ducks had better options than me.

After my next class, I trudged down the hallway, my mind barely aware of my surroundings. Someone touched my elbow. I spun, ready to duck, dodge, and weave. Katie, pretty as ever, smiled at me, green eyes sparkling.

"Hey, you," she said with a perky grin.

I nearly tripped over my own feet before recovering. "Are we speaking again?" I asked in a skip-the-bull tone. I was sick of everyone acting like my new best friends when they didn't even know who in the hell I was. The old me might have found it pretty cool. The new me had almost been devoured by a mutant house cat, had a felycan stalker, a vampire ex-girlfriend, and was under threat by a drug-dealing vampire. These days it took a lot to impress me.

"I'm so sorry for being awful to you." She hooked her arm in mine. Her skin felt warm and soothing. How many times had I fantasized about her embrace? How many times had I wished she was mine?

"It's okay." Elyssa's angry face flashed into my mind. *Screw you,* I said using telepathic brainwaves. Not that I had suddenly figured out how to communicate with my mind, but I wanted to make my feelings known to my heart which hadn't gotten the message yet. It was time to move on.

"Walk me to class?" she asked.

"What about Brad?" I thought back to our conversation in the bathroom and wondered if I should mention it. *Nah, it'll just make her cry.*

She pursed pouty lips. "We broke up for good."

Whatever. I tightened my arm around hers and we walked down the hall. When we reached her class, she gave me a sultry look.

"You've added some muscle. It's sexy." She touched my firm and no longer flabby biceps. Pressed a hand against my right pectoral.

Her shimmering halo of sexual desire beckoned to me. My essence reached for hers. I fought against the hollow craving and the beast. The tip of one tendril caressed her halo. A tiny trickle of refreshing energy flowed into me. My body demanded more. I resisted, reeling back the traitorous probe until it felt safe to move. Katie had been talking about something the entire time and didn't seem to notice the intrusion.

"It was all my fault," she said with a sad smile. Then she kissed me. It wasn't just a peck on the lips but a full-on tongue tango.

I trembled as my hunger fought for control while my body reacted predictably. *Holy shit! Katie kissed me! For real!*

She came up for breath and made an appreciative little moan. "You've changed." She pecked me on the lips again. "I like it."

"You'll be at the game?" I asked in a hoarse voice as I mentally stuffed the groping, hungry tendrils back into their cage.

"Wouldn't miss it for the world, hot stuff." She winked.

I left her and went to class, a skip in my step. I didn't feel like a million bucks—more like half a million. But I felt a lot better than I had after Elyssa kneed me in the guts. At least she'd had the decency not to crush my manhood with that powerful sexy leg of hers.

I also felt slightly better now that I'd taken in a tiny bit of energy from Katie. I halted in my tracks as it occurred to me that I hadn't had to ravish Katie to get my fix. Somehow, I'd managed to keep only a tiny tap into her aura without opening the floodgates. I'd barely controlled it, but maybe that was because of my still powerful attraction for her. Maybe it would be easier if I tried it with someone I didn't find sexy.

It could very well be the answer to my problem or the key to my night-mares. Just as I had fed on the laughing guys that one day, it might be possible to feed from positive emotions emanating from other people without tapping in so deeply they ripped off their clothes. I took a seat in Chemistry and glanced at my classmates. I wanted to practice feeding but quickly discovered the general mood was so dour and serious that I wasn't sure if it would work.

The only person with a positive vibe was Cindy Mueller, one of the smartest girls in school. She was a teacher's pet through and through. Every time the teacher posed a question, her hand shot up and waved excitedly. It wasn't ideal, but she was my best bet. I linked with her and tried to limit the flow to a trickle. But the hunger betrayed me almost immediately and ripped open the floodgates. She leapt up, looking desperately around the room all while moaning and rubbing her hips.

Mr. Heisenberg, the teacher, gaped in shock while I desperately tried to close the connection. Alan Weaver sat right behind Cindy. He stared at her, face taught with terror. I reached for his aura, hoping an opposite emotion might shake loose Cindy's psychic grip. For an instant, I felt Alan's fear and Cindy's sexual desire collide. Both their presences vanished from my mind. Cindy and Alan faced each other. She attacked him with her lips.

I had to give him credit. He didn't pass out. Cindy was skinny, wore thick glasses, and styled her hair in a fashion more suitable to the fifties, but she was probably kind of cute underneath all that geek chic. Alan leapt to his feet and locked lips with her, panting and tearing at her clothes. Cindy gripped Alan's shirt and ripped it open. Buttons scattered everywhere. Students scrambled out of their desks, yelling, shrieking, desperate to escape the madness. Mr. Heisenberg finally came to his senses and shouted at them. He rushed over to pry them apart.

Guilt dug at my insides. I had started this insane fiasco. I grabbed Alan and pulled him away from her. He wriggled like a snared rabbit, but my strength overwhelmed him. The couple stopped struggling and stood there, panting with lust and gazing passionately into each other's eyes. I felt horrible. What had I done? Had I just completely wrecked their brains?

"Really, you two," said Mr. Heisenberg in a huff. "I understand about hormones, but this is just uncalled for."

"I want you," Cindy said to Alan.

"You are a sexual goddess," Alan replied, eyes ablaze.

I wondered if I had somehow connected them to each other, causing a mutual lust, or if Alan really liked her.

"How romantic," Cheryl Horne crooned.

As Alan and Cindy continued to exclaim their intense need for each other, the bell rang. I helped Alan get his stuff, but maintained a firm grip on his arm. I was certain if left to their own devices, he and Cindy would enact some memorable pornographic scenes that would scar the rest of us for life. I walked Alan to his next class. About halfway there, he started shaking his head as though clearing it of cobwebs.

"Wow." He stopped in the hallway.

"Wow what?" I asked.

"That was intense. I've always had a thing for Cindy, but I couldn't control myself back there."

"Hormones," I said sagely.

He whistled. "Turbo-charged hormones." Alan stopped me in front of the Home Economics classroom. "I'm here."

I looked behind us and saw Mr. Heisenberg at the far end of the hall leading a similarly dazed Cindy our way. "Do you two have the next class together?" I couldn't see him baking cakes. "Why in the world are you taking Home Economics?"

He looked adoringly at Cindy. "Because she is."

"Oh dear." I sounded just like my mom whenever I'd done something awful.

Mr. Hubble gave Alan a suspicious look then let Cindy go of her own recognizance. She walked over to Alan, light returning to her formerly glazed eyes.

"I'm so sorry for sexually assaulting you. I don't know what came over me."

He took her hand. "I kinda liked it."

She smiled. "Me too." She looked down at his gaping shirt. "Oh no, I've ruined it. Maybe I can sew on some new buttons during class."

"That'd be sweet." Sweat beaded on Alan's forehead and his hand trembled. I knew the feeling all too well.

"You two should go on a date," I said. "In fact, I think Alan said he wanted to take you to dinner."

Her eyes brightened. "You do?" She squeaked, looking at him in such rapt joy my eyes got all misty.

He nodded, vocal cords obviously locked by his nerves. They walked into class, Cindy excitedly telling everyone she had a date. I wouldn't have doubted it was her first date ever. I sucked in a breath through my teeth. My own nerves were a bit jittery. I had almost caused a major disaster...a calamity even. I could have brain damaged two of the school's brightest and ruined our chances at the next Academic Decathlon.

Or maybe I'd stumbled onto something really good. I felt kind of high on life since something had worked out. But I was in so far over my head I didn't know which way was up. No more trying to figure this out on my own. Elyssa wouldn't help me. In all likelihood she'd convince herself to kill me at some point. I had to give in to Stacey.

I cringed at the thought. If it wasn't for that cat tongue of hers, a relationship might actually be kind of nice. Now that I knew what she was I felt slightly better even if it freaked me out. After the game tonight, I would find Stacey and seal the deal.

The thought made me shudder.

Unfortunately, my attempts with Cindy had barely recharged my beast. It sulked in its cage, having only gotten a light snack when it wanted a four-course supper. I wasn't about to try anymore field tests at school.

The rest of the day flashed past. Before I knew it, my teammates and I lined up and dashed between the cheerleaders for our grand entrance onto the football field. Bryan Jones met Marty Ledbetter and the referees for the coin toss. The Lanier Bobcats won the toss and took first possession.

Coach Wise motioned me over before the kickoff. "The Davis boy hurt his foot, Case. You're going in on special teams."

I had only practiced with special teams once. "What do I do?"

"Tackle their ball carrier."

I hadn't really practice tackling since I was on offense, but I had a general idea. Our team would kick the ball off a tee, and the other team would catch it and try to run it back. It seemed simple enough. My nerves flopped in my belly like fat fish. I needed to go to the bathroom for the tenth time, it seemed. I took deep breaths to calm myself. They didn't help. My enhanced eyes caught sight of a furtive shadow atop the broadcaster's booth. I recognized Stacey's smile from a hundred yards away.

"Just great," I muttered. My soon-to-be felycan girlfriend was here, but my absentee parents didn't even know I was playing. Dad was probably out hiring private eyes, and tracking the Conroys, whoever they were.

God, I hoped he and Mom were okay. I planned to tie him to a chair and interrogate him the minute he walked through the door. Despite the bizarre situation, I felt a pang of regret and wished my parents could see my moment of glory.

The whistle sounded. Momentary confusion scrambled my brain just as our kicker sent the football soaring end-over-end toward the opposition. I snapped out of my haze and sprinted forward. I locked eyes on the ball, racing after it as it arced slowly toward the other end of the field. I ran into someone and heard a loud grunt as they bounced off my body. Within seconds, I stood about where the ball would land. I realized with a shock I had been running much faster than I'd meant to. In fact, I was standing right in front of the Bobcat's receiver. He gave me a very surprised look. I gave him a sheepish grin. Horror washed over me as I realized I didn't even know how fast I'd just run down the field. This was bad. Very—

Someone smacked into my back. I sprawled into the receiver. The ball bounced off his helmet and away from us. A pile of red jerseys from our team covered it just as several more players piled on me and the poor receiver. I lay awkwardly on top of him, face-to-face. His eyes flared. I tried to look away, but found it very hard to move my helmet without dislodging all the players on top of me.

"Nice run," he said.

"Thanks." I whistled innocently.

The weight lessened and we were able to get up. Teammates slapped me on the back, hooting and hollering like I'd just bought them all camouflage camping gear.

"Spectacular, boy, just spectacular," Coach Wise said as he welcomed me back to the sideline. "I ain't never seen nobody run like that. Now get out there and give 'em hell." He slapped me on the ass.

Confusion clouded my brain. Bryan and our offense took the field, and it slowly dawned on me that we had recovered the ball on the Bobcats' twenty yard line.

My psychic stomach made angry noises in my head. I was running low on energy. I hadn't done anything to recharge since my failed attempts earlier in the day, and I had no idea how much I'd burned in that idiotic run of mine at the start of the game. I went into the huddle.

"Awesome play," Bryan said. The other players were all grins and pats on the back.

"I had too many energy drinks before the game," I said. "I'm a little jittery."

"Well, you're gonna put that energy to good use. Bulldozer left on three."

The huddle broke. The left side of the Bobcats' defense looked like a brick wall. The right side looked like an iron curtain. Their guys were huge. Most stood as tall as Nathan. To top it off, I wasn't feeling so great. The incessant churning in my guts grew worse. I heard the hike count and ran forward on automatic. Two massive defensive linemen buried our offensive line. The Bobcat linebackers leapt over the line, making a beeline for me. I dodged back to the right, nearly slipping in the grass before my cleats found purchase. The situation on that side was even worse. A sea of green jerseys poured over a gap in our line. I had nowhere to go but the center.

Bryan managed to help our center push a guy the size of a silverback gorilla to the side. I slipped into the gap. I heard the smack of helmet on helmet and saw stars. A gong rang in my ears. My feet flew from underneath me and my back kissed the earth with a thud. Bryan helped me up. My legs felt like mush. I limped back to the huddle. In the distance, I heard someone shout my name.

"Hold the damned line," Bryan said. "Not even Justin can break through their entire defense."

Technically, I could—at least when I had a full tank. Ravenous hunger rolled over me in waves. I gagged.

"You okay, Case?" asked one of the linemen.

"I feel like shit." I choked down another pulse of nausea.

"Buck up, soldier," Bryan said with a grin. "Let's push this through and you can take a break."

I nodded.

We lined up. I focused everything I had on the end zone and on my legs. The ball came. I surged forward. Something huge and green dove in my way. I jumped and heard a roar from the crowd as I hurtled over the Jolly Green Giant. A linebacker came at me from the side. I stiff-armed him and he went down. Then something crushed me from the other side.

CHAPTER 24

A feminine blood-streaked face stares at me, eyes wide and overflowing with terror. Ragged breaths tear from the woman's throat as she grips my shirt and pulls me closer. I look down at her legs and stifle a shout. Torn ribbons of flesh, blood, and bone are all that remain. A crimson trail leads down a sidewalk and into a house that seems terribly familiar. I lean toward the woman and strain my ears to comprehend the faint words coming from her mouth.

"...forty-three eleven." She gasps for breath. "Only you can do it Justin. But first you have to—"

I jerked awake to the sharp sting of ammonia in my nostrils. A dull roar echoed in my ears. The odor of dirt and grass replace the ammonia. Blurry figures hovering over me sharpened into focus.

"He's okay. Just had the wind knocked out of him," said a guy in a medic uniform.

Bryan and one of the other guys helped me stand up. The crowd cheered.

"And he's gonna be okay," said the hillbilly announcer.

They set me down on the bench and Bill Chauncey, the normal half-back, took my place. The bench creaked. On my left sat Coach Burgundy, a grin plastered on his face. He put an arm around me.

"Son, if you lose this game for us, I promise you will not like the consequences." Not a trace of friendliness existed in that grin.

"I honestly don't feel good," I said. "I'm not faking it."

We watched as the Bobcats sacked Bryan for a loss. Coach Wise screamed for special teams to try for a field goal.

Coach Burgundy squeezed my shoulder. "Boy, I don't care if you just crapped your britches. Just stay downwind of me and score. The sheriff and his boys have a lot riding on this game, not to mention a few other people who would not be happy to lose. You get what you need from Coach Howard. He's got some stuff that'll patch you right on up."

I groaned and looked over at the milling herd of coaches on the sideline. Whatever Coach Howard had wouldn't help me. That much I knew. I felt like I had stepped into a redneck version of The Godfather. And that dream—it had seemed too vivid to be my imagination and more like nightmares I'd had about the baby and the pregnant woman. I must have had a few screws in my head knocked loose from that last hit.

Special teams kicked the field goal. Our defense took the field. At least we had big louts like Nathan, I figured. The Bobcats' offense didn't look nearly as impressive as their defense, but they had a quick runner and their quarterback was a passing threat. Bryan, on the other hand, was only good for short passes. He had a good arm, just no accuracy.

What am I going to do? I felt caged. If I continued to do well, I would only trap myself further in this mess. But this was going way beyond my friends getting bad grades. No telling how gangster things would become if crooked cops lost money because of me. I groaned.

The crowd on our side booed and hissed as the Bobcats scored. I tried to open myself up to the emotional energy around me but it was too distant and too negative. Disappointment from fellow teammates washed over me like rancid milk. It brought a sour grimace to my face.

Bryan grabbed my shoulder. "You okay to come back in?"

I nodded.

Bryan handed me the ball three times. All three times I got flattened. Coach Burgundy shot me a look that made my heart palpitate with fear. Elyssa could probably take care of herself, but not Ash or Nyte. And who else would these bozos go after? To make matters worse, my teammates gave me hurt looks of betrayal. Like I was intentionally playing badly so they'd lose. How had I gone from despising these people to feeling terrible about hurting their feelings?

This is a team, dammit. Not a one-man show.

Apparently, Justin was the "I" in team tonight, and Burgundy and his buddies had bet big on my performance.

I wanted to scream in frustration, but it wouldn't do any good. The crowd on our side had gone silent. I spotted Stacey still atop the broadcasting booth, smiling in a mischievous way. She puckered her lips and kissed the air. I spotted Ash and Nyte. Ash bit his fingernails. Nyte gnawed on a corn dog. A few rows to their right, Katie's sad green eyes looked at me. She waved. Jenny and Annie sat next to her. They snickered and laughed about something. I looked for Elyssa. I didn't see her. I hoped maybe we'd lock eyes. She'd smile and inspire me to greatness. "I love you," she'd mouth silently and blow me a kiss. After that, nothing would stop me. Not even the ogres pounding us to mush on the football field.

Am I an idiot or what?

The Bobcats scored three more times. Their defensive line crushed me more times than I wanted to remember or probably would remember due to brain damage from the constant battering. Coach Burgundy was beside himself with rage by the time half-time finally arrived and the team left the field.

"Just what I thought." Nathan shoved past me and into the locker room. "You ain't worth shit, Case."

Bryan patted my shoulder pads, offered a sympathetic look, and trudged into the locker room. I let everyone else go in then slipped away to the side. I threw down my helmet and stared at the parking lot thirty yards away. Now that I played football, it seemed I measured everything in yards. I could just run away. Right now. Why should I stick around?

I could warn Ash and Nyte, and tell them to warn Elyssa. Then I would vanish. Mom was gone, Dad was good as gone, and my life here as I knew it was over. I stalked back and forth at the edge of the parking lot. Why did my conscience burden me so? I walked toward the cars. Nobody saw me. I pulled off my uniform and left a trail of jersey, shoulder pads, and helmet behind me. I decided to keep on the pants and cleats for decency's sake.

I looked for Stacey, hoping she'd show up so I could cave in to her demands and get on with my depressing life as Demon Boy McGillicuddy. I looked atop the broadcasting booth but couldn't make out any movement in the shadows. Something warm prickled my senses in the darkness to my left. The large air conditioning unit sat silent in the cool fall air. Giggles echoed from behind it. I sneaked over and peeked around the edge. My former best friend Harry and his girlfriend, who I recognized as Sally Palmer, were making out. She slapped Harry's hands away as he tried to unbutton her shirt.

"Come on, baby. You know I love you," he said.

Ravenous tendrils shot from me like heat-seeking missiles. I couldn't stop them. I felt the heat from Sally's mind, her molten sensuality like lavender-scented steam in the air. I breathed it in, my essence locked onto hers. She gasped. Her eyes went wide. She ripped open her shirt, revealing a lacy white bra. Buttons showered the concrete. Sally grabbed Harry by the shirt. Pulled him on top of her, yanking his T-shirt over his head.

"Holy crap!" His eyes widened. "What changed your mind?"

She didn't answer. She was too busy pecking his scrawny hair-speckled chest with kisses. She reached for his belt. Fear blossomed on his face. White-eyed and trembling, he wrestled her for the belt buckle.

"Are you sure, baby?"

"Shut up and kiss me," she demanded.

He did as he was told, one hand protecting his belt buckle. Energy, pure and delicious, flowed into me as they made out. Their emotions swirled together, a tornado of psychic energy flooding my ravenous psyche and filling it within minutes. I broke the connection with Sally, feeling full and satisfied on the one hand, and a little disgusted for causing and witnessing an almost pornographic scene. Harry had been my friend. It was just gross seeing him and his pale scrawny ass trying to get it on with a girl.

"I'm not ready." Harry broke away from Sally's latest attempt to remove his belt, his eyes filled with despair and fright. "I—I thought I was."

"You scaredy-cat," she said. "All that big talk, and now you tell me you're not ready?"

I left them to continue their argument and made my way back to the locker room. Along the way, I snatched my gear off the pavement and strapped it back on. Screw Burgundy. Screw Nathan and my fake friends. There was only one reason to finish this game—my real friends.

I'd figure this mess out and see it through to the end. I stood outside the locker room and watched the marching bands cavort on the field for the rest of half-time.

The team emerged from the locker room. Coach Burgundy obviously hadn't given them a cheery pep talk because they looked like a bunch of sad pandas. Some of the guys gave me encouraging slaps or punches to the shoulder. Nathan growled at me.

"You best make up for this mess, boy," said Coach Burgundy from behind me, his hand pressing heavily on my shoulder pad. He hawked, snorted, and then spat into the dirt.

I knocked his hand off my shoulder and turned to face him. "I'll do my job," I said. "But let's get one thing straight. If anything happens to my friends, you'll be making a very dangerous enemy."

He laughed like a country boy on moonshine. "Son, you're about as scary as a house cat."

You have no idea how scary cats can be, jackass.

I trotted back onto the field to receive the ball as the Bobcats kicked off. The ball fell short of me and into the waiting arms of David James, the usual receiver. He pitched the ball back to me a split second before a tsunami of green jerseys washed over him. I found the biggest, meanest looking guy on the other team and charged right at him. A smile lit his face. He had to be six and a half feet tall.

He lowered his head and reached for me with thick meaty arms. I lowered my shoulder and rammed him. He grunted and bowled into the guys behind him. They went down like dominoes. I dodged right past a guy in mid-dive. From there it was clear sailing. I coasted to the end zone while the crowd went crazy. The country coot on the PA system shouted my name like Christmas had just arrived and Santa left him a pair of assless chaps in his stocking.

The big guy I'd run over was still picking himself up. He staggered around in a drunken haze for a moment before finding his way off the field. I walked over to Coach Burgundy.

"Put me on defense."

He spat. "Defense?"

"Yeah. Seeing how effective they've been, I figure they need a boost."

He nodded. "Johnson, you're out. Case, get in there."

Trip Johnson gave me a look of relief as he left the field. "Crush them." He bumped fists with me as I took over his spot on the line.

Trip towered over me, and the Bobcat lineman across from me made Trip look like a Chihuahua. He smiled as I lined up in the shadow of his hulking mass. Apparently he'd missed what I'd done to his teammates on my kickoff return.

"What the hell are you doing out here?" Nathan grabbed my shoulder pad and spun me around.

"I'm helping, obviously. So unless you have a problem with that, back off."

Nathan clenched his jaw but did as I demanded.

The Bobcats hiked the ball. I darted between my guy and the center and tackled the quarterback before he could even back away. I decided if I did that every time, my mutant abilities would be way too obvious. The next play, I cleared a hole in the line. Nathan roared through and sacked the quarterback again. From then on it was wash, rinse, repeat. Nathan's sack stats were going to be epic.

The rest of the game terribly frustrated the Bobcats. They couldn't stop me from scoring when I ran the ball, and they couldn't keep Nathan or Steve out of their backfield since I kept knocking back their blocker, who by the way, wasn't smiling anymore.

After I scored the touchdown giving us the lead, the crowd chanted my name. It felt pretty damned good. Like they were worshipping me. The rush hit me, hot and seductive. A huge grin split my face. This was more like it. I might even grow to enjoy playing football.

The final buzzer sounded and the home crowd erupted with cheers.

Other coaches and players directed many brofists, ass slaps, and high-fives at me. Even Nathan came over, a contrite look on his face.

"Hey, Case," he said in a gruff voice. "Nice work out there." He held out a fist. I punched it lightly and we did the asteroid explosion, sound effects and all. Suddenly, the universe was a better place.

Steve and Adam gave grudging thanks as well. I felt like the man. I felt better than I'd felt in what seemed like forever. This was acceptance. Despite the coercion and outright blackmail dragging me kicking and screaming to this point, I loved it.

I showered, smiling and nodding each time players came in and congratulated me while they lathered up and desperately tried not to drop the soap. It was odd not feeling like a ninety-pound weakling in the locker room. On the other hand, the air reeked of Old Spice. I half-expected to see the Old Spice guy waltz around the corner. As I dried off, I noticed Nathan dousing his armpits with it.

"Why Old Spice?" I asked, trying desperately to block out the odor by force of will.

He gave the spray bottle a serious look. "Dude. This is the stuff of men."

I flashed back to my headaches and the strange concurrences of Old Spice invading my nostrils. Every jock on the football team probably bathed in it. Now I knew why I smelled it so often. *One mystery down. A million more to go.* I shook my head. "I'll stick with Axe, thank you very much."

He chuckled. "We're gonna head to a party over at The Creek. How 'bout you come on out?"

"Sure," I said. The Creek was an abandoned subdivision not far from my house. I'd heard of many a party out there but had never been invited to one. I dressed and checked my phone. Both Ash and Nyte had texted me congratulations. I shot back my thanks and went out to the Jetta. The parking lot teemed with players and fans celebrating the win. Most of the fans didn't seem to recognize me in my street clothes and that was okay by me. My fist was going to get pregnant if I kept bumping it with everyone I ran into.

"You were amazing!" Katie came up behind me and laced her arms around my neck. She greeted me with a kiss when I turned to face her. Not a peck. Not on the cheek. She kissed me for real, just as she had earlier in the hallway.

A hot burst pinged on my radar. I looked up and saw Elyssa standing with Ash and Nyte several yards away in the sea of revelers. Something flashed in her eyes. Was it pain? Desire? Anger? She turned away and pushed through the crowd before I could make a guess. Ash and Nyte waved, huge grins plastered on their faces, apparently unaware Elyssa had left.

"What's wrong?" Katie asked.

I stared at Elyssa's retreating back. "Nothing." I took a deep breath to diminish the knot in my throat.

I arrived at the entrance to The Creek, Katie in tow, and located the party in question by the sheer number of pickups and cars parked along the road. The party house was almost fully built, but skeletal frames and barren concrete foundations told the story of a failed project that might never be finished. Nathan shouted when he saw me and motioned me over to the beer kegs.

Katie looked at him and shuddered. Annie and Jennie squealed at her from an adjoining room. "I'll be with them." She eyed Nathan warily. I couldn't blame her. It seemed like ages ago he'd groped her and tried to steal a kiss. In a sense, that had been the incident to kick-start my strange destiny. It was clearer now—the headaches and blurred vision had all been supernatural growing pains. I was no longer Justin Case. I was something else. Something inhuman. And all these people thought I was just a person like them.

"My main man, Case!" Nathan roared over the loud music. He handed me a plastic cup filled with pee-colored beer then pulled me to the back porch where a group of people downed shots and reveled in drinking games. He eyed me for a minute and damned if he didn't actually look embarrassed, of all things. "We've been through some real crap, haven't we?"

I took a sip of the beer and grimaced before looking him in the eyes. "That would be putting it mildly."

He nodded. "I hated you."

"Are we best buds now?"

"I wouldn't go that far." He chuckled and gulped down half his beer. "I guess the point is, I'm..." he mumbled something.

I cupped a hand to an ear. "I didn't quite catch that."

A growl rumbled in his throat. "I'm sorry."

Hearing an apology from Nathan felt really good. At the same time, it hardly covered all the mistreatment he'd put me, my friends, and countless other kids through. *Baby steps*, I told myself. *Baby steps.* "I think the person who needs an apology more than me is Katie."

His face went scarlet and I thought for sure I'd just pushed the wrong button. But when his eyes focused on his beer I knew for sure it wasn't anger he was feeling but embarrassment.

"I—I suck with women." Nathan gave me a sad puppy-dog look. Actually it was more of a sick Rottweiler look considering his huge head.

"But you're a football player," I said as if one of the laws of physics were being broken. *Don't women flock to football players?*

"How do you do it?" He gazed wistfully at Katie through the sliding glass door where she gabbed with her friends. "You stole her right out from under Brad Nichols, and that dude gets chicks just for having a motorcycle."

I gave him a confused look. Was this the same Nathan I'd always known or had an alien scooped out his brains and replaced them with some random dork's gray matter? Katie had dragged me through hell and I still wasn't entirely sure if she'd suddenly fallen for me, or if it was just because of football. "I can tell you one thing for sure."

Interest kindled in his eyes. "What's that?"

265

"Girls don't like it when boys try to force them into kissing them."

He blushed even redder. "Yeah, I figured that one out."

"Girls also don't like nice pushover guys no matter what they say. The way I see it, you have to be somewhere in between."

"Not a nice guy but not a total asshole?"

"Exactly." I honestly didn't have a clue what I was talking about, but if it made Nathan a better human being, who was I to argue? "But first I think you need to apologize to Katie."

"And that way, I'm not a total asshole." He slapped me on the shoulder. "Case, you're fricken devious, man. So we're good, right?"

I nodded. "Sure. Let bygones be bygones, I always say." I'd actually never said that once in my life, but figured it made me seem magnanimous.

He leaned against the half-finished brick siding. "What ever happened to you and that Goth chick?"

"Things didn't work out," I said, my voice rough with emotion.

"*Women*," he said, as if that explained everything in the universe. Maybe it did. His face brightened. "Hey, I want to try out your advice." He led me to a group of giggling cheerleaders talking about shoe shopping. There were some older girls there too, alumni who were in college but had apparently not made the cut as college cheerleaders.

I started talking to a pretty brunette named Mandy. She had a strong Italian nose, huge eyes and smelled of vodka and peach-scented perfume. She gabbed excitedly to me about college and rushing for a sorority while she slammed down shot after shot. I mostly nodded and said "Uhuh" and "Mhm" to whatever she said.

Nathan, meanwhile, tried out my patented "Not a Total Asshole" approach by alternatively complimenting a girl and then telling her that her shoes were ugly—or something like that. Amazingly, it seemed to be working on at least one of them. Or maybe the rollercoaster of emotions simply short-circuited her brain.

Katie appeared from nowhere and grabbed my arm. "Who are your friends?" she asked in a slightly slurred voice. The cloying odor of something like cough syrup lingered on her breath.

I introduced her.

"Justin is amazing at football." Mandy struggled to keep her balance. She'd taken four shots in the space of ten minutes. "He ran over those huge guys like they were nothing. Pow!" She smacked one hand off the other for illustration and nearly toppled her drunk little self in the process.

Katie smiled, holding onto my arm for support. "He's amazing all right."

Mandy grabbed my other arm around the bicep. "Flex it!"

I suppressed a sigh but flexed.

"Girl, look at that body." Mandy rubbed my abs over my shirt. "Damn, I'd like to wash my dress on that washboard."

Katie's smile turned venomous. "He works out."

"When are you graduating?" asked Vanda, one of Mandy's college friends.

"Same time I do," Katie said as I opened my mouth to speak.

"We're going back to my parents' place for a more intimate party," Mandy said. "You should come, Justin. It'll mainly be a college crowd, but you're totally cool."

"Come, please." Vanda blinked her big eyes flirtatiously.

Katie's grip on my arm intensified. "We have other plans."

Before I could ask her what those plans were, she dragged me away and out the front door.

"We have other plans?" I asked.

"Yes...we do." She wobbled a little as we stood in the chilly air.

"How much did you drink?"

"Ugh. Too much. Someone gave us shots of something green. Annie threw up all over Jenny."

"Good times." I repressed a chortle of malicious glee.

Katie kissed me. She was a good kisser. She tasted like an apothecary's mixing bowl, thanks to whatever the heck had been in those shots. I didn't care. I still cared about her and wanted her despite the rough journey to this moment.

Elyssa's lips are so much softer.

I squeezed my eyes shut and banished her from my traitorous mind. Elyssa had dumped me. She had blown our chance to have something amazing. I could still have that with Katie. After all, it hadn't been too long since I'd thought I was in love with her. Maybe the universe was making things right for me this once.

"Are your parents home?" she asked.

"Nope."

"Want to..."

I nodded.

I drove the short distance to my house while Katie nipped my earlobe and kissed my neck. My mind reeled with what we were about to do. *She slept with Brad Nichols.* My stomach twisted at the thought. I was a virgin. She wasn't. Should it matter?

"Was Brad definitely your first?" I asked. The question surprised me because I hadn't meant to voice it.

She nodded and snuggled up to me. "We only did it once. It was a horrible mistake, Justin."

Yeah, no kidding.

We reached my house and went straight toward the bedroom. Katie wanted to sleep with me and I wasn't even using my supernatural persuasion on her. She was the first girl who wanted to be with me for real.

Except for Elyssa. A barb of pain stabbed my heart. I tried to ignore it.

We went inside. I didn't see Dad. His bedroom door hung wide open, and aside from the smooching noises Katie and I made, the house was silent. Katie pushed me on the bed and crawled on top of me. She pressed her lips to mine, tongue pressing against mine. Soft moans drifted from her throat.

The image of her and Brad Nichols flashed into my mind again. I banished it and pressed her harder against me. I ran my hand down her back, squeezing her ass with both hands. She shivered. I trembled. This was what I had always wanted. Tonight, Katie would be mine and I would be hers. This was meant to be.

Katie sat up and pulled off her shirt. Her breasts, still trapped in a lacy white bra, jiggled. *Is this for real?* I had to be dreaming.

God I wish she was Elyssa.

The beast awoke and pawed at its cage. I tried to push its insistent presence away as Katie's hands worked along my chest and sent chills racing along my skin. I could concentrate on one or the other but not both. She pressed her bare skin against mine as one of her wandering hands slid into my pants and grabbed me.

The beast broke loose. It groped for her essence before I could stop it. Her sensuality entwined itself around mine like white glowing vines. Our bodies writhed against each other, sexual need flaring into insatiable desire.

"Oh, yes," she moaned, green eyes filled with lust.

I rolled us over so she was beneath me. Her hand gripped the button on my jeans and tugged.

Another hand, a bigger hand, gripped my shoulder in an iron vice and ripped me off her. I sailed through the air and slammed into the wall with a bone-jarring crash. Pictures fell off the walls and crashed into the floor. I bounced off the drywall, rolled off the top of my chest of drawers, and landed on my back. I looked up.

A demonic face stared back at me.

Dad was home.

CHAPTER 25

Blue fire literally blazed in Dad's eyes and rage contorted his face. I had never seen him with such a horrendous expression. His face hardly looked human, as if there were two versions of his face, one overlaying another.

Katie let out a tiny peep and passed out as an unseen force sliced through our connection. Dad turned his gaze back on me, eyes emitting a cold dark fury. "What in the hell do you think you're doing?" he said through clenched teeth.

"Ouch," was all I could muster. I pushed myself off the floor. I looked at him and felt real fear, the kind where you're in a dream but moving in slow motion. "What's going on?" I squeaked out.

Dad paced the room, looking at Katie, then back at me. The glow in his eyes faded but his face remained livid. "Take her home."

"Won't she remember what happened?"

He sniffed. "She's so drunk I doubt she'll remember anything. Especially not after I cut you off."

"You're the one who did that?" I asked.

He said nothing but turned and left, closing the door behind him.

I threw on my shirt and slid Katie's back on. Amazingly, she still had on most of her outfit. I trembled from fright and the abrupt end to my carnal adventure.

I hefted Katie over a shoulder and loaded her into the Jetta. Dad stood near the doorway his face calm but sad.

"What's going on, Dad? Where in the hell have you been?" Sadness and anger choked my voice.

"I'll tell you when you get back." His voice was calmer now. "Go."

I hopped in the car and drove to Katie's house. It was late and the windows were all dark. I hoped fervently I didn't wake anyone up because her parents would *freak*. I took the keys from Katie's bag

I slid the key into the lock and slowly twisted it. The deadbolt opened without a sound. The lock on the doorknob responded with a low click. I eased open the door. The hinges squeaked. My heart thudded. I paused and listened with my enhanced hearing. I heard slow breathing. No walking or anything else to indicate someone was up and about. I put Katie over my shoulder and crept up the stairs, my intrusion aided by a nightlight in the upstairs hall and in the only bedroom with an open door. I figured out quickly that the open room was hers. The excessive amount of pink confirmed it. What was it with girls and pink?

After depositing her under the covers, I made good my escape, leaving her keys inside and engaging the bottom lock as I left.

Dad paced the foyer when I got home. He placed his hands on my shoulders and stared at me, studying me like I was a science experiment gone wrong.

"It's about time you showed up," I said. "I need some answers."

He chuckled. "No, it's about time *you* showed up." He took a step back. "I guess we need to have the talk."

"In case you hadn't noticed, I'm a little past needing to know about the birds and the bees."

"I'm well aware of that, son. This is a different talk."

I wanted to be furious with him, but felt so relieved to see him alive, I forgot to shout. "Where is Mom?" My voice broke, afraid to hear something terrible happened to her.

"I'll get to that." Dad seemed vastly altered. Confidence and authority radiated from him as opposed to drunkenness and apathy. Usually, Mom was the one I thought of as wearing the family pants.

His attitude indicated she must be okay. I grabbed a glass of water and took a seat at the table. "I'm all ears."

"I almost don't know where to start." He shook his head. "I honestly didn't think you would become like us. Like me. You're kind of a late bloomer."

"Wait a cotton-picking minute. You have the same abilities?" I guessed it should have occurred to me after all the clues I'd gathered. Glowing eyes should have been a clue as well. On the upside, that probably meant my eyes could glow too which was really cool. I imagined flicking the glow off and on in the dark so I could scare the pants off kids at Halloween.

"Of course I do," he said. "You are, after all, my son."

"And Mom's like us too?"

"Ah," he said with a sigh. "Your mother is another matter altogether."

"Okay, well find a starting point and fill me in. Am I a demon?"

He put a finger to his chin and gazed at the wall behind me for a moment, then seemed to come to some conclusion. "In a sense, yes. You are an incubus."

"What? But I thought they only seduced women in their dreams."

"Meh, that's the biblical definition. We're the male version of a succubus."

The string quartet in my head struck a note of horror. I expected to see lightning outside and hear the roar of thunder as a spooky organ played in the background. I jumped up from my chair and nearly toppled the table. "So we really are demons?" I couldn't think of anything worse. I'd rather be an evil faerie or a vampire than a demon!

"Calm down, Justin. It's not as bad as you think."

I started hyperventilating. "We're demons, Dad. Demons! Oh my God—can I even say that anymore without worrying about getting struck by hellfire? Or is it heavenfire?"

"Sit down," he said with a firm note in his voice.

I dropped into my chair. Pain gripped my heart with steel talons. Elyssa had been right about me. I was a monster, one-hundred percent evil, doomed to Hell, and straight out of the nether world.

"We're not pure demons, not in the sense myth portrays us. We are in fact very much like humans—on the outside anyway—though our needs are more like vampires. "

"I was dating a vampire." My heart hurt with the thought of Elyssa.

He quirked an eyebrow. "You *dated* a vampire? Are you sure?"

"I saw her fangs, Dad. Right after she kicked my butt."

Dad quirked both eyebrows. "Son, vampires don't date our kind. They feed on us." He blew out a sigh and ran a hand through his hair. "I think you'd better start at the beginning. I get the feeling you've gotten your-self in quite a mess."

"No thanks to you. First Mom disappears on a trip, and then you vanish off the face of the earth. Where have you been? Where is Mom?"

He blanched and put a hand to his forehead. "I'm ashamed of myself,

Justin. I've let you down and put us both in danger. Tell me when this started and everything that's happened."

I sighed and glared at him. That was no explanation and he wasn't close to earning my forgiveness. But I told him the story anyway, starting with Randy, my encounter with Nathan, the disastrous fight that turned me into a pariah, then worked my way to the gym and Stacey and my near deflowering at the hands of the woman in the grocery store. By the time I reached the end, Dad must have face-palmed ten times.

"Jesus, Mary, and Joseph," he said. "I guess you've done okay for a clueless teenager."

"That doesn't make me feel very good."

"To survive the attentions of a felycan is quite a feat."

"Was the big cat I fought a felycan?"

"No, that sounds like a moggy. Those are strays or alley cats felycans mutate into guardian forms. They use them as drones to guard or attack and they're tough to kill."

"Well someone or something cut off that moggy's head."

"You must have a guardian angel."

"Angels are real too?"

He chuckled. "I didn't mean it in that sense. Felycans are solitary creatures unless they have mates. You were obviously in her lair, and that was probably one of her moggies. As to who killed it, that's anyone's guess."

"Can felycans infect humans like werewolves do?"

"I'm not really sure what they're capable of. They're rare, and I've only met one. They do like our type though. If you weren't protected by your mother, she might have leeched your essence dry."

"How is Mom protecting me? She wasn't even there."

"There's so much to explain. Maybe I should just tell you the essentials and teach you the rest over time."

"Just what I need. Supernatural kindergarten."

"Our real last name is not Case. It's Slade."

The memory of my parents arguing popped into my head. *The Slades*, Mom had said. *Was that cowboy asking about my family?*

"Well, at least my name isn't a stupid pun."

Dad chuckled.

"You did that on purpose didn't you?"

His grin grew wider. "You might say, just in case."

I groaned and switched back to my real family name. "I overheard you and mom talking about the Slades. Do we have more Slade relatives?"

"Yes."

"Why haven't I met them?"

Dad shook his head. "If I have my way, you'll never meet my family. Justin, demon spawn have a bad reputation for a reason. In fact, it's why your mother and I took on the last name Case. We've been hiding from both of our families for years."

I hazarded a guess. "The Conroys, too?"

His eyes widened. "How did you know that?"

"The private eyes you hired. Is there a connection between them and Mom?"

"Yes. She didn't go on a trip, Justin. She left us to be with the Conroys." A tear trickled down his cheek. "Life isn't worth living without your loved ones."

I wondered how he, or I for that matter, *could* love. We were demon spawn. Was the love I felt really an illusion after all? Still, the thought of

276

Mom being in danger from the Slades or the Conroys choked me with fear. "Are the Conroys as bad as the Slades?"

Dad nodded. "They're Arcanes—sorcerers."

Elyssa had mentioned Arcanes. I snapped my fingers. "That would totally explain the frogs and rats."

"So, you listened to my voicemail."

"You're damned right I did. I needed answers and you weren't here to give them." I stood up and paced restlessly, grabbing an apple from the counter and taking a bite. "I take it Mom is also demon spawn? A succubus?"

Dad leaned back in the wooden kitchen chair. "Your mother and her family are human."

"Ooh." I winced. "I'll bet her family didn't like the idea of having you as a son-in-law."

"No more than my family wanted me to marry a human." He twirled a pen on the table, eyes giving it a thousand-mile stare. "My kind collectively calls itself Daemos, though many derisively refer to us as spawn. Had I not left home I would have been forced to mate with my sisters, my mother, and other female relatives. I would have been little more than a stud horse for breeding."

I spat apple chunks all over the place. "Mate with your sisters and mom? Holy crap, Dad! What kind of family do we come from?"

"Inbreeding doesn't affect spawn like it does humans." His eyes left the pen and settled on me. "But it's revolting and I'll have nothing to do with it."

"Good lord. Don't I have any normal relatives?"

"Define normal."

Considering I wasn't even human, I supposed my life wasn't meant to be full of typical nuclear family activities. "If Mom is human, does that mean I'm half human?"

"Doubtful. Spawn consider interspecies breeding disgusting and repugnant."

"As if sex with your relatives isn't the worst ever!"

A chuckle lit his face for a moment. "True. We hadn't seen the result of a spawn-human mating in centuries, but it's rumored the resulting children are born true—either entirely human, or spawn."

"But don't spawn have sex with humans when they're feeding?"

"Oh yes. But never mistake feeding for breeding."

"Have I told you how mental your family is?" Talk about double standards. "So I can't be half-and-half?"

"I don't think so. You appear to have inherited the skillset from my side of the family. As such, that would mean you are pure spawn. Like me, you are soulless in the strict sense of the term."

Another wave of panic hit me when I realized what he was saying. I took a deep breath to banish an anxiety attack. "I don't have a soul? Oh, God this sucks."

"Our demonic nature gives us a form of immortality in exchange for souls, or so I've been told, but we do have a demon spirit."

I fought back the dread until another thought burst into my mind. *How can I have a soulmate if I don't have a soul?* Was true love even possible for my kind? Had Elyssa been right about me from the start? This was horrible news.

I found my voice. "This makes no sense. Do vampires have souls?"

He shrugged. "Some believe they forfeit their human souls for immortality, but I'm no expert. Your mother and I escaped the supernatural life and tried to make normal lives. But you'll have nothing approaching a normal life if I don't teach you to use your powers responsibly."

"Better late than never, I guess." My dread morphed into anger. How could I have been so blind all this time? It seemed my parents might have told me something. But if I'd turned out human maybe they would have worried me over nothing.

Dad's voice broke through my stony silence. "Justin, listen to me. The world is far more dangerous than you know. When you feed on psychic energy, your activity burns bright like a beacon. Any nearby leech can feel it. That includes felycans and vampires. Werewolves can smell our kind especially well when we're leeching. While they probably won't interfere, vampires regard us as something of a rare treat. Not only is our blood like a fine wine to them, but some believe it can increase their vampiric abilities. Imagine being reduced to a living wine cask for vampires."

Everything Randy said made a lot more sense. I shuddered at the image. "Point taken."

"Also, there are ways to feed without exposing yourself. You've been going about it a bit too enthusiastically."

"I did feed on those laughing guys in the bathroom."

"Exactly. I've found comedy clubs to be a good focal point of positive energy. Passive feeding takes longer and is less satisfying but it will keep your nature hidden. That, I think, will be the first lesson I teach you."

I furrowed my brow. "Dad, the cravings are intense. Are you telling me that all the time you were with Mom you never fully satisfied your hunger?"

"She was worth the sacrifice. Our kind are not the sort who fall in love, but your mother won me over from the first." Pain knotted his features. He grabbed the pen from the table. It crunched as his fist clenched around it.

A knot formed in my throat. The pain in his eyes probably echoed my own. I found it hard to speak for a moment but I had to know. "Is Elyssa a vampire?" He hadn't said a thing about her.

"It's best you forget her," he said.

"But I love her."

"Love is powerful. Very powerful. But it can't overcome some obstacles."

"Enough with the mysterious nonsense. Is she really a vampire of some sort?"

He hesitated. "It sounds like it."

"But she goes to school. She doesn't burst into fire in the sun."

"Vampires, as a general rule, don't like the sun because it makes them lethargic and they easily sunburn, but it won't torch them."

"She didn't seem tired to me. Would SPF three-thousand sunblock do the trick?"

He offered a grim smile. "She may be a dhampyr, a very rare breed of day vampire."

"Oh, how wonderful. A rare kind of bloodsucker." I tossed the remains of my apple into the trash.

Dad stood and brushed the crushed pen bits from his hands then wiped at the spilled ink with a paper towel. "True vampires cannot breed. Only those of great age and potency can successfully turn a human into their kind. However, in the dark days it was a known practice of some old and lonely vampires to approximate families by turning a woman while she was pregnant."

I gagged. "Babies can survive that?"

"Rarely. Vampiric metamorphosis is brutal on the body. Even strong adults often die during the process."

"Did your parents homeschool you about this stuff?"

"It's certainly not something you'd learn at public school. Your mother and I left you dangerously ignorant of the facts. We'd hoped you would be a human child and that we could offer you a normal life. We were so very wrong. And for that, I'm sorry."

"You didn't even have a hint that I might be like you?"

He waggled his hand. "I suspected it was possible, but I've been away so much lately, I—I failed you."

I thought of Elyssa, eyes blazing and fangs glistening. Scary as hell but so damned sexy. "So you're saying the baby could come out as a vampire. A dhampyr. What makes it different from a normal vampire?"

"Dhampyrs have souls—they're half human. They are immortal but they can also procreate like humans."

"You look older than me, but you're immortal, right?"

"We're both immortal, son." Dad grinned. "Our immortal bodies grow and age to a certain extent because we're born and not turned. Our aging simply slows and then ceases. A mortal turned vampire, however, would not age or change from that point on."

"That would explain Randy."

"The vampire in the bathroom?"

I nodded. "He looks like a toothpick, but even with my super strength, I couldn't overpower him." I sighed. "I guess vampires are just stronger?"

Dad shook his head. "No. One-on-one, I can beat any but the oldest vampires at fisticuffs."

I snorted. "Fisticuffs?"

He held up a hand. "I'm old, Justin. Do you know how much of a pain in the ass it is to adjust to all the pop-culture changes in languages over the years?" He waved a dismissive hand. "Anyway, it's never just one vampire that you have to worry about—it's the pack. They're extremely social supers. They love to dress fancy and look cool. The Red Syndicate imposes strict dress codes on member vampires."

"Is the Red Syndicate an optional club for vampires?"

"I wouldn't say optional, exactly. It's the political arm of the vampires much like the Arcane Council is for sorcerers, wizards, Arcanes, and so forth." Dad backhanded the air. "It's not terribly important, because just like human politicians, they're all full of shit."

I snorted. "Point taken."

"Yeah, I despise politics. One reason why I ducked my family." Dad shuddered. "You're still not done developing, Justin. You just hit demonic puberty a couple of weeks ago, so don't expect to be at full strength. Every Daemos has a clumsy stage because their physical abilities exceed their reflexes and mental agility. I know you hated being forced to play football, but I think it's done wonders to get your neurons firing in time with your body."

"I realized that too." I shrugged. "Even so, I'll bet Elyssa could still kick my ass."

"Yeah, she's something else entirely." Dad put a finger on his chin. "Justin, if she is what I think she is, then you're lucky she didn't slice and dice you that night after Kings and Castles."

I gulped. "What is she?"

"Well, she's definitely a dhampyr. If memory serves, I think the violet eyes are a giveaway."

"You didn't mention that before."

"Yeah, well the old noodle is full of useless info." Dad tapped his temple.

"So, dhampyrs hate spawn?" I asked.

"Oh, no, that's neither here nor there." He shook his head. "I might be wrong, but if she's got ninja skills, and her family is in the security business, I'd bet she's a Templar."

"Huh?" I scratched me head. "Like the old dude with the beard and armor from Indiana Jones?"

Dad barked a laugh. "Not even close."

"I really thought she liked me. I guess that explains why she nearly slashed my throat and called me a monster."

"Aren't we?" Dad scrubbed at the ink on his hands but it wouldn't come off. "Like I said, you're lucky she didn't cut off your head for trying your demon tricks on her."

I shivered and tried to push the thought from my mind. "Hang on a second," I said. "This isn't just about me, it's about Mom too. Does she think you're a monster? Does she think I'm a monster?"

"It's complicated, Justin. Your mother still loves us despite all outward appearances that she's abandoned us."

"Then why did she leave?" I pounded the table in anger. A crack ran down its center.

"Her parents are very powerful in the sorcery community. Our *blessed* union came as a huge embarrassment to them. Your mother loved me despite my being nonhuman, though those were very trying times. She loved me enough to bear my children.

"Wait, did you say *children?*"

Dad nodded. "The Conroys stole something very precious from us. She couldn't bear the pain any longer and it nearly destroyed our relationship."

"What could be so precious that she'd abandon us?"

He seemed to weigh his next words carefully. "Your little sister."

CHAPTER 26

I sat there, mouth gaping in stunned silence.

"Her name is Ivy, and she's about to turn eleven." Dad's jaw tightened like a vice, eyes literally flickering with unholy blue light. "Eliza and Jeremiah Conroy, your mother's parents, took her shortly after birth. Jeremiah is a powerhouse in the Overworld and Arcane community, so no one dares go against him."

"I have a sister, my mom is a sorceress, and my dad is a demon." I slumped in my chair. "And I thought people on reality TV had it bad." I realized that all Mom's talk of auras had been for real.

Dad smiled grimly. "Like I said, son, love doesn't conquer all." He sighed. "Look, your mom left you a letter to explain things, but I thought it best if I talked to you about it."

"A letter?" My mouth dropped open. "Where is it?"

"Hang on." He went into his bedroom and returned with a crumpled piece of paper. "Just don't judge us too harshly, okay?"

I snatched it and spread it out.

Justin,

You mean the world to me and it agonizes me to have to do this, but your father and I have decided to go our separate ways. Remember when I told you about tough decisions? This is one of those. I love you so much but there's another person out there who needs me more than you and your father. I have to do this. I have to make right a mistake I should have never made. I already hate myself for it and I pray you won't hate me too.

But if you do, I'll understand.

Please don't blame your father and especially not yourself. I'm the one to blame.

I love you. Always.

Mom

I TRIED to keep back the anger, but I couldn't. "She couldn't tell me in person? Since when is a crummy letter supposed to make things right?"

"It's not, son, but she did it for a good reason." Dad shook his head sadly. "We hoped the Conroys would let her come back, but that hasn't happened. That's why I've been trying to find where they're keeping her."

I crumpled the letter again. "Why did Mom wait all this time to go to Ivy? Why didn't the Conroys take me?"

"We managed to hide from them for years, but they found us while your mother was pregnant with Ivy. Their price not to reveal our location and to let us keep you was our daughter. They forbid us from seeing her until she turned eleven, at which point your mother could return home to them."

I did some quick math in my head. "How in the world don't I remember Mom being pregnant? I was only seven, but I think that would stick out."

"All those times you mother charmed you, she also blurred your memories. Made it harder for you to remember certain things. She thought it was for the best, sparing you the pain, although I disagreed."

"You're damned right it was wrong! I have a sister. I want to remember everything about her, no matter how painful."

I thought back to the mystery pregnant woman who dashed in front of the car after my first encounter with Stacey. She had looked like Mom. I remembered the nightmare with the long dark hallway and the shadowy figure with the cane. Now that I thought about it, I remembered other times I had dreamt of crying babies and mystery pregnant women. Trying to pull it into focus was like peering through a shimmering haze.

It made sense now. My subconscious had known all along. My first encounter with Stacey had triggered Mom's protective charms and that must have jarred loose suppressed memories.

The strain of remembering caused a gentle ache in my head. I massaged my forehead with my fingers, but it didn't help. "I remember the night the Conroys came for my sister."

Dad nodded. "You attacked them with your toy sword."

"I guess I didn't win."

"Your grandfather laughed." Dad's lips pressed tight. "And then he hit you with a spell that froze you into place." A snarl contorted his face. "He told me to chain up the little monster next time."

"Why did he think I was a monster? You didn't even know what I was until now."

"He believed you were spawn and that your sister was pure human. What made him think that, I have no idea."

"Did Mom know?"

He shook his head. "Of course not. She would have told me." Something flashed on his face. Was it grief? Uncertainty? I had a sickening feeling that neither Dad nor I knew what Mom was truly up to.

"Why didn't we go into hiding again?"

"Sorcerers have ways of finding people no matter where they go. This particular geographic location interferes with tracking spells and magic, according to your mother. In the end, Jeremiah still found us."

"It doesn't make sense." I resisted the urge to put another crack in the kitchen table. "Why did the Conroys make her wait eleven years?" *And why didn't she take me with her? To protect me?*

"Eleven is the age at which most children start their arcane arts training."

"Magic?"

He nodded. "Your mother was one of the best teachers."

"Eleven years is plenty of time to brainwash a little girl. They probably figured I was too old for that."

Rage and sorrow warred for dominance on Dad's face as he nodded. His fists tightened, released, tightened, released. He drew several deep breaths as if performing a well-known ritual. As if exorcising his own demons.

I rose to my feet, a sense of purpose roaring into my veins. I would rescue my sister and my mom. Soul or not, I wanted my family united again. "I'm ready."

"For what?"

"To learn how to be a good demon. When do we start?"

"First thing tomorrow."

"No more vanishing? No more secret meetings with private eyes?"

He shook his head. "It's time I became a real father."

I walked over to him and hugged him. "Thanks."

He patted my back and squeezed me to him. "I love you, son."

For once, I didn't feel icky for saying it. "I love you too, Dad."

We stayed up talking for a while. The clock read two in the morning when we finished and Dad told me to get some rest—we'd start practice during the day when it was safer for us to be out.

Despite my exhaustion, it took a while to fall asleep. *I have a sister!* That meant I was a brother. A big brother at that. That gave me the right to beat the crap out of any guys who even looked at her, right? I was happy but nervous and full of dread all at the same time. What if she didn't like me once we met? Images of the mysterious man in the top hat played through my mind, still blurry from Mom's attempts to block the painful memories from me, but vivid enough to fill me with rage. I wanted a sister to protect and to love. I *would* save her from those monsters no matter the cost.

But I had to face reality. I was in over my head until Dad showed me how to use my abilities and I learned more about the Overworld. All the times I'd been out at night prowling for girls, I'd never thought about the dangers posed by other supers.

A gentle tap on my window snapped me from my reverie. My senses went on instant alert. I slithered out of bed and peeked through the curtains. A pair of mischievous amber eyes glowed. I groaned and walked to the front door, eased it open to avoid waking Dad.

"Stacey, what are you doing here?" I'd completely forgotten my plans to become her boo in exchange for help. With Dad around, I didn't need her help anymore.

She pursed her lips. "I know it is none of my concern, but I thought perhaps it would endear you to me if I"—she traced a fingernail down my arm and cast a sultry gaze at my crotch—"gave you certain information."

I almost told her my father had given me the four-one-one on everything she'd dangled like a carrot in front of me all this time. A part of me wanted to rub it in her face, but despite her being cray-cray level ten, a stalker, and a cradle robber, I liked Stacey. I covered a yawn with a smile. "I already know I'm a demon spawn. I know you're felycan. I know—"

"Not that sort of information, my lamb. This regards the vile vampire who took an unholy interest in you." Stacey raised an eyebrow. "Randolph?"

"Randy?" A chill that had nothing to do with her fingernails against my skin raised goosebumps on my neck. I scanned the yard for signs of vampire attack. "Why? What's going on?"

"He appeared at the party just before you left with your little wench." Her upper lip curled into a sneer. "I remained behind to watch him. He's tried to find your house many times before, but I've made sure to throw him off the trail."

As a child, I'd always gone to Randy's house to play because he hated carting his mountain of toys to my house.

"Really?" I squeezed her hand. "I had no idea, Stacey. Thanks."

Her cheeks flushed with pleasure. "Of course, darling. You see, I am superior in every way to that little tramp you took home with you."

"Please don't call Katie a tramp." I put a hand on her shoulder. "Was there something else?"

Stacey blinked. "Yes. He looked for you at the party. I searched his car and found a blood-leeching apparatus. I do believe he means you serious harm at your next encounter."

I shivered. "He just doesn't give up."

"I also saw him secretly pouring red liquid into people's drinks. I do not know if it is a truth potion to help him find your home, but it was all very nefarious."

My heart skipped a beat. "No, that's not truth serum. It's a fricking vampire steroids potion, or something like that. My god, there's no telling what that stuff will do to people!" I grabbed her shoulders. "You've got to help me!"

I ran inside and grabbed my car keys, but they were gone. Dad wasn't in his room. He wasn't in the house. "God damn it, Dad! Where are you?" No answer.

His motorcycle still stood in the garage, but the Jetta was gone. I grabbed the keys to the bike and patted the seat. "Get on, Stacey."

"Oh, how exciting." She got on behind me, pressed her softness to my back. I didn't know what was louder, her purring or the motorcycle. I didn't have a lot of experience with a hog, but my football-honed reflexes linked in my enhanced muscles. I spun the bike toward the road and sped toward the Creek.

It didn't take long to get there, or long to see that all hell had broken loose. The door to the party house lay in the yard, literally torn from its hinges. The entire house shook like a giant was moshing in the den.

I rushed inside. A snarling Jenny leapt at me from the dining room on the left. I dodged and held her at bay with a stiff arm. Eyes glowing red, face contorted with rage, she viciously snapped at me with human teeth. Apparently the V drug didn't give her fangs.

"Jenny, it's me, Justin."

She shrieked and tried to bite me again. Any semblance of humanity was gone. Not that Jenny had been all that humane to begin with. I wondered if Annie had drunk the vampire Kool-Aid as well.

I spun Jenny around and got a firm grip on her neck before she could bite me. She screamed and wriggled, but failed to break my grip. Shrieks and howls filled the house. Thuds pounded the second floor. Pushing Jenny in front of me, I walked around the corner and found bedlam.

Bodies lay scattered across the floor, many of them my football team-mates, cheerleaders, and the college kids from earlier. Annie lay half-clothed next to a spilled cup of red punch. Bryan's still form lay next to a keg. I couldn't tell if any of them breathed, or were dead.

Adam and Steve traded blows in the middle of the den, howling like madmen at each other. Two women danced in circles, oblivious to the carnage around them. Nathan growled like a dog, gnawing a leather boot someone had lost. Mandy and Vanda writhed on the floor in a spreading puddle of beer.

"What a wretched mess." Stacey watched calmly as if it was just another day at the office for her.

"Can you knock them unconscious?" I asked.

"I could certainly hit them on the head." Stacey shrugged. "Would that suffice?"

"Can you do it without killing anyone?"

Stacey quirked her lips. "They are so delicate. There is a nom drug store not far from here. Perhaps they have chloroform."

"Can you get some before they kill each other?"

She kissed my cheek, blithely ignoring the writhing Jenny snapping at her inches away. "Indeed, I shall." With that, Stacey blurred away.

I looked around for rope, anything I could use to tie up Jenny so I could stop the others from fighting, but it was a high school party, not a fetish soiree. If I hit the girl too hard, I might crack her skull or worse.

A figure blurred into the room and grinned. "There's my little buddy."

"Randy, you son of a bitch! What did you do to these people?" I would have rushed him, but Jenny squirmed and nearly took a chunk out of my wrist before I got her back under control.

"I gave them one of the bad batches of V." Randy held up a vial of reddish liquid. "It's caused problems with test subjects in the past." His hands blurred. A vial of purple replaced the red. "This is the antidote."

"Then give it to them!"

"Not so fast." Randy's grin dipped into a snarl. "When I got here, I saw you talking to that piece of shit Nathan Spelman like he was your best friend." He plastered a smile on his face. "I planned to politely ask for your blood again, but watching you just made me so fucking angry!" The last three words roared rapid-fire from spittle-flecked lips.

This caught the attention of Nathan. He abandoned the leather shoe, growled, and lunged at Randy. The vampire swatted him away without a second thought. The hefty football player flew through the air and crashed into the wall, leaving an imprint in the drywall.

"Careful!" I shouted. "You could have killed him!"

Nathan groaned. Blood trickled from his nose. *That poor guy and his nose!*

Randy snarled. "You abandoned me when we were kids, Justin. You turned me down when I asked for your blood. Now you're just one of the popular kids." Randy's crimson teeth bared. "You, my friend, are a fucking twatwaffle."

"That's a great insult. Think I'll file it away for future use." Still holding Jenny at bay, I held out my other hand and tried to calm him. "Randy, look, I'll give you some blood. Just give these people the antidote. *Please.*"

"I have a better offer." Randy's eyes glowed red. "Why don't you give me yourself, and then I'll give them the antidote." He held up a glittery ribbon. "Just wrap this around your neck."

"Is this a joke? Why should I wrap a ribbon around my neck?"

"Trust me, it'll make this go a whole lot easier." He shrugged. "But hey, if saving these kids isn't enough incentive, I've got friends on the way. They're very persuasive."

Tires screeched outside. Car doors slammed. I sidled sideways toward the kitchen to put plenty of distance between me and the front door. Since the broken door lay in the front yard, it only took a moment for me to recognize the figures walking down the front sidewalk. The female in the school girl outfit, geek glasses perched on her nose grinned maliciously at me. Behind her came the little boy in skinny jeans, and last, a brawny, olive-skinned kid who looked like a real scrapper.

I had to ditch Jenny without hurting her, but how? I looked at the ribbon Randy held and wondered what he hadn't told me about it. "Fine, throw me the ribbon."

"That's my boy." Randy wrapped it around a beer bottle and tossed it to me.

I caught the bottle with my free hand and tugged the ribbon off the top. "What will this do to me?"

"It'll make you look cute as a bell." He snickered and turned to his comrades. "Felicia, Mortimer, Blake, meet our ticket to the top, Justin Case."

The geek girl curtseyed and smirked. "How nice to meet you." She licked her lips. "Randy gave us a taste of your blood. It's totes delish."

"Ah, so someone does still use totes!" *Take that Katie!*

"God, what a mess!" the boy whined. "The boss is gonna be pissed."

"Christ Almighty, Mortimer! Stop your damned whining." Blake—I figured out his name using the process of elimination—slapped the kid lightly on the back of the head.

"Ow!" Mortimer rubbed his head and growled. "You're such an ass."

I held the ribbon towards my neck. "I have your word that you'll use the antidote on everyone if I do this, right?" *Buy a little time. Stacey will be back soon.*

"Absolutely." Randy shook the vial of purple. "Now, put on the ribbon."

"Are they alive?" I nodded towards Bryan and the others sprawled nearby.

Randy rolled his eyes. "Mortimer, see if the jocks are still alive."

"Why me?" Mortimer sniffed loudly and went up to the nearest body. He put an ear to the mouth. "Still breathing."

"How about the others?" I said.

Mortimer groaned loudly and checked several more. "Yes, they're alive." He looked up at Randy. "Did you use batch one thousand six?"

Randy hissed a breath. "No, this is nine-eighty."

Mortimer turned to me. "Nine-eighty knocks out some people. Turns the others into stark-raving lunatics." He got up and brushed off his hands. "They'll survive if they get the antidote within seventeen hours of taking the serum."

Blake cracked his knuckles. "Now, put on the damned collar, or I'll do it for you."

"Aha!" I strained as Jenny wriggled madly in my grip. "So it's a collar. Is it magical?"

Randy knelt next to Annie and gripped the girl's head. "Put on the collar or I snap her neck."

My time had just run out.

CHAPTER 27

My original plan crumbled to ash. If I defied Randy, Annie would die. The world might be a better place without the bitch, but all life is precious—blah, blah. On the flip side, Randy might be lying. If so Edenfield High would suffer a rash of funerals and have to replace the entire football team.

How could I guarantee he followed through on his promise?

A figure blurred into the room. Blake grunted and flew through a bedroom door. A tremendous thud shook the walls. Randy shot to his feet, leaving Annie unscathed. Felicia and Mortimer assumed fighting stances.

"Stacey!" I shouted.

Blue eyes glowed from a shadowy corner. Dad stepped out into the light, a grin on his face. "Well, shit, son. You got us some toys." His face morphed into something not quite human. Black claws grew from the tips of his fingers. "Let's have some fun."

"Fuck!" Randy charged me.

I wrapped the ribbon around Jenny's neck. She went limp as a noodle. I barely got her out of the way before Randy slammed into me. I flew backwards, smashing through drywall and studs until a body stopped my flight.

Blake grunted as he absorbed the brunt of momentum and smacked into the outer wall. Randy plowed through the hole I'd made, eyes burning like embers. Face contorted in rage, he charged again. This time I was ready. I lowered my shoulder like a running back and lunged.

Ribs cracked. Randy's screams trailed away as he flew back through the gap in the wall. My hackles rose, neck tingled. I ducked to avoid Blake's grasp. He tripped over me. I kicked him in the head. Before he recovered, I picked him up and threw him through the window. The glass was already smashed, so he hardly made a sound as he sailed into the night air.

I have to get the antidote! If Randy escaped, everyone would die. I hoped I hadn't already broken the vial during the fight. I ran back into the den. Dad blurred past. Grabbed Felicia by the hair and flung her into the kitchen.

I couldn't help it. God, I tried so hard, but it just came out. "Bye Felicia!"

Before the words trailed from my mouth, Dad blurred diagonally across the room. Time seemed to slow. I saw the big grin on his face as he slid on his knees, arm extended, and flipped Mortimer's legs out from beneath him. The kid vampire screeched and slammed into the concrete.

"Run! Run!" He tried to get up, but the blow to his brain disoriented him. Legs flailed and spun uselessly.

I saw Randy making a break for it. It was time for a little blurring of my own. I focused on my feet and ran. Wind whistled. I skidded around the corner to the foyer. Dove for Randy. My hand snagged his jacket and pulled him over backwards.

Arms gripped me in an iron vice. "I'm gonna kill you, you fucking demon!" Blake screamed in my ear.

"Not so damned loud!" I shouted back. I stomped his foot hard enough to crack the concrete.

"Ahhh! Agh!" Blake's screams nearly ruptured my eardrums.

Randy had made it out the door. He was halfway to the car, staggering off balance and holding his head. I dashed through the door. My neck prickled. I dodged left in time to avoid another rush from Blake. I tripped him. Before he even hit the ground, I grabbed him by his fancy-ass jeans and used his considerable forward momentum to hurl him.

He flew twenty feet through the air and slammed into Randy. The pair went down in a heap. I dashed over and felt through Randy's pockets. Liberated four vials of purple from his jacket. The contents leaked from a broken fifth vial.

Felicia and Mortimer ran screaming from the house, a blue-eyed demon roaring at their heels. I grabbed Randy by the collar and dragged him kicking and screaming behind me. Dad roared. Felicia and pals screamed like a bus full of cheerleaders falling off the Golden Gate Bridge.

"Let me go!" Randy shouted.

I let him go. He jumped up. I nailed him in the jaw so hard, he spun around twice and dropped to his knees. I dug in his other jacket pocket and found another ribbon. Before I could wrap it around his neck, one of the crazed students tripping on Randy's drug leapt on my back and tried to bite me.

Randy staggered to his feet and ran after his friends. Felicia shoved him into a black van. Blake and Mortimer dove in after him. It peeled out of the driveway, fishtailed down the road and out of sight.

"Son of a bitch!" I yanked the mindless attacker off my back and used the ribbon on him. The ends sewed themselves together and he passed out.

Dad roared with laughter. "Oh, man, I haven't had that much fun in a hundred years." He sighed, patted my back. "Good work. I'd say the football practice definitely paid off."

I glared at him, then ran back inside, dragging the unconscious victim behind me. I figured since Randy dealt the serum in drinks, I could dilute the antidote in a little water and trickle it into the mouths of the stricken students. The dancing and crazed ones were the easiest, amazingly enough. While Dad held their mouths open, I poured in the antidote. Rather than spit it out, they gulped greedily.

Within a few seconds, the glow in their eyes faded and they fell asleep. It took a couple of hours to search the house drag all the kids into the den where we treated them and let them sleep. I glowered angrily at Dad the entire time.

Once we were done, I held back my anger and calmly asked, "Where were you when I left the house?"

"Feeding." Dad sighed. "I came home. Saw my bike was gone and went looking for you. I thought you were asleep, or I never would've left without you."

"How did you find me?"

He raised an eyebrow. "Your felycan." Dad chuckled. "She must have seen me driving around the neighborhood."

"She knows the Jetta," I said. "I wondered why she didn't come back."

He shrugged. "Well, shall we go home?"

I was still pissed Randy had gotten away. "If I catch Randy, can I turn him in to the Overworld cops?"

Dad bit his lower lip. "I don't know, son. Might be best to forget about him."

I shook my head. "No. He's too dangerous." I waved him away. "Go home. Get some rest. I'll stick around and make sure the students wake up."

"Justin, if you do catch Randy, we can't contact the Templars. We can't let anyone know where we are."

I nodded. "Don't worry. I'll figure out something."

He gave me a doubtful look. "Your call. Guess I'll see you at home."

I sighed wearily. "Yeah. Just answer your damned phone if I call, okay?"

Dad took out his cell phone and turned up the volume to max. "Promise." He tossed me the Jetta keys and held out his hand for the bike keys. "No offense, but I don't trust you with my Harley."

"I don't blame you." I gave him the keys and watched him leave.

I hovered over Bryan, peeled back his eyelids. His breathing sounded normal, but I couldn't tell when or if he'd wake up. I straightened and looked at the others, deciding if a splash of cold water would help.

The skin on my neck heated. I spun toward the door.

Glittering violet eyes regarded me. She wore a black skin-tight outfit, silver sai swords sheathed against each leg. Raven hair hung in a dark curtain around her face.

She looked like a dark angel of death waiting to collect her due.

My knees went weak. I staggered back. "Elyssa?"

"You." She stalked forward, teeth bared, and jabbed me in the chest... with a finger. "You're the one they're after!"

"They?" I didn't back away from her finger. I yearned for her touch, even if it was in anger. I recovered and shot back. "I almost made a citizen's arrest on your new partner." I wished I had Randy to dump at her feet, but had to settle for dramatically pretending to do so.

"Oh, god." Elyssa groaned.

"Oh, god is right." I squared my shoulders. "I don't for a minute believe you're a dealer though. Are you?"

"Of course I'm not!" She held her thumb and forefinger a fraction apart. "I was this close to getting on the inside, but you've probably ruined that."

"Ruined it?" I laughed. "He's still free and it's not like he thinks me and you are friends."

Elyssa sighed. "I hope you're right." She looked around the room. "My god, it looks like a warzone in here."

"Aren't you going to automatically assume I killed these people and ate their souls or something?"

Elyssa rolled her eyes. "I saw you and your father fight off the vampires."

"How'd you know he's my dad?" I asked.

She tapped her left ear. "Super hearing, Justin. I waited outside while you rounded up the victims and treated them."

My mouth dropped open. "You've been watching all this time and didn't even lift a finger to help?"

"You had things well in hand."

"Yeah, but we could've caught Randy's entire gang!" I shook my head slowly. "Now they all got away."

Guilt flickered in Elyssa's eyes. "I was also curious to see what you did."

"To see if we'd help or harm?" My hopes dared to rise. "I'm a monster, Elyssa. I know that now and I accept it. But can't you see I'm a good monster?"

She threw up her hands. "Justin, I can't even right now, okay?" Elyssa checked a watch. "You have to be out of here in five minutes, or it won't be pretty."

"Five minutes?"

"I have a cleanup crew on the way. We'll make sure everyone gets home safe, okay?" Elyssa stepped back and flourished her hands toward the door. "So, get going."

"But—but what about Randy and his evil minions?" *What about showing I'm good?*

"We'll eventually catch him and he'll go to supernatural jail, okay?"

"Nothing I do will ever prove I love you, will it? That I'm not evil."

Elyssa's eyelashes fluttered. She backed up a step. "Four minutes. Better go."

I choked back a plea of despair. My master plan to prove I was good hadn't done a thing to change Elyssa's mind. If anything, she seemed cold, impersonal, uncaring. My hand ached to caress her cheek. My lips trembled to touch hers. My body shook with desire to feel her warmth.

But it wasn't to be. If this proved anything, my time in the sun had passed. "I will never find a brighter star than you," I whispered. Then I walked away, leaving what could have been to the sands of time.

Holy shit, I'm so poetic I just want to cry.

And I did the moment I got into the Jetta. Tears trickled slowly down my cheeks. I didn't sob. I didn't wail. I had forever lost the love of my life and I wanted to be a little dignified about it. So I wept big boy tears all the way home and cried myself to sleep.

CHAPTER 28

A delicious odor woke me from a dreamless sleep. My first thought was of Elyssa.

I banished it and gritted my teeth. *It's over. Accept it. Dad is home and it's training day.*

After last night's excitement, I hoped we could keep it chill. I tossed on some shorts and went into the kitchen.

Dad flipped a pancake and put some bacon on a towel. He flashed a grin. "Sleep well?"

"What do you think?" I cracked a yawn. "I'm starving both literally and demonically."

"Me too." He put a heaping plate of pancakes on the table. "Let's get the literal out of the way first, okay?"

My stomach growled. "Don't have to convince me!"

After breakfast, Dad explained a few basics to me, some of which I had already figured out on my own. When I used my superhuman abilities such as health restoration or strength, they consumed energy from what he called my *psythus*, or a psychic well. The psythus was the equivalent of a psychic stomach that stored the essence drained from others. When I leeched, I actually took parts of a human's soul and spirit from them. Dad explained the two were separate, that even soulless beings had spirit. His explanation about the two only confused me so I took his word for it. If I fed too much on one person, I could severely damage the person's soul to the point of no return and leave them in a coma or worse.

This frightened me as I thought back to Victoria and the girls who I had come so close to ravishing. I told him my concerns but he assured me I would have to be near death to leech enough soul from someone to damage them.

He told me how to probe without "hooking" as he called the latching process. Apparently I could feed off any sort of emotion, but as with food, every incubus had a different taste preference.

"There are those who enjoy pain," he said. "The things they'll do to a person while they feed are horrific."

"What are kine?" I asked, remembering the strange term Stacey had used a few times.

"It's an old term that means cattle. That's how most leeches view humans."

"That's horrible."

"One entity's predator is another entity's cattle."

I shuddered to think of what Stacey might have done to me had Mom's charm not been in place. Come to think of it, a psychic energy battery meter would be really handy. Maybe on a watch or something so I could look at the time and tell whether the old supernatural batteries were running low.

"What happens if we go to church?" I asked.

"We would disintegrate into puddles of molten flesh."

I gave Dad a horrified look and leapt from my seat. "What if I'd gone to church with a friend? Holy crap, Dad!"

He laughed. "Just kidding. At worst you'd have to listen to a boring sermon."

"Oh." I sat down. "Well, that sounds like reason enough to avoid churches."

After a lecture taking up most of the morning, Dad took me to the laundromat to practice my skills.

"Why a laundromat?" I surveyed the bored men and lethargic women reading magazines or watching *Saved by the Bell* reruns on an ancient nineteen-inch television. "Is this what you were doing when I followed you that day?"

"Yes, I was feeding," he said. "People here are in a neutral state of mind. It's easier to practice probing without strong emotions getting in the way."

I was just glad he hadn't been getting his jollies from watching old ladies. Nobody seemed to notice we weren't doing laundry while I practiced. It took a while, but I eventually got the hang of probing, dirty as the term sounded. While I could not read minds, as I had discovered long ago, I sensed emotional states. Most of the people in this place were practically comatose. No surprise there. One girl, however, rather enjoyed herself thanks to the erotic novel in her lap.

Another interesting tidbit—I could hook into a person's psyche without them immediately wanting to tear off my clothes. I had to attune to their emotional state before diving in.

"Isn't this like mind control?" I asked.

"It's dangerously close. If you can raise sexual impulses, you can make a person do things they normally wouldn't do. As it is, we can either prevent them from responding to us by keeping our hooks attuned to their state, or we can attract them."

I was a little disappointed I couldn't telepathically make them do what I wanted. It might have been funny making someone dance a jig. It didn't take me too long to figure out how to attune my state to people's auras so I could hook into them after Dad explained the process. It still required a lot of control and willpower to settle my mind into passivity.

"Once you've hooked, you can transfer the link to another person," he told me. "That's what happened to you with Cindy Mueller and that other boy."

"Were they were feeding off each other?"

"No, humans can't feed. They don't have a psythus. By linking two people you can increase the flow of energy just as you did to the young couple at the football game. Much as it sounds like magic, there are some scientific principles to psychic energy generation and so forth."

"Cindy and Alan are dating now. Cool, huh?" Ever since my accident with those two in Calculus, they'd been inseparable.

His eyes hardened. "Don't toy with people's emotions, Justin. It's wrong for one thing, and for another, the feelings you think you're creating are illusion. You can't make someone like or love another person if true feelings don't already exist."

I gave him a shocked look. "I would never do that." I actually had planned on playing matchmaker with others in school, but wasn't about to tell him now.

"Our ability to force emotional connections between people can be a dangerous power."

"Anything is dangerous in the hands of a hormonal teenager," I said with a grin.

He chuckled. "No doubt."

I practiced hooking and unhooking for a while, seeing if I could leave the individual in question totally unaffected. They seemed to know something was afoot because most would glance around as though someone had just tapped them on the shoulder. So long as I maintained a calm emotional state, I could feed with hardly a tic from the victim. The only problem with a neutral emotional state? The energy trickled slowly across my demonic taste buds with all the flavor of plain rice cakes.

After practice, we went to a hipster restaurant in downtown Decatur for some real food.

"Do dhampyrs hate us?" I asked Dad as we ate.

He pursed his lips. "I would imagine that each individual has his or her own opinion of our kind much as ordinary humans do. In general, though, spawn have earned their bad reputation."

"Elyssa's mom is a hair stylist," I said. "A hair stylist! I would never think someone like her was a dhampyr."

He shrugged. "Like anyone else, they've got to earn a living."

He made it sound so mundane. How many people could say their hair-stylist was a day vampire? I sighed. "So there's probably no chance of Elyssa and I getting back together."

"Ah, to be young and foolish," Dad said. "I hate to say it, son, but it sounds like she has some prejudiced feelings that will be hard to overcome."

I tried not to hang my head, but the weight of his words hit me like a hammer, even if Elyssa had already told me in no uncertain terms how she felt about what I was. Even if everything I'd done last night hadn't changed her mind. But there was nothing I could do about it. Just like I couldn't change into a giraffe, I couldn't control what I'd been born. Besides, dating demon spawn was probably more extreme than most people wanted to deal with.

Hey, Mom and Dad, I'm dating a soul-sucking demon!

Yeah, it was a hard thing to overcome.

We left the restaurant and walked down an alley between the restaurant and a neighboring pub, toward the parking lot at the other end. Shattered glass littered the pavement and crunched underfoot. A stray dog trotted past us, something dangling from its mouth. We reached the junction of a service entrance where four buildings backed up to each other. Dumpsters lined the paved strip. Steam drifted from the sewage covers in the middle of the service alley. I wrinkled my nose at the unwelcome odor pervading an otherwise crisp autumn evening.

A covering of leaves blew away to reveal a line of chalk. A crackle and a low hum filled my ears. I stopped and looked around, half expecting a power transformer to explode. Dad took a couple of steps forward. He bounced back as if he'd hit a wall.

"Shit." He lunged forward and rebounded again. He pressed against the air like a mime touching an invisible wall.

"What is it?"

"We've got a problem."

I still wasn't sure what the hell was going on. "What are you doing? There's nothing there."

"It's a confinement circle."

More leaves blew away and I saw the line extending in a circle around us—just like the circles behind the school.

The mysterious cowboy came from around the corner and gave us a triumphant look. "Well that was easy."

"You!" I shouted.

Cowboy Dude chuckled. "Hey, I remember you."

My fists clenched. "Shouldn't you be herding cattle and promoting cigarettes?"

He scowled. "What the hell is that supposed to mean?"

"What do you want?" Dad asked.

"The bounty, of course," replied the man. He strutted over like he was the cock of the walk and studied me. "You must be the little Slade monster everyone's so worked up about." He looked at my dad. "You, on the other hand, are wanted by the Conroys. I guess it's for the best if I turn you in with your 'son'." He flashed air quotes to demonstrate exactly what he thought about our family relations. "I'll let the authorities sort it all out."

I barely knew Cowboy Dude, but I already hated the bastard.

"I guess the Conroys got tired of me poking around in their business." Dad's eyes glowed blue. "Who put a bounty on my son?"

The man shrugged. "I don't know. I just take the monsters to the Conclave and let the authorities sort it out." He rubbed his hands together. "Now, if you'll just cooperate, I promise things will go smoothly."

I was getting really tired of this dude's insinuations that my dad and I were nothing more than monsters for him to ship off.

I stepped forward. Dad stopped me. "You can't break through it, son. It's a circle."

"A circle?"

"It's what sorcerers use to trap demon spawn, among other things." He pointed to the chalk outline on the ground.

"A chalk circle?" I pshawed. "That's stupid. Who in the world came up with that rule?"

The cowboy wizard listened to us with an amused expression on his face then lifted a large rune-covered staff and waved it around in a way that probably wasn't good for our near future.

I knew something horrible was about to happen to Dad. Before I could think, I blurred forward and snatched the staff from the man. I snapped it into four pieces. Threw the pieces to the ground. I grabbed the man by the neck. He squealed like a pig—probably just like Coach Wise preferred—as I chucked him at the dumpster. He bounced off the open lid and landed inside with a metallic clang. I blurred over to him and looked inside. He was out cold, covered in moldy lettuce and tomatoes.

I approached the oh-so-dangerous chalk circle and rubbed out a section with my shoe. Dad stepped across, staring at me with amazement.

"How did you do that?" he asked.

"I, uh, just walked across it," I said. "I felt a little static in the air, but that was it."

"You know what this means?" he said.

"That I can step across a chalk line?"

He shook his head. "You *are* part human."

"So I'm not a demon spawn after all?"

He grinned. "Oh, you're definitely demon spawn, but you have a human side too." He whistled. "And they thought half-breeds were impossible."

"The Conroys must have known something if they took Ivy."

"Maybe. Or perhaps they're just evil people."

"That goes without saying about anyone who'd steal a baby from her parents." I pointed a thumb over my shoulder at the dumpster wizard. "What about him?"

"I don't know what to do about him. This is bad news. If he found us, it means others might be close behind."

"Why would magicians need money? Can't they just make it out of thin air?"

He chuckled. "They don't like to be called that. It lumps them in with the ordinary illusionists. Besides, even the best sorcerers can't make things out of thin air." Dad stared vacantly for a moment then narrowed his eyes. "Do you have your phone?"

"Of course." I produced it.

"Let's check the Conclave's website. Maybe they have my bounty posted there."

My eyebrows threatened to fly away. "You must be kidding. They have a website?"

I typed in the address my dad gave me. Sure enough, a website for the Overworld Conclave appeared with slick professionally-designed graphics and everything. The main page listed bounties. Mine and my dad's sat at the top of the list. Most of the bounties ran around a thousand bucks. Ours were fifty grand each. I almost felt flattered.

"How can sorcerers have a website? I thought magic and technical stuff didn't work very well together."

"Technology and magic work very well together," he said. "Some of the things they can do nowadays would scare your pants off. Besides, this isn't the Arcane Council's website. The Overworld Conclave governs all supernatural beings. Or at least it tries to."

"Tries to?"

"Every faction complains that other factions have too much power. Most of the time nothing gets done. About the only thing most factions agree on is keeping the supernatural out of the limelight. Anyone caught breaking that rule is usually dealt with quickly and efficiently."

I gulped. Had I stepped over the line? Stupid question. I had dived over the line with football. That had to be the reason the Conclave had listed a bounty on me.

I went to the dumpster and, despite the horrible odor, pulled out the unconscious sorcerer. A few shreds of moldy lettuce fell off his brown leather duster. I patted him on the cheek a couple of times. He jerked awake, mumbling something about remembering his gym shorts. When his eyes settled on me, they hardened.

"How did you break the circle?"

"I'll ask the questions," I said. "How did you find us?"

"A lot of detective work."

"Tracking spells?" Dad asked.

He shook his head. "Didn't have blood or anything to track you with."

I wasn't sure what the limits of magic were in that regard. For all I knew he could wave a magic wand around and teleport to us.

"You two should just come with me," the sorcerer said. "It'll be a lot easier on you that way."

I gave him a yeah-right look. "How about you leave us alone and go away?"

He snorted. "I'm the least of your worries. Ever since the bounties on you two went public, all sorts of supers are on the hunt."

"Vampires?" Dad asked, worry creasing his forehead.

The sorcerer pushed himself to his feet and looked at the splintered mess I'd made of his staff. "Do you know how long it takes to make one of those?" He shook his head. "No, of course you don't."

Something rustled. A bit of broken roof tile fell onto the alley floor from two stories up. Dad cursed. The sorcerer dug in his trench coat and whipped out a smooth ebony stick about twelve inches long. Something cold prickled at the edge of my senses, the way it had last night before the fight with Randy.

"I just knew those sons of bitches were following me," the sorcerer said. "Lazy bastards were probably waiting for me to put you in sleepers."

I gulped. "Um, who's following you?"

Dark forms dropped from above and landed in front of us. I counted six. One shadowy figure stepped into the dim light of a lamp. He looked pretty ordinary to me aside from his abnormally ice-hued skin and his Fabio-length brown hair. He smiled. His canines lengthened into ivory-colored fangs.

Behind him appeared another familiar face.

Randy.

CHAPTER 29

Mortimer, Blake, and Felicia flanked Randy. Considering how we'd kicked their asses last night, I wouldn't have been worried if not for the dozen or more other blood-suckers backing them up.

Fabio grinned, revealing buck teeth and a quarter-inch gap.

"Christ almighty! What happened to your teeth?" I waved my hands in mock horror. "Don't vampires visit the orthodontist?"

"God, I'm so sick of your snarky little mouth, Justin." Randy cracked his knuckles. "You should've just accepted my offer last night. Now things are going to get unpleasant. I hate to do it, but you and daddy dearest are about to become the newest guests at Casa del Vampire."

"You beat the hell out of me last night." Mortimer's chin trembled. "Bad demons! Bad!"

Dad bared his teeth, eyes flickered into flame. "Yeah, kid, it's what we do."

I smirked. "Casa del Vampire? Damn, Randy, your French is terrible."

Cowboy Dude snorted. "That's because it's Spanish."

I tried to come up with a witty response and failed. "Oh."

"Yeah, dork. It's Spanish!" Randy's stained teeth gleamed in the lamplight.

"Well, screw you and your Spanish!" I shouted back.

Crimson irises glowed in response. I glanced around the rooftops and lost count of the shadows waiting for the word to pounce.

"Hold on a cotton-picking minute!" Cowboy Dude held up his smartphone to display a symbol that looked a bit like a sheriff's star. "I'm Harry Shelton, a duly licensed Overworld bounty hunter. You can't just jump my claim like this."

"Overworld?" Randy laughed and looked around. Other vampires added their scornful laughter to his. The smile left his lips. "We don't need those losers anymore. You're looking at the soon-to-be new vampire order."

"Holy farting fairies." Shelton gripped his magic wand tighter. "You smacktards can't be serious. The Red Syndicate will yank out your fangs and shove them up your asses before they let you break Overworld law. Now get the hell out of here and let me finish my capture!"

I had to admit this Shelton dude was ballsy as hell considering the odds.

Randy peeled back his lips to reveal his nasty fangs. "Fat chance, cowboy."

"I'm not a goddamned cowboy!" Energy glowed at the end of Shelton's wand. "Last chance, you blood-sucking baboons."

I couldn't help but respect the dude, even if he was an assmunch.

I tensed.

Dad tensed.

The vampires edged forward, stylishly, of course. The susurrus of fashionably torn jeans, school-girl skirts, and fabulously designed shirts blended with the stomp of expensive leather shoes. Felicia pushed up her geek glasses and stuck out her tongue at me. She looked so damned snarky, I just wanted to punch her in the face.

"Wait!" I held up my hands and the vampires paused. I looked at Fabio. "Where did you get those marvelous jeans?" That threw him off long enough for me to shout, "Run!"

The three of us retreated.

A group of vampires jumped off the roofs behind us, each one perfectly executing a three-point landing, all except for the last guy who caught the edge of the dumpster with his foot. His cry of dismay cut off with a thud when he face-planted on the cobblestones.

Now there was nowhere left to go.

Dad morphed, muscles coiling around his arms until he gained nearly a foot in height and his skin turned light blue. He brandished sharp claws and unleashed a roar.

Mortimer screamed and tried to retreat, but the bulk of vampires behind him pushed him forward.

"How do I change like that?" I asked Dad.

"Don't even try it." His usual tenor dropped an octave, verging on guttural. "If you mess up, you'll see what a real monster is."

The vampires charged. All hell broke loose. Shelton shouted a word and a blistering gout of orange flames roared past my face and blasted Blake, knocking him against a wall and charring his designer jeans. The odor of burned hair and denim filled the air.

I caught a vampire with my fist in mid-dive. Sent him flying. Ducked under Felicia's foot as she sprang off the wall at me, hissing. A vampire behind me wrapped his arms around mine in an iron grip. Another vampire swung his fist at my face. I ducked out of my captor's arms. The other vampire's fist missed me and crunched into his comrade's nose. I lowered my shoulder and rammed my would-be attacker. He flew back and thudded inside the same dumpster I'd knocked Shelton into moments earlier.

The sorcerer roasted another vamp, annihilating his long hair and leaving a smoldering, smelly mess. Fire didn't seem to kill them, but charring their hair and designer clothes really pissed them off. Shelton shouted, "Yod!" and formed a fist with his free hand. He aimed it at the vamps behind us. The would-be flankers smacked against an invisible barrier and bounced back.

Dad grabbed Fabio his magnificent hair and slammed him into the dumpster. Teeth cracked.

"Guess that's ones way to fix those nasty teeth!" I put my back to Dad's and faced another onslaught.

Mortimer dodged and dipped around my punches. I felt kind of guilty about fighting a kid, but then again, he was likely a lot older than he looked. Besides, he darted around my punches like Yoda on energy drinks. Felicia attacked from the left. She connected with my jaw. Stars erupted. I wobbled and staggered. The kid delivered a punch to my stomach that almost caused my dinner to make a return trip up my esophagus. I barely dodged another vicious blow from Felicia and caught sight of Dad as vampires swarmed him like ants.

Despite his monstrous semi-demon form, there were just too damned many vampires.

A surge of adrenalin-fueled anger burned through my veins. I lunged for Mortimer as he came in for another punch. Grabbed his throat. Slammed him against the brick wall. Felicia leapt on my back. I grabbed her pigtails. Slung her into the group of vampires that had just broken through the sorcerer's shield behind us. The impact bowled them over and gave Shelton the split second he needed to cast a wall of flames.

Shrieks and curses erupted as the flames consumed the vampire's clothes and with it, their dignity.

I spun back to dad. "There's too damned many," he said. He yanked a manhole cover and flung it like a Frisbee. Vampires flew everywhere. Dad turned to the brick wall, raised his demonic fist and punched it. Cracks formed. He slammed it again. The crack widened. Before he could hit it again, the vampires surged forward in a wave.

I blindly threw punches, unable to tell friend from foe in the melee. An orange globe shot into the air and burst into brilliant sunshine. Vampires recoiled from the light, their skin turning pink.

"Dad!" I spun in a circle as the press of bodies vanished, vampires shielding themselves from the sunlight spell. I saw him carried away, his strength and size no match for the mass of super-strong captors.

Randy wrapped a ribbon around Dad's neck, and my father went limp. He caught my eyes and smirked. "One down, one to go, Justin."

Someone gripped my elbow. I reared back and almost punched Shelton in the face before realizing it was him. Our attackers, beaten, burned, and hurting, abandoned their fight with us and guarded the retreating flank of their comrades as they raced for a black van at the end of the alley.

"Dammit, kid, let's go. This spell ain't gonna last for more than a minute." Shelton motioned me the opposite way from the retreating vamps.

"No! Help me stop them," I pleaded. "Blast them."

"I can't. I'm exhausted and there are too many of them. If they figure that out, they may come back and finish us off."

"Conjure up some wooden stakes and shoot them!"

"It doesn't work that way, kid."

I ran toward the swarm of vampires. Three of the new ones formed a wall for their smoldering, now hairless comrades. I lowered my shoulder and rammed into them. One went tumbling. The other caught a blast of fire from the sorcerer.

A pair of arms clamped around my chest. "You'll make a nice snack," said a deep male voice.

I roared, bent my knees, and sprang backwards, slamming my captor into the brick wall. His hold loosened. I rocked my body forward then drove my head back into his face. His nose made a nasty crunch. His arms loosened their hold as his hands raced for his broken nose. I spun and punched him in the eye. Kneed him in the stomach. He howled in pain and doubled over as dark blood oozed to the ground. A foot slammed into my butt. I tumbled forward and landed in a heap next to the sorcerer's feet.

He muttered something and a blue-tinged shield sprang into being between us and the attackers.

Randy waved at me from the other end of the alley. "Hey Justin, want your daddy back? I'm taking trades." He flipped me off and got into the van.

The remaining vampires backed off, heading for a black sedan that pulled into the spot vacated by the van. Felicia threw her cracked glasses at the shield and stuck her tongue out at us before following her comrades. One of her pigtails was missing and her pink shirt had acquired greenish mustard and rotten lettuce—probably from the oft-used dumpster.

"Good work, kid." Shelton slapped me on the shoulder.

"Oh, God." I dropped to my knees. "They have Dad. What am I going to do?"

"There ain't much you can do." He shrugged. "Shit. You're demon spawn. Shouldn't matter that much to you."

I stood up. Grabbed him by his coat and jerked him toward me. "You may not think we're human, but he's my dad. He raised me from birth, bought pizzas almost every Friday, and gave me my first sip of beer. He showed me my first nudie mag and took time to throw baseballs with me even though I sucked ass." I jerked him again.

"Maybe we are just lowly evil demon spawn, but he's my fucking dad!"

"I don't appreciate the way you're touching me, kid."

"You don't?" Rage boiled my blood. I picked him up off the ground by his leather duster and considered slamming him against the wall until he was ground hamburger.

"Hurt me if you want, but it won't save your dad."

He was right. It wouldn't do me any good now, I realized. Sadness cooled my anger. I dropped him on his feet and turned away to stare at the alley exit.

The sorcerer cleared his throat. "Look, I appreciate you saving my life back there. The name's Harry Shelton, but everyone calls me Shelton."

"I heard your name the first time." My shoulders slumped. "I'm Justin."

"I know," he said before hastily adding, "from the bounty notice."

"I suppose the Conroys told you all about us."

"Those stuck-up bluebloods?" He snorted. "Alice Conroy, your mother, vanished from the sorcerer community years ago. We hadn't heard a thing about her for over a decade. Suddenly she's back on the radar and the Conroys put out a bounty on David Slade and family. Now, as everybody knows, you don't mess with House Slade. But apparently Daddy Dearest was no longer considered a part of the family. So I did a little digging and found not only did Alice Conroy play house with this monster, but she apparently had you to boot. Once I figured out Case was an alias, it was only a matter of tracking you down."

"I guess you drew all those confinement circles behind the high school to see who got trapped."

Shelton grinned. "Brilliant, right? Guess I didn't figure on them not affecting you."

"Did you have any idea I was the Slade you were looking for?" I asked.

"Nah, man. You totally Jedi mind-tricked me."

"No, I really didn't know I was a Slade until yesterday." I bared my teeth. "And I'd appreciate it if you'd stop referring to us as monsters, your prejudiced son of a bitch."

Shelton gave me a thoughtful look. "I'll admit your father doesn't seem like the typical spawn. And you." He shook a finger at me. "Something is very different about you. I always thought spawn and human mating produced pure spawn." His eyes lit up. "But in this case it didn't. Am I right? You're part human. That explains how you could break my circle."

"Guess I'm only part monster."

Shelton smirked. "Don't be so hard on yourself, kid."

"Since I'm part human, will you help me?" Every wasted second beat painfully in my chest.

"I guess I owe you one."

"*That* is putting it mildly."

"Just doing my job." Shelton shrugged. "If I do assist, we can't involve any other Arcanes. Your kind doesn't have a lot of admirers."

"Is it just me or is the supernatural community full of racist pricks?"

He smiled. "Look, you don't know much about the political map, obviously. Spawn are not nice...err...people. Vampires, on the other hand, are usually pretty civil—excepting those bloodsuckers we just fought." He frowned. "Mostly, everyone loathes spawn because they're a bunch of demonic jerks."

"What's the deal with the vampires we just fought? Are they against the Red Syndicate?"

Shelton straightened his rumpled collar. "Who the hell knows? Looked like a bunch of kids to me. The Red Syndicate likes vampire candidates in their mid to late twenties, usually." He picked up the bits of his staff off the ground and looked at them mournfully. "If I'd had my staff I probably would have been more help."

"Just magic it back together again," I said. "It's just a lousy stick."

"Right, well I wouldn't expect you to understand a thing about magic."

"Can't you just say *reparo* and fix the thing?"

He sighed. "This ain't Harry Potter, kid. There aren't any magic words, only willpower and ability." He unscrewed a cap from the bottom end of the staff and withdrew a silver cylinder.

"What's that?"

"An arcgenerator and magic processor."

"What the heck do you need that for?"

"For magical energy and complex spell computations, obviously."

"In a magic staff?"

He rolled his eyes. "Do you honestly think I could make every physics calculation myself? I preprogram my best spells on an arctablet and transfer them into my staff or wand processor. The arcgenerator can lay down some serious juice if I need to put on the hurt."

"Why do you keep putting arc in front of your words?" I asked.

"Technology plus arcane magic equals arcnology." He tapped a module on the cylinder. "This is the MPU or magical processing unit."

"How did Merlin and pals do it in the old days?"

"What the original gangstas did is nothing compared to what we can do now."

"So your little wand doesn't have enough power, I guess." I made a sad face. "Maybe if you put a big glittery arc-star on the end it would work better."

"Ha, ha." Shelton shoved the generator into his coat pocket. He examined the wand for a moment then handed it to me. "See if you can turn it on."

I rolled it around. "I don't see a power switch."

"There isn't one, kid. Hold it by the thick end and imagine it being on."

I wasn't sure how to imagine it being on. I held it out and waved it around. Nothing happened, but something tingled in my hand. I thrust it in front of me. Still nothing, except it felt like ants crawled across my flesh.

"Guess I was wrong," said Shelton and took it back.

"I think the generator is going bad. I could feel the electrical current in my hand."

His forehead wrinkled. "You felt something?"

"Like ants all over my hand."

"Holy buffalo in a skating rink on disco night." He looked me up and down. "You're a strange one. Nobody but a human with magical talent should feel anything coming from the wand."

"Well, my mother is a sorceress."

He let out a low whistle. "Hot damn, you're right." He bit his bottom lip and narrowed his eyes in thought. After a moment, he motioned me to follow him and walked toward the street. "I'm going to suggest something you probably won't want to hear."

I clenched my fists but went with him. "I'm going to save my dad."

"Maybe you should appeal to the Arcane Council as the son of Alice Conroy for help. You have a blood claim. They have to listen."

"I thought sorcerers didn't like spawn and besides, what about the bounty?"

"Since you share a bloodline with a sorceress and your father, they may be forced by law to step in. There is precedent."

Becoming embroiled in a political fiasco did not sound like a valid option. Not while Randy used my father for twisted experiments. Just the thought knotted my stomach in agony.

"I might as well ask the Slades for help," I said.

"Terrible idea," Shelton said. "First of all, they disowned your father, and second of all, they'd find out about you and probably kidnap you for themselves."

"And the Conroys wouldn't do that?" I almost blurted, "Like they did with my sister?" Thankfully, I stopped myself. Shelton apparently didn't know about her and I intended to keep it that way.

"They couldn't. We have a code of ethics."

"Ethics? That's a laugh." I stopped in the shadows at the end of the alley and watched people as they went about their lives, oblivious to vampires, spawn, or sorcerers. I sighed. "Look, just point me in the right direction. Who took my dad?"

"Think this over, kiddo. If you go rushing in there without help, you'll end up like your dad. Imagine those fanged creatures sucking on your neck for years, decades even. They'd keep you alive for a perpetual dessert."

I shuddered. "You could help me." I could only think of one other person who might help, but the thought of asking her frightened me almost as much as the idea of going in alone.

Shelton shook his head. "Hey, I'm grateful to you for saving my life, but I won't rush willy-nilly into a vampire stronghold without backup. If you're not going to listen to me, you're on your own."

"How do I find the vampires?"

He pulled out a smartphone. "Give me your email address and I'll shoot you over what I know."

It seemed so bizarre giving my email address to a sorcerer, of all people, but I did. "Just don't add me on Facebook."

He met that remark with a wry grin. "You got spirit and a whole lot of teenage denial. Good luck."

I made it back to my car, receiving a few surprised looks from pedestrians along the way. Soot and dirty vampire blood covered my skin and clothes. I didn't have time to shower and change. I had to go to my last best hope. If she turned me down, I would have to go in alone.

CHAPTER 30

I drove to the old industrial park in Scottdale, the suspected lair for my slinky stalker felycan friend. Despite her vanishing act last night, she'd sort of helped me against Randy and pals. Maybe she'd help me rescue my dad if I got on my knees and begged.

According to Shelton's email, the vampires who took Dad were still possibly rogue and not members of the Red Syndicate. He didn't have any specific numbers, just a guess that the vampire lair hosted close to a hundred bloodsuckers.

I climbed out of the Jetta and stood in the cool night air, letting a gentle breeze carry nearby scents to me. I reached out, feeling for a hint of Stacey's presence, but found nothing. That didn't mean much since my range didn't seem to extend very far. Otherwise, I would have sensed the vampires who attacked me and Dad before they'd ambushed us. I dashed between two crumbling red-brick warehouses. Sprinted up the wall to my left and then leapt from wall to wall until I propelled myself to the roof. I crouched, listening for the sound of feline pads stalking my way or the unmistakable odor of a moggy.

Still nothing.

I waited for an hour, moving from building to building in the large complex as stealthily as I could, keeping a constant vigil on the other rooftops. If I hadn't been so frightened of running into another moggy, it might have been fun. Instead, I almost crapped myself at every innocent noise. Finally, I heard movement and ducked low as a figure leapt over the lip of the roof across from me and landed lightly on its feet. The curvy figure silhouetted against the moon was most likely Stacey, but I didn't want to take any chances. She stood upwind of me which was good. Felycans probably had a superb sense of smell.

She made a gentle mewling noise. I heard the padding of dozens of feet and froze. Had I possibly missed another moggy? Cats burst from every direction, all running and meowing like crazy, nearly giving me a heart attack. Stacey laid packages on the roof and the thankfully normal-sized cats dug in. It was fresh meat, but what kind I couldn't tell. I hoped it wasn't human flesh. I gagged at the thought of those strays chowing down on ground man-burger.

Stacey stooped and petted the cats as they fondly rubbed against her legs. She spoke to each of them and called them by name. I sprinted to the edge of the roof, leapt the gap. She jumped back, planted her feet, and faced me, hissing and baring hands with feline claws.

"Whoa, there, tiger." I backed away. She gave a start of recognition and lowered her hands. "Girl, you give a whole new definition to crazy cat lady."

"You scared me half to death, darling," she purred.

"You're not a scaredy-cat are you?" *I'm here all week, folks.* "I hope you're having a mice evening."

She laughed and walked toward me, claws retracting into normal-looking fingernails. "How did you find me?"

I decided not to go into details about following her. She might get angry considering someone had killed her moggy thanks to me. "First of all, thanks for the help last night."

She pursed her lips and narrowed her eyes. "I saw your father and decided he was better suited to help you."

"I appreciate that more than you know."

A languid smile curved her full lips. "Do go on."

"I have a bigger problem now."

"Why am I not surprised?" Stacey's smile faded. "My lamb, you *are* trouble."

I decided not to mince words. "Those vampires weren't happy we kicked their asses last night. They want to use my blood for some kind of vampire serum and came after me and my father. I got away, but he didn't."

"I cannot help you." Fear flashed in her eyes. "I am but one lonely soul."

"One lonely soul, my demonic ass. I know what you're capable of. My dad told me. You can make an army out of these cats."

"I refuse to send these innocent creatures to their deaths." Her voice rose in indignation. "Do you think I'm a bloody monster?"

I didn't answer. I didn't know what to say.

Large tears welled in her eyes. "You do think I am a monster, Justin." She sniffled. "How very unkind!"

I took her gently by the shoulders. "No I don't. I just didn't realize how you felt about your pets."

She pushed me away. "They are not my pets. They are my companions."

Very crazy cat woman, I decided. I sat on an air vent and dropped my head into my hands. I didn't know what to do.

Stacey came behind me and stroked my hair. It felt oddly relaxing, like being scratched behind the ears. "I am sorry about your father," she said after a moment. "I have not known family for a very long time." She sighed. "It would be lovely to have a companion. Someone to hunt with and to enjoy my feline friends."

"Is that why you want me?"

"Indeed. You are very close to my kind in nature even if you cannot shift."

"I like cats," I said, "but you and I would never get along."

"Oh, I see." Jealousy crept into her voice. "You are still quite taken by the female dhampyr."

"Elyssa." Pain cracked my words. "I'm sorry, Stacey. It just wasn't meant to be. You need a guy who can, um, love cats as much as you do." *And what guy would ever admit to that?*

"There are so few of my kind left." Her shoulders slumped. "I would love to have children someday."

"Stacey, do you eat people?"

"Absolutely not." She made a gagging sound. "Who would want to eat humans considering the vile rubbish they consume?"

"But you do feed on human energy."

"Do not we all?" She came around to stand in front of me. "Vampires feed on human blood. We feed on emotional energy, you and I. Even noms feed on each other in emotional ways by loving, hating, killing." She gave a delicate shudder. "We are all each other's prey, my dear. The strong conquer the weak."

"Noms." I rolled my eyes. "Supers even have a derogatory nickname for normal humans."

"Vampires, and some supers call them nom-noms because they feed on them."

"So I've heard." I felt the conversation derailing so I jerked it back on track. "Don't you scare noms half to death so you can feed off them?"

"It is part of what I must do. Otherwise my feedings would be most bland."

"You like to play with your food before you kill it."

"I admit I do enjoy a fresh kill, but I neither kill nor eat humans." She looked into the distance. "I suppose others of my bearing have different tastes. I truly have no idea since I haven't seen another of my kind in years." She shook her head. "No, I only feed on their fear. Then I drop them back into the ocean of humanity and let them scurry away."

I gave her a suspicious look. "My dad said to never trust felycans, that you're fickle."

"Well, I am female, Justin." She smirked. "Perhaps you can trust me, or perhaps not. I suppose it depends on what your goals are."

"Look, I like you Stacey. You proved that you're a good person by helping me last night." I held out a hand. "Can't you please do something, anything to help me save my dad?"

She sighed and gazed at the cluster of cats lounging indolently on the roof, tummies full of raw meat. "I know several tomcats who may be willing to fight with you, but it will be their choice. Once I transform them into moggies, there is no going back. It is also very difficult to keep them suitably fed once they are larger."

I decided to play dumb, just in case questions arose about the moggy that lost its head. "You can make them larger?"

"Oh yes. I am surprised your father neglected to tell you."

"Elyssa might have told me I was demon spawn, but I really didn't believe her until Dad confirmed it yesterday. He didn't have time to fill me in on every little detail about other supers."

"Of course not." She patted my hand. "I honestly know little of your kind, but I do know your brethren are very unpleasant to deal with." She shuddered delicately. "Your psychic energy, however, is positively top-notch. In any case, my lamb, I was pleasantly surprised to make your acquaintance."

"You tried to force yourself on me. To feed on me. You call that making my acquaintance?"

She wrinkled her nose. "That I did, and I am very sorry. But you are so delectable I could just dandle you on my knee."

I didn't know what dandling was and I had no desire to find out. "What were you going to do to me?"

"I would have taken some of your essence just as you do to your prey. I can smell your delicious aroma whenever you are near." She sniffed the air in my direction and grinned. "It excites me so. I do wish we could come to an arrangement. Perhaps," she said, tapping her chin, "I can help you in exchange for my original terms."

I really didn't have a choice. "I suppose. But nothing permanent."

"You ask me to risk so much for so little. Could you not give us a chance? I promise you our affair would be absolutely delightful." She almost sounded like Mary Poppins.

I sighed. "Stacey, kiss me."

"You are so forward, good sir."

"Very funny. I just need to see something."

She leaned in. Her breathing grew heavy, eyes closed. Our lips met. Hers were soft and feverishly warm. Her tongue pressed against mine. I braced for the unpleasant sandpapery feeling, but her tongue felt normal. Hot. Willing. I pulled her closer, trying to feel something in my heart, anything that would make me want her besides raw physical need. Something that would make me agree to this bargain without hesitation.

One of her hands stroked my hair. The other raked fingernails lightly down my back. She kissed my neck and traced my ear with her tongue.

It definitely didn't feel rough. In fact, it felt pretty amazing. Her soft breasts pressed against my chest, and my hand wandered down the curve of her back, reaching her firm bottom and squeezing.

My body reacted, brain number two springing awake in anticipation of ravishing this shapely temptress. I jerked away. What teenage guy worth his salt wouldn't be aroused after kissing like that? But it hadn't been magic. It hadn't burned through my veins with a desire to consume her and make her part of me. Despite the physical allure, her kiss had been but a pale reminder of the fiery earth-shaking touch of true love. Whether I had a soul or not, Elyssa affected a part of me beyond the physical. I would never have that with Stacey.

"Why can't I get her out of my mind?" I shouted to the sky in exasperation.

Tears welled in Stacey's large amber eyes. "You are too in love with her," she said. "I even kept myself fully human to make it more comfortable so my tongue would not cause a rash."

"I'm sorry, Stacey. I really am. But I'm willing to make a bargain with you anyway if you'll just help me."

She stood and walked away to stare out into the darkness. "I will not help you, Justin." Her voice quavered and she sniffled. "I suppose I am doomed to never find true love." She pressed the back of a hand to her forehead with a melodramatic flourish.

"Just because we aren't meant to be together doesn't mean we can't mess around."

"But I want you to love me and adore me. I want a man to come home to. Someone I can hug and kiss and make merry with." She sobbed.

I knew exactly what she was talking about. Except I wanted a girl, not a guy, of course. And I would never call a rundown place like this home. I hugged her. She turned and buried her face in my chest.

"Stacey, I want you to be happy. We didn't really get off to a good start, but I'd be willing to do what you want. How about we can, uh, date or whatever for a year, provided I survive this?"

I heard a tiny meowing and looked down to see a small black figure rubbing against my legs. I picked up the familiar feline. "Captain Tibbs!" I said. "I should've known you'd find a better gig."

"You are acquainted?" Stacey asked. She took the little cat and kissed him on the nose. "Do you know this man, little one?"

Captain Tibbs meowed a few times. Stacey looked at me with tenderness in her eyes. She put Captain Tibbs on her shoulder where he took a seat and purred while he licked his front paw.

"I will help you."

"What changed your mind?"

"Nightliss told me how you bravely saved her from the jaws evil hounds."

With all the other crap that had been going on, I'd almost forgotten about the episode. It seemed so distant with all the other worries in my head. "I couldn't them hurt her." And to think I'd thought *she* was a *he*.

Stacey pressed a palm to my cheek. "How heroic of you. You did not even possess your demonic abilities, did you?"

"No." I gave Captain Tibbs a look. "Why do you call him—I mean her —Nightliss?"

"That would be the English equivalent of what she calls herself. Besides, Captain Tibbs, as you called her, is a rather ridiculous name." She smiled sadly and looked me up and down. "You are a filthy mess and your odor is most disagreeable. Go home and clean up. I will request the help of the tomcats. Those who agree will be the help you receive from me. I expect nothing in return. If I cannot have your love, I will only be miserable in a relationship built on convenience."

It was a very melodramatic and very British way to put things, but it was a better outcome than I'd hoped for.

I kissed her on the cheek and hugged her. Nightliss batted at my ear from her shoulder and meowed. "Thank you. Thank you."

Stacey looked at the cat. "You are so insistent, little one."

Nightliss meowed again.

"Why is it so important?"

The little cat responded with a range of yowls and mews that astounded me, her green eyes moving back and forth between me and Stacey.

"Well, Nightliss is quite convincing." Stacey frowned. "It is rare to find cats much concerned beyond their next nap or hunt."

Nightliss batted her ear.

"Yes, I will consider it!" Stacey huffed. She looked at me. "Remember, only those tomcats who say yes will help you. It may be none at all."

"I'll take what I can get." I wondered how she interpreted all those sounds coming from Nightliss. It seemed impossible. Then again, I should've been able to believe in anything by then. I scratched the ears of a few nearby cats, discreetly checking if they had the proper parts dangling between their legs. I needed to impress the tomcats. Get them on my side.

"You know Elyssa can never love you back," Stacey said in a sad voice. "There is no pain like unrequited love."

I choked up and faced away from her. "Tell me about it."

CHAPTER 31

I left for home to take Stacey's advice and shower. She told me she'd
meet me back at her place the following evening. I had driven
about a mile when the Jetta sputtered and stopped. I cursed and
hit the steering wheel. It took only a second to identify the problem. I
was out of gas. With all the supernatural crap hitting the fan around me,
I had forgotten the most mundane of things. I didn't know what to do
except get out and run home. I'd have to make sure nobody saw my
clothes. They looked like I'd come from a slaughterhouse and then gone
mud sliding.

The shortest way to my place was to hightail it through Clarkston, an
even more rundown part of town. I didn't know any backyard routes so
I took to the back streets, hoping I knew where I was going. I ran past
closed stores, boarded up homes, and mini-marts with thick bars on the
windows. I had just passed the public bus terminal when I heard a faint
noise that made me stop in my tracks.

It was the sound of fear. A bottled up scream that might come from a
gagged mouth. The wrongness of it struck at my heart and I couldn't
resist the pull. I sprinted toward the source, some hundred yards away

SWEET BLOOD OF MINE

behind a nearby strip mall. Two young thugs held down a girl who couldn't have been any older than I was. Her eyes flared in terror.

"Let her go," I said before even thinking about it. It was rather stupid considering I didn't know if they had weapons.

The taller of the two turned and immediately confirmed they did indeed have weapons. He held a pistol cocked sideways in typical gangsta fashion. "You best get outta here, fool. You ain't got no business with us."

His companion stood behind the girl with a leer on his face. "Sucka don't have a clue, D.J. School him."

"Let her go." I mapped out the route which was least likely to get me shot.

The armed thug's finger twitched. I blurred left. The gun exploded. Time seemed to slow. I cut right. Grabbed his gun arm, and slammed him in the shoulder. His arm snapped like a twig. I took the gun, gave him a dirty look, and tried to eject the magazine like the badasses do on TV. Unfortunately, I didn't really know what I was doing, so I suffered a moment of awkward confusion while I fiddled with the stupid thing. Finally, I just flicked on the safety.

"What the hell?" said the other thug—the one who wasn't screaming about his broken arm.

"Guess you should've listened." Anger growled deep in my throat. Something shifted inside me. Pain exploded in my head and the world went red. Blood rushed to my head in rhythm with the timpani thundering of my heart. My forehead felt like it was cracking open. Like something sprouted through the bone.

The thug screamed at an impossibly high pitch for a man and fled. The girl passed out. The dude with the broken arm was too busy sobbing in white-faced agony to think about running.

I staggered. The pain receded. Faded to nothing. I hadn't had these awful headaches for a few days. Maybe my growing pains as a demon spawn weren't over yet. Whatever the case, aspirin wasn't going to cut it.

I picked up the girl and ran her to the front of the shopping center where a group of teens frantically shouted someone's name. Aware of just how bad it would look if a filthy guy walked up with an unconscious girl in his arms, I placed her on a nearby bench and hid behind the corner. "Over here," I shouted. I heard their footsteps and exclamations as they saw their friend. Then I was off again.

What a rush.

I took stock of my location and angled for home. It felt amazing to have rescued someone. Despite my low energy levels and the hunger that groaned in my body, I felt energized.

Foolishly, it gave me hope.

I finally arrived at home and stripped off my ruined clothes. After a shower I put on some jeans and a black T-shirt, figuring I might as well try to camouflage myself while I reconnoitered the location Shelton had given me in his email. If Stacey came through, I had to be prepared.

Someone knocked on the door. Hope surged. Maybe Dad had escaped. Maybe Shelton had decided to help me. Or it might be Nyte or Ash. I had several missed texts from the two of them.

I looked through the peephole and saw an empty stoop. I turned away. Another knock. I spun back and looked. No one was there. Somebody was playing games. That might be very bad. It could be more vampires or bounty-seeking sorcerers. I peered through the hole once more and a pair of violet eyes stared back at me.

I opened the door without thinking. Elyssa stood there, her eyes neutral rather than filled with hate or disgust.

"I know about your father," she said.

"How could you possibly know already?"

"I've had eyes on this group of vampires for a while." She remained still, watching me carefully. "After you kicked their asses last night, I figured it was only a matter of time before they looked for payback."

"You knew, but you didn't warn us?"

Elyssa tapped her temple. "Use your brain, Justin. Just because I locked up that low-level punk last night, did you think this was over? That the rest of the organization behind him would just let it go?"

She was right, so I shifted tactics. "Well, congratulations, they got my dad." I stiffened my upper lip. "One monster down, one to go."

"Oh, come off it, Justin. You can't get him back. The vampires who took him are rogues, so we can't even ask the Red Syndicate for relief."

"Why do you say that?" I was furious with her for sounding so callous, but a part of me couldn't stop thinking about touching her lips. *Stop it, you moron!*

"The Red Syndicate has an official image to uphold in the supernatural community, even when it comes to demon spawn. They'd demand his release otherwise, or at least turn him in for the bounty."

"That's funny. I can't believe evil blood-suckers would be worried about their public image. "

"Vampire politics are tricky. They drift whichever way the wind blows. Most of the time, they're the ones who make it blow in the first place." Her gaze wandered from my left eye to my right, then down ever so slightly. "Even if they consider your father a rogue, they'd treat him according to law."

"And what about my father's family? They'd stand by and do nothing?"

"They would, considering they disowned him."

I waved her in. Her eyes grew guarded, but she came in anyway. I noticed she had two short sai swords sheathed on her thighs like last

JOHN CORWIN

night. They looked a lot like the ones she'd constructed for Kings and Castles.

She wore the same form-fitting uniform from last night. The stretchy material pressed against her curves. Her red lips beckoned from a snow-white complexion. Silky raven hair cascaded across her shoulders.

My ninja goddess.

I cleared my mind of such thoughts and tried to make myself hate her. "Well, aren't you just armed to the teeth?"

"In my line of business it doesn't pay to walk around in my underwear."

Now *that* was a sight I'd like to see. *Stop it!* "I have to try to save my dad. You know I can't just leave him."

"I mean, he's demon spawn." She cocked her head slightly. "You're demon spawn."

"And?" I threw up my hands. "Do I have to repeat the speech I gave Shelton?"

"Who?"

"For fucks sake, Elyssa, he's my dad." I clamped my mouth shut. *Nothing you say will convince her. Accept it and move on.*

Her eyes narrowed. "There are other avenues to freeing him. We could petition the Overworld Conclave for intervention."

"You said 'we'. Does that mean your family will help me?"

"Oh, hell no." She shook her head vehemently. "They don't even know I'm here."

"Do they know about me?"

"They're aware of you now, thanks to this hubbub over your dad."

"And?"

"And what? They won't hunt you down if that's what you think. Mom was not exactly happy to find out she styled the hair of a spawn and didn't even know it." Her lips curved into a sad smile.

"That's kind of creepy, now that I think about it," I said. "Finding out your hair dresser is a vampire. Did a vampire turn her while she was pregnant with you?"

Elyssa scowled. "Mom is a dhampyr like me, Justin." She slashed a hand through the air. "We're nothing like those creatures."

"Wait a minute. Vampires are creatures but you're not? Hypocrite much?"

She leaned against the back of the couch eyes flashing dangerously. "Just because a vampire raped one of our ancestors doesn't mean we're anything like them. We do something positive with our abilities. Dhampyrs are *not* vampires."

"So you're telling me you couldn't help being born a dhampyr?" I made a surprised O with my mouth. "Damn, I had complete control over my creation. I picked my parents out of a catalog because they were the most evil people I could find. God thought it was a good choice for me."

Her mouth dropped open a fraction. "Where do you come up with this shit?"

"I could ask you the same thing, you supernaturalist!" I'd aimed for a supernatural parallel to racist, but my effort fell flat.

"Huh?" Her forehead pinched. "We swore an oath to protect mortals from supernaturals. From leechers like spawn."

"Are you with the supernatural police squad? Should I call you Deputy Elyssa?"

"We're Templars," she growled.

Well, that confirms what Dad suspected. I acted like I didn't know. "Like the knights?" I laughed. "You run around killing vampires and demons?"

"It's not like that. We don't go around killing anyone. We simply take care of the outlaws and rogues despite our dislike of..."

"Monsters like me?"

She met that with a protracted sigh. "It's just the way things are."

I paced into the kitchen and grabbed some water. My insides churned with the desire to punch her for her prejudice, kiss her because I still loved her, or maybe both. I doubted I could lay a hand on her before she gutted me.

I took a gulp of water. "I'm not going to beg a bunch of lousy politicians to help free my dad. If it works anything like human politics, it'll take forever. No telling what Randy and his asshole friends are doing to Dad right this moment." I chugged down the rest of the water to quench my burning thirst, but it didn't help. It wasn't that kind of thirst. "I already have someone to help me anyway."

"Who?" she said in a scoffing tone. "Your little cat woman? What good will she be?"

"At least she wants to help!" I yelled. I gritted my teeth and lowered my voice to a snarl. "Nobody else gives a damn because they think we're monsters who don't deserve to live in peace. We're blamed for being born what we are." The anger fled from me as despair settled in. I groaned and sank into a chair. "We can't help how we came into this world, Elyssa. What matters is what we do while we're here."

She put a hand on my shoulder. I ached to touch her hand. To feel real solace in that touch. But it was an empty gesture.

"Justin, please listen to me. I don't want to see you hurt."

"Says the girl who almost cut my throat."

"No. Says the girl who saw how you helped those students last night. You don't deserve to die." She removed her hand and stepped in front of me.

"Look, I have to go." The hunger and her presence were unbearable. "Can you at least tell me what I have to expect?" Aside from basic politics, location, and estimated numbers, Shelton's email told me nothing about what other dangers lurked, or even how I might break into the vampire stronghold.

"You're really going to do this no matter what, aren't you?"

I nodded, trying to look grim and determined while inside I felt scared and alone.

She huffed out an angry groan. "Stubborn idiot. Fine." She pulled a printout from a pouch at her side and laid it flat on the table. It detailed the layout of a building, marked entrances with slashes and enemies with red dots.

"You knew what I'd say, didn't you?"

She sighed. "Of course. You're either stubborn, stupid, or blindly optimistic."

"All of the above."

Elyssa rolled her eyes. "God, you're worse than me."

"I think it's adorable you prepared a battle plan for me." I looked it over. "You're so girly."

"Can we cut back on the snark for a minute, Justin?" She huffed and jabbed a finger at the map. "My plan requires stealth and a lot of luck. Also, it'll work best if we execute during daylight hours. The rogues will be asleep aside from a few sentries."

"So—wait a minute. Did you just say 'we'?"

"I'll help you."

My eyes misted. I turned away and wiped them so she wouldn't see me go soggy. "Thanks." I cleared my throat. It was difficult to speak over the knot. "Why help a monster?"

"Even if things between us didn't work out due to you being a demon and all—" Her voice broke. She paused, swallowed. "I don't want to see you killed."

"I don't want to see me killed either. I also don't want to see you hurt."

"I've got my big-girl panties on. I'll be fine."

I laughed despite the conflicted emotions coursing through me. "Why a daytime attack?"

"Vampires hate sunlight because it weakens them and they get a really nasty sunburn since their skin can't adapt to the ultraviolet rays," Elyssa said. "It also hurts their eyes."

"What's the best way to kill them?"

"Beheading, usually. If they lose enough blood they'll die, too."

I made a face. "Yuck! I just don't get how they can drink blood. It's gross for a whole host of reasons, not to mention it's unsanitary." I paused and looked at her. "Do you have to drink blood?"

She shifted uncomfortably. "I'd rather not talk about it."

"You know all about my kind. I know almost nothing about this Templar and dhampyr business."

After staring blankly at the wall for a few seconds, she sighed. "I guess you deserve some explanation."

"It would be nice after having a knife pressed to my throat." I raised an eyebrow in challenge.

She looked down at the table. "We need human blood to survive, just like night stalkers—that's what we call normal vampires. We can subsist on other mammalian blood, but it isn't as nutritious, so to speak."

"Nothing like Flintstones vitamins, eh?"

A brief smile lit her face and vanished like the sun behind a cloud. "We don't drink directly from humans. It's forbidden. The Templar organization provides us with blood packs."

"Can you eat normal food?"

"We have to eat it for our human side to survive."

"Dad told me vampires love spawn blood like a woman loves her chocolate. Is it the same for you?"

Her violet eyes sparkled and she gave my neck a long look. "I've never tasted it." She clenched a fist. "I don't understand how I could have missed what you are all that time. I can usually sense it right away."

"My mother put a charm on my aura. I guess it camouflaged me just enough."

"No. You don't understand. The minute I spilled your blood it was all I could do not to…"

"You vanted to suck my blood?" I said in my best Count Chocula imitation.

She shook her head in wonder. "I had never smelled anything quite like it. So sweet. Just the aroma made my skin tingle, like chocolate. I can't imagine what it would taste like."

"Are you saying you only wanted me for my blood?" Doubt crept into my gut. What if my sweet blood had been the only reason she'd fallen for me in the first place?

Her body tensed. She bit her upper lip and turned her gaze back to the map. "Maybe we should get back to planning your father's rescue."

I grimaced. *Stubborn girl.* "What did you have in mind?" I pushed away the doubt for another time. More important matters required my attention.

"What was I talking about before?" She tapped her chin and gazed at the map. "Oh yeah. Night stalkers." She gave me a drawing of what looked like the grandpa vampire from the Munsters. Underneath, a few paragraphs outlined interesting factoids about vampires.

"Is this what passes for Templar literature on vampires?"

"No, I made that one just for you." She raised an eyebrow. "Want a crayon to color it with?"

"Cute." I chuckled and read. "How can you tell a vampire's age?"

"Well, if his bones are like iron, then he's probably old. They get a lot tougher with age."

"That's helpful. I'd like to know how old one is before I attack."

"The vampires who have your father are a bunch of young rogues. They're rebelling against the establishment for more freedom."

"Raging against the machine for what? More freedom to kill?"

She shook her head. "Vampires don't like to kill. It would be very messy. They have willing humans who keep them fed for the possibility of being turned or for the high it gives them."

"Yeah, who wouldn't want to live forever?"

"It boils down to population control. Immortals can't add more humans to their ranks without outpacing their food source. The rogues disagree with the policy."

"Maybe they want all their friends to live forever."

"Probably. In any case, they rebelled because they hate old vampire politics."

"Sounds a lot like human politics."

She quirked an eyebrow. "Just because they're supernatural doesn't mean they're any better at life than the rest of us."

I had so many questions I wanted to ask about her, her family, and their mission. But all that had to wait, so I asked her to get down to brass tacks and explain the plan. She'd mapped out several routes and possible locations where my dad might be within the building. I was amazed at her military prowess. She broke down an impossible mission into manageable chunks and almost made it seem possible.

"We prepare tomorrow and start at dawn the next day."

"Isn't that a school day?"

She blew out a breath. "If we fail, I don't think it'll matter."

I raised the question I'd been dreading the answer to. "What do you think our chances are?"

She compressed her lips into a thin line. "Slim to none."

CHAPTER 32

Elyssa looked at the time. "I should go. I have…responsibilities."

"Beasts to slay? People to save?"

One corner of her mouth lifted in a wistful smile. "Let's just say that my absence will be noticed."

I knew that feeling. Her absence left an aching void in my heart.

She stood up and turned to leave. I walked her to the door and opened it. She stopped just over the threshold and offered a hopeful smile.

"We'll get him back, Justin."

Then my sexy ninja girl turned and walked to her car. I wanted to race after her. Spin her around and kiss her. I wanted her back so badly that the effort of not chasing her stabbed my heart until tears welled in my eyes. Long after the taillights faded into the distance, I closed the door and prepared for bed.

I passed out the moment my head hit the pillow. Surprisingly, I didn't have a single nightmare or dream, for that matter. Real life was already a big enough nightmare, and the future didn't look much brighter.

I woke up feeling moderately less depressed than the day before. A shower and a shave later, I left and went to the laundromat. The people there were just as perky as the last time. Boredom etched tired faces. Their emotions read like flat-lined heart monitors and tasted like unsalted pretzels.

After a trickling diet of unsatisfying blah, a couple of old women came in, gossiping and laughing about some poor woman named Matilda who apparently was not as great a cook or lover as she thought. Neither of them looked like God's gift to men, either, with pink curlers and polyester clothes. They reeked of baby powder. On the other hand, their emotional states were just dandy. I tapped into both of the gossipers and my much-needed helping of tastier emotional nutrition trickled in. My nerves calmed and the worry creasing my forehead into an origami swan released its death grip on my chest.

But I wanted more and I wanted it faster. I pulled harder. The women noticed. They licked their lips and preened their hair. One of them pressed hands to her hips and pursed her lips. I realized with horror I was about to resuscitate their elderly sex drives.

I did *not* want anything to do with that. I grimaced and throttled back before I instigated grandma porn that would destroy the minds of everyone present.

After getting my fix, I went home to wait for Elyssa. I studied the map she'd given me last night in the hope I might discover a minor detail that would make things easier. I apparently didn't possess her skill with analytics, however, because it all looked like a jumble of lines and dots. I gave up. My phone rang. I answered without checking who it was, thinking it must be Elyssa.

"Hey, Justin," said Katie.

My brain flat-lined for a moment. I hadn't given her much thought since the party. It seemed ages ago I'd suffered my Katie-induced meltdown. "Uh, hey. What's going on?"

"I hadn't heard from you since Friday. I must have been really drunk because I don't remember a thing." She paused. "I do remember us kissing—"

"Yeah, you were really drunk." I thought fast. "But, um my dad's sick so I haven't had a chance to call." I was pretty sure "kidnapped by vampires" would not fly well with her.

"Oh, no. I hope it's nothing serious."

"He's puking all over the place. I feel kinda bad leaving him alone. How about we get together later this week?"

"Promise?" She drew out the word in a throaty, sexy voice which I had never heard her use before. What the hell is it with women? The minute you don't give a crap about them, they suddenly want you.

"I promise." I left out the clause which abdicated me of said promise should vampires kill me or Elyssa decide she want me again, and hung up.

"Hasn't that girl caused you enough trouble?" Elyssa said in a withering tone.

I jumped so high I hit the ceiling and left a dent. "Christ almighty! You scared the shit out of me." Drywall dust floated around my head in a halo.

"Sorry." She didn't look sorry at all. Elyssa set a black leather scabbard on the table. "I brought this for you, just in case."

I unsheathed a silvery rapier from the scabbard and admired it. It was beautifully designed, the blade engraved with tiny knights killing all sorts of evil creatures like me. "Wow." I sheathed it and gave her a quizzical look. "Why don't we use guns? Or is it required we go old-school on vamps?"

She shrugged. "Tradition. There are those who prefer projectile weapons, but not my family."

"What if the vamps have guns?"

"I'm sure some do. Bring a gun if you want, but it won't do much good unless it blows a huge hole in them."

"What about a headshot?" I'd killed thousands of virtual enemies in video games, but real-life shooting sent a shudder of horror down my spine.

"I suppose if you blew off their head it would kill them. Vampires can regenerate almost anything else provided they're well fed."

I examined the blade. "Silver?"

"Steel with a thin silver coating," she said. "Silver won't outright kill anything, but it does stop a super from healing as quickly."

"Why not make a bunch of silver bullets?"

"It would be prohibitively expensive."

"Well, at least some myths have a basis in fact even if you can't insta-kill a vampire like Blade does."

"Blade." She snorted. "What a joke." She pulled a couple of sheathed knives from a duffel bag and added them to the pile on the table. The last item she removed was a black ninja-like outfit, hoodie and all.

"Are you sure you guys aren't really ninjas?"

"Ninjas *are* a lot cooler." A tiny smile fought its way onto her stern face.

I reached out a tentative hand and touched hers where she'd let it rest on the table. "If we survive this, I'd really like to know more about who you are and what you do," I said.

She sighed and pulled her hand away. "If we survive this, we can't hang out or pal around, period. My parents may not hunt you down, but that wouldn't stop my brothers from stepping in. They have a thing for protecting their little sister." She blew out a breath and looked annoyed.

"I get it," I said. "Two older brothers, Templar Knights, no less. I'll bet being a little sister has been quite a tribulation for you with those two beating the snot out of anyone who gave you a cross look." I laughed. "No wonder you got so ticked off whenever I tried to protect you."

She blessed me with a genuine smile. "I'm not a weak little girl who can't stand up for herself."

"Most girls aren't Templars either."

"On that we can agree," she said. "Come on. Let's see how you handle a real sword."

We went into the backyard and fenced. She was far better than me, although I'd never practiced against someone who used two short swords, or anyone who used real swords for that matter. The fencing classes I'd taken years ago were of some use. After an hour, my muscles adapted to the feel and balance of the weapon. It really was a superb piece of work. My reflexes were quick, and my body supernaturally agile, but Elyssa's well-tuned muscle memory knew exactly what to do in situations I'd never faced. I thought she might take off my head if I didn't use every ounce of skill available.

"Are you really trying to kill me?" I barely deflecting a two-pronged attack from her short swords.

"Do you think the vampires will stop and give you a breather?" She shoved both of her swords against mine. Her foot swept mine from beneath me. I thudded on my back, her sword at my throat. It reminded me uncomfortably of the dagger after the K&C tournament.

I pounded my fist on the grass. If the vampires were this good, I was screwed. Having my ass relentlessly kicked by a girl was not the best thing for my ego either. After countless lost bouts, I finally earned a draw from her. We both panted from the exercise.

"You're not bad," she said as we sat on the porch swing to recover from the intense workout.

"If by not bad you mean I'm a notch above useless, then thanks."

She shook her head. "No, I really think with some practice you could beat me."

"And your brothers are better than you?"

"Much better. And stronger."

"Great." I drew out the word for a full three seconds. "I hope they don't figure out where you are."

"They're out of the state right now on assignment."

"Isn't this an interesting sight?" said a male voice.

Elyssa and I leapt to our feet, swords at the ready. Shelton smiled back, his staff pointing at us.

"How did you find me?" I asked.

"I'm a bounty hunter."

I put down the sword. "No, you're a sorcerer."

"There's no reason I can't be both, kiddo."

"Who is this?" Elyssa asked.

"This," I said, waving my hand at Shelton, "is Harry Shelton. He tried to capture me and my dad for the bounty."

Her eyes narrowed. "What is he doing here, then?"

"Yeah, what are you doing here?" I asked him. "You said you wouldn't get involved."

He shrugged. "I got to thinking about things. About how you got out of my containment circle—"

"He got out of a circle?" Elyssa asked.

Shelton gave Elyssa an appraising look. "It held his dad just fine. But not him."

351

"That's impossible," she said. "You can't escape a circle if it's done properly."

"Like I said, his dad was good and trapped, but he stepped across the line like there was nothing to it."

Elyssa's forehead crinkled. "That doesn't make any sense."

"Sure it does," Shelton said. "He's part human."

"Justin is part human?" Her eyes filled with disbelief.

"Yeah, just don't let it get around," I said. "Don't want to ruin my inhuman rep."

"What does that mean?" Elyssa said to Shelton. "I've never heard of half-human demon spawn."

"Good question," Shelton said. "Wish I knew the answer."

I cleared my throat dramatically. "I hate to break up all the discussion about my humanity or lack thereof, but why are you here, Shelton?"

"Well, kid, I felt terrible about leaving you to do this on your own. I dug into the politics of this situation and it turns out some rogues took your dad."

"I already told him that, thank you very much," Elyssa said.

"Well, if you'll let me finish, little lady, you might find out where I'm going with this." He rested his gaze on her for a moment before continuing. "Since they are rogues, there is nothing politically preventing a sorcerer from taking action against them."

"You're going to help?" I said.

"I'm thinking about it." He nodded his head at Elyssa. "First, maybe you can explain why Little Miss Templar is here."

Elyssa and I looked at each other awkwardly. I finally answered.

"We used to date."

"Before I knew he was demon spawn," she amended hastily.

"You weren't complaining," I said.

"That was before you tried to rape my mind!"

Shelton held up his hands. "Whoa, boys and girls. Let's get back to the matter at hand and leave the lovers' spat for later."

"We are *not* lovers." Elyssa crossed her arms and scowled.

"You Templars think you're so much better than anyone else, don't you?" I said.

"Enough!" Shelton roared. "I'm not gonna involve myself if you two don't shut up and act professional."

I narrowed my eyes and took a couple of steps toward Shelton. "I know you're not here just from the goodness of your heart, bounty hunter. Spit it out. What's really in it for you?"

"You saved my life, kiddo. Easy as that."

"Sorry, but I'm calling bull." And then something occurred to me. "Is the Red Syndicate offering a bounty on the rogues?"

Elyssa pulled out her smartphone and tapped on the screen. "Yes they are." She showed me a website. "Over two grand each."

"You've gotta be kidding me," I said. "Does every supernatural group have a website?"

"Not every supernatural group is stuck in the Dark Ages," she replied.

I looked back at Shelton. "Money is your game, huh?"

He had the gall to smile back at me. "Okay, so there are bounties. I admit I'm not doing it entirely out of the goodness of my soul."

"I should have known," I replied with an eye roll. "Anyone who'd capture a father and son for a bounty just because the in-laws don't like them is a lousy person."

He gave me a hurt look. "I'm not that bad. Besides, you'll need the extra help."

I put my hand on Elyssa's shoulder and regarded him with narrowed eyes. "I won't lie. I can use all the help I can get. The difference is I trust Elyssa with my life even if she thinks I'm a monster. You, on the other hand, are a mercenary. If things get a little hairy, I can't count on you because all you care about is money."

Shelton held up his hands. "Jumping Jesus on a pogo stick. Cut me some slack!"

I ignored him and continued. "We plan to sneak in and out with my dad. If we're lucky, we won't even have to talk to a vamp, much less fight one. How does that figure into your bounty hunting?"

"I don't plan on running in guns blazing, kid." He leaned on his staff. It was not the same one I'd destroyed, but looked similar, if a little more worn around the edges. "I want a stealthy hit and run, too. I figure I can capture a few rogue vamps along the way and bounty up with the Red Syndicate."

"If you come with us, you'll have to stick to our plan," I said.

"Make him swear on his soul, Justin," Elyssa said.

Shelton blanched. "C'mon, you can trust me. I promise."

"Swear it on your soul," I said.

"Look, if something happens and I accidentally break that pledge, it could strip me of my powers."

"I don't know you, Shelton," I said. "I can't risk Elyssa's or my father's life on the possibility of you going off plan. Either leave or swear you'll follow mine and Elyssa's orders and not purposefully do anything that would compromise our operation."

Elyssa retrieved a thick piece of chalk from her pouch and drew a neat infinity symbol on the porch concrete. "Swear it and seal it, sorcerer."

"Damned Templar goody-two shoes." Shelton cursed a blue streak and dithered, staring at the symbol. Finally, he walked over and repeated the pledge. Elyssa made him repeat it with her exact wording. Shelton cut the tip of his pinky finger and pressed a drop of blood into the center of the infinity symbol. The air popped and I heard the same electrical crackle I'd heard from the circle he'd tried to trap me and Dad in.

"Damned self-righteous Templars," he muttered.

"Pig bounty hunters." Elyssa bared her fangs with a grin.

With a team like this, I was more certain than ever we were going to die.

CHAPTER 33

"**A**re you really going to ask for help from that little felycan tramp?" Elyssa asked as we hopped into the black van she'd driven.

I'd told her where my Jetta was so I could recover it. It also happened to be very near Stacey's hideout. "She's actually a decent person once you get to know her."

"Never trust felycans. They're finicky and dangerous. One of them almost killed my oldest brother, Michael."

"Wow, they're that strong?"

"This one was. He broke into several animal shelters and let all the animals go."

I frowned. "What's wrong with that?"

"He also severely injured security guards and staff, not to mention clued some of them in to his supernatural abilities."

"I take it that's a bad thing."

Elyssa gave me a *Duh!* look. "Spreading knowledge of the supernatural to mortals is forbidden. It's one of the first laws the Overworld Conclave enacted."

"I haven't exactly had time for Supernatural 101."

"The Overworld Conclave is the worldwide supernatural government." Elyssa honked at a car in front of us. "Stop texting at traffic lights!" She blew out a breath and continued on the previous subject. "Every year they hold a caucus where delegates meet to decide on rules."

To see a Templar ninja get road rage brought a grin to my face. "Delegates from different supernatural groups?"

"The major groups. Loners like your kitty cat friend don't normally participate." Elyssa gave me a pointed look. "Doesn't mean they don't answer to the law, though."

I gripped the *Oh-shit!* handle above the door as she veered around a curve. "And that's where you come in."

Elyssa gunned the van around a slower car on a two-lane road with double yellow lines. "We're considered the only impartial party to the Conclave. Every nation has its own police force. I guess we're kind of like the supernatural version of Interpol."

Damn she's a scary driver! I sucked in a breath, but somehow kept my train of thought. "With swords. And ninja outfits."

She grinned. "Kinda cool, huh?"

I laughed. "Man, I feel like a baby. Supernatural nations, the Conclave, Templars. It's enough to give me a supernatural headache." I pinched the bridge of my nose. "Do the spawn take part in the Conclave?"

"Yeah, they're major players, but their internal politics are even more complex than vampires if you can believe it."

"I can believe anything at this point. At least I have super cop to protect me."

357

She flashed a brilliant smile and stared at the road. After a moment, she spoke again. "I meant to thank you earlier."

"For what?"

"For what you said to Shelton about me."

"Oh." I pondered it a minute, trying to remember exactly what I'd said. Then I saw the Jetta sitting in the dark to the side of the road. "There it is."

She pulled off and I hopped out with a red gas tank in hand.

"I won't go any closer to her lair," Elyssa said. "She'll sense me and freak out."

"I don't blame her." I grinned. "I'll bet you're not even a cat person."

"I prefer dogs." She got out of the van and held out her hand, palm up. "I'll take your Jetta back."

"Why?"

"Because if she delivers some moggies to you, you'll need the van."

"Will moggies freak out if you're around?" I asked in all seriousness.

Elyssa shrugged. "I'm not a felycan expert but I don't think so. Whatever the cat woman tells them to do, they should do."

"I hope so." The last thing I needed was giant alley cats savaging someone's toy poodle.

"I have no idea how to fit those creatures into the plan," she said with a protracted sigh.

"Backup."

"If we need backup, it'll probably be too late."

"Stop being so optimistic." I hopped in the van. "See you back at the house?"

Elyssa flipped open the fuel door to the Jetta and nodded.

I drove the short distance to the old warehouses and sensed Stacey nearby, though something felt alien about her presence. I clambered to the top of one of the buildings and scanned the rooftops. Goosebumps crept up my spine. The hair on the back of my neck stiffened. I spun. Something huge crashed into my chest and hammered me into the ground. Feline fangs glistened inches from my face. Did everyone have fangs except for me? A pair of amber eyes bore into mine. A rather large black panther with incongruously blonde-tipped fur frosting its ears sat atop my chest.

A tongue eclipsed my view and licked my nose. I sputtered. The huge cat licked my cheeks, a rumbling purr thundering in its chest. I wiggled. Managed to dislodge the big cat and scrambled to my feet. The panther yawned wide and gave me something approximating an amused grin.

"Stacey?" I said.

The big cat stretched. Bones popped. The huge paws shrunk and the black fur retracted. The panther yowled and roared over the sound of cracking bones and the mushy sounds of muscle and sinew rearranging itself.

I winced and flinched at every moist crackling pop. My gag reflex kicked in.

"Are you having an episode?" A very naked Stacey walked towards me without the least hint of embarrassment. I couldn't stop looking at her soft curvy bits, jiggling and swaying with her catlike stride.

"I think I might have one now," I said in hoarse reply. I tried to remember why I'd come here in the first place. Oh yes, the moggies. "Did any of your companions decide to help me?"

"Indeed, my dear. Two tommys have risen to the occasion."

Stacey's nakedness had made something else rise to the occasion. I shook my head and tore my eyes from her chest. "Two tommys?" I was a little disappointed there were only two, but then again, I'd probably need a cattle truck to haul any more of them. Two shadowy figures appeared, leaping though a hole in the roof. They stood as tall as lions. Bony ridges ran along their spines, their paws wide and disproportionate. Although they looked clumsy, they flowed along the roof with deceptive grace and speed. Black and white spots adorned one's hide. The other sported orange fur striped with black. They looked the same size as the original moggy I'd encountered, with the same bony spine protrusions, scruffy fur, and thick whiskers.

"So the dhampyr girl is helping you," Stacey said in a low growl.

I didn't bother asking how she knew. "She is."

"I find that very surprising. Her kind does not usually mix with ours."

"She's a good person."

An amused smile lit Stacey's face. At least I think it did. I was trying hard not to stare at her boobs.

Stacey noticed. "Are you a good person, my lamb?"

"I think so, my little kitty cat."

"You are simply too much." She scratched the orange moggy behind the ears. His golden eyes narrowed in pleasure and a deep purr rumbled in his throat. "This is Marmalade, and that is Dots."

I wrinkled my forehead. "You've gotta be kidding me. Did you give them those names?"

"That is what they were called before they fled their uncaring masters."

"Lovely."

"They *are* quite lovely. Give them the respect they deserve and they will honor you with loyalty and service."

"How do I tell them what to do? Do I need to learn cat language?"

"Oh no, my precious." She giggled. "Simply tell them what to do."

I decided to test that out immediately. "Come here, Marmalade."

He looked up at Stacey. She took his great head in her hands and kissed him on the nose. "Who's my good boy?" she cooed.

He licked her cheek and trotted over to me where he sat by my feet and stared curiously into my eyes. I reached out cautiously and scratched his huge ears. The resulting purr sounded like Dad's motorcycle. His fur was rough and spiky, and his jaw stretched wider than a normal feline's. Otherwise he was just one big fluffy ball of love.

"They don't mind the daylight, do they?"

"No, but how stealthy can they be in broad daylight?" Stacey pursed her lips. "You mean to attack during the day?"

"That's the plan," I said.

She pshawed. "The vampires will be at their weakest then, true. But they are not foolish enough to leave themselves open to attack during the day. I would suggest a night attack. Many of them will be out and on the prowl instead of at home asleep."

I hadn't thought of it that way. "But Elyssa says a daylight attack is best."

She growled. "I am sure the girl has some trifling background with such matters, but I speak from true experience."

"You attacked a group of vampires before?"

"They were using cats for extremely distasteful experiments."

"What?" I said, shocked. "Were they making vampire cats?"

"Indeed. They *were* scientific-minded vampires. I taught them the error of their ways."

"Good lord, I can't imagine having to deal with vampiric cats."

"They were so distraught." She sniffled and wiped away a tear. "Those that did not die, I had to lull into the eternal sleep. Every moment of life was a danger to other felines. I could not let such a plague spread."

I wrenched the discussion back to the topic at hand before curiosity derailed my train of thought. "Are you absolutely sure about a nighttime assault? If we mess this up, we're dead."

"I do not think you stand much of a chance in either case. Explain your current plan to me."

I gave her the quick version of Elyssa's plan, noting with pride that I'd gone at least one minute without looking down at her chest.

"The girl has a very logical mind," Stacey said after a moment. "I do believe, however, that a nighttime foray will be more successful, especially if you execute it this evening."

"Tonight?"

"It is a new moon. The lycans are at their lowest strength and the vampires are at their greatest. They will, as you say these days, be partying it up." The idiom sounded funny coming from Stacey's proper British lips.

"There's something to all that full moon myth stuff then?"

"I suppose there must be, for as long as I have walked this earth, the full moon and new moon celebrations have always been just so."

"When were you born?" I asked.

"I was born under the greatest queen the world has ever known. In fact, I served her quite faithfully until our kind had to go underground again."

My mind dug through its pathetic store of British history. "Queen Elizabeth?"

"Heavens no, dear. I'm not so old as to have been around during Elizabeth the first. I speak of Queen Victoria." She sighed. "Those were such golden years."

"Wasn't she the big prude?"

"Indeed."

"But you're so, umm..." I wasn't sure how to put this delicately. "Stacey, you're kind of on the slutty side. No offense."

"Yes, I have become quite fast and indecent over the decades. My biology, however, forces me to take action lest I am left childless and bereft of love for all eternity."

"You also use a lot of flowery words. Sometimes I don't even know what you're talking about."

"Indeed." She put a hand to her bosom. "Change comes hard to supernaturals and most of all to the British."

"What would you do if you had to assault the vampires?" I had the map with me so I pulled it out and showed it to her.

She examined it in silence for a moment. "Stealth is the correct approach. In this, I agree with the girl." She sighed and glanced at the star-filled sky. "Though it pains me greatly to admit it, Justin, you are the closest thing I have to a friend or a companion in this world. I have grown somewhat fond of you and I believe this girl leads you to your doom."

"Are you sure you weren't an actress back in the day?"

"A thespian? Why, I would never associate with their ilk."

"If we go with your idea of a night assault, what would you suggest?"

Nightliss mewed and ran up to her, her large green eyes serious as she yowled a mouthful to her mistress.

"Yes, little one?" Stacey's brow furrowed. They meowed back and forth for a moment before Stacey nodded. "Nightliss is quite insistent. She will scout out your father's location. Once found, she will tell me where you should look."

"Won't that require you to be there?"

"Indeed it will."

"But I thought—"

"I do so enjoy the looks of confusion that cross your lovely young face. Of course I will come despite the presence of that–that guardian girl you so covet."

"Ah. Um, welcome to the team then." I hoped this wasn't leading to a terrible mess. I might witness a cat fight of epic proportions. "Does this mean you'll come back to my house with me?"

"I will meet you there in one hour's time."

"Am I taking the moggies with me?"

"No, I will bring them myself."

"I really appreciate you helping me, but could you please not start any fights with Elyssa?"

She purred. "Do not worry yourself. I am sure she and I will get along fabulously."

I did not like the smirk on her face when she said that.

CHAPTER 34

"**Y**ou what?" Elyssa yelled after I arrived home and told her about our new partner.

"We need all the help we can get," I said. "Just don't go waving your swords in her face, please."

"A night raid? With a felycan?" She threw up her hands. "This is suicide."

"But it makes sense, doesn't it? If the vamps will be out partying, we'll have fewer to deal with."

Her violet eyes flashed. She snarled and snatched the map from me then slammed it on the table. She jabbed her finger on one of the many colored dots on the map. "These markers, as I explained earlier, are where their sentries will be *during the day*. The majority will be sleeping in the main chamber of the basement. We know exactly where nearly every vampire will be during the day. But at night they'll be awake, wandering all over the place."

"Or maybe they'll be off their guard like she said."

Elyssa stared so hard at the map that I thought it might burst into flames. After several moments of silence she blew out a breath through tight lips. "I just don't know." She shook her head and stared out the sliding glass door leading into the back yard. "Why would you involve her after all I told you about felycans? She might hang us out to dry."

"She helped me with Randy last night, and said she'd help rescue Dad before I even knew you were going to show up. At least hear her out." I felt more and more out of control of this rescue operation. In fact, I hadn't been in control since Elyssa offered her help. Sexual superpowers or not, even I didn't stand a chance against women. They took over everything.

"Do you realize how difficult it is to switch strategies on such short notice? And Shelton may not be able to help now."

I snorted. "Well I trust Stacey more than him, that's for sure."

"He has his own agenda, but at least he swore an oath he can't break without hurting himself."

"Should I email him about the possible change in plans?"

"Let's wait until I hear what this little slut has to say."

"Hey, wait a minute. Are you jealous?" Hope sparked in my heart.

She glared at me briefly then looked away. "Don't be stupid. I just don't want us getting killed."

"So, you do care."

Elyssa stiffened. "Your guest is here."

Stacey's presence felt off-kilter to me and I knew it was because she'd arrived in panther form. I hoped she transformed outside. All that bone crunching and popping made me want to throw up. The sliding glass door opened and Stacey, dressed in black workout pants and T-shirt stepped inside. Nightliss scampered through after her and hopped on the kitchen table.

"Thanks for wearing clothes," I said with a tinge of regret.

She dropped a black sack on the table. "It was inconvenient to carry them in my mouth. But I knew the girl might have delicate sensibilities."

"Delicate sensibilities, my Templar ass." Menace filled Elyssa's voice. "This had better not be a trick. If I get a whiff of betrayal coming from your feline ass, I'm gonna shove my sword up it."

Stacey gave a feral grin. "I would like to see you try, Templar."

Elyssa stalked toward the shorter woman. "Anytime."

I squeezed between them and shoved them apart, somehow nailing both of them right in their boobs. Thankfully, they were both too intent upon staring each other down to notice my inadvertent grope.

"This isn't very helpful," I said. "Can we please agree to be civil until this is over?"

Stacey shrugged. "I am not the one behaving untoward."

"I don't trust her," Elyssa said.

"Why would she go so far out of her way to betray us?" I said. "Someone would have to be really mean to do that."

"I've heard stories of her kind."

"Yeah, well in case you hadn't noticed, you're helping demon spawn. Honestly, if stories were all you had to go on, who would you trust more, a crazy cat woman or an incubus?"

Stacey giggled.

Elyssa rolled her eyes and backed off. "This goes against everything I know. But we'll hear her out."

I sighed in relief. "Okay, Stacey, the floor is yours."

Nightliss leapt up to Stacey's shoulder and perched there. Her huge green eyes gazed intently at each of us. Stacey scratched the cat's ears. "My little friend here will find Justin's father and scout out the location of sentries. Depending upon what she finds, here is what we'll do." She leaned over the map and went through a short but detailed summary of what she'd explained to me earlier.

Nightliss meowed occasionally, seemingly to support or correct Stacey's statements. Elyssa peered at the little cat, a look of utter disbelief that the feline had anything to do with the planning process.

The plan mirrored Elyssa's aside from the timeline and the inclusion of a housecat scouting the compound for us. Somehow, Elyssa kept her mouth shut.

After Stacey finished, Elyssa stared into space for a few moments before speaking. "Email Shelton. Tell him we're hitting the compound tonight."

"The plan is good?" I asked.

She clenched her fists and her face reddened. She muttered a few indelicate curses which were not very kind toward cats. "Yes."

Stacey purred.

Shelton replied almost immediately to my email, surprised, but still ready to be part of the team. He showed up thirty minutes later. I checked the clock. We were cutting it close. According to Stacey, the vampires needed time to wake up, throw on some fancy clothes, and shift into party mode. Most of them slept from dawn to around sunset. It seemed kind of funny thinking of bloodsuckers getting all spruced up for a night out on the town. Then again, I figured they weren't much different from the rest of us schmucks.

"What kind of an operation are you running here?" Shelton asked when he surveyed the motley crew. "This is nuts."

I felt like correcting him because I wasn't the one running it. "You're welcome to back out if you want," I told him. "But you have to do it now."

He looked from Elyssa to Stacey and then to me. "Let me hear this new plan of yours."

"You're quite young for a sorcerer," Stacey said.

He shrugged. "I'm old enough."

"You, young man, are not a year over twenty-five."

"Your point being?"

"One quarter of a century is hardly enough time to obtain proficiency."

"How would you know?"

She tapped her temple. "I have my sources."

"That's all very well and good," I said, "but I've seen him in action. Anyone who can shoot fire out of a stick is okay by me."

"My wand is hardly a stick, kid."

"And I'm hardly a kid to you, kid. You can stop with the condescension right now."

He chuckled. "Fair enough." Shelton dropped into a chair at the kitchen table. "All right, show me this new miracle plan Goldilocks thought up."

Stacey pursed her lips. "Goldilocks, eh?" She ran a fingernail down his neck. The hairs stood on end. "Shall I see if baby bear is home?"

Shelton cleared his throat uneasily. "The plan, please," he said in a choked voice.

Stacey purred. "Of course, magic man."

By the time she was finished, Shelton looked pretty peeved. "How am I supposed to get any bounties with this plan?"

"If all goes well, you won't even be needed," I said.

"Exactly my point. I won't get in a lick of action."

"This isn't about you." Anger heated Elyssa's words. "It's a rescue operation, not a bag and tag."

"Are the bounties valid if they're dead or alive?" I asked.

"I'm no murderer," Shelton said, "although rogues are officially off the protected list. Still, living vamps are worth more. Guess their elders have plans for them."

"How do you plan to take a vampire alive? The flames you shot at them didn't seem too effective."

"I wasn't exactly prepared for vampires when I came after you," he grumbled. "Vamps don't like fire but I hadn't programmed my wand since the last time I used it."

"Programmed it like a remote control?" I laughed. "I still don't understand how that works."

"It's way too complex to go into now, kid—I mean, uh, Justin. There's an energy cost to using magic just as there's a cost to using an arcphone. It all boils down to physics. If I can offload some of the overhead on a computer, then it helps me. Hell, you give me enough juice and I can create a hell of a blast or burn an entire building to slag."

"Fine, fine, I get it," I said, already bored with the lecturing tone of his voice. "But what spells are you planning to use against the vamps?"

"Ultraviolet bursts."

Elyssa shook her head. "Effective, but highly visible. We can't use those in a stealth operation."

"What would they do to vamps?"

"A powerful enough burst will knock them out or immobilize them," she replied. "But the flash will light up the place like a strobe light."

"Actually, the spell I've coded should be no worse than a flashbulb," Shelton said. "And one flash can take down multiple targets, provided it bursts right in their faces."

"Not feasible," Elyssa said, shaking her head. "Not unless we're in trouble and need help."

"Aw, come on. It works great in the simulations."

"Emergency use only."

"You backing out or sticking around?" I said.

He mumbled something.

"What was that?"

"I'll come."

"Remember your oath."

"Believe me, if I go against an oath like that, I'll incur so much negative karma that it'd wreck me."

"I thought things were complicated enough using computers and magic. Now you're saying karma is involved too?"

He grinned. "Karma is a magic all unto its own. It's like a piggy-bank of positive or negative equity we carry around, indirectly affecting everything we do."

"Great," I said. "One more thing to worry about." I caught motion from the corner of my eye. Nightliss batted around the string of the blinds to the kitchen window. "How does Nightliss feel about prowling through a den full of vampires?" I asked.

Stacey regarded me with those vertically slit pupils of hers. "She thinks it will be rather exciting."

I thought of something nobody had mentioned. "How are we going to prevent the vampires from sensing us? I can sense people once I get within a few yards of them."

"Vampires can smell spilled blood," Elyssa said. "They can hear the pulse of a beating heart from ten feet away." She spoke of vampires as if they were in no way related to her.

"Why didn't anyone mention this before?" I said. "How in the hell can we sneak through a building full of vampires if they can hear our heartbeats?"

"When I am stalking something, nothing can sense me," Stacey said.

"I have a masking spell I use," Shelton said.

"Templars learn to block others from sensing them," Elyssa said. "I'm sure spawn have defensive measures as well. I had just assumed you knew how to do it."

"No," I said. "I'm still a newb. Dad never told me anything about hiding myself."

Elyssa pulled out her smartphone and started punching keys. Shelton did the same.

"Please tell me you're not Googling for an answer," I said.

Elyssa gave me a guilty look.

"Well, my spell might work," Shelton said. "But I can't just use it on you. I'd have to stay within a few feet of you for it to remain effective. However—" He pulled out a pouch and rummaged through it. After a moment he pulled out a gold chain and stared at it. "Ah, damn. No, this won't work. I thought I'd programmed one of these with the correct enchantment, but it's gone stale."

"Stale?"

"Yeah, you gotta keep renewing enchantments or they wear off over time."

"Can you freshen it up?"

"Not without a few hours to do it in."

I groaned. "What am I supposed to do then?"

"There's a simple version of this spell you might be able to do. Mine is one-way, meaning they can't detect me, but I can detect them with the proper spells. The simple version is like throwing up a wall of insulation between you and them, but you won't be able to sense them as well."

"He can't do magic," Elyssa said. "He's demon spawn."

"There are demon spawn who can do magic," Shelton said. "But usually only if they've been around a long time."

"He hasn't been around long at all."

"Actually," Shelton said, giving me the same look he'd given me after letting me hold his wand a day earlier, "I think he can. Can't hurt to try."

"Fine," she said. "Waste your time. But I think we're going to have to keep you closer to us than we'd planned so you can keep him masked."

"We need some quiet," he said. "Let's step outside."

We stepped on the back porch. I nearly had a heart attack as two large shadows in the back yard shifted. Then I remembered the moggies.

Shelton pulled out some chalk. "First you need to draw a container, like a circle, around you and close it."

I sketched a circle which more closely resembled a warped oval.

"Now you need to close it by pressing your thumb against it and willing it closed."

"How do I will it closed?"

"Just think about the circle and wish for it to be closed."

I pressed my thumb against the chalk and wished for the circle to be closed. Nothing happened.

"Think 'circle close'," Shelton said.

This whole exercise seemed pointless and silly, but I kept thinking that phrase over and over again. The air around me crackled faintly.

"Nice job," he said with a big smile. "You just did your first magic act."

"Seems pointless," I said.

"Believe me, it's not. There are a lot of different ways you can close a container, but this is all you need for this spell. After a minute or two, you should feel a slight buildup of pressure in your ears."

I nodded. "I feel it."

"Okay, that's what magic feels like when it can't escape your container. Now you need to focus on what you want it to do."

"Like put up a wall?"

"Exactly. But we need to be careful here. We want you to block out your heartbeat and psychic emanations without blocking all sound. Otherwise you'll be deaf and possibly blind to what's happening around you."

My stomach fluttered nervously. I didn't want to render myself senseless by accident. "How do I block things selectively?"

"Listen to your own heart and imagine it as being silent to everyone."

I closed my eyes and listened. The moggies purred nearby. Car engines and tires echoed from the streets. I heard indistinct talking from the kitchen and the sound of Nightliss batting around the cord to the blinds. I filtered those noises one by one until I heard my heart thudding in my chest. It sounded rather panicked and I couldn't blame it. Things were about to get real.

After a few moments, the sound of my heart was the only noise I heard. I imagined it being shielded from the rest of the world. Buffered by my will. I concentrated on it for what seemed an hour when I realized I could no longer hear my own heartbeat. I opened my eyes. Shelton gave me a thumbs up.

"I did it?"

"Yes you did."

"Is your hearing sensitive enough to hear my heart beating?"

"I was using a little bit of magic to eavesdrop."

"Oh yeah. Guess you would be."

"Now we need to do the same with your psychic emanations."

I remembered something Dad had told me while learning how to feed. I evened out my psychic hook, as he called it, just as I would before sneaking into someone else's psyche. Making it neutral, he had termed it. Then it would be no more noticeable than background noise.

"That was quick," Shelton said.

"I didn't need magic for that one," I said.

He compressed his lips and nodded. "After this is over, maybe you'd like to learn some real magic."

I cocked an eyebrow. "You think I'm capable?"

"You seem to be a natural at it."

I wondered if that might have to do with my mother's side. I rubbed away the chalk line with my foot and felt a release of pressure from my ears as the magical energy dissipated into the air around me. We went inside. Stacey and Elyssa looked at me for a moment. Stacey clapped her hands and laughed with glee.

"You did it," Elyssa said. She cast a questioning gaze on Shelton. "How is this possible?"

The sorcerer grinned. "He's got potential."

She grabbed my arm and put a head to my chest. I wanted to press her entire body against me. I drew in her scent: sword-cleaning oil and leather underneath the sweet smell of a spring day. Just her warmth against my chest made my pulse quicken. She pulled away, a hint of softness in her eyes, and shook her head. "I've never heard of demon spawn who could do this."

"He's a special case."

"Special in the head maybe."

"Hey." I playfully punched Elyssa in the arm. "That's not nice."

Elyssa returned a sad little smile. "We're all special in the head for going through with this crazy plan." She sighed. "Lock and load time."

Everyone nodded their assent and their faces tightened. I felt an intense urge to visit the bathroom. Instead, I grabbed the keys to the van.

"Let's roll."

CHAPTER 35

We drove southeast to a part of Edgewood on the border of ghetto and hipster. The rogues had taken over an old school, gutted it, and turned it into large luxury lofts ago. According to Elyssa's information, a huge basement lay beneath the lofts, now used as sleeping chamber. The resulting building looked oddly out of place, as the original designer had an obvious enthusiasm for all things gothic. The retrofit only enhanced the design. Points and spires adorned the roof. Gargoyle faces leered from the marble window frames. A large dark-stained wooden door guarded the main entrance with all the effectiveness of a drawbridge.

In short, it looked like the perfect place to find vampires.

Foot traffic was light this time of night, although plenty of non-vampiric revelers drank at a bar across the street. Melodies from an indie band at another venue down the way echoed in the cool night air. Stacey took her pack or pride or whatever the term was for a group of mismatched feline creatures to a dark adjacent lot. She would help Nightliss into the building so the little cat could scout it for us. I parallel-parked the van on the street.

Shelton poked his head out the sliding door on the side and whispered something that sounded like "fizzle" while flicking his fingers. The closest street lamp made a faint pop and went out, leaving the van hidden in darkness.

Elyssa stared hard at the rogue compound and scribbled on a notepad. She was probably doing something important like mapping out alternate routes or maybe even writing a goodbye letter to her parents in case we all died. I felt pretty useless so I leaned over her shoulder. She was drawing her name with little hearts around it.

"Seriously?" I said.

She flinched and gave me a dirty look. "I'm waiting to hear back from the felycan."

"She has a name, you know."

"You're becoming kind of attached to your little cat woman, aren't you?"

"I'm getting really tired of people judging others just because they're not pure human."

She turned away from me and drew a crooked heart next to her name. "Oh, I'm sorry. I hope *Stacey* comes back with some good intel."

"That's a lot of vamps." Shelton pointed up the slight rise to the gothic structure.

A gaggle of vampires, all dressed to kill, or at the very least to drink blood, waltzed toward a stretched Hummer. I had to admit the vamps knew how to style. I peered at them with my enhanced eyesight to see if I might recognize Randy and pals, but they were too clustered together to get a good look. Then I noticed Mortimer looking mournfully on from the front door. Poor kid would never look old enough to drink alcohol no matter how old he really was. And forget faking a driver's license.

The sliding door on the street side of the van jerked opened and my heart froze. Stacey climbed in. Nightliss followed and jumped on her shoulder. The little cat rubbed her cheek against hers and meowed happily.

I took a deep breath and uttered a few choice curse words at the surprise entry.

"Less than twenty vampires remain in the compound," she said, her face more serious and composed than I'd ever seen it. "My little one was able to go into the basement which is now one cavernous room filled with beds and partitions. A locked door at the back of this area blocked her way, but one of the resident cats told her he had hunted rats down there before. The vampires only recently locked that door. I would bet my tea and crumpets on your father being somewhere down there."

Elyssa crossed her arms and gave Nightliss a pointed look. "When you say 'down there', do you mean that door goes to more stairs?"

"Indeed. Apparently the building was once an old church even before it became a school. There's a crypt beneath the basement."

"Stupid vampires and their flair for the dramatic," Elyssa said.

Stacey gave her a toothy grin. "Why, my dear, you *are* speaking of vampires. Why do anything at all if you cannot do it in style?"

I gave Stacey a funny look. She hardly sounded like a seductress when she broke into the Queen's English. And the incongruity of her attire only added to the bizarre vibe I got from her. Really, she should have been born French.

"How do we get into the door?" I asked.

"More importantly, what kind of door and how is it locked?" Elyssa said.

Stacey smiled sheepishly. "While my kin could detail a mouse down to the number of his whiskers, they are not so very good at detailing mechanical things such as locks. Nightliss said the door seemed quite sturdy, though admittedly most do for one of her delicate stature."

Elyssa dug through her pouch. "I guess I can handle it." She pulled out what looked like a lock-pick kit.

"Nightliss also says that one of the vampires accessed it while she was there and jabbed his finger at something on the wall next to it."

"An electronic lock?" Elyssa tossed the lock picks back into her pouch. "Just great."

"It could've been an intercom." Shelton gave me a look. "If it's magnetic, a hex ought to do the trick, though."

"So you'll need to come?" I asked.

"Unless you're up to it."

"Even if he I do it," Elyssa said evenly, "it might take him too long."

"Yeah, well dragging around an extra person is gonna be even tougher to hide." Shelton handed me a bit of chalk. "An experienced caster wouldn't need a container, but you don't know how to aetherate your own internal well. Just make a circle and close it like before. When you feel a little pressure in your ears, you should have enough juice. Concentrate on the keypad and imagine throwing that built-up energy at it. It might help to use a word to focus your effort."

"Like fizzle?"

He chuckled. "Exactly. The magnetic lock should die at least temporarily."

My stomach flip-flopped a couple of times. Every time we got closer to the objective, we found another snag. Except this one was pretty major. "Maybe I should practice on a street lamp."

"That's a brilliant idea," Elyssa said. "Let's go into the middle of the street, draw a big chalk circle, and blow out some light bulbs right in front of the place we're about to invade."

"No, I mean go somewhere else I can practice."

"We don't have time."

Stacey marked a copy of the map that Elyssa had given her with the sentry locations and other items of importance. There were no direct routes to the basement, and the best entry point appeared to be the service door in the back as Elyssa had predicted in her first version of the plan.

"Drive us around to this parking lot." Elyssa jabbed a finger at the map after examining Stacey's edits.

I started the van and pulled out into the street. The parking lot was the same one Stacey had used to hide the moggies. I parked and took a look around. A sturdy chain-link fence separated this lot from the vampire compound. A cat the size of Nightliss could get through, but not the rest of us. I was about to wrench a hole in the links when Shelton put a hand on my arm and shook his head. He took out his wand and examined the metal links. The runes on the wand glowed. Static electricity charged the air.

He aimed the wand at a link. The metal bubbled and melted away like solder. He ran the wand up the length of the fence, leaving a neat incision in the metal. He repeated the process next to one of the support poles. A rectangular patch of fencing fell to the ground with a rattle. We winced.

"I should have caught that," I said. "Crap."

"It wasn't that loud," Shelton said. "Plus the metal would've been scalding hot."

"Maybe you two would like to set off fireworks while we're here," Elyssa said in a cross voice. She stared through the trees bordering the grounds at the service doors.

I belted on the swords and knives Elyssa had so thoughtfully given me and made sure I still had the chalk from Shelton in my pouch. Worry knotted my stomach while fear slithered its cold fingers into my bowels. I had to clench my teeth to stop them from chattering. Then, before I charged in with my emotions broadcasting my presence, I made sure I quieted my psyche so it wouldn't give us away the moment we entered the place.

Elyssa seemed very calm and unperturbed as she watched me go through my preparations. She untwisted the buckle to the sheath holding the sword on my back and smoothed my shirt down. What was it I saw in her eyes? A hint of regret, maybe? Concern? Then the spark vanished and she was all business again. She walked toward the compound without even looking to see if I was behind her.

A delicate hand took mine. Stacey's eyes brimmed with worry. She stood on tiptoe and kissed my cheek. "Good luck."

I gave her a hug. "Thanks."

Nightliss rubbed against my leg and meowed.

"She will go with you and scout ahead." Stacey picked up the small cat and kissed her nose. "She is so brave and quite insistent on seeing this through. One might think she likes you, Justin."

Nightliss purred and gave me a half-lidded gaze.

Shelton slapped me on the shoulder. "Come back in one piece, Justin." He offered a grin that didn't quite reach his worried eyes.

"The moggies will be ready to come in if you need rescuing," Stacey told me. "We will be listening on the wireless contraptions."

By that, I assumed she meant the cheap walkie-talkies Elyssa had brought along. I just hoped their signal could carry from underground. I gulped and trotted to catch up with Elyssa, who stood at the edge of the lawn leading to the service door. Grass carpeted the open area for thirty yards or so where a paved driveway led to steel double doors. A sidewalk ran the perimeter of the compound, lined by saplings which hadn't grown large enough to hide much of anything. Thankfully, only a single lamp above the service door illuminated the area, and the moonless night offered the cover of darkness. Still, vampires had excellent vision.

Should one of them stare forlornly out the back windows of the complex because he couldn't go party tonight, he might spot us. Mortimer came to mind.

We blurred across the open area at a full run, reaching the doors within seconds and putting our backs against the wall. Elyssa pressed slowly down on the outside door handle until it clicked open. It sounded like a cannon shot from where I stood, but the noise from the lively crowds at the bars across the road hopefully camouflaged it. We crept inside. Nightliss trotted between us and into the wide corridor ahead. Wooden pallets with furniture and other odds and ends leaned haphazardly against the walls, giving us some cover in case someone came looking for the one with their favorite Snuggie on it.

Nightliss dashed ahead and vanished at the far end of the corridor. I wasn't sure how the little cat would tell us if something dangerous lurked around the next corner since neither of us spoke meowish, so I followed Elyssa's lead and kept low and quiet. We reached the propped-open doors of the next entryway without incident. We peeked around the corner. The first sentry Stacey had marked should be patrolling the nearby vicinity.

The interior of the compound was simple. The building formed a large rectangle with a hallway that ran the perimeter on all three upper levels. The basement could be reached via the elevator from the front lobby, by a service elevator in the back hallway, or by the door that was halfway down this hallway on the right. The service elevator would be too noisy, so we needed to reach the basement door.

Nightliss sat and stared at the doorway, the tip of her tail twitching up and down. She looked to us and then waved her paw at the door to the basement and meowed.

"What does that mean?" I asked.

"I have no idea but I don't see any sentries," Elyssa said.

Nightliss hissed as Elyssa started down the hall. I grabbed her arm and brought her back. "Just wait a minute."

As if on cue, the basement door swung open and a vampire dressed in cargo shorts and a kickball T-shirt stomped into the hallway with a half-empty blood bag clenched in his hand. He punched the metal door and left a dent in it. Nightliss dashed between his legs and down the stairs. The vampire didn't seem to notice.

"Freaking assholes, leaving me here to guard," the vampire muttered as he stalked down the hall toward us. "You need to learn how to dress," he said in a whiney voice. "God, I hate Britney. I swear I'm gonna pee in her blood supply."

Elyssa and I crouched behind a pallet and waited until the disgruntled vampire disappeared around the corner at the other end of the hall.

We made our way down to the basement door and stepped onto the stairs. The corridor was so dark I could hardly see anything. I groped for Elyssa's arm and hit something a bit softer.

"What are you doing?" she whispered.

"I can't see."

"Are you kidding me? Adjust your eyes."

"My night vision kind of sucks." I hoped that whatever night vision had tried to turn on the night the moggy attacked me would work automatically because I didn't know how to manually turn it on.

She sighed. "You are such a newb." She grabbed my hand and led me down the stairs. It almost felt like old times.

We reached the bottom of the spiral staircase dozens of stairs later and peeked into the well-lit basement. Huge chandeliers hung grandly down the center of the ceiling with a disco ball hanging awkwardly from the bottom of the middle light fixture. Marble columns ran up the two-story walls and arched across the dome-like roof. Bunk beds and cots lined the sides in neat rows with a walkway splitting the cavernous room in half. It looked like a giant army barracks. Some areas had cubicle partitions, probably for privacy or silence.

Several leather sofas surrounded a huge television screen at one end of the chamber. Several gaming systems, and all the accoutrements for Guitar Hero were neatly tucked away on a svelte glass entertainment center. It was awesome. Felicia pranced around in a Dance Central dance-off versus two guys. *Take a Chance on Me* by ABBA boomed from the huge sound system.

Vampires really know how to have a good time.

Elyssa caught me staring longingly at the entertainment center and pulled me down into a crouch just in time to hide from two more male vampires as they rounded a corner and walked past, animatedly discussing how to beat some game which involved catapulting birds at pigs.

We stayed low and dashed across the open space to the left side of the basement where a long cubicle-style divider hid a mess of electrical cords. Behind the divider and a few feet down stood the door Nightliss had meowed about to Stacey. The little black cat looked at me with wide green eyes and extended a paw toward the door.

"I never realized cats were so smart," I said in a low whisper.

Elyssa ignored me and pulled out a penlight so she could study the arched doorway. The solid hardwood and hefty metal hinges looked formidable. The lock was old-fashioned—something a skeleton key might open. I felt incredibly relieved. Then I noticed two metal plates at the top and bottom of the door jamb. A conduit ran from the plates, along the gray marble wall, and up to the ceiling. I stifled a groan as my relief turned into a pang of worry.

"Magnetic," I whispered.

Elyssa nodded and studied the keypad to the left. She gave me a pointed look.

I pulled out the chalk, trying to keep the tremors from my hands. *Everything* hinged on me being able to hex this thing. I drew a circle around me and willed it shut by pressing my thumb against it. The air crackled, indicating I'd at least done that part right. I waited. After a few heart-pounding seconds, the pressure in my ears built to a point where I knew there had to be enough magic around me to do the job.

Staring at the keypad, I willed it to malfunction. Nothing happened.

"Fizzle," I said. Nothing again. "Poof." Still nothing.

Elyssa gave an exasperated sigh and examined the sturdy metal conduit. She pulled out a knife and pried at it.

I willed all sorts of terrible things upon that blasted keypad, but nothing happened. My hair felt like it was standing on end, probably from the magical energy hanging uselessly around me. Elyssa peeled the metal conduit away and stared at the thick wires inside it. I gave up my attempts, giving the keypad one last dirty look and flipping it a bird.

"Just die already," I hissed through clenched teeth.

A thick blue bolt lanced from my middle finger and into the keypad. It sparked and smoked. The magnetic latch went dead and the door click open a fraction, held in place by the old original latch. That would have been great except the electricity springing from my middle finger arced into one of the power strips on the floor. Loud pops and sizzles echoed across the room. The sound system boomed one last time and went silent. Light bulbs in the chandeliers exploded. Vampires yelped in surprise. The basement went black.

CHAPTER 36

"My perfect game!" Felicia wailed into the darkness. "Who the fuck just ruined my dance-off?"

"Santiago, you Spanish son of a bitch!" A male voice shouted. "Did your hairdryer trip the breaker again?"

My eyes automatically went into night mode this time. I'd expected a greenish hue like military goggles, but a gentle blue nimbus touched my surroundings instead.

Elyssa whispered a string of curses and grabbed my hand. Nightliss scooted down the spiral staircase ahead of us. I was just swinging the door shut behind us when a hissing and spitting Nightliss dashed back up the staircase and scuttled through the closing door.

I flashed a confused look at Elyssa. "I wonder what got into her."

"Can you see?" Her irises emitted a violet glow.

"Yes. Are my eyes glowing too?"

She rolled her glowing eyes. "Yes."

"Awesome."

"Will you take this seriously?"

"This is my way of trying not to shit my pants," I said. "I'm scared out of my wits."

She took my hand in both of hers and squeezed. "Everything will be okay."

I covered her hand with mine. For a moment, the world seemed to slow. My nerves calmed and it seemed like we might actually pull this thing off. I raised her hand to my lips and kissed it.

"Thanks."

She opened her mouth to say something then gave the door a startled look. "I think they're coming this way."

We jogged down the stairs. The rancid odor of rotting meat drifted into my nostrils. I hadn't noticed it at first due to being scared out of my wits and all, but my nose notified me in no uncertain terms that something stank. Big time. I gagged.

"Good lord. You think they're putting dead bodies down here?" I shuddered. "I thought vampires tried not to kill people." At least I knew why Nightliss hadn't stuck around. My upgraded senses added an extra dimension to the stink I really didn't appreciate. Especially since I'd heard all odors were particulate.

Elyssa whipped out a couple of bandanas and handed one to me so I could cover my nose. Women always seem to have the answers to life's little inconveniences hidden in their purses, or in this case, utility belt.

The faint scrape of something against stone emanated from below. Elyssa slowed. I followed her lead. We reached the bottom and peered through the arched door frame. The ceiling in the crypt rose about ten to fifteen feet high. Marble coffins and niches lined the length of the corridor. The floor alternated between carved rock and dirt. The bandanas covered up the worst of the wretched smell but only barely.

I had hoped to find a simple room with my dad in it. From the look of things, this crypt wasn't going to make it easy. I had flashbacks to Indiana Jones and imagined finding cobweb-covered skeletons and a rolling boulder trap. I would have gladly traded the foul odor for a boulder trap any day. Elyssa edged forward and went left to the end of the corridor. I followed and peeked around the corner. Several more coffin-lined corridors led off of the next one.

She grunted. "This place is a maze."

Scraping and shuffling echoed off the walls but it was hard to tell where the sound came from. "Is that my dad?" I asked her.

"I don't know." Her forehead creased with worry. "Come on."

We went a few more steps. The odor seeped through the bandanas in a nauseating wave. I expected to find a pile of rotting victims at any moment. We wended our way through the maze of corridors and finally reached what seemed to be the center. The rocky walls retreated several feet to either side of a squat marble tomb in the middle. Further back, a light shined from within a stone building.

"He must be in there." I gagged on the rancid stench.

Elyssa squeaked and went rigid. Her hand tightened on my wrist so hard I expected to hear the bones crunch. I followed her gaze. Bodies littered the floor. Flies buzzed around the corpses. They appeared black and oily to my blue-tinged night vision which made the gruesome scene all the worse. My heart raced. My face felt hot from fear and outrage at the slaughter of these poor people. The corpses ranged in age from the young to the elderly. Many wore ragged clothes, possibly homeless when they were alive or just rotted from age.

"They're all dead," I said in a hoarse whisper.

A grunt echoed. One of the bodies jerked upright and turned our way, its sunken eye cavities staring blindly in our direction. I had to squeeze my ass cheeks to keep my bowels from emptying. The sound of shuffling bodies echoed in the chamber and I realized that had been the scraping noise I'd heard earlier. More corpses jerked upright, heads swiveling toward me.

Elyssa's grip tightened another notch. "Not quite." She stared at me in alarm. "Are you still masking your heartbeat?"

"I think I let that slip when I saw the dead bodies."

"Oh, God." Elyssa spun back the way we'd entered. "We've got to get out of here. We've got to run. Now!" Her voice was a whisper, but the alarm in it supercharged my growing fear.

The animated corpses jerked like broken puppets to their feet all the while making horrible gurgling and wheezing noises from rotting vocal cords.

We spun and raced back through the maze.

"Zombies?" I asked.

"Vamplings," Elyssa said. "These idiot vampires have been trying to turn humans into vampires but they're too young or they don't know how."

"But they look dead."

"They're mostly dead, all right. The human side of those people died when the turning failed, leaving the monster side completely in charge. Now they're just empty, mindless shells that crave blood. Think zombie meets vampire and that's a vampling. From the looks of them, they haven't been fed in weeks."

I tried desperately to cover up my thudding heart, unable to scrape together enough presence of mind to do so. I didn't have time to stop, make a circle, and focus. Angry shouts echoed from ahead.

"Half the breakers are fried!" Someone shouted. "I swear to god, I'm gonna kick Santiago's ass!"

"No, my friend," a voice with a Spanish accent answered. "I dried my silken locks over an hour ago."

"Bullshit," Felicia shouted. "Did you plug that European hair dryer into our outlets again?"

"You hurt me, my friends, so I go." The Spanish vampire sounded sad.

"You'd better go!" Felicia shouted.

Elyssa and I screeched to a halt.

Her eyes widened with panic. Mine felt like they bugged out of my head.

"Maybe we should just fight the dead ones," I said. "They look rotten enough to punch through."

"You don't understand," Elyssa said. "With the human side of them gone, they have no sense of self-preservation or self-limiting beliefs. The worst part is, they're relentless. They'll never stop coming unless they're a pile of bloody gore." She scanned our surroundings. "We've got to hide until the vampires go back upstairs."

"Whoa wait a minute!" Footsteps clomped down the stairs. "The keypad is fried. Looks like someone tried to burn it out and nailed one of the surge protectors nearby."

"So much for surge protection," Felicia muttered.

"What the hell is going on?"

Randy's voice sent a nasty chill down my spine. Part of me wanted to rush from cover and pound him to a pulp. The other part didn't want to get swarmed by vamps and turned into an eternal snack pack.

"Why do we have to be on guard duty, Felicia?" Mortimer whined. "It's the new moon."

"Shut up, Mortimer." Felicia growled. "You'll get the vamplings riled up."

"Good lord, they stink something fierce," Mortimer said. "We need to talk to Maximus about some Lysol."

"Shut up, Mortimer," Randy snarled.

Blake piled on. "Mortimer, you're a whiny little bitch."

Two other voices I didn't recognize joined in bashing the vampire kid.

Elyssa stopped me and held up six fingers. My heart raced even faster.

"How many can you take?" I whispered.

She frowned. "Three, maybe four, if I kill them."

"I might be able to handle three."

More footsteps clomped down the stairs. "Did you guys find the breakers?"

"Scratch that," Elyssa said. "Sounds like four more just joined the party."

We looked for a hiding place, a niche, anything. A guttural scream gurgled through the chamber. I turned to see the vamplings shambling toward us at a horrific clip, their eyes focused on the only thing in existence that mattered to them: blood.

Elyssa pulled her swords. I followed suit.

The vampires raced around the corner and skidded to a stop. Glowing red embers burned in their eye sockets as they stared at us, then at the vamplings coming up behind us.

Randy's lips spread into a smirk. "Justin! If you'd texted me before you came to visit, I could've baked some cookies." He turned to Elyssa. "If I didn't know any better, I might think you're a Templar." He folded his arms and feigned a hurt look. "So, about letting you into our network—that's gonna be a hard *no*, since you're a liar and all."

Elyssa smirked back at him. "On the upside, I don't have to pretend to like you anymore."

Blake cracked his knuckles. "Hot damn, I want some payback."

Felicia gripped Mortimer by the arm. "Call Maximus."

Mortimer nodded. "I'm on it." He raced back toward the stairs.

Dim emergency lighting flickered on, the lights racing through the crypt corridors in all directions.

Felicia flashed a wicked smile. "Give yourselves up and we'll call the vamplings off."

"As if you control them," Elyssa shot back.

I pulled out the walkie-talkie and clicked the button in the emergency pattern I'd arranged with Stacey. I heard static, but that was it. We were too deep for the signal to get out.

The first vampling, formerly a young man with a backwards ball cap on, reached Elyssa. She spun and hacked. Its head rolled off but the body didn't fall. I swept my rapier across its legs. The sword wasn't sharp enough to slice the bone, but the sheer brute force in my swing crunched through them. The body flopped with the sickening noise of maggot-riddled flesh smacking a sidewalk.

Another reached us. We hacked at arms and legs, but I could tell it wouldn't be enough. There were too many of them. The path behind us where the vampires stood narrowed, making it impossible to skirt around them. The path widened and split around several coffins in the center, joining again on the other side before turning sharply and back toward the wide-open area with the tombs. Right now, rotting vamplings jammed the path.

"Just give yourself up," Randy said. "I might even let your girlfriend go."

"Your sorry ass is next!" I shot back. "Where's my father?"

Felicia giggled. "You're so feisty!"

Blake pounded a fist into his palm. "Come at me bro!"

I shoved a coffin off its pedestal, blocking a mass of vamplings. Elyssa's arms whirled, swords a silver blur blending the creatures near her into chop-suey. The image of a shadowy figure, a flash of silver raced through my mind. Had Elyssa been the one to kill the moggy that night? Was she my mysterious savior?

I didn't have time to think about it. A rotting woman in a filthy yellow dress came from my side. She opened rotted jaws wide to reveal a maw of jagged teeth and blackened fangs. Maggots writhed in one of the empty eye sockets and in the green pocked-marked flesh.

I ducked beneath a lunge. It crashed into a vampling behind me. I lunged upward, shoving them both in opposite directions. They sailed through the air, splatting noisily against the walls. I grabbed the sword in time to hack through another one. The sword blurred in a Z pattern, dissecting the vampling into harmless chunks. I tried to ignore the clothes, the eyes, anything that humanized these walking corpses so I wouldn't think about who they'd been before the vampires had turned them into these god-awful things. I didn't have the luxury of guilt.

They are not alive. They are not *alive.*

This was worse than cleaning out grease traps times a zillion.

A laugh from Randy boiled my blood. I grabbed a vampling by the throat and hurled it into the onlookers. Felicia shrieked. Randy and pals shouted and ran as the monster chased them in circles.

Elyssa screamed. One of the creatures had leapt onto her back, locking its legs around her midsection. It sank its fangs into her right shoulder where it joined with the neck. Another went for her throat. The sword in her right hand clattered uselessly to the floor.

"No!" I rammed one creature with my shoulder. It plowed into the vamplings behind it, knocking them down. I dropped the sword and grabbed the one on Elyssa's back by the head, tearing its fangs from her. The rotten flesh felt slimy and disgusting under my fingers. I yanked hard enough to rip off its head, then flung it with all my might at the nearest attacker to keep it at bay.

Elyssa staggered. Her black shirt went dark where blood soaked it. She lost her grip on her other sword. I jammed my sword into the sheath on my back, or rather, tried to and missed. It clattered to the floor. I ignored it and picked up Elyssa.

Randy leapt up and down on the head of the vampling I'd thrown at them. Felicia and the other vampires bared their fangs. With Elyssa down, I didn't have a chance of breaking through their blockade. The vamplings didn't seem interested in attacking them, probably since they weren't warm blooded.

The other vampires stared hungrily at us, smelling the blood in the air. The vamplings gurgled with desire. The only place to go was further back into the crypt. I dodged around the coffins in the center, threading my way past several vamplings. I offered silent thanks to Coach Wise for all the football practice, and churned my legs as fast as I could. Gurgling howls of rage and hunger followed behind.

Unless the crypt had a back exit, there was no escape. Incandescent bulbs hanging from overhead wires offered dim light in the tomb. A brighter light shone within a small mausoleum ahead. I sprinted to it and looked inside.

Dad's limp form lay next to the wall. Chains secured his wrists. A bolt and thick padlock secured the barred door. At full strength I might be able to break it. But I was exhausted from the fight and slowing with every step.

I prayed Dad wasn't dead. Crusted blood stained his neck where the vampires had feasted. Someone whimpered. I looked behind him and saw a half-naked girl, filthy and frightened out of her wits. A single chain attached her ankle to the wall. Crimson stained the metal cuff where it chafed her ankle raw.

"Help me," she said. "Please, God, you have to get me out of here."

"Those animals," I growled.

Elyssa groaned. Her head lolled. I looked back at Dad and the girl again. "Vampires are chasing me. I'll come back if I survive."

"Don't go!"

I shook my head. "You'll be safer in here, believe me."

"Please come back!" Her wails of despair chased me deeper into the crypt.

Guilt twisted my stomach, but there was nothing I could do. Dad and that woman were trapped in their prison, but safe. I had to recuperate. I had to make sure Elyssa was okay.

It soon became obvious that the crypt had been carved from a natural cavern. It widened to about fifty yards across, stalagmites jutting from the floor, impeding my footing. The sounds of dripping water echoed ahead. I skidded to a stop at the edge of an underground lake. Stalactites hung from the cave roof, some coming so low as to almost touch the water. The cave ended on the other side of the lake. We'd reached the end. I wondered if the vamplings could swim and quickly realized it wouldn't matter. They probably didn't need to breathe, so they'd just wade in after us and pull us under.

Discarded beer bottles, beach towels, and a stack of foldout chairs gave the impression the vampires used this as their own underground beach. I didn't see how anyone could enjoy the cold, damp environs. Florescent lights hung haphazardly from wooden beams overhead. The vampires might dress great, but they sucked at carpentry.

I slumped to the floor, weak, empty of hope. My insides churned in agony from the hunger. I tore off mine and Elyssa's bandanas and rested her head gently on my knees. I pressed two fingers to her neck and checked her pulse.

"Justin," Elyssa said weakly.

I choked back tears at the pain in her voice. "How are you, babe?"

She reached her hand to my face and caressed a cheek. She gagged. I pulled her toward me in alarm only to find tears in her eyes.

"I don't think we're going to make it," she said.

"Sure we will." I took a deep breath to drive away the anguish.

"I still love you," she said between sobs. "I never stopped loving you."

"I love you too." Happiness trickled into my heart. "You don't know how I've ached to hear you say that."

She pulled my face down to hers and kissed me. "Forgive me."

"For what?"

"For wasting all the precious time we could have had together."

"It's not over yet." I projected a hopeful note in my voice. "We can make it out of this."

She shook her head. "The venom in the bite is paralyzing my muscles. I'm too weak to fight it off. By the time it wears off, it'll be too late."

I held out my wrist to her. "Take my blood."

She looked at me with tremulous eyes. Her nostrils flared as they took in the odor of my blood. She pushed my hand away weakly.

"I can't," she whimpered. "I can't."

"You're a better fighter than I am, and I'm at the end of my strength. Take my blood and recharge yourself."

She sniffled and pushed my arm away again. "I'm too weak. I might kill you."

"I don't care. If it means you might be able to rescue my dad and get out of here, I don't care." I caressed her cheek. "My only regret would be never seeing you again."

Tears flooded from the corners of her eyes. "I won't do it. I can't. The vampling bite is infectious. The Templar Blessing might negate the curse, but if I bite you, it might spread the infection. It could turn you into a vampling, given enough time."

"Then infect me. I don't care!"

"I do." She shook her head. "Escape, Justin. *Live*."

"What good is life without you, Elyssa?" My throat ached, eyes stung.

Her grip on my arm loosened. "I can't feel my arms anymore." She drew in a shuddering breath. "Feed off me. Survive."

"No." I could hardly speak, hardly think. Tears blinded me and dripped away.

"It's your only chance to save you and your dad," she said weakly.

"I'll figure out another way. I'll search in the lake. Maybe there's another passage."

"It's too late."

I heard the vamplings shambling closer. Heard Randy shouting my name.

"Justin! Oh, Justin!" He laughed. "Just give yourself up and I'll let your girl go."

"You can't do that," Mortimer said. "She'll tell the authorities about this place."

Elyssa reached for my shoulder with a trembling hand. "If you love me, you *will* do it, Justin. Do it for me. Survive for me. Please."

Elyssa lowered her defenses. I felt the hot pulsing of her essence hovering right before me, unshielded and vulnerable like a precious flame in the dark. But it felt so much different than what I'd felt with other women. They were dim candles compared to this blazing sun. I tried to resist but the hunger clawed at my barriers. I fought the madness and the pain as the need to drink her essence hammered at my defenses. I gritted my teeth against the pain. Squeezed my eyes shut. I would not do it.

"Stop, Elyssa. Stop it! I won't kill you to save myself."

"I love you," she whispered, and shivered violently.

My walls crumbled. The beast howled in victory and greedily pulled her essence into me. Love cascaded into my heart in a golden torrent of

SWEET BLOOD OF MINE

sunshine. I tried to stop the hunger, tried to cut myself off, but my depleted reserves drew her essence in like a dry sponge draws in water.

Tears flooded my eyes, blinding me as I drank in the essence of the girl I loved. She smiled at me one last time. Then her arms went limp and light in her violet eyes flickered out.

CHAPTER 37

I lowered Elyssa's body gently to the ground, sobbing, rocking back and forth from the agony ripping through my heart.

"No, Elyssa, no." The pain was unbearable. I doubled over as grief wracked me and ripped my heart to shreds.

The sound of putrid flesh on stone echoed nearby. I clenched my teeth and glared at the vamplings. Felicia, that evil vampiric bitch, stood behind them, goading them on.

Randy sneered. "Aw, did your girl go bye-bye?" He laughed. "You've got balls, Justin. Raiding our stronghold was a bold move, Cotton. But it didn't pay off."

I didn't know who Cotton was. I didn't care. All I wanted in that moment was to kill that mother fucker. The agony in my heart blazed into searing rage, a volcanic eruption charring the heavy weight of grief to ash. I stood and faced the horde. I roared in mad fury. Blue flames cascaded before my eyes. Pain erupted in my head. I staggered backwards. A nuclear explosion detonated behind my eyes, pressing against the insides of my skull. An agonized roar filled the chamber. It sounded like the roar a monster would make. Some part of my mind realized the alien roar was my own.

My blue-tinted night vision went red.

Bones popped and cracked and my clothes went tight as a drum skin. After a short eternity of pain in every molecule of my body, the red in my vision receded and I looked to see the vamplings mindlessly shuffling toward me. My body felt strange and elongated. I looked at my too-large hands and saw blue-tinged flesh and blackened claws. My head felt off kilter. I reached up and touched horns protruding from my forehead. Something hung heavy from my backside.

Fury overpowered all rational though.

DESTROY. CONSUME!

The beast was in control.

I towered over the mindless creatures before me. They would not withstand my might. My clawed hands shredded the closest attackers. I backhanded the next so hard into the cavern wall it exploded like a rotten melon. One came up behind me. I wrapped my tail around its neck and squeezed, popping off its head and batting the remains into the lake behind me.

I roared and clawed and punched and hammered the creatures mindlessly. Within a minute, only quivering bits of flesh and putrid juices remained where before there had been close to twenty vamplings. I bellowed in triumph, the guttural echo bounding off the cave walls.

Meanwhile the rational side of me asked what the hell was going on with my body and wondered where in the hell my tail came from. But the rational side of me seemed to have no say in the beast's actions.

"I can't even!" Felicia shouted.

"It's just him, you idiots!" Randy charged me. I towered nearly two feet over him. With a contemptuous backhand, I sent him flying into the lake. I turned to Mortimer, Felecia, and the others and unleashed a roar that blew their carefully groomed hair straight back.

They screamed and fled, tripping over each other in their haste to get the hell out of Dodge. A dripping wet Randy ran close behind them. The creature I had become gloried in the coming chase. They were succulent prey. I would hunt them and drain their essence until only empty vessels remained.

THE INFERNAL MASTER AWAITS!

I launched myself after them.

Elyssa! shouted the rational voice in the back of my head. *I can't leave her.* The creature raced ahead mindlessly, gaining quickly on the fleeing vampires, claws clacking on stone.

I love Elyssa! I love her. Don't leave her!

The beast slowed and turned back to the limp form lying at the edge of the lake. It was just an empty vessel. No essence to rip from the body. No possibility of an exhilarating chase as predator tracked prey. Why should this corpse matter? The real prey was escaping!

She is my love. My reason for existence!

LOVE IS NO REASON.

Love is everything, you warthog-faced buffoon!

POWER IS EVERYTHING.

Power is empty without love. I imagined the first time I'd kissed Elyssa. Saw her brilliant smile. Felt her loving touch. *Without her, life is meaningless.*

Tears sizzled in my eyes. The beast relented. All thought of the chase vanished and my fury melted into agonizing grief. I rushed back to her and knelt by her side. A reflection in the water caught my eye. I leaned over it. A monster stared back at me. Blood-red flames danced where my eyes had been. Ebony horns spiraled upward from just behind my hairline and my skin was blue. The gasp that escaped my huge mouth sounded monstrous and threatening.

I turned back to Elyssa and felt for her presence. But there was nothing. Not a spark or a breath of life. More tears sizzled in my eyes, flashed to steam by the dancing hellfire. I reached for her essence with all I was worth. Instead of burning life, I felt the cold absence of death. My huge shoulders shook with grief. I had killed her. The rational part of my mind clawed for supremacy with the big dumb beast I'd become but I couldn't break through. The beast roared and renewed its efforts.

And then I felt it, a tiny whisper of life. I reached for it gently. There was so very little of it I was almost afraid to touch it, a glowing ember of hope in the howling winds of despair. I feared my overwhelming presence might snuff it out like a bucket of water on a spark. The merge was such a delicate matter, but the beast did it on pure instinct. As its fury abated, so did the barrier separating my rational self from the rest of my mind. I merged with the wisp of life.

This time I didn't pull, I *pushed*.

I pushed with all the might and love I had in me. I thought of her laughing. Of those violet eyes looking into mine as I pulled her to me for a kiss. Of her soft lips against mine. Of her warm body pressed against mine. Of the happiness in a simple smile on her face. *Elyssa, come back to me.*

The energy left me at first in a trickle and then in a steady flow. A demonic howl of hunger burned my throat and wracked my insides. I ignored it and pushed harder. As the essence left my body, the agonizing hunger increased. My body rippled, cracked, and popped as bones reset and muscles shrank. My clothes hung loose and torn from my smaller frame. The horns detached from my forehead and clattered to the cave floor. The fire in my eyes poofed out with a whoosh.

"I love you," I said in my own voice. "Please come back to me."

The pulsating energy flow leveled out and no matter how I tried, I couldn't push any more into her. I stopped trying and hugged her to my chest. She felt cool. I put my head to her heart and listened. A faint thumping beat in her chest. Hope blossomed in me, but we still weren't out of the woods. The long walk back to the main crypt still lay ahead and I didn't know if the vamps might be waiting with backup.

I rinsed the rancid gore off my hands and arms in the lake. My shoes were stretched and misshapen with large holes torn at the toes. One of the horns that had been attached to my head lay nearby. I grabbed and examined it. I touched my forehead where the horns had been, but the skin felt smooth and unblemished. The horn was about two feet long and sharp at the end. I could probably kill a vampire with it. I put it in the sheath where my sword had been and picked up Elyssa. She whimpered but didn't open her eyes.

The walk back seemed to take forever. Muscles cramped and burned with every step. My stomach growled and burbled while supernatural hunger clawed at my sanity. I wanted to run, but I also didn't want to waste what little supercharged energy I had left if the vampires showed up again. I reached the tomb holding Dad and looked inside. He groaned. The girl next to him brushed the hair from his eyes and begged him to wake up. She saw me and shrieked. Then she realized it was me.

The lightbulbs outside the mausoleum blinked out. Apparently, the vampires thought darkness would slow me down.

I ignored the new development. "Did you see where the vampires went?"

She nodded, a wild look in her eyes. "They were screaming like crazy and running so fast they kept bumping into each other. It was like the Devil himself was chasing them. I'm pretty sure they're gone."

"Good. Let me see if I can break you out of there."

Her eyes widened in hope. I took out the horn and placed it in the gap between the padlock and the hasp. I gripped the base of the horn and jerked. The metal groaned. I jerked again and the latch gave way a little more. I adjusted the horn, braced my feet, and pulled long and hard. The padlock screeched and popped open. After pulling it off, I yanked the door open.

Dad groaned and peered at the girl through cracked eyelids. He jerked away. "No, I won't do it," he said in a weak, groggy voice. "Let her go."

"Dad, it's me." I knelt in front of him.

His eyelids fluttered open. "Justin? How?"

"Don't worry about it. I'm gonna get you two out of here."

Dad sniffed and wrinkled his nose. "Brimstone. We're in terrible da..." He trailed off and his head lolled.

I tugged where the chains were bolted to the wall but I might as well have politely asked them to release my dad. I didn't have enough strength left in me to do anything. I looked at the girl. The demonic hunger clawed my insides and demanded food. But I couldn't do it. I was so hungry that I might lose control. She seemed to sense the predatory intent in my stare and cringed against the wall like a rabbit facing the wolf.

I tore my gaze from her and examined the padlocks securing the chains. They were old-timey padlocks, but thick. Even at full strength, it would be hard to rip them open.

Elyssa's lock picks.

I unzipped her pack and dug through it until I found the little pouch with the tools in them. I didn't have the slightest idea how to use them. I dumped them out onto the wooden floor of the tomb and sorted through them until I found one that looked like a skeleton key. I grabbed it and jammed it into the lock. After twisting and fiddling with it, the old mortise lock clicked and the padlock popped open.

I pumped my fist. "Yes!"

After a few minutes I had freed the two prisoners. The girl cried gratefully but didn't go quite so far as hugging me when she saw the ravenous look in my eyes. The hunger bordered on unbearable but I had too much to worry about to give in. Dad was too weak to walk on his own and too heavy for the girl to carry. Elyssa was still unconscious as well.

"I hate to do this," I said to the girl, "but I have to leave you here with them."

"Can't you take me with you?" she asked. "Please. I've been trapped here for days, maybe weeks."

"There are more vampires upstairs. If I try to lug two people with me, I'll be too weak to do anything but watch as they finish us off." My stomach made a loud almost mournful noise. "Plus, I'm so hungry right now, I don't think I can resist much longer."

"You eat people?" she said in a whimpering whisper.

I laughed despite the situation. "No. I feed on emotions."

"I feel very emotional right now."

"I know. But in my condition, I might also have sex with you and drain you of everything."

She cringed even farther away. That simple prey-like movement increased my desire to pounce and take her. Every demonic fiber in my body demanded it. I closed my eyes and tried to collect myself. Elyssa depended on me. My dad depended on me. Feeding on this girl would help me save them. Maybe I could control myself. I stepped toward her, hot essence cowering just feet away from me and pulling me like gravity. Her sacrifice would save those I cared about the most.

You're a monster.

"No!" I shouted, backing away from the girl. "I'm not a monster."

"You don't look like one," she said in a quavering voice. "None of them did."

I shook my head violently, as if that would clear it. It only made me dizzy. "You stay here," I said. "I'll go for help."

She whimpered but nodded. I held up a finger, indicating to hold on a minute, and jogged over to the spot Elyssa and I had lost our swords. I grabbed them and brought them back to the girl. She took one of Elyssa's sai swords and held it with both hands. I put Dad and Elyssa in the back of the tomb, away from the door, motioned the girl back in, and shut it.

"Remember, the vamps can see in the dark, so stay in here until I get back."

"I can't believe this is happening to me." Fresh tears trickled down her cheeks. "I can't believe vampires are for real. And they're not even as beautiful as Edward."

I should've known she was Team Edward. "Pretend they're kidnappers if that makes it easier. Kidnappers with night vision goggles."

She nodded. "Okay." Some of the fear in her eyes diminished. "Thinking of it like that kind of helps, actually."

I ignored the desire to roll my eyes and grabbed my sword from the floor. It felt heavier in my hand than I remembered it, probably because I was almost spent, both naturally and supernaturally. My night vision dimmed and brightened as I walked. My heart hammered at the thought of losing myself in the pitch black. Was I running on a quarter tank? Less? If I ran into Randy and pals, I'd have to rely on fear and intimidation. A fight would be suicidal.

I reached the stairs leading up out of the crypt with no sign of vampires. I trudged up the spiral staircase, careful to keep as quiet as possible. I reached the door to the main sleeping chamber and peered inside. The power had returned. Lights hummed overhead. *Sexy and I Know It* thundered from the speakers. Otherwise, the place looked empty.

I tried to run but ended up trotting across the room, thanks to my weary legs. I reached the long staircase leading up to the first floor. Shouts echoed from above but I couldn't make sense of them. I heard a feline roar and then a scream. The moggies must be inside, I realized. I huffed and puffed my way up the stairs and peeked into the hallway. Felicia and another vampire backed away from a black panther.

"Who the hell let a panther loose?" the other vampire said.

Felicia shot him a scornful glare. "It's not a panther, you idiot. It's a felycan."

"A what? I'm new to this crap. I don't know what a felycan is."

"A werecat, you moron."

"Oh crap. Like a werewolf? Those things are mad strong. Maybe we should run away."

Felicia's scornful look turned thoughtful. "I think you might be right this once."

They turned to flee when a bright flash popped in their faces. Their red eyes rolled into the backs of their heads and they collapsed in a heap. Shelton walked over to them, whistling a cheerful tune as he secured them with silvery zip ties.

"Shelton, Stacey, I need your help." I hobbled toward them.

"Holy crap, kid, you look like hell," Shelton said. "You guys were gone forever, so we brought in the cavalry to get you out."

Stacey morphed in mid-stride and rushed to me in all her naked glory. "Where are your father and Elyssa?"

"I was too weak to carry them up. I need help."

She cried out with a high-pitched mewling that hurt my ears. A moment later, the moggies padded into view. One bled heavily from a gash in its shoulder.

"Oh, my poor dear." Stacey examined the wound.

The moggy rumbled a reply and rubbed against her leg.

"He is so brave." Her eyes misted. "They will go with you to retrieve the fallen."

"Take these." Shelton pulled leather straps out of the man purse he wore over his shoulder. "Strap them to the moggies." He handed them to me while doing his best not to stare at Stacey's nude form.

Something small, black, and furry did a figure-eight between my legs. Nightliss looked up at me and meowed.

"She smelled danger and came to warn us," Stacey said. "We would have been down sooner, but were stalled by several vampires."

"Speaking of which," Shelton said, "you've gotta hurry. Some of them escaped and I wouldn't doubt they've placed calls to whoever's in charge of this place. We might be able to whip a few youngsters, but not a horde of them."

I summoned my remaining strength and hobbled down the stairs. Shelton and Stacey took up positions outside. It took the better part of fifteen minutes to make it all the way back down to the tomb. The girl cried out and hugged me. She leapt back, fear returning to her eyes. I probably looked like hell, eyes glowing pale blue with hunger.

When she saw the moggies she screamed and jumped on my back, arms in a death grip around my neck.

"They're with me." I struggled to loosen her grip. "Help me strap on Elyssa and my dad."

She let go. "My god, those are big, scary cats."

"They're friendly." I put Elyssa and Dad stomach-first on the backs of the moggies then used the leather straps to fasten them. The big cats took off like they weren't carrying anything, leaving me and the girl behind. She stared into the darkness ahead and shivered.

"Please don't eat me," she said in a plaintive voice.

"Stick close. I can see in the dark."

I had to give her credit. Despite the constant trembling in her hand, she didn't scream once. I couldn't imagine being led through a pitch black crypt with a soul-sucking demon spawn as the guide. When we made it into the light of the sleeping chamber, she cried with relief and hugged me.

"Thank you, thank you."

"There are more people waiting upstairs," I said. "We still have to escape."

She nodded. We continued onward and upward. I stepped out into an apparently empty hallway. I had just turned to motion for the girl to follow me when I heard a hissing noise. I looked left. Five vampires, murder in their glowing red eyes, streaked inhumanly fast down the hall toward me.

CHAPTER 38

S helton stepped from a niche in the wall and raised his staff. Stacey, back in panther form, stepped from a niche in the opposite wall and roared. The moggies were nowhere to be seen. I assumed they were delivering their cargo to the van.

"There's a van in a parking lot across the back," I told the girl in a rush. "Run to it. Unstrap the man and the girl from the big cats and put them into the van. Now go!"

She nodded and skedaddled.

Shelton raised his staff and shouted, "Yod!" At first, nothing seemed to happen. The vampires raced down the yards of empty hall straight for us. About fifteen yards from us, they slammed into an invisible barrier. Hollow booms resounded in the hall, sounding like a maniac pounding on timpani drums. Bloody outlines of vampire faces hovered in the air as their bodies slid to the ground in a collective heap. Then the thick dark blood which seemed to be hanging in midair, splashed to the floor.

"Duy wov," Shelton barked, and a blinding light flashed above the vampires.

Most of them conked out immediately, but one staggered to his feet and turned to run. Stacey streaked over, batted him with a massive paw, and sent him flipping through the air to thud onto his back. She leapt on his chest and opened her mouth as he screamed and wriggled like a caught dormouse. A dull yellowish light flowed from his eyes and mouth in a vortex and swirled into Stacey's eyes. His screams sent chills down my spine. I turned away.

After a moment, Stacey released his unconscious form and stalked over to me.

"Watching her feed gives me the creeps," Shelton said. "Half of them are scared witless by the time she gets to them, though, so I'll bet it's good stuff."

I felt the lure of female essence and saw the unconscious form of Felicia. I couldn't hold back any longer and latched on. The vampire bucked and moaned, but the sleeper bracelets Shelton put on her kept her unconscious. Her essence was colder than that of a normal human, less satisfying, but it gave me enough energy to go on.

"We should go now," I said.

Shelton stared at the unconscious and groaning vampires longingly. "I don't suppose you could help me take a couple back to the van?"

"Are you kidding me?" I said through clenched teeth. "We need to leave."

Stacey rubbed against me like a giant housecat and made a cooing noise that sounded very strange coming from a panther.

Shelton sighed. "Well, I'll grab what I can."

The yowl of a feline in pain echoed down the hall. Randy stepped into view, teeth bared. He held Nightliss by the neck and growled my name. "Oh, Justin!"

Stacey morphed into human form. "Nightliss!" Fear filled Stacey's eyes. "Let her go, you monster!"

"Felycans and their stupid cats." A smirk twisted Randy's bloodied face. "How in the hell does a demon spawn even get an Arcane, a felycan and a Templar to help him? It boggles my fucking mind!"

"Look, let the cat go, and I'll give you what you want. I'll give you my blood." I held out my hand beseechingly. "Just don't hurt her."

Stacey bared fangs. "I promise if any harm comes to her, I will tear you to shreds."

"As long as you stay right there, there's no need for kitty to get hurt." Randy cupped a hand to his ear. "Ah, what's that? I think I hear the cavalry coming."

Oh, shit.

"Oh, shit." Shelton said.

Maybe most people wouldn't give up their life for a cat, but I wasn't about to abandon Nightliss. She'd been the entire reason Stacey decided to help me in the first place. I couldn't just leave her. Randy also had to know that little cat was the only thing standing between him and an ass-beating of epic proportions.

Nightliss hissed. Ultraviolet light flashed. Randy shouted in alarm. The cat dropped from his hands and ran for the door. I blurred across the room. My uppercut met Randy's jaw. He flew in the air. Before he hit the ground, I slammed his chest with both hands. His body crunched into the floor.

"You almost killed Elyssa!" I roared. I picked him up by his left arm and leg, spun him in a circle, gathering speed, and flung him against the wall. Brick cracked, and red dust drifted through the air.

"Remind me not to piss you off," Shelton said.

I stared at Randy's unconscious form, panting with pure rage. Whatever energy I'd stolen from Felicia was nearly spent, and vampire reinforcements were on the way. I grabbed Randy by the collar of his stylish leather jacket and dragged him behind me. "Let's go."

"What spell did you use to save my sweet kitty?" Stacey asked Shelton.

His eyes flashed. "I didn't use a spell. I thought you did something."

"I possess no such ability." Stacey turned her gaze on me.

"Sure wasn't me," I said. "I thought it was Shelton too."

Stacey raised an eyebrow, then morphed back into panther form. We raced back to the van, Shelton huffing and puffing, but unable to keep up. We slowed, Stacey baring a panther grin.

Shelton shot her a dirty look. "I ain't got supernatural strength, okay?"

Randy groaned, so I punched him in the back of the head to put him back to sleep.

We reached the van and found the girl standing ten feet from it and shaking in fright. She ran to me, gibbering like a person covered in spiders. She shielded herself from the van with my body and pointed over my shoulder. "V-vampires in there!"

I gave Shelton a dirty look. "I hope they can't escape."

"Nah, I got 'em locked in sleepers."

"Those plasticuff things?"

"Yep. Arcane's best friend. They can't wake up until I release them."

I dropped Randy. "Here's one more bounty for you."

Shelton raised an eyebrow. "Really? You don't want to turn him in to the Templars?"

I shook my head. "I'd be willing to bet the Red Syndicate isn't too happy with the rogues. Their punishment might be even worse than a cushy jail cell."

Shelton snorted. "I like your style." He slapped sleepers on Randy. "I'll make sure to let the Syndicate know he was badmouthing their elders. Talking about revolution."

"Will that piss them off?" I asked.

He grinned. "Big time."

Elyssa and Dad were still strapped to the moggies, so we untied them. I lifted Elyssa into the back very gently and pulled her against me. The vampires snoozed in a heap near the back doors. Stacey morphed back into her naked human form right in front of the girl whose name I still didn't know. The girl gave a little squeak and fainted.

"Truly, it's for the best," Stacey said with a smile. She slipped back into her clothes and climbed into the passenger seat.

Shelton closed the sliding doors and hopped behind the steering wheel. "Where to?"

I doubted a hospital would do much good. "My house."

"You got it."

On the ride back, I stroked Elyssa's cheek and whispered in her ear. She didn't respond but at least she was breathing. I hoped I hadn't severely damaged her mind. For all I knew, she'd never wake from this coma. I clenched my teeth to keep the tears at bay.

Dad groaned a few times but seemed otherwise okay. I figured he had to be weak from not feeding, not to mention the obvious health effects of vampires sucking his blood. Both he and I would have to feed at some point. It would take all of my self-control to keep from hurting anyone. I stared hungrily at the sleeping girl. I wasn't sure what to do with her.

"I'll take care of her," Shelton said in a grim voice, startling me out of my reverie.

"Don't kill her! Maybe we can mind wipe her somehow."

"Geez, you think I'm a murderer? The Arcane Council has a program for ordinary people who have seen too much of the supernatural side. We can help them adapt to the terrible realization they're just a bunch of normal idiots."

The tension left my shoulders. "Good."

We reached my house. Shelton took Dad inside. I carried Elyssa in and put her on my bed. She was a mess. Blood crusted her shoulder and she had bits of rotten vampling flesh spattered on her clothes and skin.

"I do so hate to leave you, dear," Stacey said. "But I must get my companions back to shelter. They are exhausted and wounded."

I hugged her and kissed her cheek. "Thanks for everything. You're a true friend."

She laughed and pressed a hand to my cheek as a tear welled in her eye. "I am rather glad I didn't eat you, you precious little man."

"Wait, I thought you didn't eat people."

She giggled. "Not in *that* way."

Nightliss rubbed against my legs and meowed.

Stacey frowned. "And so it begins? What, pray tell do you mean, little one?"

Nightliss looked up at me and purred.

Stacey shrugged. "She is quite an intelligent little cat." She slid out of her clothes and graced me with a seductive smile over her shoulder before transforming into a panther. Nightliss hopped atop a moggie, and the strange crew raced into the early morning darkness.

"That's a damned fine looking woman," Shelton said. "Scary as hell though."

I gave him a suspicious look. "I could have sworn I recognized those magic words you were using against the vampires."

"You must be a real nerd then."

"Ooh, the pot calls the kettle black. Who in the world would use Klingon words for their spells?"

He grinned. "It ain't so much what you say as the intent." He shrugged. "Plus it sounds cool."

"Yeah, I guess so." I yawned so hard my jaw cracked.

Shelton slapped me on the shoulder. "Get some rest. Not much you can do right now."

"Unless the rogues know where I live."

"The vamps don't know where you live, as far as I know, so I think you're safe." He pressed a hand to the floor and closed his eyes for a moment. "You've got two ley lines—kind of like high-voltage power lines for magic—running under this area. It's why your mom chose this place to hide. The magical interference is off the charts. I'll set some anti-vamp wards. They should last quite a while with the juice flowing under this place."

Relief melted some of the tension in my muscles and forehead. "Thanks, Shelton." I followed him back outside and watched him set the enchantments in place.

He brushed his hands together when he finished. "If a vamp crosses these lines, they'll get a blast of ultraviolet right in the noggin."

"One less thing to worry about," I said.

He nodded. "Sleep well." Shelton climbed into the van and drove away. I felt very alone all of a sudden. The two people I cared about most in the world were unconscious, maybe in comas, and all the super powers I had couldn't bring them back

I went inside and cleaned off, changing into some jeans and a T-shirt. Elyssa smelled just awful but my muscles trembled with fatigue at the thought of picking her up and bathing her. My stomach howled in unison with its supernatural counterpart. I had to do something about food and psychic energy before anything else. The sky turned pink in the east as I went back outside. I found a little café not far from the house and ordered a waffle. A group of old men laughed and traded stories over steaming cups of coffee.

I smiled and hooked into them, filling my psychic batteries with a trickle of warm feelings and good memories. After topping off, I went back home and found Dad stumbling through the kitchen. His face was white as death, hands cold and clammy. Ravenous hunger glowed icy blue in his eyes. His face had that demonic bony look to it, the same as when I'd followed him to the laundromat days ago.

He had to feed but I was afraid he might hurt someone, and I didn't want him going after Elyssa if he lost control. I had no other choice. I reached for his essence. He sensed mine and jerked it toward him greedily. I fell to my knees as he siphoned my replenished energy at incredible speed. Dad was like a starving infant, sucking furiously at a nipple. I felt myself growing woozy.

"Stop, Dad." I staggered to my feet and took him by the shoulders. "Stop!" He seemed to be in a trance. I focused every ounce of remaining strength in me and punched him in the nose.

He yelped and crashed backwards into the kitchen table. Anger flashed across his face. He leapt to his feet, fists clenched, his once-again hazel eyes glowing. Then he seemed to see me for the first time and gasped. The draining sensation stopped. I fell back to my knees.

"Justin?"

"That would be me."

He helped me to my feet and checked my eyes. "Are you okay? Did I hurt you?"

"I'm tired," I said. "But otherwise okay." Strength seeped back into my muscles as my remaining psychic energy leveled out.

He looked around the house in confusion. "How—how did I get home? Where's Linda?"

"Linda?"

"The girl. The vampires wanted me to feed off her so I'd stay healthy."

"She's taken care of."

His eyes grew large in horror. "You didn't—"

"No, I mean she's fine. The Arcane Council has some sort of treatment program for the supernaturally exposed."

"Thank goodness." He slumped into a chair. "You rescued me?"

"I had help. A felycan, a sorcerer, a housecat, and a Templar."

His eyebrows threatened to climb off his forehead. "Sounds like the start of a bad joke. How in the hell did you even get them to cooperate with each other?"

"Now that," I said, "is a long story." I looked at my bedroom. "And I have to take care of some business before doing anything else."

He walked over to me and offered his hand. I took it. He reached his other arm around and gave me a firm hug and a kiss on the cheek. I squeezed him back and pulled away. Tears glistened in his eyes.

"Geez, Dad, no need to get all weird on me."

He wiped away the tear and grinned. "I'm proud of you, son. Very proud."

I felt my own eyes clouding up and wiped them furiously. "Thanks." I gave him an awkward pat on the shoulder and went into my room.

Elyssa hadn't stirred since I'd left her. I fought back more tears and decided to clean her. I pulled off her boots and clothes, leaving a lacy black bra and matching panties. I figured if a girl was going to fight vampires, she'd do it in her best underwear. She looked beautiful despite the filth and blood.

I drew a bath and put her in it, leaving on the underwear. If she regained consciousness, I didn't want her to kill me for taking liberties. I took a rag and gently wiped the grime off her face and arms. After cleaning the crusted blood off her shoulder, the bath water looked like raw sewage. I drained it and examined her shoulder. The twin fang marks were puckered and raw. My heart sank. If her body was recovering, then those should have healed by now.

After the water drained, I used the hand shower to wash her down again. I dried her off and decided to remove the soaked bra and panties. I put her in my Darth Vader T-shirt and Chewbacca boxers. Then I tucked her into my bed. I put my ear to her mouth and listened for any signs of life besides breathing. I found none.

I sat next to her for several minutes, tears trickling down my cheeks. I didn't know what to do. I didn't know how to contact her parents, and even if I did, they might descend upon me in holy vengeance. A light bulb sparked on inside my head. I found Elyssa's pouch buried under her clothes and emptied it. Her phone clattered atop the pile.

I flicked it on only to discover it was password protected. My heart dropped another notch. If I could contact her family, I could have them meet me somewhere. That way I would be the only one in danger. Or, I could tell them where to pick her up and watch from a safe distance.

But how would I know if she recovered? I doubted her family would send me a postcard. I paced back and forth, straining to think of something I could do. I tried to guess her password, using her name in upper and lower case, and the name of her mom, Leia. No luck. I dropped the phone on the bed and sighed.

Dad was making coffee in the kitchen. I wandered in, face screwed up in misery and told him about Elyssa.

He was incredulous. "She's the Templar dhampyr?"

"Yes." A long sigh escaped me. "We're in love."

His incredulity increased as indicated by his jaw dropping open a fraction. "Tell me exactly what happened."

I gave him the four-one-one. Told him how I'd fed off her and then reversed the flow in an attempt to revive her.

"That's not possible," he said. "You and I can feed off each other because of what we are, but we can't give back what we take."

I shrugged. "Somehow, I did." I thought for a moment. "I don't know if it makes a difference, but I transformed into some kind of monster."

He sucked in a breath. "Explain."

I told him about the creature that had erupted from me and slaughtered all those vamplings. Dad blanched. Seeing someone who supposedly knows a lot more about this stuff than me go sick with worry didn't inspire a lot of confidence in my actions.

"What is it?"

He dropped into a chair. "You *spawned*. That's why I told you morphing takes practice, or you can lose all control."

"Well, we are called demon spawn, right?"

"Right. We're called spawn for a reason. You literally spawned or manifested into your demon form." He leaned forward. "You must never let it happen again. I can't believe you didn't go on a rampage and kill everyone."

"I almost went Incredible Hulk, but thinking about Elyssa brought me back."

"You were lucky. Very lucky. Only older spawn can manifest and maintain control. I still can't fully manifest at will, and even if I did, I would probably rampage."

I shuddered with fear at what might have been. "I was furious when it happened. I lost control."

"That's how it starts. You were starving, outnumbered, and angry. In this case it was a defense mechanism."

"Well, it worked."

He nodded thoughtfully. "Like I said, you were lucky." He ran a hand through his matted hair. "You took out all the vamplings?"

"I think so."

"Thank God. Those things would spread like a plague if left uncontained and they can infect animals too. Those idiotic rogues are going to make a horrible mess if the Conclave doesn't step in and do something about it."

"Vamplings can spread vampirism?"

He waggled his hand. "They spread the vampling curse. It's like a zombie virus, killing the host, turning them into a mindless vampire zombie." Dad shuddered. "Vampires have control over turning a human into a vampire. Vamplings have no control or will for that matter, only hunger. Anything they infect will die and leave an animated corpse. Even animals. All we need is a vampiric rat infestation again."

"What about Elyssa? Did they infect her?"

"Templars have a sort of immunity from most infectious curses. I think you'd see black veins and other signs if your girl was infected." He frowned. "The venom, on the other hand, probably weakened her. Maybe that's why she hasn't come to."

"Or she was dead after I fed off her." My heart locked in agony. "I think I wrecked her aura. Maybe damaged her brain too."

"Let's not jump to conclusions. Maybe we can find a healer."

"A healer?" I relaxed but only slightly. "Is there anything I can do to help her?"

He sighed. "I'm sorry, son, but I don't know what you can do. Let me see if I have any contacts who can help." Dad scratched his head. "The trick is finding a healer who doesn't hate spawn."

I decided not to tell him about my plan to return her to her family. He might not agree with such an idiotic plan. "Well, maybe you should clean up. No offense, but you stink."

He chuckled. "I think you're right."

I went into my room and sat down at my computer. Elyssa looked even paler than before. Her face felt cool to my touch. A tear tumbled from my eye and splashed on her cheek. Nobody could help me now.

And Elyssa would probably die.

CHAPTER 39

S uper powers, magic, and blood that vampires would kill for—all of it for nothing. Elyssa's hold on life dwindled and I couldn't do a thing about it.

The answer came to me in a flash. I knew what might fix her. I had the answer flooding through my veins. My sweet demon-spawn blood. I hoped it was as wonderful as the vampires made it out to be.

Elyssa was forbidden to drink from humans—not that I was entirely human—but I knew a way around the restriction. She drank from blood packs. Why not from a coffee mug? I found one of Dad's big coffee mugs with the words *Mondays Suck!* emblazoned on the front. Somehow having the word "Suck" on it seemed appropriate.

I took a knife. Positioned my hand over the mug. Gritted my teeth and sliced my skin open. It hurt like hell but I didn't care. Thick cherry-red blood dripped into the mug for a second or two. Then it stopped and the blood in the cup congealed into a coagulated lump. My hand had already healed. I groaned. Super-healing was going to make this painful and difficult. Then I remembered something. I dug through the gore-coated ninja outfit Elyssa had given me and found one of the silver-coated knives. She hadn't mentioned whether silver would slow my healing abilities, but now was as good a time as any to experiment. I rinsed the glob of blood from the mug, set it on the counter as I took hold of the silver blade.

If the kitchen knife stung, the silver knife scalded my skin. I slashed my palm and whimpered. Blood poured freely into the mug without slowing. Silver apparently kept my blood from coagulating. Just before the mug overflowed, I grabbed another one and placed it underneath my hand. When the second mug was full, I staunched the flow with a wad of paper towels. My hand felt like I'd rubbed it raw with fiberglass shards and pressed it against a hot stove.

I wouldn't be blinging out with silver pimp chains anytime soon.

After taping up my hand so I wouldn't gush blood all over the place, I took the steaming mugs of fresh blood into the bedroom.

Fancy a hot steaming cup of blood, dear?

Elyssa's nostrils flared when I placed a mug under her nose. Her eyelids fluttered but didn't open. I propped her head up on my knee and put a mug to her face. I started to feel a bit ill as I faced the reality of what I was about to do. I buckled down my nerves and trickled some blood into Elyssa's mouth. She coughed. Swallowed.

I gagged hard and averted my gaze.

Within a few seconds, she had gulped down the entire mug. I put the second to her lips and let her drink it down. Then I took a napkin and wiped the blood 'stache off her face.

I could already imagine the *Got Blood?* billboard.

I pressed the back of my hand to her cheek. It felt slightly warmer. Maybe it was just wishful thinking.

The minutes ticked by but Elyssa didn't move. A cold knife of fear twisted in my stomach. What if her body was still alive, but I'd destroyed her mind? Dad had warned me that was possible. Elyssa had been weak. Poisoned by the vamplings. And then I'd sucked her dry. Left nothing.

Tears flooded my eyes.

I'd killed the girl I loved and left only an empty shell.

"No, no, no," I moaned. What had I done?

I ripped the bandages off my hand. The blood had clotted and the wound was healing despite the silver poisoning. I grabbed the knife. I would pour the blood straight from my hand and into her mouth. She could suck me dry. I didn't care. Life had nothing left for me to care about without Elyssa.

I slashed my hand, crying out at the pain, and held it a few inches over her mouth. She gulped the steady stream of blood. I cut my hand again and again as it tried to heal. The pain was so overwhelming my hand went numb. My skin blanched from blood loss.

The room spun. I felt cold. Sleepy. I shook my head, fighting the urge to pass out.

I lost.

I JERKED AWAKE.

Something or someone watched me. I looked left. Tear-filled violet eyes gazed back at me.

"Elyssa?"

She smiled and caressed my cheek. "I'm here."

I sat up. Crusted blood glued the sheets to my hand. I peeled away the sheet and looked at my palm. Some of the multiple cuts had healed.

"What did you do to yourself?" she asked.

"What I had to do."

She pushed herself up and gripped my hand. She went into the bathroom and stared at her blood-stained lips. After cleaning her face, she emerged with a sad look.

"How much blood did you give me?" She looked green. "Did I feed directly from your flesh?"

I shrugged. "No, I let the blood pour into your mouth. As for how much, I have no idea. I passed out."

She gently took my injured hand and kissed it. Her eyes glistened. I wrapped my other arm around her waist and pulled her to me. I pressed my lips to hers and tasted salty tears. I wasn't sure if they were mine or hers. After a moment of joyful kissing, I checked her shoulder and was relieved to see the vampling bite had healed.

She jerked upright and put a hand to her cheek. "Oh crap. I've got to text my parents. They're probably flipping out right now."

"What will you tell them?"

She grabbed her phone and entered the password: *Justin*.

"My name is the password?"

She flushed crimson and gave me a stern look. "Not another word."

I couldn't suppress a grin as she tapped out a text to her mom: *Vampire trouble at Morningside. Taken care of. Lost my phone or I would've texted sooner. Sorry.*

"Will they buy it?"

She sighed. "I think so. It's not the first time something like that has happened." She leaned back against the headboard and focused those beautiful but tired eyes on me. "Remind me to tell you about my zero assignment sometime."

"Zero?" I scratched my head. "What did you do? Nothing?"

She chuckled. "I wish. It's all part of why I ended up in your high school."

A question that had simmered at the back of my mind burst out. "Are you the one who killed the moggy a few nights ago and saved me?"

Confusion clouded her face. "Huh? Why would I kill a moggy?"

Unless she was still dazed from almost dying, her expression convinced me. "Oh, nothing. I must have had a nightmare after I passed out. Are you feeling okay?"

She nodded. "I thought we were going to die."

"So did I."

"I've never been so scared."

I squeezed her hand. "You were scared? You didn't look scared."

"*You* looked totally scared," she said.

"No I did not."

She grinned. "You were wetting-your-pants scared."

"If I had to rank that on my all-time scare list it would probably rank a five. Maybe a six."

Her mouth dropped open. "You've got to be kidding me. A five or a six? What would you rank a ten?"

"Clowns."

She giggled. It was music to my ears. "What do you want to do today?"

"How about a movie?"

Elyssa snuggled up to me. "A movie?"

"You heard me. I've been chased by the undead, fought vampires, freed my dad from a crypt, and brought my super-hot Templar lover back from the dead by letting her drink my blood. Man, I need something normal."

She pursed her lips. "I'm your super-hot lover?"

"Yep."

"Want to prove it to me?"

I locked the door to my bedroom. Took her in my arms. Kissed her and the world fell away.

"Do you like the *Princess Bride*?" I asked.

"It's my favorite movie! Do you have it?"

Did I win the lottery or what? I kissed her again. The heat from her lips ran through my chest and tingled down to my toes. I came up for breath. "Of course I have that movie."

She smiled and pecked a kiss on my nose. "We should watch it."

I grinned back at her. "As you wish."

EPILOGUE

The little black cat sat atop one of the warehouses used by the felycan woman, gazing out at the dawning day. The long wait, it seemed, was nearly over. But was she strong enough to reveal herself? Could she help the world survive long enough for Justin to mature and grow?

Nightliss didn't know.

At least now, there was hope.

I HOPE you enjoyed reading this book. Reviews are very important in helping other readers decide what to read next. Would you please take a few seconds to rate this book?

Be among the first to know about new releases. Join my newsletter at johncorwin.net!

ACKNOWLEDGMENTS

To my wonderful support group:

Alana Rock, Barbara Kuhl, Becky Hammer, Chelle Magliozzi, Dana Prestridge, Hazel Godwin, Karla Ileana, Keren Hall, Karen Stansbury, Nicole Passante, Nita Banks, Pat Owens, Sheri Feikert, Terri Thomas and Jennifer Smith.

My amazing editors:
Annetta Ribken
Jennifer Wingard

My awesome cover artist:
Regina Wamba

You guys rock!

ABOUT THE AUTHOR

MEET THE AUTHOR

John Corwin is the bestselling author of the Overworld Chronicles. He enjoys long walks on the beach and is a firm believer in puppies and kittens.

After years of getting into trouble thanks to his overactive imagination, John abandoned his male modeling career to write books.

He resides in Atlanta.

Connect with John Corwin online:

Facebook: http://www.facebook.com/johnhcorwinauthor
Website: http://www.johncorwin.net
Twitter: http://twitter.com/#!/John_Corwin

BOOKS BY JOHN CORWIN

THE OVERWORLD CHRONICLES

Sweet Blood of Mine

Dark Light of Mine

Fallen Angel of Mine

Dread Nemesis of Mine

Twisted Sister of Mine

Dearest Mother of Mine

Infernal Father of Mine

Sinister Seraphim of Mine

Wicked War of Mine

Dire Destiny of Ours

Aetherial Annihilation

Baleful Betrayal

Ominous Odyssey

Insidious Insurrection

Assignment Zero (An Elyssa Short Story)

OVERWORLD UNDERGROUND

Possessed By You

Demonicus

OVERWORLD ARCANUM

Conrad Edison and the Living Curse

Conrad Edison and the Anchored World

Conrad Edison and the Broken Relic

Conrad Edison and the Infernal Design

STAND ALONE NOVELS

Mars Rising

No Darker Fate

The Next Thing I Knew

Outsourced

For the latest on new releases, free ebooks, and more, join John Corwin's Newsletter at www.johncorwin.net!

Made in the USA
Monee, IL
14 December 2020

52998315R00256